END OF THE LINE

END
—OF THE—
LINE

Kem Parton

Copyright © 2005 by Kem Parton
All rights reserved

Published by
Book Republic Press
857 Broadway, 3rd floor
New York, NY 10003

Library of Congress Control Number
2005921680

ISBN 1-58042-190-3

Book Republic Press is an imprint of Cardoza Publishing

This book is a work of fiction. Names, characters, places, and incidents are products of the author's imagination or are used fictitiously. Any resemblance to actual events or locales or persons, living or dead, is purely coincidental.

To Beth—
Others may have made greater contributions
to the manuscript, but none of them went
through childbirth for me.

PART ONE

- 1 -

Even by Arizona standards, Canyon Demonio was hot and desolate.
The surrounding desert sported a water table with no legs and relative humidity measured in negative numbers. According to local folklore, birds flew upside down over Demonio because they could find nothing below worth shitting on.

Though the name *shithole* had many proponents on the railroad, the official listing in the Transcontinental Railway Company's timetable remained "Demonio Station," as it had for nearly a century. Consisting of only an aging signal tower and a weathered location placard, it was, in reality, only a phantom station, a reference point on a railroad timetable that allowed train dispatchers to separate this vast wasteland into manageable chunks.

The dominant feature of this barren landscape was a railroad bridge, a steel-girder monster spanning the eight-hundred-foot chasm between the canyon walls. It was flush with the canyon rim and had no superstructure or guardrails. Under the tracks, the bridge's structural support consisted of two immense steel I-beams driven into separate concrete pilings in the canyon floor three hundred feet below. Two dozen steel cross-members spread out from each of the twin I-beams like Chinese fans, evenly distributing support for the five-thousand-ton trains that thundered overhead.

Although nearly a century old, the Demonio Bridge remained the sole improvement to the desert that engulfed it, an iron fragment of humanity in an apocalyptic landscape. The godforsaken setting seemed particularly fitting to Casey. If you were planning to send a train to hell, this was the perfect point of embarkation.

Kem Parton

Casey found the isolation strangely appropriate. After all, revenge was a lonely and socially stunting career choice. He had no contemporaries with whom he could discuss the pros and cons of mercury switches, no buddies with whom he could swap recipes for nitrate-based explosives. Years of meticulous planning in relative seclusion had led to celibacy and a nasty habit of talking to himself. The celibacy he could handle. The one-man conversations were another matter.

"Only crazy people talk to themselves," he said out loud, smiling at the unintended irony of his words.

While his sanity had received mixed reviews in the past, he knew he wasn't your textbook psychotic motivated by inner demons or strange voices. He had a higher calling—*vengeance and immortality*. He'd soon be driving a spike through the heart of the Transcon Railway empire and redefining the Casey Jones legend once and for all. Even if he was a little eccentric, Casey rationalized, being immortal would take the edge off.

He figured it was too damn hot to waste energy on self-analysis. Though well into autumn, the midday Demonio sun was oppressive and he still had a lot of work to do.

He parked his white Ford pickup on Transcon's right-of-way, then checked his watch. The next train, a southbound heading for Phoenix, was due in thirty minutes. It would never reach its final destination.

Casey opened the tailgate on his pickup and dragged a pneumatic rail cutter to the edge. The machine was little more than an industrial-strength grinder with two umbilical air hoses connecting it to a compressor in the pickup bed, but once positioned on top of the rail, it would cut through the 136-pound steel in a matter of minutes.

The rail cutter was every bit as heavy as he remembered. Its weight shortened his natural stride, and he stumbled slightly as his steel-toed boots dug into the crushed-rock ballast. Fresh and well packed, the ballast rested atop dozens of rock layers that had long ago been ground to dust under the weight of a million freight cars. The dirty-white cinder was so unvarying it looked as if it had been quarried from a single boulder.

End of the Line

After pacing off a distance roughly half an engine-length from the bridge, Casey clamped the rail cutter in place and went to work. He made the first cut in less than five minutes, slicing cleanly through the rail until the grinding wheel was spitting up splinters from the wooden crossties underneath. Then he repeated the process exactly twelve inches away from the first cut.

The foot-long section he'd cut was still held in place by four spikes. He rocked it back and forth until the spikes eventually released their grip, then discarded it without ceremony, covering the useless hunk of steel with enough ballast to make its presence undetectable.

As he wiped the sweat from his brow, back aching, Casey reminded himself that terrorism wasn't all press clippings and groupies. It could be hard work, a fact he'd be sure to pass on if he ever decided to start a mentoring program.

He stood up to stretch, popped a piece of gum in his mouth for a quick pick-me-up, and glanced over at the signal tower. Just as he'd expected, the system's fail-safe mechanism had detected the missing rail section and directed the tower to display its most restrictive signal. It had dropped from green to red.

Casey knelt over the rail and applied a two-foot strip of black duct tape over the missing section, then examined his handiwork from all angles to ensure that the tape blended with the rail. Finally satisfied that the camouflage would be undetectable from the elevated vantage point of a locomotive, he dipped into his pocket and retrieved a precut length of copper wire to bridge the gap created by the missing section. He reached for the roll of duct tape, but only a small sliver remained, its adhesive rendered useless by the cardboard backing on the spindle. Casey chided himself for being so careless.

He removed the gum from his mouth, separated it into two equal clumps, then used them to paste both ends of the wire to the rail, tricking the system into thinking the rail was continuous. The tower responded immediately by upgrading the signal from red to green.

Casey looked at the hodgepodge of gum and duct tape. *The right tool for the right job.*

He stowed the rail cutter in the bed of his pickup and removed a reclining lawn chair and a Styrofoam cooler. He unfolded the chair twenty feet from the broken rail and placed the cooler within arm's reach. It was a waiting game now. He twisted the top off a longneck, sat down, and set about completing his ensemble.

Rail buffs, known as "foamers" in the industry, were common fixtures on the right-of-way. A few finishing touches and Casey would look the part. Average height, average weight, and no distinguishing marks—he was a police sketch artist's nightmare. His features had been slightly dulled by exposure to sun and diesel exhaust, making them even less remarkable. He'd been blessed with the kind of face that one easily forgets, and he did everything in his power to groom himself to that standard.

Casey set the beer between his legs and reached into his shirt pocket for a small vial of zinc oxide, applying a liberal amount to his nose. To complete his ensemble, he donned a 35mm camera and a pair of wayfarer sunglasses. He laughed at the appropriateness of his disguise. Railroad management held foamers in utter contempt, viewing them as train groupies, parasites that huddled around derailment sites like buzzards over a fresh kill. The railroad police would shoo them away, only to see the flock reform just off the right-of-way.

Train service employees held an entirely different view. Engineers enjoyed celebrity status in foamer circles, and they went out of their way to pander to their fan club.

Casey leaned over and retrieved a train lineup and manifest from his back pocket, locating his target, a 70-mph automotive-transport train. According to the manifest, it consisted of two crewmen, four locomotives, and fifty bi-level autoveyor-type railcars. Each autoveyor was carrying twelve sport-utility vehicles.

Casey calculated that ten million dollars was a conservative estimate for the locomotives, rolling stock, and freight. All in all, measuring Transcon's impending loss against the price of the duct tape and copper wire, it would be an excellent return on his investment.

Not that the money mattered. The damage figures were irrelevant, nothing more than a handy way to keep score. More importantly, he was going to kill two Transcon employees. How could you put a price on that? He allowed himself to fantasize about the contorted expressions he'd see on the crew members' faces when they realized that death was imminent. *Truly,* Casey hummed, *the best things in life are free.*

He decided to fill the remaining time by taking care of administrative matters. He flipped open a cellular phone and depressed a button set on speed dial.

"Hello," a voice answered on the first ring.

"The Axeman cometh," Casey said, then terminated the call.

He flipped the cell phone closed and checked his watch, mentally making note of the time. Not that he'd easily forget the first defining moment of the rest of his life.

The approaching headlight snapped him to attention. Even in the midday sun, its intensity made the train's approach impossible to miss. It would be here in less than a minute.

He studied the oncoming train. *Exquisite.* It lacked the inertia of a heavier freight but made up for it in speed and exterior design. The unpainted steel mesh and smooth lines of the bi-level autoveyor cars evoked in him a profound emotional response.

Trains had always thrilled him, the raw power and size of the beasts sometimes even exciting him to a state of sexual arousal. Casey wrote off the odd physiological response as natural—a phallic reaction to the ultimate phallic symbol, symptomatic of his lifelong love affair. His devotion to his railroad mistress was every bit as intense as it was difficult to comprehend. Sadly, he knew this love was unrequited. Had the object of his affection been a woman, she would long since have obtained a restraining order.

Casey watched the train close the distance. If the sight of a foamer in the middle of nowhere wasn't enough to pull the engineer's eyes away from the roadbed, Casey figured a friendly gesture ought to do the trick.

As soon as the engine was close enough, Casey raised his right arm over his head and pumped it up and down repeatedly, as if tugging on an invisible rope, knowing the engineer would recognize the universal hand sign that foamers use when they want to hear the horn sound. His effort was rewarded by the lead locomotive's mating call: two long blasts of the horn, one short, and a final long burst of the whistle. The horn was cut short as the lead wheels, spinning at 70 mph, hit the missing section of rail. The freight train was doomed.

The locomotives hit the gapped rail at full speed, the flanged steel wheels easily crushing the wooden ties beneath them. Splinters spewed sideways and rained down on Casey, still sitting just a few feet away, close enough to see the scared faces of the conductor and engineer.

The initial jolt had propelled the conductor headfirst into the windshield, the inch-thick glass fracturing under the force of his skull into bloody spiderwebs that spread out from the point of impact.

The lead locomotive slipped inside the rails, splitting the iron pathway before it like opening a zipper. Rail spikes were ripped from their ties, their heads snapping off and strafing the right-of-way in a machine-gun arc.

With no rails to guide them, the four locomotives skidded on top of the ties as they tested the bridge. The lead engine veered right, the others alternating direction in accordion fashion, whiplashing the much lighter railcars behind them. The cars immediately behind the last engine became airborne and started a bumping wave that rolled back through the train. With a final jerk, the knuckle tying the cars to the four-unit locomotive consist parted.

The locomotives caromed halfway across the narrow bridge before failing the tightrope walk. The cars had acted like the tail of a kite, preventing the engines from succumbing to the lateral forces caused by the uneven roadbed, but losing this rudder, the locomotives tumbled onto their sides, their momentum carrying them off the edge of the bridge, still coupled together as they followed each other like lemmings over a cliff.

Without a roadbed to restrain their horsepower, the ungoverned diesel generators squealed faster and faster, emitting a whining eulogy that Casey was certain only he understood. The locomotives were singing him their swan song. Seconds later, the singing stopped, replaced by a thundering crash echoing off the canyon floor. Casey watched the spectacle is if in slow motion, his camera poised.

End of the Line

As the cars dog-piled on the bridge, their connecting knuckles parted easily, sending each car on a personalized path of destruction. One by one, fifty cars careened into space, toppling over the canyon wall. He held the button for continuous feed until he'd exhausted an entire roll of film on the epic derailment. He made a mental note to pick up more film and duct tape at Wal-Mart, one-stop shopping for the aspiring terrorist.

He peered over the side of the canyon at the tangled wreckage, studying the large silver coffins smashed on the rocks below. The locomotives had been buried under the hail of cars, which were crushed like discarded aluminum cans. Several of the autoveyors had split open, scattering their cargo of crumpled SUVs on the canyon floor—a yuppie graveyard. Somewhere beneath the five thousand tons of steel lay the conductor and engineer. Casey was certain they were as dead as he could make them.

Of course, he had no intention of climbing down the sheer canyon walls to verify this. An inspection of the wreckage would be a depressing waste of time. He had zero compassion for the train crew. By Casey's reckoning, in the railroad food chain, train service employees were the equivalent of plankton. The train itself was another story. The sight of this superb piece of equipment mangled beyond recognition nearly brought tears to his eyes.

Shaking off the rising depression, Casey reminded himself that after seven long years, his plan had finally reached the execution phase. His "vengeance and immortality" shtick might lack the eloquence of a proper mission statement, but few would be able to argue with the results. Within days, the nation's most vital transportation system would be brought to its knees, and perhaps the nation along with it.

It was Casey Jones one, Transcon nothing. In a week's time, he'd be farting through silk.

He stowed his gear in the bed of his pickup before doubling back to police the area. Of his jury-rigged rail, only the gum remained. The wire and duct tape had been whisked away in the wake of the train.

He reached down and removed the gum, now filthy from the diesel soot and dirt that coated the rail. He rolled it around in his fingers until it was reduced to a small black ball. Turning around for a last look at the smashed train below, he absentmindedly popped the gum in his mouth.

"Rest in pieces," he said as he chewed, smiling at the bitter flavor the rail had added, certain it was the taste of victory.

As he slid back into the driver's seat of his truck, the giddiness of success prompted him to sing aloud.

"I've been working on the railroad, all the livelong day . . ."

– 2 –

San Bernardino Yard was a tangled maze of tracks, the byproduct of a century's worth of piecemeal overhauls conducted at decade intervals. The collective result was a switchman's nightmare, described by locals as a working model of chaos theory built entirely out of Rubik's Cubes.

The primary reshuffling of cars was accomplished in "the bowl," thirty parallel tracks that gradually decreased in length from top to bottom. Seen from the air, it resembled a large bowl, hence the name. As aerial observers were in short supply in the late 1890s, the nickname for this particular yard feature survived for many years on a leap of faith.

Twin switching leads ran along the ends of the bowl tracks, then branched off in a dozen different directions, guiding locomotives and rolling stock to the car shop, roundhouse, scale track, locomotive washrack, and other destinations on the periphery of the yard. As was proven on many occasions by local switch crews, it was technically possible to get from any one location in the yard to another, as long as you were willing to throw the two dozen switches necessary to line the path.

Every track was imprinted on Division Superintendent Cal Farranger's mind like a map. He walked through the bowl tracks, performing the same daily inspection he had for the last eleven years. If something were out of place, he'd know it instantly.

The only good thing about the yard layout, thought Farranger, *is that it is so inherently flawed, even Transcon can't make it any worse.* He half wondered if he wasn't selling the new owners short, but considering the damage they had managed to inflict in the first six months of their takeover, who was to say how badly they could screw up the yard if they really put their minds to it?

Six o'clock in the morning and with only one cup of coffee in him, Farranger was still feeling fuzzy. Normally as he made his rounds he'd be thinking about the switch lists he would be marking up for the three daylight yard jobs coming on duty in a matter of minutes. But today his mind was fixed on the terrible train wreck that had taken place the previous day at Demonio Canyon Bridge in Arizona.

Two of his men had died yesterday.

Good men. Wallace Colvin and Sam Montilli. Farranger knew them well. The first time in ten years they'd had fatalities on the line. A real horror story. His was a risky business, but railroaders were trained always to be on high alert, checking for potential weaknesses in the system. Still, so many things could go wrong.

Maintaining the tracks was essential to the safety of the railroad. Of course, there'd be an investigation to find out what caused the accident, and make sure it never happened again. Initial indications were that the crewmen had died because of a broken rail. If that were true, Cal was certain that Transcon's penny-pinching refusal to spend money on track maintenance was to blame. Farranger would damn sure read every word of that official report.

He seriously doubted that Transcon would own up to its incompetence. If his short history with the new owners was any indication, Transcon would figure out a way to shift the blame to the train crew, then sue the dead crew's estate for damages. It was a stunning display of managerial arrogance, and Farranger vowed he'd not let the Transcon management team get away with it, even though technically, he was one of them.

Transcon had kept him on after the acquisition of the California Western because he knew the line. One day he had been running his own shortline railroad, the next he was just one of twelve Transcon division superintendents, managing his small part of a massive eighty-thousand-mile rail network that ran coast-to-coast. As superintendent, he was grand marshal of the parade of trains rumbling through Southern California and Arizona, the biggest transshipping point on the West Coast.

Grand marshal, nursemaid, whipping boy.

End of the Line

At least he was for now.

He'd known from the beginning his days were numbered. It was only a matter of time before Transcon replaced him with one of their own, a twenty-something MBA who had never even whiffed diesel fuel. From the feel of things lately, it was going to be sooner rather than later.

At five-foot-eleven, Farranger was well aware that he fell below average height for a railroad officer. The rail industry had long subscribed to the theory that size mattered, at least when it came to physically enforcing the rules on its union workforce. Farranger had never needed to use strong-arm tactics, but he could remember dealings with some pretty ornery conductors when a few extra pounds would have come in handy. What made Farranger stand out among his rail brethren was that he had none of the traditional scars. Not a scratch. This was a spectacular accomplishment in an industry where seniority could reliably be determined by whoever had the fewest fingers or the most prosthetics. The past twenty years had taken their toll, however. His sharp, lake-colored eyes were heavily lined with wrinkles.

Stepping across the steel rails of the yard, Farranger noted with annoyance that the track 12 switch was rusted and inoperable. It should have been nothing, no more than a minor note. But his mood lent meaning to the most insignificant signs of decay.

Nearly finished with his inspection, Farranger cut through the middle of the bowl, making his way toward an old passenger terminal that served as division headquarters. As he crossed 10 track, he saw a lone figure wearing a railroader's cap standing between the rails of an empty track twenty car-lengths away.

The figure in the cap was concentrating so intently on his cell phone conversation that he was oblivious to his surroundings and the danger he was in. He took no notice of Farranger, who was now heading toward him at an increasingly brisk pace.

"Hey," Farranger yelled at the top of his lungs. "You're in the foul. Get off the tracks."

The lone figure responded with a dismissive wave, turned his back to Farranger, then cupped a second hand over the cell phone to shut out the background noise.

That tears it, Farranger thought to himself. *I might not be able to stop Transcon from screwing up my railroad, but I'll be damned if I'm going to be ignored in my own backyard.*

Farranger increased his speed to a run, lowering his body as if he were lining up on a tackling dummy. At impact, he was running at full sprint. He upended the unsuspecting man, sending him flying to a face-first landing on the ballast.

Standing up, Farranger regarded the man with disdain, until he noticed the railroader's cap had flown off, revealing a mass of brown-gold hair. The stunned woman rolled over on her back to see her assailant. She recovered her composure quickly enough to flash Farranger an angry what-the-hell look.

With the low squeaking of steel wheels, a sixty-ton gondola car rolled over the spot that the woman had been standing on only seconds before. Still disoriented from the body block, her face registered a vague understanding of what had happened.

Too close for comfort, Farranger thought with a shudder. A few seconds later, and she'd have been dead. A shame, too. As the road crews would say, she was nice scenery.

"Your field of vision would be greatly improved if you'd pull your head out of your ass," he said angrily. He removed the radio packset from his belt. "South end yard engine, if you guys are through bowling for broads in 8 track, can you make a pickup?"

"Roger," a voice answered between two bursts of static. "We're about to put in for beans anyway, so we're already headed that way. Oh, yeah, we brought the stuff you asked for."

Farranger turned to the woman who was just beginning to sit up.

"Who the hell are you, and what are you doing in the yard?"

"I'm Megan Langford," she managed. "I have business with Superintendent Farranger."

Farranger paused at her reply, suppressing his natural instinct to identify himself. Pissed as he was, he would allow himself to have some fun with her.

"Farranger works in the terminal building." He motioned to the three-story passenger terminal just beyond the bowl. "You'll know him. He's the only guy around here that wears a tie."

End of the Line

Megan rose, slapping the dust off her canvas jacket and blue jeans. Straightening, she craned her head to look past a boxcar toward the nineteenth-century building he'd identified. When she turned back around, her rude benefactor was already walking away from her.

"I'm not finished talking to you," Megan yelled out after him.

Of that, Farranger was certain. But he was finished talking to her, at least for now. He replied with the same dismissive wave she had given him earlier. Given his foul mood, it felt particularly satisfying.

His delight was short-lived, replaced almost instantly by guilt from having treated her so shabbily. His first thought was to go back and apologize for his ungentlemanly behavior, then sternly explain the dangers of a railroad yard in a manner that would stick. It would have to wait though. A quick glance behind him found the woman was halfway to the terminal tower. Since she would be looking for him, he could make amends there.

Farranger continued his rounds, contemplating the bitter truth of the dangers of railroading. Train service was hazardous to your health, a truth so universally accepted that a newly hired employee was instructed to eat before his first shift so he wouldn't have to die on an empty stomach. Farranger could personally vouch for the truth behind this odd custom, having attended more funerals than retirement parties. But it was something you learned to live with—for the most part. Those that couldn't handle the danger quit and did something else for a living. If you'd been at it so long that railroading was in your blood, you left train service and took another job on the railroad—division superintendent, for instance.

Farranger watched silently as a switch engine arrived, stopping half a car-length away from his position. An older man in coveralls dismounted from the locomotive's front platform. Farranger was pleased to see that the switch foreman was carrying the material he'd requested. Barry Lounds had brought a fusee, the railroad equivalent of a common road flare. The fancy name allowed vendors to charge twice what it was worth.

"What are we celebrating, boss?" Lounds asked.

"It's Sim's eighty-first birthday today." Farranger took the fusee from the foreman's hand, then walked toward the front of the locomotive. Reaching down, he grabbed one of four thick black rubber hoses extending from the engine. The hose had a nonstandard attachment, a custom extension he'd designed himself. "I think we should light it up in style."

"You sure you want to do this?" Lounds asked him.

"Get me a torpedo." Farranger passed a hand sign to the engineer, who nodded from his place behind the control console. Seconds later, a stutter of air hissed through the brakeline.

The switch foreman shook his head in mock disapproval, then pulled the requested item out of his pocket and handed it to Farranger.

Slightly bigger than a can of snuff, the torpedo had a four-inch flexible metal strip on the end that attached to the rail, with a small charge inside designed to explode harmlessly under the rolling wheels of a locomotive. It was designed to alert an unwary train crew that track repairs were in progress dead ahead.

Farranger used the torpedo's metal strip to attach it to the fusee, then dropped them both down the air hose. As he gently tapped shut the butterfly-valve angle cock that allowed airflow through the hose, he could feel his foul mood dissipate.

Lounds laughed. "This is gonna be one of those special beer-ad moments that helps us all bond, isn't it?"

"Oh, yeah." Farranger curved the air hose around the front of the engine until the three-story terminal control tower was directly in the line of fire.

Somewhere inside the control tower sat eighty-one-year-old Lucas Sims, lord of all he surveyed. As yardmaster, Sims was afforded a panoramic view of the yard through an eight-foot-high window that extended the full length of the floor. The tower was a quarter mile away, but it was a big target.

"Jeez," Lounds said nervously, his laugh fading as he realized where Farranger was aiming. "The old man has heart trouble, doesn't he?"

"Believe me, it's gonna take a lot more than this to send Luke Sims off to his great reward," Farranger said, then quickly opened the angle cock valve to supply air to the hose. The fusee and torpedo combination exploded out of the makeshift air cannon, tumbling in a mortar-round arc toward the tower.

His aim was true. The fusee sailed over twenty car-lengths before striking the front glass of the yardmaster's station, exploding on impact. Even from a distance, the sound was so loud, it had to be deafening to Sims on the other side of the tower's protective glass.

Seconds later, an irate voice roared over the radio. "This is Sims, God damn it! Which one of you small-peckered piss ants did that? If that's the south end job, I've flushed things that put in more work than you. Over."

Farranger reached for the packset radio on his belt and depressed the transmit button, but let the laughter of the switch crewmen crowd the airwaves for a few seconds before responding.

"Number One, this is Farranger. Over," he managed before his own laughter overtook him.

"Go ahead, Cal. Over," Sims said, obviously unaware that Farranger had been an accomplice in the assault.

"Sorry about that. We were testing one of these new self-propelled fusees, and it got away from us. Over."

"Don't give me that shit!" Sims boomed over the radio with renewed anger. "I taught you that trick twenty years ago. Over."

"How's my aim, Sims?"

"A little off to the left, Cal." The yardmaster's angry tone quickly faded. "Me, I'd have hit dead on. But then, I'm used to handling big hoses. Over."

Farranger smiled. Sims had never been known for humility, or tact. Not that he needed any. Yardmaster Sims was the only man in the yard who had no fear of Transcon. Protected by a 1954 labor agreement, Sims was completely immune to being downsized. The new owners had tried to force retirement, but to no avail. The only way they'd get Sims out of the tower would be to pry his dead fingers off the microphone.

Still laughing, Farranger bid the yard crew farewell and headed toward the terminal tower. Exiting the bowl tracks, he carefully navigated his way alongside the mix of broken concrete and dirt that served as the main parking lot in the San Bernardino Yard.

The condition of the asphalt was symptomatic of a much greater maintenance problem.

Everywhere he looked he could see decay resulting from Transcon's neglect of the physical plant. Track repairs that weren't postponed were canceled altogether. Temporary speed restrictions became permanent, seriously reducing the velocity of trains between terminals.

Parked directly in front of the tower was the one piece of decay he could personally claim credit for, an old hyrail truck he used when making on-track inspections. Like everything else in the yard, the hyrail had seen better days. The engine had been replaced twice, the body provided a full accounting for the 480,000 miles displayed on the odometer. Its four hyrail guides, the flanged steel wheels that allowed it to run over railroad tracks, were rusty and looked inoperable. Still, he loved it.

Farranger opened the driver's side door, then reached under the seat for a plain navy jacket that was soiled from months of hibernation in the back of the truck. As he threw on the jacket, a shrill tone came from one of the pockets. He reluctantly reached inside for a Transcon-issued pager.

The LCD caller indicator announced PHIL ADASHEK on the screen. A chill went down Farranger's back. Phil Adashek, Transcon's VP of operations, was the greatest evil perpetrated by new owners against the former California Western Line. Nicknamed the Axeman for his ability to trim the corporate fat, Adashek seemed personally dedicated to downsizing his most productive employees.

The page could mean only one thing: Buried somewhere between the lines of a balance sheet was a decision that yet another position in Farranger's territory was expendable. This shortsighted thinking from Transcon had already cost him three of his best trainmasters and the division engineer in charge of maintenance, and he'd never once been consulted before a cut was made.

He bounced the pager in his hand as if checking the weight, then heaved it toward the bowl tracks and certain destruction. It was a futile action, but he found it satisfying nonetheless.

His radio crackled again.

"Cal, this is Number One. Over."

End of the Line

Cal pulled the mobile packset off his belt and flicked the knob. "Go ahead, Sims. Over."

"You just lose another pager?"

"Yeah, must have slipped."

"Well, it ain't gonna make Mr. Adashek go away. He's upstairs in your office."

"The Axe—" Cal stopped himself, remembering he was on an open radio frequency. "Adashek's here?" he asked.

"Roger that. Upstairs in your office," Sims replied.

"Understand. Farranger out."

"Best get the tie, Cal. Number One out."

Cal looked up at Sims through the tinted glass on the second level of the terminal tower. He nodded at the old man, then reached into his right jacket pocket and retrieved a crumpled blue tie—his corporate camouflage. It was pre-tied with a double Windsor and loosened just enough so he could slip it over his neck.

Tightening the knot around his neck, he couldn't help but feel a little silly. Formalities like ties hadn't been necessary on the California Western. Getting the freight over the road had been the only thing that mattered. As long as the customers got their cars on time, everybody was happy.

Congratulations, he told himself. *They've finally turned you into a suit.* Small consolation that it wasn't much of a suit, or that it didn't even fit particularly well.

Megan Langford watched Farranger through the glass doors on the ground floor of the terminal building. "Aw, shit," she huffed as she saw him don the tie, instantly realizing just who it was that had jerked her around at their previous encounter. Division Superintendent Farranger's smug condescension was an indignity she would make him pay for tenfold. Up to that point, she had planned on being reasonable.

She studied her adversary closely. He had the athletic frame and rugged good looks that usually drew her to a man. If he wasn't management, she might even fool herself into thinking she could be attracted to him.

By Megan's estimate, Farranger didn't look like the typical management goon, and he certainly didn't dress the part. There was something else, too. The standard management grimace, that get-back-to-work-or-I'll-fire-your-ass expression that Transcon seemed to issue its field superintendents with their first check, was missing from his face.

She had to remind herself that appearances could be deceiving. By virtue of his position alone, Farranger was a foot soldier in Transcon's army of union-crushing bastards. In Megan's book, he was the enemy.

As he approached the entrance, she psyched herself up. If she'd learned anything during her short tenure as a union officer, it was never to show any sign of weakness to management. Now that she was the regional general chairman to two thousand West Coast trainmen, this was especially true.

Farranger may have saved her life twenty minutes ago, but her mission was the same. She held him responsible for the death of two of her membership at Canyon Demonio. If Farranger thought she owed him something, or that their previous encounter meant she'd be a pushover, he'd be sadly mistaken.

- 3 -

As he crossed the lobby of the decrepit terminal building, Farranger saw the young woman he'd tackled in the yard briskly coming toward him. He noticed that she had made herself at home, helping herself to some coffee from a makeshift station in the lobby.

He was tempted to reprimand her for using amenities reserved for his switch crews, but decided he'd already antagonized her enough for one day. Besides, the ceramic mug she'd borrowed to drink from belonged to Switch Foreman Lounds, who would be thrilled at the idea. It would be the closest he'd gotten to a woman's lips in twenty years.

Megan moved toward Farranger with long aggressive strides. Without her railroader's cap, he noticed how well her gold-hued hair framed her slightly flushed face. She rolled right up to him without breaking eye contact. As he expected, the tie had been a dead giveaway. She knew who he was.

"Division Superintendent Farranger," she said coldly. "I hereby render notice of grievance filed by the Railway Transportation Union in the deaths of Wallace Colvin and Samuel Montilli in the Canyon Demonio disaster."

Great, Farranger thought, *an RTU rep.* She was the first female union rep he'd ever encountered. Her eyes were a deep hazel, and he found her pretty in an unadorned way. He felt himself momentarily transfixed in her strong gaze.

She shoved a sheaf of paperwork at his chest and blundered on. "This notice doesn't preclude civil action and in no way impinges on the right of the families to secure relief through any extralegal avenues . . ."

Though Farranger remained silent, his message somehow got through. *Dial it down a few notches, girl.* He realized it wasn't aggression he was getting from her, but nervousness.

Taking a deep breath, she started again. "I'm Megan Langford, regional general chairman of the union."

"Cal Farranger," He extended his hand in greeting, but the woman made no attempt to complete the handshake. She only looked down on his outstretched hand as if he were a leper. Cal left his arm hanging in the air for two uncomfortable beats before sheepishly retracting it.

Nice-sized chip on her shoulder. Farranger had seen it before in women railroaders. So determined to claim their rightful place in a male-dominated industry that they wound up trying too hard. Normally he would cut them some slack. Not this morning.

"You finished?" he asked, intending it as a reprimand. He held the grievance notice as though it were a piece of litter he had just picked up and would dispose of the next time he passed a garbage can.

"Not even started."

"Uh-huh," Farranger said, staring at her coldly. "Did you know Sam or Wally?"

The woman faltered, dropping her gaze. "I never met either of them."

Farranger's broad jaw tightened. "Wally Colvin hasn't any family to speak of. Living alone in an eight-hundred-square-foot double-wide out in Needles. Had a German shepherd, though, and I guess the dog might be considering suing."

"It's not a trivial matter."

"No, it sure isn't." He turned away and headed toward the stairwell at the edge of the lobby. The stairwell was protected by a secure door with a push-button lock. Once behind it, he'd be rid of her.

"Two union brothers are dead," she sputtered. "The train turned over because Transcon's too cheap to pay for proper track maintenance."

Farranger ignored her and continued toward the stairwell door, increasing his pace.

End of the Line

"The talk is that Phil Adashek and his resident lap dog, Cal Farranger, have decided to blame the crew to cover their own asses," she called after him. "Care to comment on that?"

Farranger recoiled in disbelief. *All right, maybe it was aggression.* The woman was out for more than a grievance notice. She wanted to nail him, find someone to blame for the wreck. He wasn't going to give her that.

He continued toward the door.

"Tell me, Farranger," she yelled now, "how many employees are you willing to kill for the sake of a few dollars?"

An image of Sam Montilli's genial smile flashed through Farranger's mind. He turned around, his own face reddening.

"Langford," he snapped between clenched teeth, "you're new to this job, so let me help you out." She started to speak, but he cut her off, reaching the end of his patience. "You're pissed because you think the roadbed's falling apart and isn't safe to run trains. Half of your employees are out of work because the short-haul business is gone. The other half are never allowed to lay off because it's cheaper to have just a few employees and work them to death than it is to spread the work around and have to pay benefits. Worse—"

"Listen—" Megan interrupted, but he held up his hand. She had to be stopped.

"Worse, every time something goes wrong, Transcon figures out a way to blame it on the employees. Does that pretty much sum it up?"

The woman fell silent, uncertain how to respond. Because, Farranger thought grimly, there was nothing left to say. He had taken the words right out of her mouth.

He paused, weighing his next words carefully. "I don't disagree with any of that. Your big mistake, Langford, is that you assume I'm in a position to do something about it."

"But . . . you're in charge of—"

"I'm not in charge of anything," Farranger said, his voice firm. Painful as it was to admit, it was the truth.

Her hazel eyes flashed. "Mr. Farranger, I demand an immediate conference with you to discuss specific grievances. Per section 10, paragraph 23b of our schedule agreement," she recited.

Man, she must have the whole damned agreement memorized. "Suit yourself," he said. "I don't have time to talk to some roundhouse lawyer with her panties in a knot. I'll send Yardmaster Sims down. You can talk to him. He's a little hard of hearing, though."

She stared at him as though she were about to erupt. "Damn it, Farranger, we've got a contract! You can't just ignore me the way you ignore repairs."

"Fine. Put your grievances in a letter. File a time claim. Do whatever it is you union people do instead of actual work."

He turned his back on her, half expecting her invective to continue as he punched in the combination to the secure door. Instead, he was startled by a minor explosion just a foot to the right of his head.

"What the hell?" Cal blurted unconsciously.

Looking down, he saw shards of a ceramic coffee mug strewn about the floor. He stared open-mouthed at Megan for a moment, then shook his head, suppressing his urge to laugh. Say what you want about the union, but they knew how to underscore a point.

"Well, aren't we spunky?" Cal said to the still seething union rep, holding the door to his escape half open.

"You will not ignore me," Megan demanded as she grabbed a second coffee mug as reserve ammunition.

Cal believed her. This woman was 100 percent piss and vinegar. From the look on her face, she was ready to kick his ass right there, right now. Sizing her up, he figured he could win a physical confrontation, though he might lose a testicle in the process. Perhaps it was time to reconsider his approach.

"You have legitimate grievances, Chairman Langford." Cal held up both hands, palms out. The gesture was less an olive branch than a shortstop for anything else she might throw. "If I still have a job at the end of the day, I'll be happy to sit down with you and discuss your issues at length."

Farranger observed his peace offering had only slightly pacified the union rep. She didn't appear to be entirely convinced about his change of heart.

"Fine," Megan acknowledged, as if she were carefully weighing her nonexistent other options.

End of the Line

"And how exactly will I get a hold of you?" she asked suspiciously.

Cal flashed a Cheshire grin. "Page me."

Sprinting to the top of the stairs, Farranger scanned the yard through the window. Depressing. The tracks were less than half full. In the days of the California Western, nearly all the yard's switching tracks had been crowded to capacity.

Transcon had decided it was a good idea to trim down operations. Almost as soon as the ink was dry on the California Western acquisition, the new owners had started running off what they called "low margin" local business, eliminating rail access to a number of industries that had been loyal California Western customers for decades. Many of these former customers were now bankrupt or barely solvent. As far as Farranger was concerned, it was shortsighted thinking at best. He couldn't fathom how Transcon figured they'd make more money by turning customers away.

From the top of the stairs, Farranger could see into the yardmaster's station, illuminated only by the daylight spilling from the big bank of smoked windows looking out onto the yard. Sims had busied himself behind an underutilized computer terminal, his stooped shoulders hunched toward the screen, his thinning white hair matted to his scalp. Farranger was pleased to see that. Sims normally didn't trust computers, preferring to eyeball the yard. With sixty years of experience, he was an expert at directing the switch engines, placing every car where it belonged without ever looking at a freight manifest. The grand master in a three-dimensional chess game.

"Morning," Farranger said, entering the office.

Swiveling around in his chair, Sims grinned at him. "It's my eighty-first birthday, and I'm still alive. What do you think of that?"

"Congratulations," Farranger chuckled. "If you make it till noon, I'll win the pool."

"Damn it," Sims replied, a smile pulling at his lips. "I thought you stopped that pool crap last year. I'm getting a little tired of you guys betting on when I'm gonna die."

"Not me, Sims. I keep betting you're going to live another year. I've won the pool four years running."

"Well, don't put any money on me next year," Sims sighed, his tone serious now. "The man upstairs wants me to die."

"God's not ready for you yet, Sims. Besides, what are the chances of a yardmaster going to heaven?"

"I ain't talking about *that* man. I'm talking about that bastard Adashek. He's waiting for you upstairs."

"He's slumming." Farranger suspected it was going to be a very bad morning.

"He's been trying to kill me, you know," Sims said.

"What did he offer you this time?"

Sims frowned. "Two years' pay and a trip to France."

"The bastard!" Farranger laughed.

"Damn it all, it ain't funny. He raises the ante damn near every week. You know what that means when you've been railroading as long as me?"

"Let me guess. You'll die of the railroad curse on the next full moon."

"You might think it's bullshit, Cal, but I'll be dead inside a month. That's a fact."

Cal found Sims's superstitious nature mildly amusing. Retirement was thought of as a death sentence to most railroaders, and it was an odd curiosity that most of them did die almost as soon as they left the industry. After years of working the bizarre hours demanded by the vagaries of train schedules, they had difficulty adjusting to regular hours and the sudden loss of purpose. Sims had been trying to convince Farranger for years that it was a curse of the first magnitude. Cal had considered it utter nonsense for a long time, but after seeing it happen continually over the past three decades, he could no longer be sure.

"If it makes you feel any better, Sims," he smiled, trying to shake off a sense of foreboding, "you can come up to the tower eight hours a day after you retire and pretend you're working. Come to think of it, I'm not sure I'd be able to tell the difference."

End of the Line

Sims shook his head slowly. "It ain't gonna happen, Cal. I'm protected by the yardmaster contract. I'm bulletproof." He shifted his gaze to meet his coworker's. "You ain't, though."

Farranger felt his stomach tighten. "What's that supposed to mean?"

"The Axeman didn't fly all the way out here for tea. He's gonna fire you, and he wants to do it in person. Damn shame, too. You're the best boss I ever trained. You should've cooperated."

Farranger's unease turned to rage. "Canyon Demonio wasn't the crew's fault!"

Sims nodded in agreement. "Gap in the rail is what I hear. The odd thing is Cisneros ran a geometry car over that section less than twenty-four hours before it happened. He must have missed something."

"Cisneros doesn't miss anything." This was new information to Farranger. Cal reconsidered the Demonio accident for the first time. Juan Cisneros was the most tight-assed track inspector he'd ever met. No way in hell he missed a defect that could derail a train.

Sims's face clouded over. "Could've been the track anyway."

"Maybe," Farranger sighed. He didn't articulate the thought tugging at him. *Sabotage.*

Sims seemed to read his mind, and rejected the suspicion with a wave of his hand. "They laid light rail off to Arizona. You know whose bright idea that was, don't you?"

He did. The son of a bitch who was waiting up on the third floor. The Axeman.

"Reducing overhead," Farranger said bitterly. "We lost fifteen million dollars of freight and killed two good men."

"Damn shame," Sims said. "We haven't had a fatality in almost ten years, not since—"

"Not since I killed my conductor," Farranger completed the sentence wryly. "Is that what you were going to say?"

"Wasn't your fault, Cal."

"Tell that to his widow," Farranger muttered. Turning away, he surveyed the yard below.

Sims rose from his chair and crossed to the window.

"The delivery just came." He poked his foot at a cardboard box on the floor with the railroad police emblem stamped on its side. It had already been opened. "The cinderdick brought it in this morning," he went on, using the old railroader's term for railway police.

Farranger felt a rush of dread. He knew what was in the box—the Canyon Demonio crew's personal effects.

But except for a small cellular phone, the box was empty.

"Not much to show for a lifetime," Farranger said.

"The rest of their gear's still buried on the canyon floor," Sims noted. "Don't think we'll ever find it. The phone's got to belong to Montilli. Colvin didn't believe in them."

"I guess I need to pay a visit to Montilli's next of kin. See if Colvin's damned dog has a home. Unless you want to do it."

Sims shook his head.

Trying to conceal his emotion, Farranger slipped the phone into his jacket pocket. Pretty appropriate for a lifetime of railroading, he thought. A condolence visit will be my last official act.

- 4 -

Though Casey had never been to Yermo, California, he found it to be hate at first sight. Other cities rate temperature on a comfort index, but he was certain Yermo used a spontaneous combustion meter. It was a dry heat in the sense that the planet Mercury had a dry heat.

The nuclear-testing-site quality of the Yermo landscape caused him to rethink his recent convictions. Just yesterday he was certain Canyon Demonio was the most godforsaken place he'd ever seen. But after one glimpse of Yermo, he mentally downgraded Demonio to a distant second. If Demonio was a shithole, Yermo was where it drained to.

Casey reminded himself he wasn't on a sightseeing tour. Yermo was a target of opportunity, nothing more. Located six hours west of Canyon Demonio and three hours east of LAX, Yermo was perfectly situated for his needs. He could drive in, take care of business, and then fly out before nightfall.

In the pristine air of the desert afternoon, sound carried more reliably than the distortions of light, and Casey heard the screech of steel as it rolled through the Yermo yard long before he could see the train.

Then it came into view, its flat metallic skin shimmering behind the waves of morning heat. That would be the M-BALA-01, four diesel locomotives with a train of sixty cars behind, at least forty of which were tankers hauling chlorine gas.

Ducking below the concrete culvert at the edge of the yard he waited, pen to paper. As the train bore down on him, he wrote with a flourish, then tucked the note in a small leather pouch.

When the four-unit locomotive consist at the head of the train passed by, he crept out of the culvert, climbed the steep bank of ballast, and hopped aboard the end of a boxcar. Slipping into the narrow space between the cars, he was safely hidden from the crew.

Invisible.

That Yermo existed at all was a tribute to the railroad. Yermo squatted at the intersection of lines from Los Angeles, Bakersfield, and Needles, California. Without the railroad, Yermo might have become just another windblown, gypsum-mining ghost town. But as it happened—a direct result of its location—Yermo was home to one of the largest railheads in California.

A hundred tracks crisscrossed the Yermo yard. The two main lines running along the northern edge dispersed freight to a thousand destinations on the Transcon system, each a more desirable locale than Yermo. Escaping this desert wasteland was a priority for every trainman working the road, and Conductor Lance Botone was no exception.

Botone was on the M-BALA-01, a manifest train bound for Los Angeles. It rolled slowly from departure track 4, held at the yard-limit speed of 10 mph before stopping short at the red signal that governed movement out of yard limits.

He picked up the radio handset from his post inside the lead locomotive's cab and dialed in the frequency for Yermo Hightower. "Yermo Tower, this is Conductor Botone on train M-BALA-01. Respectfully request permission to highball. Over."

"Roger, BALA," blared the yardmaster's voice over the speaker. "Wait for clearance. Yermo Tower out."

Botone recognized the voice of Yardmaster Al Yeck, a man he'd decided must be the missing link between apes and really ugly apes. Botone had first met him when Yeck was only an engineer, and not a particularly good one, either. Rumor had it that Superintendent Farranger only promoted Yeck because he didn't trust him behind a throttle—one of the few management decisions

End of the Line

Botone ever agreed with. The steep Cajon Pass, the most treacherous run on the entire system, was no place for mediocrity. Best to have Yeck in the tower, where he couldn't hurt anyone.

Botone glanced at Engineer Paulie Fredericks, at ease behind the control console. They were both middle-aged and slightly overweight, with thinning gray hair and no interest in their appearances. The two men dressed almost identically, both wearing steel-toed boots, jeans, flannel shirts, and "birth control" safety glasses, so called because it was unlikely that anyone wearing them would ever find a mate. The crew had nearly sixty years of seniority between them.

"'Respectfully request permission to highball?'" Fredericks mocked his conductor. "You're kissing up to the yardmaster now?"

"If you're going to kiss ass," Botone retorted, "make it a French kiss."

"If you're in so tight with management," Fredericks said, "how come you didn't get us a better train? This is the third dog I've had in a row. Why can't I get one of those seventy-mile-an-hour intermodal hotshots? I always get stuck on dogs that only do forty-five."

"You take what's on the lineup, Paulie," Botone replied, with all the patience he could muster.

"This is gonna suck, and you know it," Fredericks said. "I've spent the last four trips on dogs. It doesn't seem right."

"You said three trips just a minute ago," Botone reminded him.

"Hell, I've worked so much lately, I can't keep it straight. I've been marked up for the last ninety days. Ninety! Transcon's too damn cheap to hire more engineers, so the crew caller won't let me lay off."

"Yeah, I'm in the same boat," Botone said. "But think of the money you're making. I pulled nearly four thousand the first pay-half of the month."

"Money won't do me any good if I die of exhaustion."

Botone thought Paulie looked spry enough, but decided not to argue with him on this point.

The engineer now gave the control panel his full attention. He centered his reverser and checked the continuity in the brakepipe. "What do we have tonight, anyway?" Fredericks asked.

"Sixty-some cars. Mostly tanks of chlorine, flammable liquids—"

The engineer cut Botone off in midsentence with a wave of his hand. "I've got an engine to run. I don't care about any of that Hazmat stuff unless I'm taking my yearly rules test. Just give me the tonnage, and you can go back to sleep. I'll wake you up if we need to throw a switch."

A familiar voice cut through the static coming over the yard channel. "Train M-BALA-01, this is Yermo Tower. BALA has permission to highball. Over."

"Roger, Yermo Tower. Highball. Train M-BALA-01 out," Botone responded.

The signal governing movement to the mainline flashed green.

Fredericks responded immediately by releasing the independent brake, placing the reverser lever in forward, and advancing the throttle to Run Two of a possible eight. As soon as the slack stretched out of the train, he notched up to Run Three. Not a moment after the engines were on the main line, he started fidgeting with his safety glasses.

Botone could see his engineer's discomfort, but he was afraid to say anything for fear of triggering another round of complaints. It didn't matter. Fredericks was pissed off.

"And another thing," Fredericks continued, turning to his partner. "Why the hell do I have to wear safety glasses? I never leave the cab."

"Railroad rules are written in blood, Paulie," Botone shot back. The cliché was hoary, but he hoped it would silence the engineer.

"Some idiot got his eye put out fifty years ago doing something stupid," Fredericks ranted, "and I have to suffer for it?"

Botone didn't answer, but he removed his safety glasses and shoved them into his pocket. This time, Fredericks smiled. He took his glasses off, too, letting them dangle from the neck strap.

Relaxing somewhat, Botone focused his eyes on the iron pathway before them. All the switch-stand reflectors indicated green. His train was already lined for the main track, so he wouldn't have to leave the cab to throw a single switch. As he peered ahead to double-check this minor stroke of luck, he decided that this might not be such a bad trip after all.

If one intended to create a disaster, the BALA's flammable liquids and poisonous gas were just what the doctor ordered—Dr. Mengele, anyway. Casey had done his research carefully, and had determined that the BALA suited his need perfectly. By his estimate, the BALA was more than a superior choice; it was the Love Canal on wheels.

As the head end of the BALA passed the Yermo hightower and swung onto the main line, Casey pressed himself against the ladder. It was here that there was a risk of the yardmaster spotting him—the moment of greatest exposure.

Casey held his breath as the thirteenth boxcar rumbled over the switch from departure track 4 to the main line. No challenge was raised, no warning shouted from trackside—he had made it undetected.

The train would remain steady at 10 mph, until the last car cleared the Yermo yard limits. Then the engineer would advance the throttle until a track speed of 45 mph was attained.

Once fifty of the BALA's cars were occupying the north track, Casey was completely out of view of the tower. He released his grip on the ladder and stepped out on the knuckle connecting his boxcar with the tank car behind him.

He looked beneath it, visually tracing the hard rubber air hoses that connected the cars and spanned the gap between them like suspension cables from a bridge.

Taking a deep breath, Casey reached beneath the boxcar for the angle cock, carefully tapping the lever shut with the palm of his hand. Shutting it too quickly would shock the brakepipe and create an unintended application of the brakes. It closed without incident. The air brakes were now bottled on the rear two-thirds of the train.

Still in position over the angle cock, he lock-wired a small leather pouch to its base. In the pouch was his love letter to Transcon.

His personal declaration of war.

Yesterday's derailment at Canyon Demonio had been just a dress rehearsal. Until Transcon was told otherwise, the missing rail at Demonio would be written off as a track defect or maintenance blunder. But this time, the message would be unmistakable.

"Chlorine gas," Casey mused. "When you care enough to send the very best."

The BALA's cargo would be deadly, even when diluted over the wide-open spaces of suburban San Bernardino.

With the pouch secure, it was time for Casey to leave the conductor and engineer to their fate. Casey edged back out to the ladder and climbed down to the lowest rung. The train was speeding up, already at 20 mph. The eight-foot drop to the rapidly descending shoulder of the track mound would be treacherous. But since the train would never be slower than it was at this moment, waiting would be worse. With no hesitation, he jumped. He managed a full three steps before losing his footing in the ballast.

Hitting the ground, he rolled head over tail twice. Cinders flayed the skin of his arms raw, but he did not even lose his sunglasses. When his forward momentum stopped, he quickly sprang to his feet, suddenly aware that he'd managed a stuntman-worthy tumble. In self-recognition of this minor feat, he arched his back, flinging his arms over his head like an Olympic gymnast dismounting the pommel horse. Casey gave himself a ten and bowed to the applause of an invisible crowd.

The BALA creaked out of the yard, toward its date with destiny. As the train pulled away, Casey started the long jaunt to his truck, an anonymous figure in the brown dirt of a Yermo afternoon.

- 5 -

Farranger headed for his tiny office, bracing himself for the confrontation with Phil Adashek. The room on the third floor of the terminal tower was barely large enough for two people to sit comfortably, yet Sims had decided to use it as a storage closet. Even though the door—which had been removed as a courtesy to Sims—was off its hinges and resting against the wall beside the door frame, Farranger hadn't lost any privacy. Everyone, including Sims, gave him a wide berth when he was in there. Farranger had always hated paperwork, and filling out reports for corporate in the cramped confines of his office turned him into a real Mr. Hyde.

Seeing the Axeman comfortably seated behind his desk made entering the loathsome office even worse. The bastard had no qualms about taking over his turf.

Do I knock? he wondered. But there was no door.

"Hey, come on in, Cal," Phil Adashek said, easing himself to his feet. He carefully dusted off his designer pin-striped suit, smiling to give Farranger the full glare of chemically whitened teeth. "I come bearing bad news," he went on, still smiling. He waited a beat for some reaction from Farranger, who merely moved around to the opposite side of his desk. "It's about the reorganization I've been spearheading. I've got ten divisions now, not twelve, which means I've got two more division superintendents than I need."

The smooth shit. When is he going to drive the blade into my heart? Adashek gave Farranger the creeps. His movie-star good looks appeared to be the product of tanning salons and plastic surgery. Farranger couldn't call to mind another railroad man who buffed his nails. But then Adashek wasn't really railroad. He was corporate jet.

"Hey, Phil," Farranger challenged. "Why don't you come out with what you came here to say?"

"You'll land well, I know it," Adashek said, brimming with false enthusiasm. "There's a whole new world out there, with the New Economy. They're crying for top-flight executives like yourself."

Farranger looked down at his own nails, grimy with soot from the yard. "Let's put aside the idea of a railroad vice president extolling the virtues of the Internet economy," he said flatly. "Because I'll grant you it isn't the railroad it used to be, now that you've got your hooks in it."

If Adashek was firing him, Farranger was going to make him to do it with the gloves off.

"Our problem is your refusal to cooperate on Canyon Demonio. The shipper lost ten million in freight and demanded some heads. Calling it crew error was simply a business decision."

Farranger's thoughts were a maelstrom of disgust and regret. Only slime like Adashek could destroy reputations so casually, just to save face with a shipper.

"If you're giving them heads, why not start with the real culprit?" Farranger asked. "It wasn't Colvin and Montilli that cut the track-maintenance budget to the bone."

Adashek's smile froze on his face. A direct hit, Farranger noted. He didn't feel like being subtle. He held the Axeman responsible for the derailment, and wanted to make sure Adashek knew it.

"This must work out great for you, Adashek," he continued. "You rape the maintenance budget to show abnormally high short-term profits, then cash in all your stock options before the railroad implodes and move on to destroy the next company."

For a fleeting second, the Axeman looked startled, but quickly recovered.

"Transcon's making more money under my leadership than ever."

"Only until the track falls apart. I've seen what you call leadership. You've run off half our customers in less than a year. Now you're killing crews."

"I don't expect you to understand, Farranger. The customers were all low-margin anyway, so there's no harm done."

Farranger heaved a sigh. "So according to that theory, we can run off all but one of our shippers and charge him a billion dollars a car?"

Adashek ignored the comment.

"It's kind of sad, Cal. For someone who's been working for a railroad for twenty years, you show a stunning lack of knowledge about the business."

"Enlighten me," Farranger replied, doubtful there was anything Adashek could tell him about railroading.

"These local customers you've fallen in love with are bad business. We actually lose money with these mom-and-pop operations with their two-car-a-week switches. They might have been profitable for a bottom-feeding operation like the California Western, but Transcon is a long-haul carrier, a pipeline for one-hundred-car trains that run a thousand or more miles without slowing down to get switched out at every damn terminal along the way."

Cal felt a little queasy, and not nearly as righteous as he did moments ago. Adashek wasn't wrong. Farranger had seen the manifests from the cross-country shipments that terminated in L.A. Transcon made more money on one coast-to-coast through freight than all of his local customers combined. It might not be morally right to cut his local customers off at the knees, but it probably was a solid business decision. And Adashek was all business.

"You know I'm right, too, don't you Farranger?"

Cal said nothing.

"And yet you won't get on board." Adashek leaned forward, then lowered his voice. "Must be tough for you, eh, Farranger? You went from having your own personal kingdom to being my butt boy."

"I'm not your butt boy."

"And that's the problem. Since we're bearing all, do you want me to be completely honest with you?"

"Are you capable of being completely honest?"

Adashek ignored the insult.

"There is such a thing as being too much your own man, Farranger. You have the best numbers of all the superintendents that work for me. Under other circumstances, I'd not only keep you, I'd find a way to promote you."

"I'm not looking for a promotion. I just want you out of my hair so I can run my railroad."

"No," Adashek shot back. "What you want is to turn back the clock and run things the way you have for the last twenty years. That isn't going to happen. This is the twenty-first century. We can't be sentimental about inefficient customers, subsidizing them with below-market rail service to keep them from going bankrupt."

"Those inefficient customers kept the California Western in business for over a hundred years."

"Barely," Adashek retorted. "And that was when you ran a nonunion short line. Now that the RTU has unionized your workforce, they have priced themselves out of the local business market. If you weren't so cozy with the rank and file, you could see that."

Cozy. Farranger almost smiled at the suggestion, considering how he'd just treated the RTU rep downstairs.

"You realize, Phil, that these men you hold in such contempt are the ones that actually move the freight."

"At too high a price," Adashek replied. "Tell me, Farranger, do you know what a railroad runs on?"

"Number two diesel fuel?"

"Ah," acknowledged Adashek. "There's that high school graduate insubordinate wit I've grown so fond of. No, Farranger, a railroad runs on discipline. When there's an operating failure, the crew has to be disciplined as an example to the workforce. The union seems to think it runs the railroad, but I'm going to show them otherwise."

"By bad-mouthing a crew that didn't do anything? Something happened in Canyon Demonio, damn it! Aren't you interested in knowing what it was?"

"Of course. But we're informing the shipper it was crew error. That's not negotiable."

"I've known Sam Montilli for ten years, and he was a good hand. He had a wife and four kids."

"Spare me the working-man's-friend drivel."

"Why fire me before the investigation's concluded?"

Adashek paused before responding, a taunting wait-for-it smile playing on his face.

End of the Line

"Because I can."

Farranger was speechless. Life as he knew it was over.

"Clean out your gear, Farranger," Adashek ordered. "I want you gone by the end of the day. If you're on the property tomorrow, I'll have the special agents arrest you for trespassing."

-6-

Inside the lead locomotive cab of the BALA, Conductor Botone fought to stay awake. "Summit, clear block," he grumbled. The rules required him to call each signal on the trip south, but they didn't say he had to be thrilled about it.

"Clear," Paulie Fredericks responded, acknowledging the last signal before they crested Summit and began heading down the steep Cajon Pass. He could already see the massive brown cloud of smog surrounding L.A. looming on the horizon.

Botone reached down for the clipboard of forms used to record signal aspects and train speed when passed. He wrote "Summit/green" on the first blank line, then glanced at the speedometer on his side of the cab. The gauge read 45 mph.

"You can slow down any time, Paulie," he said, only half joking. "The speed down the pass is twenty-five."

"I've got six pounds of air on the train brakes. It's just taking a little time for the brakes to set on rear cars. Relax. If we're not down to speed by the time the rear car crests the grade, I'll squeeze off a few more pounds of air."

Botone watched the barren San Gabriel mountaintops pass by his window. He estimated their speed by mentally timing the old telegraph poles alongside the right-of-way. Another look at the speedometer wasn't reassuring. They weren't slowing quickly enough. His pencil began tapping nervously against the clipboard, but he knew better than to challenge the engineer.

"I hear the company's been doing a lot of speed tests out here on the mountain, Paul."

Fredericks remained tensely silent, staring intently at the control panel.

End of the Line

"They caught a couple of guys last week with a radar gun, just as they were slowing down for the mountain."

Still not a word from Fredericks. The engineer seemed oblivious to what Botone was saying, but, frowning, grabbed another eight pounds of air.

Almost instantly, the slack ran in on the train. The cars behind the turned angle cock, those without brakes, rammed the rest of the train. The force nearly knocked Botone out of his seat.

"Christ, Paulie! What the hell are you doing?" he gasped, regaining his balance.

"Got a problem with the brakes," Fredericks replied tersely, his eyes still riveted on the controls. He placed the train in emergency with a full twenty-six pounds of air. "Get a hold of the dispatcher. Tell him to get everybody clear. I just put us in emergency, and we ain't slowing down."

"Emergency! Emergency! Emergency!" Botone bellowed into the handset. He was amazed at the calmness he felt. He allowed three seconds for everyone to clear the radio before saying, "This is M-BALA-01 in emergency at milepost 3173. Our speed is . . ." He paused to recheck the speedometer. "Thirty-four miles per hour." He'd actually read 37 mph, but Fredericks's federal certification card would be suspended if they reported more than 10 mph over the authorized speed.

Seconds later, they reached 40 mph. And were still accelerating.

"M-BALA-01, this is DS21," the voice blared over the speaker. "What's your situation?"

Botone fixed his eyes on Fredericks, who placed the dynamic brakes in full dynamic, ignoring the red-lining amperage. The dynamics engaged, converting the rotary motion of the locomotive wheels into an electric current that was ultimately released as heat. Designed primarily for tweaking speed and increasing fuel efficiency, the dynamic brakes had no appreciable effect in stopping the train.

"Tell them I'm in full dynamic brake and full emergency application of the train brakes," Fredericks said. He looked grim. "The independent brakes on the three locomotives are set and the wheel sanders are on. I'm out of tricks and we're still speeding up."

Botone spoke evenly into the packset, priding himself on staying cool. "Approaching mile marker 3175, speed 50. Make that 55 mph, full dynamics engaged."

Botone felt his gut churn as he went to stand behind Fredericks. The primary braking system on the individual cars had failed. The brakes on the three locomotives were still functioning but were no match for the combined momentum of sixty loads barreling down a steep grade. Botone could already smell the independent brake shoes on the engine burning up from the stress. His fear turned to horror as he watched the speedometer rise, sweeping past 60 miles an hour. The grade would be steep for the next eighteen miles.

Botone grabbed the radio handset. "DS21, this is BALA!" he yelled. "Do we have a clear track?"

"This is DS21," the dispatcher shot back. "You're clear for the next eighteen miles, then you come to a thirty-five-mile-per-hour speed restriction at milepost 3190."

Fredericks and Botone exchanged panicked glances.

"We're screwed," Botone said.

Fredericks nodded in agreement. "Yeah, we are. We'll be doing at least eighty when we hit that curve. We'll be all over the countryside. Think we should jump?"

"At this speed? We're talking a closed-casket funeral for sure. I think I'd rather take my chances in the cab."

"Me, too," Fredericks agreed. "I'd just as soon live the extra ten minutes."

"BALA, this is DS21," the radio blared again, the handset turned up to full volume. "Recommend you put your reverser in reverse position and bring your engines up to Run Four slowly."

Botone felt sure that he'd noticed a tremor in the dispatcher's voice, and the advice baffled him. He looked to his engineer.

"It means they've written us off." Fredericks's voice went flat. "Putting the engines in reverse at this speed will unwind the traction motors. The axles will lock up and derail the locomotives. We'll be dead inside a minute."

"Then why?"

"Because they'd rather have us crash up here on the mountain than spill poison all over San Bernardino."

End of the Line

"You think the dispatcher is trying to kill us?" Botone asked, incredulous.

"No," Fredericks gasped. "As far as the dispatcher's concerned, we're already dead."

"**R**unaway!" Sims's voice shouting from the second-floor stairwell broke the silence in Farranger's office.

The instant he heard the distress call, Farranger bolted out of the office, stopping just short of a collision with Sims, who'd made his way to the top of the stairs.

"We got a runaway!" Sims exclaimed, his glasses slipping down his nose. "BALA going down Cajon Pass with no brakes."

The Axeman's face remained impassive.

"What's the situation?" Farranger asked.

"Sixty loads, mostly chlorine gas," Sims replied. "Going seventy-five miles an hour. They got a clear track all the way to the hard curve just past Baker Siding. It's a six-degree curve, Cal, they'll roll those damn tank cars for sure."

Fifteen, maybe twenty minutes, tops, Farranger figured. "What's the operations center doing?"

"The dispatcher told them to put the train in reverse, that son of a bitch."

"Standard procedure," the Axeman interjected. "That crew doesn't have a chance. No sense in taking a populated area with them."

"You might feel differently if you were on that train," Farranger snapped. He turned to Sims. "You think the crew fell for it?"

"The crew's Fredericks and Botone. They're no rocket scientists, but they're not gonna put a seventy-five-mile-an-hour train in reverse."

"It's up to us then," Farranger said. "We'll have the crew cut away from their train, then drop the cars in Baker siding. Get a hold of the nearest special agent and have him meet me at the lead switch. Call the Feds. We need a Hazmat response team on standby."

"Anything else?"

"Have your switch engines clear the road crossings. I'm gonna be hauling ass out of the yard and I don't need anybody in my way."

"Got it."

"After you get that set up, meet me out at the site if it's safe."

"Hey, Cal," the Axeman spoke up. "Just where do you think you're going?"

"To do my job," Farranger barked. "I'm still on the clock until five."

Farranger's mind blazed, not thinking about Adashek now, but about the chain of tasks that remained ahead. He needed a second pair of hands. He considered Sims, concluding in an instant that the octogenarian wasn't in any kind of shape to wrangle a runaway.

He turned to Adashek. "Care to come along, Phil? You might learn something about railroading."

Adashek backed away. "No, thanks."

Farranger shook his head. "If we don't get to it first," he said, "it's going to come to us." Then he took off, taking the stairs downward three at a time.

"What in the hell did he mean by that?" Adashek asked Sims.

"He meant for you to say your prayers," the old man said. "Chlorine gas is heavier than air. If Cal doesn't get to that train, you and I ought to be inhaling a fatal whiff of the stuff, oh, I'd say in about a half hour from now. You, me, and the rest of San Bernardino County."

– 7 –

Farranger raced down the yardmaster's station, flicking the channel selector on Sims's radio to the local road channel.

"BALA, this is San Bernardino. Over."

A long beat of silence. Then, beneath crackling static, a human voice.

"This is Botone on the BALA. That you, Cal? Over."

"Roger. Cut your engines away from the rest of the train. We'll drop the cars at Baker siding after you pass on straight track."

Before Botone had a chance to reply, the six-watt dispatcher transmitter hijacked the weaker radio on the locomotive. "This is DS21. Dropping cars is not—repeat *not*—authorized. Over."

Farranger was furious. He knew that dropping cars was considered a dangerous switchman's shortcut, banned for the past twenty years, but it was now the only logical course of action. The train would still derail, but it would be a controlled derailment. The cars would glide along the flat roadbed and remain upright instead of tumbling over at the curve. And if Farranger could get the locomotives and runaway cars on different tracks, he might be able to save the lives of the crew.

"DS21, this is Farranger. We're not sacrificing these men for the sake of your rules."

"Negative, Cal. There's no crew present at Baker Siding to throw the switch."

Farranger took a few deep breaths to calm himself. *All right,* he thought. *I'll just have to do it myself.*

He clicked through to the dispatcher. "Put the switches in Baker Siding on manual control. I'll do the rest."

He thought about putting the switches on manual himself, once he reached Baker Siding, but a safety feature would electronically lock the switch for a full five minutes during the transition. Five minutes the BALA didn't have.

"This is DS21. I need authorization to go manual, Cal. Over."

He glanced over his shoulder at the stairwell, hoping Sims and the Axeman would remain upstairs, then hailed the dispatcher again, lowering his voice. "This is Farranger. I'm acting on the direct authority of Phil Adashek. If you don't place the switches in Baker Siding on manual throw, you'll be fired before the end of the shift. You understand? Over."

A few seconds of silence passed. Farranger figured the dispatcher was trying to find out if Phil Adashek really was at the San Bernardino Yard.

"This is DS21. Switches placed in manual throw. Over."

"Roger, DS. Farranger out."

"Cal, you gonna be able to make it in time?" Botone asked, finally breaking through the radio traffic.

"I'll make it," Farranger insisted, praying he was right. "Uncouple your locomotives and make quick work of it. Kick the pinlifter and get back to the head end. Farranger out."

He ran down the last flight of stairs to the lobby, nearly out the door before he saw Megan Langford waiting to pounce on him. He'd completely forgotten about her. He blew by without uttering a word. He had bigger problems at the moment.

Cal dipped into his pocket for his keys as he ran to his truck and jumped in, but before he could turn them in the ignition, the passenger door opened. He turned in surprise to see Megan Langford sliding in next to him. Talk about picking the wrong ride on the wrong day.

"Put your seat belt on," he ordered. He didn't have time for an argument.

Before she could comply, Farranger gunned the engine in reverse, turning the wheel hard to the right. Megan was thrown sideways, her face landing squarely in his lap.

"Is this the union's new negotiating position, Ms. Langford?"

End of the Line

Cal didn't wait for an answer. He threw the truck in drive and jammed his foot on the accelerator. The pickup gave a greasy lurch forward, and as the momentum swung the door shut, he switched on the truck's dashboard radio.

"We've got a runaway," he shouted, cutting off what looked to be a world-class scream. "BALA coming down the pass without brakes."

At least he could credit the union woman with the ability to switch gears quickly. The shock and surprise on her face were replaced with a look of grim determination, and she buckled herself into the passenger's seat.

"There," she said, pointing to a trackside road that led out of the yards.

Farranger threw the steering wheel into a hard right. He grabbed at the dashboard radio and missed. Langford held up her hand.

"You drive. I'll handle communications."

The pickup bumped over a culvert, throwing both of them against the roof liner.

"BALA, come in, BALA. Over."

A static-filled pause, then a male voice. "Who's this?"

"Megan Langford. I'm with Cal Farranger."

"This is Engineer Fredericks on the BALA. Botone went back to pull the pin."

Farranger grabbed at the handset, wanting desperately to know what kind of brakes were engaged on the runaway. But he had to maneuver the truck across a waste-strewn section of yard, and he couldn't wrestle the wheel and the radio at the same time.

It didn't matter. Megan was one step ahead of him. "How are your brakes?" she said into the handset.

"Got emergency braking on the head end of the train, and full dynamic brakes. Feels like the rear of the train ain't got no brakes at all. The locomotives are set, but the shoes smell like they've mostly burned off."

"Damn it!" Farranger said. "Tell him to goddamn release his locomotive brakes. He's going to need—"

Megan cut him off, talking into the radio. "BALA? You're going to use those locomotive brakes to slow yourself down after we drop the cars in the siding. So we need to you to release what's left of them."

"Roger." Fredericks sounded sheepish.

"And hope like hell there's enough left of the shoes to stop you," Farranger muttered, completing the thought.

Megan continued. "You'll also need to ease up the dynamic brake to give your conductor enough slack to pull the pinlifter."

Farranger glanced over at her. Say what you will about the union, this woman was a real railroader.

He wrenched the wheel to the left, and the truck went into a wide-arced skid, bumping up an embankment through a gap in a chain-link fence. With a bang, it landed on a crumbling back road in an industrial backwater of San Bernardino.

As the pickup slammed down and he accelerated, Farranger realized he had been too quick with his admiration of Langford's railroading skills. There was a serious omission in her directions to the crew, a deadly error that was about put a man's life in danger.

Fredericks only did what he had been told to do. However, when he moved the independent brake handle to the release position and placed the dynamic brakes in idle, Megan's instructions caused the three locomotives to lurch so violently that Fredericks lost his balance, nearly colliding with the control console.

At that moment, Botone was squatting underneath the guardrail on the rear locomotive. He'd just managed to yank the pinlifter to release the knuckle between the locomotive and the first car, when the violent jolt jarred him off the platform.

What the hell?

Slammed backward like a rag doll, Botone landed in the narrow chasm between the rear locomotive and the first boxcar on the runaway section of the train. Inches below him, the track bed whizzed by. His back was pressed against the boxcar's access

End of the Line

ladder, his legs caught in the small space between the pinlifter and the locomotive platform, as if someone were holding his legs for sit-ups. Only the five-foot iron bar on the pinlifter handle had kept him from falling between the cars.

Botone glanced behind him, looking for leverage. With his back jammed against the ladder, he thought that if he did it slowly, one rung at a time, he might be able to shimmy up high enough to untangle his legs. It seemed workable. Until he saw the knuckle.

He'd done his job too well. The pinlifter had lifted, uncoupling the cars from the locomotives, and the knuckles were steadily inching apart. Heart racing, Botone put his hands behind him and pushed upward, working his way up the ladder. The first two rungs were easy, but the growing distance between the boxcar and the locomotives was sharpening the angle of his arms.

As his flexibility reached its limit, Botone released his grip with one hand. His body twisted sideways, his legs still caught in the pinlifter. He was now facedown, watching the ties beneath him fly past at 70 mph as the cars continued to move apart, pulling the slack out of his body, suspending him between the cars as if he were being stretched on a medieval rack. One end or the other had to give.

A searing pain was shooting through his ankles, and with his sweat-drenched palms, he was losing his grip on the ladder. He mustered every last ounce of his strength and contracted his body, then yanked his legs inward with a final heave. The pinlifter rotated slightly, just enough for his feet to pass through. His left foot freed easily, but his right turned sideways and snapped at the ankle.

His legs dropped like a cut clothesline and hung uselessly just inches above the rails. Botone clung to the ladder with both hands, watching in horror as the locomotives pulled away.

Ignoring his throbbing ankle, Botone climbed the ladder. He judged the distance, deciding he might be able to leap to the locomotive. He'd only have one chance.

Steeling himself, Botone took a deep breath and made a lunge for the locomotive. His good leg landed on the base of the engine's knuckle, but before he could gain his balance, the momentum threw him forward, his face slamming nose first into the guardrail. He heard the sickening snap as the cartilage gave way. Blood spurted down the front of his shirt. He didn't care.

He had made it.

He struggled to his feet and looked back at the runaway cars that had nearly carried him to his death.

Relief gave way to anger. Botone limped to the lead unit as fast as his battered, middle-aged body could carry him, opened the cab door, and confronted his engineer.

"Son of a bitch!"

"What the hell happened to you?" Fredericks asked, seeing the blood on Botone's shirt.

"Some goddamn train jockey almost killed me, that's what happened to me," Botone said. He sat down heavily in his chair. "I had to jump my ass back here. I almost didn't make it."

"On account you were weighed down by your big brass balls," Fredericks said. He didn't add that Megan Langford had failed to warn him to make sure the conductor was clear before he disengaged the dynamics.

"Son of a bitch," Botone said again.

"Well, it's a good thing you didn't die," Fredericks said with mock solemnity. "Because I think there's going to be a much better opportunity coming up fairly soon."

Megan Langford felt as though she were on the ride of her life. She just hoped it wasn't the ride that would end it.

Farranger had his pickup cranked up to 60 mph, rocketing through blank, empty industrial neighborhoods.

"Fredericks to Farranger," a voice called over the radio. "How far ahead of the runaway do we need to be before we can drop the cars? Over."

Megan looked over at Farranger. Being on a paved road at least meant he could free a hand for the radio. She passed over the handset.

End of the Line

Farranger spoke into it. "You need to be ten seconds ahead of the rest of your train by the time you get to the first switch at Baker Siding."

"Roger. Ten seconds. Any idea how fast we need to be going to make that happen by milepost 3190? Over."

Farranger paused, the radio handset idle in his grip.

"What's going on?" Megan asked. "You're planning to switch the cars onto a siding while the engines pass on straight track, right?"

She knew Farranger was driving as fast as he could so they would beat the train to the switch at Baker Siding. She also knew that the locomotives needed to be ten seconds ahead of the runaway cars because Cal would need that time to safely throw and line the switch between the detached locomotives and the rest of the train. The only thing she didn't understand was why he wasn't answering the engineer's question.

Then it dawned on her. Two railroaders trying to do math. Not a pretty sight. Neither Farranger nor the engineer were capable of figuring a time/distance problem.

"This is BALA," Fredericks called again, his tone more insistent. "Let me ask it another way. What's the fastest speed we can travel and still stay on the rails?"

"Best guess is 85 mph," Farranger replied. "What's your current speed?"

"Ninety-one."

Farranger was pushing the pickup to its limit, and each bump was making Megan's teeth rattle. *I'm in a truck with a madman*, she thought, as the back roads and commercial byways of San Bernardino flew past. She couldn't believe they were anywhere near a railroad, and it came as a surprise when they sped out from behind a vacant lot directly in front of the right-of-way.

Skidding wildly at full speed, Farranger swung the truck so it sat directly atop the tracks, screeching to a stop in the middle of a road crossing. He grabbed his packset. "BALA, what's your location?"

"Passing mile 3183 at ninety-three miles an hour."

"Damn!" Farranger pounded his fist on the dash, then looked at Megan. "We're not gonna make it."

Megan could almost see the wheels turning in his head. She'd seen that look before. He had to have been a conductor at one time. Good conductors make plans and execute them. Then, when the first plan goes to hell, they make a new plan.

"Do the hyrails work?" Megan asked.

Farranger nodded, his face flashed with inspiration. No further explanation was necessary.

Cal lined the truck's tires over the rails beneath them, then reached under the dashboard and pushed the HYRAIL DOWN button on the dashboard. The flanged wheel guides, attached to a small electric motor, lowered in contact with the rail.

With mounting horror, Megan realized the scope of their new plan. *A conductor as well as a madman. Bad combination.* They were now on the same track as the BALA, rapidly closing the distance between them with every passing second.

Farranger locked the steering wheel in the centered position, took his hands off the wheel, and stepped on the gas. The hyrail glided smoothly on top of the rails, quickly exceeding the maximum safe speed of 60 mph.

Megan's mouth went dry.

Farranger had placed them directly in the path of the runaway train.

As if sensing her apprehension, Farranger broke the silence.

"Hey," Cal shrugged, looking over at Megan with his most reassuring expression. "It was your idea."

– 8 –

Farranger rounded the six-degree curve at a dangerously high speed. The pickup's inside wheels came up several inches off the rail, and it canted at a ten-degree angle to the roadbed before slamming back down on the tracks. The sudden impact jarred Farranger out of his recklessness. He couldn't let fear put their lives at risk.

He glanced over at Megan, and the most peculiar thought popped into his head. *What was her story?*

"What?" she said self-consciously, looking back at him.

His quick scan revealed no wedding ring. Given her temper, he wasn't surprised. He doubted any man had a chance with her, even one that was self-destructive enough to want one.

Megan seemed to be reading his mind. "Pay attention, cowboy," she said.

Slightly flushed, Cal instinctively straightened up in his seat, tightly gripping the hyrail's locked steering wheel as if he still had control over it.

The truck came out of the curve and sped over two thousand yards on straight track before passing the switch at the south end of Baker Siding. Within two minutes, they covered the mile from there to the north switch at the other end of the siding. Farranger checked the right-of-way, disappointed to see that no railroad employees had shown up to pitch in. He'd have to do it alone.

He looked over at Megan. *With her help.*

Scanning the area, he spotted a beat-up pickup parked twenty feet from the north siding switch, just off the right-of-way. The tailgate was down, and three men were crowded at the end of it, staring at the hyrail.

Farranger studied the men and their vehicle. They had binoculars and a piece of equipment that looked like a police scanner. A shotgun was mounted on the rifle rack inside the cab, and a bumper sticker directly below the rear window proclaimed, MY OTHER CAR IS A LOCOMOTIVE. Seeing all this told him everything he needed to know.

"Foamers," he said in disgust.

Megan gave him a nod of recognition. "What are they doing here?" she asked.

Farranger pointed up the mountain. "I imagine they came to see the big derailment."

Megan followed his finger and saw the headlight of a locomotive flickering as it passed through the hills before them. She looked at Farranger in alarm. They'd stopped directly in the path of an oncoming train. The locomotives were still two miles away, and barreling toward them at high speed.

"The siding's rated at 50 mph, which means the cars ought to derail at the switch," Farranger explained. "But the locomotives burned off most of their brakes, so it might take a while to get the engines stopped. Get behind the wheel and back up—fast."

Without waiting for a reply, Farranger opened his door and jumped out of the truck, landing on the roadbed. He heard Megan cussing him under her breath. If he'd misjudged her, she'd leap out right about now and scurry to safety.

But he hadn't.

After only an instant's hesitation, Megan slid over to the driver's side. The truck shot back in reverse, tires screeching. Farranger let out a sigh of relief. She had moxie.

He scrambled to his feet and hurried to the north siding switch.

He grabbed his packset and shouted into the radio, "BALA, this is Farranger. I have you in sight. Here's the drill. Wait until you're halfway down the siding to apply the brakes, and I hope to God that you haven't burned them all off. You don't want the cars catching up with you. That curve's still there."

"Roger. Halfway."

Farranger thought for a moment. Once the locomotives passed on the straight track, he'd line the cars into the siding. The runaway cars should derail at the siding switch, or a few cars into the

End of the Line

siding. But that didn't mean they would stop. Their momentum would carry them several hundred yards without regard for what track they'd be crossing. If the engineer was in too much of a hurry to set his brakes, the derailing cars might overtake him. It would probably take half of the mile-long siding before the six-thousand-foot runaway section would finally skid to a stop.

The lead locomotive was now only a half minute from the north siding switch. Farranger glanced once more behind him. The foamers were still there. Looking the other way, he spotted the hyrail truck. Reverse gear made for slow going, but Megan had managed to back up to the south siding switch. She should round the curve in plenty of time to avoid the runaway. Whatever else happened, he thought, at least she'd be in the clear. The depth of his relief surprised him.

He readied himself at the switch, a high-stand with a tripod supporting a throw lever at waist level. He wished he had more time. The lever hung like a water pump handle and had to be rotated in a circular arc of nearly 180 degrees. It was difficult to move and painful even for his callused hands. Under ordinary circumstances, a dispatcher would line the switch remotely with the aid of an electric motor. Manual lining was generally reserved for emergencies.

The electric motor would take a full thirty seconds to line the switch. Farranger would've been content to let the dispatcher drop the cars, but he couldn't. The locomotives and the runaway cars were less than 10 seconds apart.

The locomotives were closing fast, close enough that Farranger could see the wide-eyed faces of Botone and Fredericks behind the crew window. The runaway section was close behind them. He inserted a switch key into the lock, and felt a rush of panic when the lock refused to turn. He quickly realized his error. He had mistakenly inserted an old California Western key instead of a Transcon key. He made the swap and the lock opened on the first try. Heart pounding, he stationed himself behind the switch stand, gripped hard on the handle, then waved at the crew.

The four-unit locomotive consist sped over the switch points, blasting a blanket of diesel-heated air in its wake. The rest of the train was rushing behind, now less than ten car-lengths from the switch.

Taking a deep breath, Farranger gave the switch a heave, but the manual throw didn't budge.

Mustering all of his strength, Farranger tried again. He managed to force the switch lever through only half of its arc. He braced his foot against the extended ties that served as a mounting platform for the switch and gave it one last push.

The cars loomed almost on top of him now. He felt the ground shaking as they clacked over the rail joints and hit the switch, teetering dangerously as they forced their way into the siding.

For a split-second, Farranger was afraid they were going to derail right on top of him, that he'd thrown the switch underneath them. Then the first two cars rolled into the siding.

The switch had lined in time.

He backed away, moving to a safer position near the foamers, and breathed a sigh of relief. A derailment wasn't optimal, but in this case, the lesser of two evils. With a sliding derailment, cars end-to-end, the chances of the hulls breaching on the tank cars was relatively low. It was a risk, but he was confident the tanks would remain upright on the straight roadbed and gradually lose their momentum.

He shuddered to think what might've happened if the runaway had made it to the hard curve at the other end of the siding. At that speed, the cars would roll sideways and rupture for sure. Instant five o'clock news.

"BALA, this is Farranger," he relayed. "How you doing? Over."

"Not much braking left, Cal. We ain't gonna stop before the curve, but we ought to get down below thirty-five miles an hour."

At least the crew was safe, Farranger told himself as he waited for the cars to enter the siding and begin to derail.

It didn't happen. And he watched with growing alarm as the first six entered the siding, somehow still on the rails. In fact, it looked as if the locomotives on the main track were racing the runaway section, which was coming up fast on the outside.

They're not going to derail at all, he thought with mounting horror.

Conductor Botone had reached the same conclusion. His panic came through clearly on Farranger's road channel.

End of the Line

"She ain't stopping, Cal! We're gonna meet them cars coming out the other end of the siding!"

Farranger shuddered. They would crash in less than a minute, and he had no idea how to stop them.

- 9 -

The pickup's radio had told Megan most of the story, and her eyes confirmed the rest. The BALA's locomotives were halfway between the siding switches. The engineer had managed to slow them down, but he'd burned off most of the brake shoes. They were coasting now.

She knew the crew was right. There was no way to stop the engines before the south siding switch, and her best guess was that a third of the runaway train would be coming out of the siding when the locomotives struck. Certain death for the crew. But at their current speed, no more certain than if they decided to jump.

The locomotives and the runaway cars were heading straight for her, closing the distance fast. She'd have to time this perfectly. She thrust the truck into forward and floored it, racing across the south siding switch just seconds before the runaway cars crossed back onto the main track. The six-thousand-foot train now filled the entire siding and was snaking out both ends onto the main track.

She drove straight toward the locomotives for another eight hundred feet before common sense won over bravery. Taking her foot off the gas pedal, she pressed the HYRAIL UP button under the dash. The hyrail guides lifted, and the rubber tires bounced hard against the crossties. The right front tire exploded under the pressure.

The truck lurched to a dead stop.

Megan threw herself out of the truck, scrambling to put as much distance as she could between her and the inevitable crash.

I'm not going to make it.

End of the Line

She heard the locomotives slam into the truck, and was thrown to the ground. Her hands flew to her ears, the sound deafening. The impact sent hyrail parts flying across the right-of-way. A flanged wheel landed only a few yards from where she lay sprawled in the cinders.

The pickup was crushed like an aluminum can, but most of its frame was now fused between the rail and the lead locomotive, creating a two-ton steel chock for the locomotive's lead wheels.

Sparks flew from the devastating friction.

The engines began to slow, making a piercing, grinding sound.

My God, Megan thought, surprise and relief flooding through her. *It worked.*

Farranger had been watching Megan's heroics from a hundred yards away, heart pounding, cold sweat breaking across his forehead. Just after she'd leapt to safety, the pickup was crushed by the locomotives, and a gusher of sparks erupted under the rails.

At least her foolhardy gamble had paid off. The locomotives stopped just half a car-length short of the south siding crossover and the eight runaway cars that had already veered back onto the main track. The locomotives would never have stopped in time without the truck to check their progress.

Farranger's relief that the crew was safe was short-lived. Once a third of the runaway cars crossed back onto the main track without incident, his last hope for a smooth derailment was lost. The six-degree curve rated at 35 mph was a mere two thousand feet beyond the siding. When they hit it, they'd lose their grip on the rail and slam to the ground at almost 90 mph. The chlorine gas tanks would rupture, the deadly contents spreading over a five-mile radius in a matter of minutes. It looked as if Langford's selfless act of courage had been wasted.

But then an idea came to him. The foamers.

He approached the one who was snapping pictures. "I need your shotgun," he yelled. Without waiting for a reply, he raced over to the pickup and grabbed it out of the cab.

"So, mister," the foamer called after him. "You plan on stopping a mile-long train with a shotgun?"

"Yeah, I do." Farranger walked past him to the edge of the siding.

The foamer followed, standing silently behind Farranger as the cars rushed into the siding.

As each one entered, Farranger performed a detailed roll-by inspection. The cause of the runaway was obvious. The brakes on the rear of the train had malfunctioned.

He propped the shotgun against his shoulder, moved right up to the cars, and stared down the muzzle. The shotgun wasn't exactly a precision weapon, but it would do the job. He needed to put as much lead out as possible and hope like hell some of it hit the mark.

He targeted the air hoses between the cars. If he was right, he'd diagnosed the BALA's problem as a turned angle cock that bottled the air somewhere in the train. A direct hit on any air hose would release the air from the bottle. The fail-safe system would do the rest, setting an automatic emergency application of the train brakes.

Holding the gun as close to the speeding cars as he dared, he lined up his shot just three feet from the air hose.

And pulled the trigger.

The blast was followed by a hiss of air. The brake shoes clamped down, the application of forty-five cars' worth of additional brakes.

The runaway slowed immediately, but its momentum carried it forward. The brake shoes locked the wheels of the train so they slid atop the rails without turning. In less than a thousand feet the train speed was cut in half. The train rolled around the speed-restricted curve at less than 30 mph, then slowly came to a stop.

"I'll be damned," the foamer breathed.

End of the Line

The crew watched as the rest of their train exited the siding in front of them and then came to an easy stop.

Megan sprinted past the crushed pickup, surprised how calm she felt. The truck was mangled beyond recognition, a fate she no doubt would have shared if she hadn't had the sense to jump out at the last moment.

A small part of the hyrail lay crushed under the lead traction motors of the locomotive. Part of the twisted frame extended out in front of the locomotive nose. The pickup had done the job.

Half a car-length to spare, she thought, her switchman's instincts preventing her from measuring in the more conventional feet or yards. Somehow, the close call comforted her.

As she approached the lead locomotive, the two men inside waved at her from the conductor's window. When she got closer, their faces registered amazement as they realized it was a woman who'd saved their asses.

Grabbing both handholds alongside the three steps on the conductor's side of the locomotive, Megan pulled herself up to the catwalk that curved around the front of the locomotive.

"Who the hell are you?" Conductor Botone asked, as she opened the interior door to the cab.

"Gentlemen, I'm Megan Langford, regional general chairman of the Railway Transportation Union," she said. Maybe her rank would dispel any bias the crew might have about female railroaders.

Botone continued to stare at her.

"Well, Chairman Langford," he finally said, "You've got our vote."

-10-

"I need a lift," Farranger said, turning to the old foamer in the driver's seat of the pickup. He didn't wait for a reply, just hoisted himself into the open bed.

As they sped off, he shifted uncomfortably on the wheel well, the uneven surface amplifying every high spot on the ballast.

"That your truck?" the old foamer yelled through the rear window, gesturing toward the wrecked pickup.

"Used to be!" Farranger hollered back.

His gaze fell on the block of metal that had once been a Chevy pickup. Above it, Megan Langford and the train crew were huddled together behind the window of the lead locomotive. He'd need to talk to the train crew, but there was something he wanted to do first.

The old foamer slowed as they neared the locomotives.

"Keep going," Farranger instructed, motioning him to drive south along the right-of-way. As a matter of safety, he'd have to set a few hand brakes on the cars. While the shotgun-initiated emergency application of brakes had stopped the cars, it wasn't a permanent condition. Within a couple of hours, the air holding the brake shoes against the wheels would bleed off. Left alone, the cars would start rolling downhill again.

He continued another sixteen car-lengths before he saw it. "That'll do," he abruptly called out to the driver.

The foamer had stopped just past the fourteenth car from the head end of the runaway. Farranger jumped out of the back of the truck, eyes fixed on the boxcar's rear angle cock. From a distance, he'd thought it was turned. It was. But now he could see that there was a leather pouch lock-wired below it.

End of the Line

He yanked it off, loosened the drawstring, and reached inside, pulling out several photographs and a folded sheet of paper. He stared at the photos, sequential shots of an auto train derailing.

At Canyon Demonio.

Transcon had listed the cause as human error, and Farranger had guessed faulty track maintenance. Then, when he heard that the track had been inspected just hours before the accident, his suspicions had been aroused.

The pictures told the story. The shots were entirely different than the ones that had appeared in the media after the accident. These hadn't been taken after the fact; they'd been snapped by an eyewitness.

Farranger unfolded the sheet of paper. A note. Its words were chilling.

> *To the Transcontinental Railway Company*
> *This time everybody gets to die with me.*
>
> *- Casey Jones*

The reference in the note was clear enough. Casey Jones was a railroad legend. An Illinois Central engineer who'd sacrificed his own life to save the lives of a trainload of passengers. But the name was too obvious to be any sort of clue. It was like some madman signing a communication with the name Superman.

A shiver ran up Farranger's spine. The frightening images of the Canyon Demonio train wreck flashed in his mind.

Sabotage.

He shoved the note and photos back into the pouch and hitched one last ride on the foamer's truck back toward the BALA's locomotive. He spotted a Chevy Blazer traversing the ballast, and recognized the two figures in the cab—Sims and the Axeman, riding shotgun.

Cal reached the locomotives just as Sims pulled up. Langford and the train crew were now standing on the catwalk on the conductor's side of the engine. No one made any motion to detrain, or even to acknowledge the Axeman as he got out of the vehicle.

Farranger assumed the brush-off was Megan Langford's work. As a union officer, she'd no doubt urge her members not to speak to management on the basis that anything they said could be used against them in a disciplinary hearing. In this case, it was a prudent precaution. If need be, Farranger thought, he'd talk to the train crew later.

Adashek inspected the train wreck scene, pausing by the pickup, which was still wedged under the locomotive. He looked up at the union formation on the catwalk.

"Any of you three want to tell me what happened?"

Megan spoke up sharply. "Mr. Adashek, I represent these men. Please direct your questions to me."

Farranger waited to see how she'd hold up against the Axeman's barrage.

"Don't play your union games with me, Langford," Adashek snarled. "I'll tell you exactly what happened here. The engineer fanned his brakes on the mountain and let his air bleed off. Isn't that right, Mr. Engineer?"

Farranger was surprised. Adashek's explanation was wrong, but it wasn't a bad guess.

Sims, still sitting inside the Blazer, looked at Farranger for confirmation. Farranger shook his head.

Fredericks tried to respond but Megan cut him off. "Don't say anything."

Adashek scowled. "You men can play mute all you want," he said, clearly fed up with the stonewalling. "But as of this minute, you're all out of service. I'm also demanding the surrender of your engineer certification card per FRA, part 240."

"It was sabotage," Farranger interrupted in a steely voice.

All eyes turned to him, riveted.

Adashek frowned. "What did you say?"

"It was sabotage," Farranger repeated. "Someone turned an angle cock between the cars. He also left his calling card." Farranger tossed the leather pouch at the Axeman.

Momentarily speechless, Adashek opened the pouch and peered inside. "What the hell is this?"

"I'd say it's a warning," Farranger replied.

"Jesus," Adashek grunted, examining the photos. He glanced at the note. "Casey Jones? He's got to be kidding."

Farranger gestured around him. "This look like a joke to you?"

Sims cut in on them. "Cal! It's him, and he wants to talk to you!"

"*Who* wants to talk to me?"

"Doug McClure, the CEO. He's on the San Bern Yard channel."

"Turn it up," Farranger said. "Let's all hear what he has to say." He walked over to Sims, who passed him the microphone through the window.

"This is Cal Farranger. Over."

Static crackled over the line, and then Doug McClure's voice came through loud and clear. "This is Doug McClure in the operations center. I've been watching the show here. Hell of a job, Farranger. Damn fine piece of railroading. Is the crew all right?"

Farranger gave the shell-shocked train crew a quick inspection. "Nothing a bottle of scotch won't cure."

"Any idea what caused the runaway? Over."

"Yes, sir. Looks like an Andrew's raid. But I don't think it's wise to discuss it over an open frequency."

"I see," McClure replied. "Okay, Cal. Then I'll see you tomorrow morning at the operations center here in Dallas. Over."

"Understood. Farranger out."

"McClure out."

Adashek looked puzzled. Farranger had no doubt as to the source of his confusion.

"The Civil War turned railroad sabotage into an art," Cal offered. "The most famous was the Andrew's raid. Any real railroader would know that."

Farranger handed the microphone back to Sims. *I'm on the job again,* he thought, then turned back to the Axeman.

"So, I guess you'll have to get back to me on this whole firing thing?"

- 11 -

Farranger circled through the maze of one-way arrows and inclined planes at Transcon's Dallas headquarters parking facility, the events of yesterday still weighing on his mind. The early-bird flight from LAX had touched down at DFW over an hour ago, but he was still running late. *Not fashionably late,* he chided himself, *just late.*

He finally found a free space on the basement level, where the damp, poorly lit atmosphere lent an almost Gothic quality to the gray concrete support pillars.

This was Farranger's first trip to corporate, but he could already see why the five thousand employees here called it the House of Knowledge. The eight modern buildings of glass and steel spreading over six square miles of rural Dallas more closely resembled a junior college than the headquarters of a Fortune 100 company. The Central Operations Center, the COC, was the largest and most important of these buildings, and looked like a domed sports coliseum.

He strode toward what he hoped was the main entrance. Checking his watch, he picked up his pace. He arrived at a set of double doors, frustrated to see that they were guarded by a security panel. No one had bothered to tell him he'd need an access card. He'd have to wait until someone emerged.

To his relief, the door opened almost immediately, flung open by a man wearing coveralls and dark wayfarer sunglasses. Probably a contract maintenance man, Farranger thought, hoping he could cajole the guy to admit him. The name on the coveralls read CHUCK. He walked with an uneven gait and lugged a heavy toolbox.

"Sorry about that," Casey said, after nearly colliding with Farranger.

"I needed a way into the building anyway," Farranger replied.

"You don't have a card?" Casey asked, his tone slightly suspicious. "I'm not supposed to let anyone in without one."

Farranger hesitated, wondering if he should make up some story.

The man stared at him for a moment. "I suppose I could let you in. You can't be too careful, though. A lot of crazy people running around."

Farranger nodded. There was more truth in that remark than the guy realized. "You don't happen to know where the operations center is, do you?" he asked.

"Straight ahead," Casey offered, pointing. "You can't miss it. It's a big target."

Odd choice of words, Farranger thought, nodding again.

Casey smiled back, and then disappeared through the doors to the outside.

Farranger passed through another set of double doors into the Central Operations Center and stopped short, looking about admiringly.

The COC floor was the size of two football fields, an impressive facility by any standard. From this centralized location, train movements for the eighty thousand miles of track on the Transcon system were managed.

Eight theater-sized screens on the rear wall displayed an abundance of information: the on-time performance of passenger trains, system weather, coal and grain shipment forecasts, intermodal loadings, locomotive utilization, CNN, and Bloomberg Financial News. A wealth of information for anyone who cared to look up, though few had time. Beneath these screens sat the busiest employees on the railroad.

Row after row of train dispatchers, like vendors at a swap meet, were crammed into two hundred dehumanizing "pods," identical in size and shape save for a few photographic reminders of home and an occasional Dilbert cartoon. Each dispatcher was staring intently at the four computer consoles detailing the territory they'd been assigned to dispatch. The nuances of Transcon's coal and grain profitability were lost on them. They had a railroad to run.

Ranks of managers were seated behind them, empowered with the more global concerns of selecting the right number of locomotives for each particular location and deciding which customer was going to get screwed so another could be served. Like the dispatchers, their positions were "hot-seated," each minuscule cubicle of real estate theirs only for the tenure of the eight-hour shift.

Although Farranger was more than impressed with the size of the facility, he was appalled by the working conditions. The place had the atmosphere of B. F. Skinner's rat-crowding experiment gone horribly awry.

"Excuse me," he called out to a young runner hurrying past.

"Yeah?" the young man said, slowing down his pace.

"Where's the main conference room?"

"Up there." The youth pointed to the second floor, where a skybox with tinted glass gave its occupants a clear view of the pod of dispatchers below.

"Thanks," Farranger smiled. He pointed to some minor construction underway in the dispatching section. "What's going on over there?"

"Oh, they're double-stacking the cubicles."

"You're kidding."

"I wish," the young man sighed. "Gotta go back to work," he added, and ran off.

Farranger arrived at the main conference room sixteen minutes late for his appointment with Doug McClure. A group of people were seated around a massive oval table, something akin to what King Arthur might have had if he'd used Eddie Bauer as his decorator. He headed for the only empty chair, doing a visual check of the attendees as he walked.

Doug McClure was there, of course. Farranger had never met the CEO in person, but he recognized him from a picture in Transcon's annual report. And he had a lot of respect for the man. McClure had an excellent reputation. He was a railroader's railroader, hiring out as a switchman and working his way up through the ranks to CEO by the time he was thirty-five. Moreover, he'd accomplished something no other railroader had been able to do in two centuries: create a national railroad.

Many had tried, but only McClure had succeeded. At the age of forty-five, his place in railroad history was already secure. In an industry rich with empire builders, he'd shamed them all, creating a rail empire that dwarfed everything that had preceded it. Virtually all the U.S. rails worth owning were now under one management. His only shortcoming, in Farranger's mind, was his choice of a man to run his empire—the Axeman.

Phil Adashek was there, too. Farranger didn't recognize any of the other men seated around the table; they were probably semisenior corporate butt boys, he decided.

He almost did a double-take as he noticed the woman seated next to the empty chair.

Megan Langford. Dressed in a cream-colored blouse and dark blue pantsuit, she looked crisp, yet revealed a hint of glamour. Her golden hair hung freely. Quite a transformation from the last time he'd seen her. What was she doing there?

"You're late, Farranger," Adashek said, smirking.

And you're an ugly SOB, Farranger thought, sinking into the empty chair.

"You didn't miss much," Doug McClure interjected. "Ms. Langford was just giving us an eyewitness account of the Cajon incident."

Farranger nodded at Langford. She gave him a cold glance. Union versus management. The good will from yesterday's Baker Siding incident apparently had evaporated.

"Cal," the CEO addressed him, "this is Deputy Director Jack Kelly of the FBI. Jack's been assigned to catch our saboteur."

Farranger acknowledged the man across the table. Kelly looked to be in his midforties, with boyishly handsome features. *Deputy Director Kelly.* Cal reasoned that anyone that had risen so high, so quickly, must have done so on a track record of high-profile successes. But he obviously wasn't a railroader, and that made Farranger nervous. To catch this crazy guy, Cal was convinced they were going to have to think like him.

"Here's the situation," McClure went on, addressing the entire group now. "We've got a nutcase with a thing for wrecking trains and killing people. Our good friends in the union are rightfully concerned about the safety of the workforce. Our current labor agreement expires in seven days, and the union's promised a nationwide strike if this maniac isn't caught."

Farranger scanned the group. Everyone looked surprised.

Except Langford.

"I've convinced the union that this is a localized affair, confined to the southwestern United States," McClure said emphatically. "They've agreed not to strike, if we provide them full access to all security measures taken to protect the workforce. The Southwest is Ms. Langford's territory, so they've made her liaison." The CEO paused, then offered Megan an olive branch. "I think it's an excellent choice."

"I'll start preparations right away, Doug," the Axeman chimed in.

"Actually, I'm putting Cal in charge of security," McClure corrected him. "He's familiar with the area, and he's already proven his worth at Cajon."

Adashek looked annoyed. "As the operational vice president, I—"

McClure cut him off. "You have plenty of other things to do. Do you have some objection to my decision?"

Farranger held his breath. Adashek was clearly unhappy. Usually quick to try to micromanage any situation, he now just shook his head.

McClure turned to Farranger again. "You'll be in charge of protecting the railroad. You have carte blanche to put in place any measures you see fit to protect our people."

"If I come across anything suspicious, should I report it to Deputy Director Kelly?"

"Security doesn't mean investigation," Kelly interjected, looking directly at Farranger. "I want it clearly understood that there will be no civilians involved in this investigation. Stick to guarding trains. I have fifty highly trained agents assigned to the case. It's been my experience that civilians tend to get in the way. I don't mean to sound hostile, but I want to be perfectly clear on this point."

"Clear as a bell," Farranger grinned. He decided not to say another word. He fully intended to try to find this guy himself, repaying a debt he felt he owed to Sam Montilli and Wally Colvin, and see that the son of a bitch who thought it was cute to label himself Casey Jones got his just punishment.

"Let me explain," Kelly offered in a kinder tone. "I have the top forensic laboratory in the country at my disposal. Even as we speak, some of our best people are combing every pebble at Baker Siding, Canyon Demonio, and Yermo. If there's so much as a toe-nail, we'll find it."

"Why Yermo?" Adashek asked.

"Whoever turned the angle cock on that train did it in Yermo," Farranger added before Kelly could answer.

"What makes you say that?" Adashek scoffed.

"The angle cock had to be turned after the air brakes were tested in Yermo but before they were found defective at Summit."

"Why couldn't they have been turned at Summit?" Adashek asked.

"Because it had to be done at a speed slow enough to allow detraining," Farranger explained. "I pulled the speed tapes on the BALA. They left Yermo, got up to track speed at forty-five miles an hour and maintained that speed all the way to Summit. If you jump off a train at that speed, you die. Whoever did this, did it at Yermo."

An awkward silence followed. Farranger hadn't intended to make Adashek look foolish, he just wanted to move things along.

"We concluded as much," Kelly added. "We can actually take it a step further. We know the exact point he got on the train, where he got off, and based on tire tracks have a good notion of the kind of vehicle he used."

Cal was impressed. He had no idea how the feds could figure out where someone got on or off a train. It was a neat trick, but Kelly didn't look like he planned on sharing how it was done.

"It sounds like we have more than we do," Kelly cautioned. "This case is not going to be solved with insight; it will require brute-force trial and error."

The railroaders around the table looked uniformly confused.

"For those of us laymen," McClure felt he was speaking for the whole group, "What exactly do you mean by 'brute-force trial and error?'"

"The universe of suspects is large," Kelly started. "The most obvious choice is a disgruntled employee, ex-employee, or someone who simply doesn't like Transcon. This could be a customer that felt slighted, someone who's lost family in a crossing accident or whatever. Based on my initial review, there are quite a few who fall into the 'don't like the railroad' category."

Adashek and McClure shifted uncomfortably in their seats. Railroads were not popular, Transcon especially so.

"So to reduce this universe of suspects to a single person, we need a way to eliminate the rest. Thankfully, our perpetrator has provided us with exactly what we need."

"The note," Cal surmised aloud.

"Written in his own hand," Kelly confirmed. "We need only match it to an existing handwriting sample and we have our suspect. This, unfortunately, is where the brute force comes in."

"My God," Megan concluded, "you're going to manually compare handwriting with everyone in North America until you have a match?"

"Thankfully, there is nothing manual about it," Kelly chuckled. "We have an automated way of comparing handwriting on a large scale, and I think we can narrow it down a bit more than the general population. But you're essentially on the right track."

"How long will that take?" Cal asked skeptically.

"Depends on how automated the records are. For example, Transcon's computer database records the social security numbers of its employees. Using that number, we can cross check with various agencies that keep records that include scanned handwriting samples—say a computer-recorded driver's license signature, for example. You'll be happy to know that in less than fifteen hours we've been able to determine that 99.99 percent of the Transcon workforce certifiably isn't Casey."

"And the other one-hundredth of one percent?" Cal asked.

"The computer program is accurate to a point, but generates about one false positive every ten thousand samples," Kelly replied. "These have to be checked out manually. Most can be dismissed—either dead, too old, too young, wrong sex, etc. Any doubt and we send a field agent out."

"And this works?" Cal said skeptically.

End of the Line

"We've done this before," Kelly said coldly. "With the number of agents assigned, and what we know about the perpetrator, I believe we will have exhausted the universe of possibilities in twenty-five days."

Farranger had no doubt the agent was telling the truth, but still felt uncomfortable. A lot could happen in twenty-five days.

"Do you have any theories?" Adashek asked, shifting the deputy director's attention away from Farranger.

Farranger didn't hear Kelly's answer; he was distracted by a commotion he'd noticed on the COC floor down below.

As he watched through the skybox window, the frenzied activity level hit a new plateau. One by one, the corporate propaganda and business statistics slides on the huge screens were replaced with live signal charts—functional layouts of individual dispatcher's territories, complete with all tracks, switches, and signal indications. With growing horror, Farranger saw that every one of the hundreds of signals that were being displayed indicated "red."

Cal returned his attention to Kelly, who was still talking, predicting early capture, and apparently being persuasive enough to earn reassured looks from the group.

"He's shutting down the whole system," Farranger murmured, still staring at the screens.

No one heard him. Kelly continued on.

"Our profiler has determined that we are dealing with a sociopath. He is very intelligent, with perhaps genius IQ. He has delusions of grandeur, and in layman's terms holds a grudge. The good news is that this is the type of person that likes to plan things meticulously, months in advance, leaving no detail to chance. So unless he's been planning out every attack for years, it will take him weeks to regroup for another . . ."

Farranger stood up, cutting Kelly short.

"Look," he said, pointing to the signal diagram displayed on the screens behind Kelly. Eleven heads turned. "He's not finished. Every signal on our system has defaulted red."

"What does that mean?" Kelly asked, looking bewildered.

"It means," the astonished CEO interjected, "that five thousand trains aren't moving."

"Four thousand, to be precise." The disembodied mechanical voice echoed eerily from the room's hidden speakers. Everyone in the room reacted with a startled jump. "But I'll get around to the rest of them in due time."

McClure jumped to his feet. "Who said that?" He turned his head and gazed at the back of the conference room.

"Just call me Casey. If you'd be kind enough to sit down, Dougie, I'll continue."

The CEO complied, sharing a puzzled expression with everyone else in the room.

Farranger was stumped. His imagination couldn't conjure the precise way the room had been bugged. *How is he doing it?*

"Christ, can't you figure it out?" the voice laughed. "Look up at the wall in the corner of the room. That's right. You're on camera. Please don't make any sudden movements. If you do, I have various devices spread around the room guaranteed to blow you to kingdom come. As you already know, I have no aversion to killing."

"Who are you, and what do you want?" Kelly demanded.

"Don't talk; just listen."

"We can't help you if we don't know what you want," the Axeman spoke up.

"Don't patronize me! And no one's talking to you anyway, Adashek. Hell, if I gave you enough time you'd destroy the railroad yourself."

Farranger exchanged a glance with Langford. Whoever this guy is, he thought, he knows plenty about Transcon.

"I suppose I'll have to give you another demonstration to prove my resolve," the voice continued. "Please direct your attention to the glass that separates you from the dispatchers below."

As all eyes turned to the window, four small charges exploded simultaneously. The glass shattered into countless pieces, four hundred faces below turning up toward the ceiling as the tiny shards cascaded down to the COC floor.

No one was hurt, but the explosion had fully captured everybody's attention. The dispatchers below, not hearing the explosion that shook the window loose, were more shocked than frightened, the collective assumption being that Transcon's half-ass quality control was to blame.

End of the Line

"Pretty impressive, huh? You might want to look at what's left of the detonators, Mr. Kelly. I'm rather proud of them. Tell me if you think they look like the work of a sociopath."

Kelly looked grim but said nothing as he headed for the window.

"Not now, you fool! After I've finished. This demonstration is by no means over."

- 12 -

Farranger remained in his seat, trying to stay calm. The bedlam down on the COC floor was leaking into the skybox conference room through the shattered partition, the murmur of three hundred dispatchers providing a background of white noise for the group held captive at the round table.

"If you think your trains will crawl without signals, let's see how they do without dispatchers," Casey said. "Please direct your attention to the Montana dispatcher below you."

Those in back stood up. Everyone else swiveled in their chairs to view the floor of the operations center below. A dial tone replaced Casey's amplified voice. A series of touch-tone beeps sounded over the speakers, followed by a muffled ringing.

A dispatcher in the middle of the fourth row slid off his radio headset. He reached over to the far side of his workstation and grabbed a cubical mounted telephone. Farranger could almost read his lips as he spoke into the receiver.

"Montana DS," he answered.

"Hello. Would you please raise your hand so the folks in the main conference room can see you?"

The dispatcher looked up toward the conference room. A dozen heads peered at him through the broken glass. Though clearly puzzled, he did as requested and raised his hand.

As everyone else stared in mute confusion, Farranger rushed to the edge of the shattered partition and gestured wildly at the dispatcher to disconnect the phone.

His effort was wasted.

In the next second, the dispatcher's handset exploded.

The man's head simply evaporated, globs of blood and brain matter spattered in all directions.

End of the Line

Pandemonium erupted on the COC floor. Workers screamed in terror, trampling one another as they scrambled for the exits.

"Sorry about the little mess," Casey said. "How many dispatchers do you think are gonna show up for work tomorrow, Dougie?" His voice broke into a menacing chuckle. "I've got twenty of these death phones scattered throughout the system. I'm betting my ability to reach out and touch someone is going to keep attendance low."

Farranger felt his heart racing. "We have to—"

"Shut up!" Casey thundered. "Don't think I've forgotten about your little stunt at Cajon Pass, Farranger. Interference has its price."

Farranger slumped back into his seat. *Whoever this guy is*, he thought, *he knows about my role in heading off the BALA disaster.*

"We're gonna play dial-a-corpse again. But just to prove I'm a stand-up guy, I'll give you a chance to play the hero, Farranger. All you have to do is answer a simple railroad trivia question, and I'll save the poor sap who's next on my list. Failure to answer within fifteen seconds will be taken as an incorrect answer. Understand the rules?"

"I understand." Nausea welled in Farranger's gut. He caught Langford's terrified glance.

"I can assure you the other party won't be able to hear you, so don't waste precious time trying to warn him."

What Farranger heard next made his heart stop.

"San Bernardino. Sims here."

Oh, God, Farranger thought.

"Please hold for a call from Cal Farranger."

Farranger's mind went into overdrive, searching for some way out.

Casey Jones muted the phone line. "All right, Farranger," he chortled. "Answer correctly to keep the old fart in the tower from getting a face full of C-4. The category is railroad history. What is first on Engineer Casey Jones's last engine and last on his first engine?"

What the hell? As Farranger racked his memory, Casey softly hummed the *Jeopardy* theme song over the hidden speakers.

How did the song go? *Around the turn old Casey flew, a-spittin' steam from his 382.* But Casey had two engines. The other was . . . what? The 638. Could the answer be that simple?

"Time's up, Farranger. What's your answer?"

"Thirty-eight," Cal replied, "The last two digits on his first engine and the first two digits on his last engine."

"My favorite number," Casey enthused. "And correct. I'm impressed."

Farranger's hopes soared.

"Unfortunately, I can't accept your answer. You didn't phrase it in the form of a question."

The familiar touch-tone pattern came over the speakers again. Then the line went silent.

Farranger's heart turned to lead. He heard Megan Langford gasp and catch her breath.

"You should've known better than to go up against me, Farranger. Thanks to you, Lucas Sims is sounding his whistle in that great roundhouse in the sky."

Farranger thought of the times he'd heard Sims vow that they'd have to pry his dead fingers from the tower microphone before he'd leave.

Sims was dead because Farranger had failed him. It was no different from the Demonio crew, or his conductor years ago when he last worked as an engineer. Everybody who counted on him wound up dead.

He tried to shake off the guilt and grief, and concentrate on the crisis at hand. "How do we know Sims is dead?"

"Excuse me?"

"You could have botched it the same way you botched Cajon. Let me call San Bernardino Yard to verify."

"Sure, get the morbid details from your people if you want. Meanwhile, I have a few administrative details to iron out."

Farranger grabbed a phone on the conference table, but then hesitated.

"Relax, Farranger," Casey said. "The phone's safe. I have something more elaborate planned for you."

Farranger began dialing.

End of the Line

"As for you, Dougie," Casey continued, "I have but one simple demand: break Transcon up into its twelve former railroads. If you don't comply immediately, blood'll be flowing like diesel fuel."

"That would take months . . . years," McClure stammered. His body seemed to sway with the weight of the madman's words.

"Tell you what. I'm running a few mileposts ahead of schedule. I'll give you twenty-four hours."

"We can't possibly—"

"The choice is simple. Break Transcon up, or I'll do it for you. And I'll break it into a lot more than twelve pieces. The union's already about to bail out on you. I'll have your entire workforce run off by the end of the week."

"We don't make deals with extortionists," Kelly interjected.

"No? Well, deal with this," Casey laughed. "When this railroad shuts down, so will the rest of the country. No Transcon means no coal. I figure the power plants will run out of fuel in three days. The lights go out, and America's back in the Stone Age. Can you deal with that, Mr. Kelly?"

The room was deathly silent.

"Of course, that won't matter," Casey continued. "By the end of the week, forty million people will be out of work, too poor to afford electricity anyway. Without raw materials, factories will be forced to shut down, the price of commodities will skyrocket, and the financial markets will tumble. I especially can't wait for the riots and looting in the streets."

Farranger slammed down the receiver.

"So what did you find out, Farranger?"

"That a psychopath just killed a good railroader."

"In my book the only good railroader is a dead railroader. And there'll be a lot more good railroaders before I'm done."

Farranger flopped back in his seat.

At almost the same instant, there was a mild pop from a distant explosion. The sound was barely audible, but the effect was immediate. The COC floor and conference room were momentarily engulfed in complete darkness before the emergency generator kicked in, casting an eerie haze over everything.

Seconds later there was another explosion, a deafening roar that filled the conference room. Drywall exploded inward from all directions. Farranger gripped the arms of his chair, but McClure, Adashek, and Langford were thrown out of their seats. Farranger knew the first set of explosives had been strategically placed, blowing the circuits in the primary lighting system. The second wave must have targeted the conference room only. Contact explosives hidden behind the wall panels had gone off.

He bent over and helped Megan to her feet. She was covered in plaster and dust. She leaned into the curve of his arm. Buckling, she started to crumple to the floor. He gently eased her back into the chair.

A chilling silence fell over the room as the air began to clear. Just as Deputy Director Kelly opened his mouth to speak, the operations center speaker system crackled to life and a western guitar began playing the introduction to *Fulsome Prison Blues,* with Casey singing his own lyrics in a poor imitation of Johnny Cash.

> *"I hear the train a-comin',*
> *A-clangin' on its bell.*
> *In the canyon of the Devil,*
> *I sent a train to hell.*
> *I'll take a pound of flesh*
> *for each mile of track.*
> *This time it'll be different,*
> *now that Casey Jones is back."*

The message played in a recurring loop for nearly three minutes, until someone in technical support mercifully figured out how to shut it off.

No one was seriously hurt, but the frightening noise and falling plaster dust had left the group totally unnerved. *We're lucky to be alive,* Farranger thought. A slightly larger charge, and they'd all be dead. This madman, this Casey Jones, could have easily killed everyone in the room.

So why didn't he?

End of the Line

"Are you all right?" Megan asked him, looking straight into his eyes.

Chaos. Adashek was shouting, to no purpose that Farranger could see. Everyone in the room was struggling to keep their composure.

Waiting for the next explosion.

"Break up into teams," McClure shouted. "Call as many field offices as we can, and tell them *not* to use their phones!"

"That won't be necessary," Farranger said. "I didn't call San Bern Yard. I called our communications center and had them shut down the entire phone system. Anyone dialing a Transcon number will get an out-of-service message until all the phones can be checked."

"Thank God," McClure sighed.

"You can do that?" Kelly asked, clearly impressed.

Farranger nodded at the director. "Big railroads have their own telecommunications systems. Our microwave relays are installed alongside the track, and we control all of it from our main computer complex in Lincoln."

McClure took control. "Okay, here's the plan. Phil, I want you to handle the media and our major shippers. Farranger, you take over operations in the COC. I know you'll do everything possible to ensure the safety of our people. And make sure Ms. Langford has complete access to any security information she needs."

Farranger glanced at Megan, who was still trying to regain her composure. At the moment, Farranger considered her collateral damage. He flashed her a friendly smile, certain he could ditch her at the first available opportunity.

"We'll all reconvene tomorrow morning on the COC floor," McClure instructed. "If there's any truth to these threats, I want to know about it first. Questions?"

"I have a question," Kelly said. "That stuff about shutting down the country . . . is that actually possible?"

The railroaders exchanged knowing looks.

Farranger broke the uneasy silence. "Half the electrical plants and factories in this country are rail-served. And we move enough grain to feed half the world. We're talking the Great Depression, part two."

"That can't happen," Kelly vowed, as if only to convince himself.

Farranger frowned and looked down at the chaos on the COC floor, at the four thousand deadlocked trains displayed on the screens.

"It's already started."

-13-

Farranger charged through the double doors of the operations center, almost running into the two EMTs wheeling a gurney through the doorway. A lifeless form lay under the sheet. Farranger felt sickened by the senselessness of the Montana dispatcher's death.

He arrived at the COC floor to find it in complete disarray. It was hectic under the best of circumstances, but Casey's attacks had pushed the term *chaos* to a new level. A dozen railroad police formed a ring around the operations floor, but their presence didn't inspire confidence. They were called to guard the secure electronic exit doors because the access pads had been disabled from the inside by senior managers trying to keep the day shift intact.

Management had reacted quickly to stem the tide, but not quickly enough. Half the seats on the operations floor were empty. Others would have followed their lead, but were herded back to their stations by floor managers spouting weak reassurances or threats of dismissal.

Farranger paused at the threshold, taking an overview of the damage. A thick layer of sawdust had been spread around the Montana dispatcher's cubicle, darkened by the pool of blood underneath. The surrounding cubicles were vacant.

Sick at heart, Farranger wove his way through the occupied workstations, making a silent inspection of morale. Many key stations were unmanned, abandoned by employees too traumatized to continue their shifts. Those who remained had fear in their eyes.

Great—I've assumed command of a crew on the verge of mutiny.

Farranger elbowed his way down a crowded aisle toward the largest and most ornate cubicle, with a sign posted over it that read SYSTEM OPERATIONS DESK. Inside, a harried-looking man was glaring at eight computer screens and popping antacid tablets like candy. He was flanked by two clerks and a dozen phones.

"I hear you're the one who runs things around here." Farranger smiled as he approached the System Operations Director, relieved to recognize one of the suits from the meeting upstairs. He wouldn't have to waste precious time explaining himself.

"At least for twelve hours a day," the man replied, tearing his eyes from his screens to extend a handshake. Cal clasped a hand that trembled slightly, betraying an otherwise calm demeanor. "I'm Marlin Rice. Most folks around here call me SYSOP."

Farranger stuck out his hand. "Cal Farranger."

"And I'm Megan Langford from the Railway Transportation Union." Langford stepped in and moved up beside Farranger, as if to prove they were on equal footing. He wasn't particularly annoyed by the intrusion, but he was sure that he would be before long.

The SYSOP all but ignored her, acknowledging her with only a slight nod before turning to Farranger. "I guess you're the boss, Farranger. So what's the plan?"

"I want the mandatory thousand-mile inspection performed on the locomotives at every terminal, not just at the thousand-mile point. Same thing for the rolling stock. I also want additional inspections—journal bearings, brakelines, every single vulnerable point."

"You got it."

"That's it?" Megan asked. "What about the interchange sites where we get cars from other railroads?"

Farranger had just been about to issue that order. He flashed Megan an icy look, biting his tongue, then nodded at the SYSOP. "How much of our signal system is left?"

"Eighty percent of the lights are out. The tech guys are tracing the problem, but it's going to take a few hours."

Farranger was surprised the delay wasn't greater. "Get our signal maintainers reassigned and have them check the twenty percent that is working. And I want those territories dispatched manually until they're finished. Use Direct Traffic Control or

End of the Line

Non-signaled Track Warrant Control, whatever works best for your crew here."

"What the hell for?" Megan asked. "Why spend time on the signals that are working? We should be concentrating on getting the bad ones fixed. 'If it ain't broke—'"

"We don't know it 'ain't broke,'" Farranger snapped. "It might be broken in a different way—like giving a green signal instead of a red one. Don't you find it a little odd that this psycho just left part of the system alone?"

Megan ignored Farranger's logic and edged past the SYSOP. She moved to one of the computer screens and began studying the data pouring in.

Without another word, Farranger walked away and headed for the track-maintenance desk, breathing a sigh of relief when he glanced back and saw Langford still scanning the computers. He had work to do. The war would be starting in less than twenty-four hours.

"You in charge of track maintenance?" he asked a young man sitting in the track-maintenance cubicle.

"Yes. Are you Farranger?"

Farranger nodded. The young man was clearly unnerved by recent events, but other than a slight quiver in his voice, he held together well. "I want all capital expansion projects canceled," Farranger said. "Have all the track gangs reassigned to track inspection."

"What are they looking for?"

"Any signs of tampering. Every switch, bridge, culvert, and appliance. Anything with a moving part."

"We can't do that. We've got a hundred thousand culverts, tons of bridges, and nearly a million switches. It'd take months to check them all."

"Then the sooner we get started, the sooner we'll finish. Get on the horn and have your people recall every furloughed and seasonal maintenance employee. And while you're at it, tell them I want the furloughed engineers and conductors, too. It's going to take twice as long for the trains to get over the road without signals. We'll burn through our rested crews fast."

"You're talking thousands of employees. That'll cost a fortune! Adashek's gonna shit."

"And that's a problem because . . .?"

The man flashed a wide grin. "No problem," he said. "No problem at all."

Farranger scanned the operating stations, trying to decide where to go next. He spotted Langford leaving the SYSOP's desk. She was heading his way.

"One more thing," he said. "See that woman heading toward us? Delay her as long as you can."

The young man looked up the aisle, his eyes registering approval. "You want to stay away from that?"

"I'm afraid that's one of nature's crueler optical illusions. Just keep her busy. Start an argument or something."

"How am I supposed to do that?"

"Believe me, it won't be difficult," Farranger sighed, already moving away. "Say something bad about the union. That always seems to work."

Still unfamiliar with the COC layout, Farranger scrambled from one workstation to another. Issuing orders on the fly, depending on the signs over the cubicles to guide him. He nearly overlooked a station called Asset Protection, a fancy name for railroad police. He ducked his head inside.

"We need to find every available K-9 that's trained to sniff explosives," he said to the uniformed cinderdick he found there. "Use them by the pack to sniff out every facility we've got. Run them until their paws bleed if you have to."

"Okay," the special agent said. "You got it."

"And have our people put together a package for the local law enforcement and media in every town we run through—things to look for, how to tell if something doesn't belong. We've got eighty thousand miles of track, and we need every pair of eyes we can get."

"Uh . . . we can't do that. Adashek ordered a complete press blackout."

"Unbelievable." Farranger started to say something else, then spotted Megan coming toward him again, well within earshot. He didn't want to give her another reason to complain to him about management.

End of the Line

Farranger quickly excused himself and took a shortcut back to the SYSOP's desk, a path that forced him to pass directly beside the ruins of the Montana dispatcher's cubicle. By the time he reached the SYSOP, Megan was only two steps behind him, and the expression on her face told him that his attempts to shake her hadn't been nearly as subtle as he'd thought.

He was about to give the SYSOP further instructions, when a balding man in a blue pin-striped suit walked up to him.

"Mr. Farranger? I'm Julian Haskins, VP of human resources. I came down to see if there's anything I can do to help."

Farranger looked Haskins in the eye, half expecting to see some sort of demon. The man who'd laid off half the men in Farranger's division was asking what he could do to help. Farranger was tempted tell him he'd done enough already.

"We're critically short of dispatchers," he said instead, motioning to the COC floor. "Do you know of any managers who used to be dispatchers?"

"There's probably a few dozen of us scattered around the marketing and the business units."

"Good. They need to take a leave from their current positions and get down here to fill in."

Haskins nodded, looking around at the empty dispatching chairs.

"Do the same thing with every company official who's ever worked as a conductor or engineer. Put them back in train service."

"You can't do that," Megan interrupted. "It'd be a contract violation. Management can't take our work from us."

"If we don't get the cars over the road, there won't be any work for anyone," Farranger snapped. Could her loyalty to the union's outdated work rules really be so unflagging in spite of this crisis?

"You don't get it, Farranger. Management working craft positions constitutes a major dispute. Try it and my people will walk."

"Just whose side are you on? We're under attack, and all you're doing is throwing obstacles in my way."

"I'm trying to watch your ass for you, Farranger. You don't want the situation to get even more complicated because Transcon's not honoring the contract, do you?"

"I can't worry about contracts when a maniac's killing our people. There's only one way this psychopath can shut the railroad down, and the union seems to be playing right into his hands—"

Farranger stopped himself short. Arguing was pointless, and Megan was only trying to help. "Major dispute" was union lingo for any action that warranted a strike, and management officials working union positions was an absolute taboo. Neither Langford nor any other union representative could waiver on this point.

Farranger thought long and hard. "Mr. Haskins," he finally said, "demote every management employee who's ever held a position in train service and have them sent back to the craft."

Haskins looked dumbstruck, but Megan nodded in understanding.

"Make sure they know," Farranger went on, "that their management positions will be reinstated as soon as the crisis is over."

The VP cracked a smile.

Farranger looked at Megan. "Satisfied?"

"Absolutely."

"Need anything else?" Haskins asked.

"Yes. When you get done, take an empty chair for yourself." Farranger gestured toward the dispatching cubicles.

"I haven't dispatched in thirty years," Haskins objected.

"Perfect. It's been that long since we've dispatched like this."

Haskins stormed off, muttering to himself. Farranger couldn't quite make out the exact words, but it was evident the man hadn't completely forgotten the more colorful terms employed by railroad dispatchers.

Farranger worked late into the afternoon. He hurried from station to station to make sure his orders were being executed, cringing at the updates. He tried to tamp back his panic. *The whole network is going to freeze up!*

Already the system was showing signs of gridlock. The trains were moving at only a third of normal velocity. Detroit's automakers would be the first casualties. Their "just in time" supply

End of the Line

chain left little room for error if parts and raw materials stopped flowing.

Megan stayed on Farranger's trail, second-guessing every move he made and questioning the productivity of his security measures. Unfortunately, she was right. Protecting every weak point on the eighty-thousand-mile system was an impossibility.

Being right doesn't make Megan Langford any less a pain in the ass. Quite the contrary, Farranger thought dryly.

"I need to report to the union," Megan told him. "Think you can you handle things till I get back?"

"Gee, I don't know. I might have a hard time making decisions without the constant buzz of your voice in my ear."

"Just don't stray too far," she smiled. "I'll need an update when I get back. Remember, your CEO said 'complete access.'"

"Yes, ma'am," Farranger muttered. *At least now maybe I can get something done.*

As he turned his attention back to his work, a nearby clerk waved his phone receiver in the air. "Call for you."

Farranger noticed the phone's green handset didn't match the off-white cradle, a sensible replacement given what had happened to the Montana dispatcher. He raised the receiver to his ear, glancing up at the second-floor skybox windows with the eerie sensation that he was being watched. "Hello."

"Adashek here. I need a status report so I can deal with our customers. Anyone hit particularly hard?"

"Detroit's already in trouble. The automakers have a short turnaround. They'll be shutting down production lines before the night's out."

"Understood." The Axeman abruptly hung up.

Frustrated, Farranger shook his head and returned the phone to its cradle. At some point, when the crisis was over, he'd have to square off with Adashek. But he couldn't worry about that now. He had plenty to worry about, like trying to defend a rail system that had millions of vulnerable points. And he had the horrible feeling that the man they were calling Casey Jones knew them all.

Adashek immediately dialed another number. "Brandon, this is Phil Adashek. Sell short thirty thousand shares each of Ford, GM, and Daimler Chrysler. Use the usual discretion."

"Jesus, Phil, you watching the news? CNBC is doing a hatchet job on Transcon."

"What about?" Adashek gazed out the glass window of his office to one of the COC floor monitors displaying the news. It was Bloomberg, not CNBC, but the message at the bottom of the screen was no doubt the same: gridlock.

"Something wrong with your computer system, Phil?" the broker asked. "They're reporting your trains have road crossings blocked all over the country. They had one guy interviewed—I think he was the mayor of some Podunk town in Oklahoma—he said you guys have a train blocking the main road and no one can get in or out of downtown. What gives?"

"Yeah, it's minor, a computer glitch with our signal system," Adashek lied. "It should be cleared up soon."

"They're also reporting an explosion in your operations center."

"Blown fuse in one of our main electrical panels, nothing serious. Are you a broker or a press agent?"

"Thought I was your friend, Phil, just filling you in so you know why your stock is down three percent in heavy volume. But I'm sure you've got it all figured out."

"Don't worry about Transcon," Phil admonished. "We're a widows and orphans stock. Just short the big three like I told you. Call it a hunch, but I'm figuring a twenty-percent drop in share price by this time tomorrow."

-14-

Dallas Siding was only five miles from Transcon's operations center. The siding was a desolate outpost, the midpoint on a low-traffic branch line surrounded by Texas scrub. Other than a daily road switcher that served local farmers, the area drew no visitors. Casey was sure he was the first tourist.

But it wasn't just a pleasure trip, and he certainly couldn't be leisurely in his pace. He needed to finish working the cars in the siding before the daily road switcher arrived to make a pickup.

He pulled a stencil off the gray, covered hopper car, then backed up a few paces to make sure the dimensions and placement of the freshly painted number conformed to the other forty cars in Dallas Siding.

Satisfied with his paint job, he ducked under the hard rubber hose running from the hopper car to the diesel tanker truck he'd parked on the right-of-way. He'd already transferred three thousand gallons of diesel fuel through the top of the hopper's center fill cap.

Like most of Casey's equipment, the tanker had been stolen from the railroad—Transcon had been more than accommodating in providing the means of their own destruction. But using the railroad's equipment was more a case of economics than poetic justice. His mission was an expensive one, funded by his own personal grubstake. Ironically, his railroad severance package was footing the bill. The paradox amused him to no end.

The gray hopper was carrying two hundred times the amount of ammonium nitrate used in the Oklahoma City bombing. In addition to pacifying his infantile fascination with blowing things to bits, detonating the hopper would be devastating, causing the deaths of tens of thousands and plunging the entire country into fearful anarchy. Not bad for a day's work.

Casey read the fuel-flow gauge on the tanker: four thousand gallons. Perfect. After shutting off the pump, he disconnected the hose from the top of the car, armed the detonator inside, and tightened down the eight bolts securing the fill cap. He quickly restored the fuel hoses to the mounting brackets that ran the length of the truck.

The gray car was nearly identical to the other quarter-million covered hoppers in North America. Its only distinguishing feature was a graffito of an upended champagne glass, signed THE RAMBLER. Casey felt a strange kinship with the anonymous graffiti artist. This railroad hopper would serve him in a similar manner, as a canvas for his deadly masterpiece.

Using a screwdriver and crowbar, he removed the brick-sized electronic ID tags attached to the side of the hopper, stashed them in a green duffel bag, and carefully attached counterfeit tags in their place—the only truly delicate part of the operation. The tags were electronically coded. He had no replacements if they were damaged during installation.

Casey was so focused on his work that he didn't notice the special agent's car approaching alongside the right-of-way until it was practically on top of him. The sound of crunching ballast finally caught his attention.

He reminded himself to stay calm. Cinderdicks weren't like some flunky security force; they were the law on railroad property. They had the authority to carry weapons and make arrests, but the necessity for either rarely presented itself. Most railroad freight came in the form of bulk commodities, and its sheer weight normally defied theft. A seventy-five-ton roll of steel was certainly valuable, but it couldn't be transported without access to, say . . . a railroad. Which was one of the reasons why America's most wanted hadn't earned any fame for train robbery in nearly a century.

The appearance of the special agent posed more of a nuisance than a threat. Casey could easily explain himself as a mechanical employee performing some kind of maintenance function. He wouldn't necessarily have to kill the guy. *Then again,* he thought, *where's the fun in that?*

End of the Line

He watched nonchalantly as the patrol car pulled up beside the stolen tanker and stopped. The special agent got out, a man who had to be approaching retirement, with graying hair and a waistline expanded by too many doughnuts. The nametag on his chest read DUMARS.

Agent Dumars ignored Casey, his attention focused on the tanker truck. A bad sign. Someone had probably reported it stolen. Still, Casey wasn't particularly worried, even when the agent copied down the license plate. He'd put too much effort into his plans to let some overweight cinderdick ruin them.

The agent ambled toward him, showing no visible sense of alarm. The only weapon drawn was a pen with which to write down the answers to routine questions.

"Good morning, sir," the special agent said politely. "Mind if I ask what you're doing out here?"

"Working," Casey replied, in a union-employee tone meant to convey that the special agent didn't have a real job. "Topping off generators for some reefer cars."

Dumars scanned the line of cars going down the siding. There were, in fact, several refrigerated boxcars on the track. "Would you mind showing me your registration and DOT license?"

"No problem. They're in the truck."

Casey moved casually toward the cab compartment of the tanker, Special Agent Dumars in tow. He resisted the urge to move more quickly, lest the agent conclude he wasn't a union man.

He stepped up on the tanker's running board, reached through the driver's-side window, and grabbed a pry bar—a five-foot-long railroad crowbar made of solid iron that weighed thirty-five pounds and had a sharpened wedge on one end for removing spikes.

My samurai sword.

As he turned and leapt off the running board, Casey rammed the blunt end of the pry bar into Dumars's chest.

The agent doubled over in agony, but made a weak attempt to reach for his gun.

Casey swung the pry bar with all the force he could muster, breaking Dumars's arm. Casey continued the attack, sweeping the agent's feet out from underneath him and pressing the sharp end of the tool to his throat.

"If you'd be so kind, Officer," he said, his tone sickeningly sweet, "please roll over on your stomach and allow me to apply your handcuffs. I'd hate to have to kill you over something so minor as a stolen truck."

The special agent quickly complied. Casey grabbed the handcuffs off the helpless man's belt and clamped them around Dumars's fleshy wrists.

Once he had the agent safely secured, Casey finished cleaning up loose ends. He sang in a flat, twangy voice, imitating his favorite mountain singers.

*"Casey Jones was a son of a bitch,
Ran his train into a whorehouse ditch."*

Agent Dumars's moans forced Casey to sing louder.

*"Casey held his air hose in his hand,
Said 'Look at me girls, I'm a railroad man.'"*

When the noise continued, Casey lifted Dumars into a sitting position.

"Mr. Dumars, is it? I'm working on a little something. Would you mind helping me out?"

The agent said nothing, but a slight pressure in the groin from Casey's pry bar solicited a nod.

"All right, then. Give me your honest opinion and don't pull any punches. Be brutal."

Casey backed up two paces, took an Al Jolson stance, and started to sing.

*"Casey lined a hundred whores up agin' the wall,
Bet a hundred dollars he could spike 'em all.
Spiked 98 until his balls turned blue,
Took a shot of whiskey and he spiked the other two."*

End of the Line

He walked back to Dumars. "Well, what do you think?"

Dumars gasped in pain, but he nodded approval.

Casey couldn't help but notice that the special agent had been staring at the hopper. Diesel fuel still trickled down the side of the car.

"You just had to go and figure it out, didn't you?" he asked.

The pained expression on Dumars's face gave way to horror.

"That's a real shame," Casey deadpanned. He hefted the pry bar like a javelin. "Now I'll have to kill you."

Casey maintained a remorseful expression for as long as he could stand it, but he couldn't keep a straight face. "Ah, I'm just messin' with you," he said, giving the agent a tight-lipped smile. "I was going to kill you anyway."

-15-

It was almost evening before Farranger finally left the COC and headed for the parking garage. *A long hard day.* Blood on the tracks, Sims and the Montana dispatcher murdered. Farranger was weary beyond belief. But he still had to figure out where he parked his rental car. Scanning the concrete maze and its hundreds of tightly packed vehicles, Cal realized he had no memory of where he'd parked.

My God, Farranger thought, I can't even remember what color the damn thing is.

"Abandoning your post, Farranger?" Megan called out, hustling up behind him.

"No," Farranger replied, growing even more irritable. "The COC just got an unusual report, an AWOL five miles north of here."

"Train crew?"

"Nope, special agent. I'm going out there to check it out. If I can find my car."

"You're supposed to find the bad guy, but can't find your own car?"

"I see the irony, believe me. But I'm only in charge of security. The FBI's supposed to be catching him."

"They don't have a clue what they're up against. This guy obviously knows the railroad. It's going to take a railroader to catch him."

"I don't think there are any real railroaders left." Poor Lucas Sims, Farranger thought, his heart sinking.

"Except you."

Farranger was so surprised by the compliment that he quickly changed the subject. "Seen any Feds running around?"

"I've seen them *sitting* around. They're holed up in a conference room, combing the personnel files on every employee who's ever worked for us."

"Grunt work—"

"Farranger!" The Axeman's shout echoed off the walls of the parking garage. The man speed-walked up to them, his normally smooth demeanor decidedly ruffled.

Farranger turned around and waited for Adashek to catch up. *I don't think I've ever seen the Axeman with his hair mussed,* he thought, with a glint of satisfaction.

"Do you have any idea how much your security measures are costing us?" Adashek blustered.

"I'm cutting corners wherever I can, Phil." *For example, I haven't ordered security for your office.*

"One day into this, and we've already got shippers demanding blood," the Axeman complained. "The factories are running short on inventory and the power plants are threatening to ration power."

"And no one knows that there's more bad news to come." Farranger's temper flared. "Care to tell me why you ordered a press blackout?"

"Public relations is not your concern. You have Doug's support now, but that won't last forever."

"Then I guess we can take up where we left off."

"Is that a threat?" Adashek demanded.

"Take it for what it is," Farranger said. He turned his back on Adashek and again scanned the garage for his car.

"Try using the remote access to home in on it," Megan suggested.

Farranger depressed the UNLOCK button on his electronic key ring. An instant later, two aisles away, the Ford Taurus exploded in a blinding flash of light.

Farranger, Megan, and Adashek were knocked off their feet by the blast. Flying shrapnel broke windows and set off car alarms.

As the dust and smoke cleared, the three stood up and moved cautiously to view the wreckage. The roof of Farranger's rental car was peeled back like a convertible. The driver's-side door had been blown off its hinges, and the interior was black as tar.

"So I'm not the only one who doesn't like you," Adashek smiled with remarkable calmness. "This Casey Jones fellow seems to carry a grudge. My guess is that one of the two of you will wind up killing the other by the end of the week."

"Let's hope it's not the wrong one," Cal muttered.

"There's a wrong one?" Adashek smiled at what must have seemed like a win-win situation from his perspective. Without waiting for a response, he walked away briskly, leaving Cal and Megan in the dust of the smoldering wreckage.

Asshole, Farranger thought to himself. From the disgusted look on Megan's face, her thoughts mirrored his.

Farranger examined the damage, his mind racing. In five seconds there would be police, explosive experts, a mind-numbing round of questions to answer.

No way. The lead he was pursuing was more important. He realized there was no tomorrow deadline to meet. The war had already started.

I've got to get out of here.

He turned to Megan Langford. "Have you got a car?" he asked. "It looks like mine is going to be in the shop for a while."

Slumped wearily in the passenger's seat, Farranger broke eight blissful minutes of silence only reluctantly. "Thanks for the ride," he said.

"I'm starting to feel like your car service," Megan said. "Maybe we can try not to demolish this one."

Megan pulled to a stop at the end of Dallas Siding, where a large diesel tanker truck was blocking the right-of-way. Except for the tanker and a small signal shack, the siding was barren. Farranger looked both ways when he heard the warning bells of a railroad crossing going off in the distance, but there wasn't a train in sight. He got out of the car to make a quick inspection of the tanker.

"So what's the big emergency?" Megan asked, following him. The siding didn't exactly look like a hotbed of activity.

End of the Line

"A special agent called in four hours ago to report that he'd found a stolen tanker truck," Farranger explained. "That was the last anyone heard from him. They found the stolen truck, but no agent, no patrol car. He just vanished."

"What does our police force think?"

"That he just forgot to check in, or that his radio isn't working."

"But you don't believe that?"

"Who else but our guy would steal a diesel tanker truck? They're only used for fueling locomotives."

Farranger circled the tanker, inspecting it on all sides.

Nothing.

"Casey Jones must have a locomotive somewhere," he said, thinking out loud. "He steals a tanker truck full of fuel but gets caught in the act by one of our special agents. It's the only thing that makes any sense. But if that's true, where's the special agent?"

Scanning the area around the siding, Farranger spotted the flashing lights of the distant road crossing, still clanging its warning. As he traced the overhead catenary lines from the crossing to the nearby signal shack that housed its electronic brains, it hit him.

He raced to the signal shack, fumbling through his assortment of brass skeleton keys. He selected the smallest one and unlocked the door, then eased it open.

The sunlight pouring in revealed a grisly sight. Inside, dozens of signal relay boxes were clicking like telegraph keys. Several relays had been knocked off their mounting shelves, which explained the malfunctioning warning system at the crossing. Agent Dumars was pinned against the rear wall of the shack by six railroad spikes that had been driven through his body. Blood had poured from the wounds, run down the wall, and pooled at his ruined feet.

Farranger stood frozen in shock, unaware that Megan had walked up behind him.

"My God," she murmured.

Too late, Farranger turned and tried to push her out the door.

But she couldn't tear her eyes away. When Farranger grabbed her by the arms and held them tightly in front of his chest, trying to stop her from hyperventilating, she broke free and stumbled outside, where she dropped to the ground and retched.

Farranger and Megan sat on the rear bumper of her car, numbly watching as the FBI and a dozen railroad and civilian police officers scoured Dallas Siding. Megan's shaking had finally subsided, her breathing had returned to normal, and the color was slowly returning to her cheeks.

Kelly approached them with a determined look. "The two of you stay put," he ordered. "You'd better believe I'll be talking to you."

Cal didn't relish the prospect. One day into this mess, and he already had a lot of explaining to do. Kelly would question them for hours, even though he was sure they didn't know anything useful. He wondered if Megan was up to it.

"Are you all right?"

She nodded, turning her head away.

"You don't have to be strong all the time, you know."

"Sure I do," she replied, staring down at the ballast. "People are counting on me. They elected me to represent them. How do you think they'd feel if they knew I threw up at the first sight of blood?"

"Is that what this is about? Hell, I'd have thrown up myself except I didn't want to look bad in front of you," Farranger said, smiling.

"Like you give a damn what I think."

"As a matter of fact I do," he said, realizing suddenly that he meant it.

"Why? Because you want to sleep with me?" Megan's tone was laced with sarcasm.

"Where the hell did that come from?"

End of the Line

"Experience. I'm a woman and I work on the railroad. That's usually all it takes." Megan stooped down and grabbed a handful of pebbles from the ground, throwing them one by one.

Back at the COC, Farranger would've loved to have taken the union leader down a peg. But seeing her now, the idea didn't seem so appealing.

"How do you manage to walk with that huge chip on your shoulder?" he asked.

"Me? You're the one who 'can't waste any time talking to some roundhouse lawyer with her panties in a knot.'"

"That *was* a pretty good one, wasn't it?" Farranger grinned. "Something about being called Adashek's lapdog somehow brings that kind of thing out in me."

"You're not his lapdog. You're not even from the same kennel." Megan smiled for the first time in an hour.

"You're too hard on yourself, you know. Anyone who tries to stop a 150-ton locomotive with a pickup truck hyrail has to be pretty amazing. Stupid, but amazing." Farranger paused, growing serious again. "Any idea how lucky you are that you weren't killed?"

"It wasn't luck, it was a calculated risk."

Farranger had to laugh. There hadn't been time for calculation.

"Like I said, I'm a woman and I'm on the railroad. A day doesn't go by that someone doesn't hit on me, including management." Megan turned to look into Farranger's eyes, her smile fading. "So you can understand why it's important for me to know that you don't value my opinion because you want to sleep with me."

"I guess I wouldn't mind sleeping with you," Farranger admitted. "But that isn't why I value your opinion."

Megan laughed.

"Look, if it makes you feel any better," he went on, "the only fantasy I've had about you so far is strangling you."

"Hold on to that anger, Farranger," Megan replied. "When you find this Casey Jones creature, you're going to need it."

-16-

"DS23, this is Spokane Local reporting dead on the Hours of Service law. Five minutes to work. Over."

"Roger, Spokane Local. I show you dead, eleven hours, fifty-five minutes on duty. Pull your train into Smallwood Siding and wait for the relief crew. Over."

Casey Jones turned the volume down on his packset radio, marveling at his luck. Smallwood Siding was less than two miles away. Under federal law, a railroad crew was forbidden to turn a wheel after twelve hours on duty. Management counted the crew as "dead."

So did Casey.

It would be another few hours before Transcon's twenty-four-hour deadline was up, but the opportunity presenting itself was too tempting. After a ragged flight to his truck in L.A. and twenty hours of continuous driving, he figured he owed himself a pleasant diversion. He sped through the streets of Spokane's seedy industrial section, his eyes alternating between the rough road and the train lineup he was holding under the truck's dim interior light. If the train schedule was accurate, a southbound loaded with freight for a company by the name of Consato was due to pass Smallwood Siding in twenty minutes.

Casey reached the road crossing that led to Smallwood Siding in two minutes, then slowed to 15 mph as he bounced over the right-of-way, anxious for his first glimpse of the Spokane Local. He slowed even more as he passed the caboose at the rear end of the train, admiring the craftsmanship of the car. Cabooses were almost extinct. This was a particularly fine specimen.

End of the Line

He stopped just before the caboose at the siding switch. The target showed the switch lined for main track movement. After a little unexpected difficulty with the switch lock, he snapped the mechanism apart with his pry bar. It wasn't exactly a subtle solution, but it freed the switch for hand throw. He wasted no time in lining the switch for siding movement.

Stepping away from the switch, he made a quick inspection of the freight. Apart from the caboose, the rest of the local didn't impress him. Two locomotives, twenty boxcars, and a few open-top gondolas.

Casey sighed. *It's not much of a train, but at least it's mine.*

After parking his truck near the two-unit locomotive consist, he got out and donned a white hard hat, gripping his pry bar tightly in his hand. He climbed the ladder in front of the engineer's window, then slunk around to the nose door at the front of the engine.

Casey entered the cab, the color of his hard hat announcing him as a track-department supervisor. "Hello, boys," he greeted the three-man crew, instantly sizing them up. "Good night to go dead, huh?"

With lightning speed, he jabbed the engineer in the temple with the blunt end of the pry bar, crushing his skull. The man slumped over lifelessly in his chair behind the control console.

The conductor and the brakeman froze, looking at him goggle-eyed.

"Let that be a lesson to you," Casey said, tapping his hard hat with the pry bar. "Safety first."

The brakeman was too petrified to move, but the conductor made an awkward charge for him. Casey put both hands on the pry, holding it parallel to the floor until the conductor was close enough, then pushed it forward as if he were bench-pressing a barbell. The blow struck the conductor across the bridge of his nose, breaking it and severely damaging his right eye. The stunned conductor fell backward against the rear wall.

Casey hovered over him, brandishing the pry bar over his head like a spear. He plunged the sharp end into the man's throat, pushing it out the back of his neck.

Twisting the pry bar free, Casey turned to face the brakeman.

The two men stared at each other for a short moment. The brakeman broke contact first, his eyes dropping to the packset radio on his belt.

"You touch that radio, I'll kill you where you stand." Casey stepped forward, within striking range.

"You're going to kill me anyway." The brakeman's voice quivered with fear.

The comment stopped Casey in his tracks. He *was* going to kill the man, but he hated to be predictable. "Okay, but I bet you don't know *how* I'm going to kill you."

Before the brakeman could answer, Casey delivered a series of nonlethal blows, breaking bones in every extremity. Satisfied that his victim was now sufficiently immobile, he dragged the brakeman to the electrical panel behind the engineer's seat, opening it to reveal a 660-volt knife switch about a foot above the floor. The switch was cocked in the up position, like an upside-down tuning fork.

After pulling the switch down halfway, Casey positioned the still-conscious brakeman's wrist between the switch and the contact points. He kicked the rubberized switch handle up again with his black work boot, keeping a firm pressure on it as the current completed its circuit through the knife to the brakeman. He finally released it when the man's body stopped convulsing.

"Bet you never figured on electrocution, smart-ass."

Casey checked his wristwatch. He'd been having so much fun, he'd almost forgotten the time. The Consato train was only a few minutes away.

He propped the engineer up in his seat and duct-taped his left hand to the air brake handle, his right to the throttle. It was the same position the original Casey Jones's body had been in when it was found in the cab of his famous Cannonball.

Sending a message.

Casey backed up a couple of paces for perspective. Everything on the Spokane Local was ready.

He turned off the locomotive headlights, released the air brakes, placed the reverser in the reverse position and the throttle to Run Eight. Since the throttle and brake were taped to the dead engineer's hands, manipulating the controls made Casey feel a bit like a puppeteer. Struck with the image, he considered branching

End of the Line

out into ventriloquism, briefly toying with the idea of making the engineer appear to speak while he drank a glass of water.

But time was short.

The brakes hissed their release, and the local shoved its twenty cars north out of the siding to meet the southbound Consato train on the main line.

Casey detrained.

He returned to his truck and waited, watching the right-of-way. The southbound Consato train didn't see the darkened local coming toward it until it was too late. Casey heard the frantic blast of its whistle.

With a relative speed of 80 mph, the trains came together in a tremendous thunderclap.

The heavier locomotives of the Consato train crushed the local's lighter caboose and boxcars, jamming them inward. The mangled cars compressed into a solid mass of metal, creating a makeshift ramp that catapulted the Consato's locomotives thirty feet into the air. As the engines slammed back to earth, the ground beneath Casey's truck quaked. The cars behind the Consato's engines skipped off the right-of-way, slicing through power lines and telephone poles before skidding across the asphalt road crossing and rolling over a dozen vehicles parked in a factory lot adjacent to the right-of-way.

Heading away from the siding in his truck, Casey made one last hurried survey of the wreckage. The Consato's engine was lying on its side, its malfunctioning horn still blasting its warning.

-17-

Farranger had been at Transcon headquarters for twenty minutes, still reeling from the news of Casey Jones's preemptive strike in Spokane. Despite Adashek's best efforts to keep the media in the dark, the news outlets all had video footage of the wreck. Looking up at the theater-sized screens that were displaying CNBC, CNN, and Bloomberg, he could see the crash in full color, in triplicate.

The CNBC news anchor was reporting five crew fatalities, a fact Cal had confirmed with the SYSOP. The cat was most definitely out of the bag, and Transcon's falling stock price reflected the event. Transcon was down 5 percent in the first hour of trading.

That Transcon was tanking was predictable, but Casey's actions were not. Farranger couldn't understand why Casey had traveled halfway across the country to attack this specific train. There were a hundred locals between Spokane and Dallas—what made this one special? Farranger barely had time to ponder Casey's motivation when all hell broke loose.

Casey had jumped his own deadline.

At precisely 8:30, fifty culverts and four key bridges blew up simultaneously. The explosions cut the main line to pieces, completely isolating Detroit's auto industry and severing critical routes to the nation's coal reserves in West Virginia and the Powder River Basin. Hundreds of trains carrying coal and automotive parts lay idle on the crippled tracks, creating ten-mile logjams behind each break.

Casey Jones had targeted two of the nation's most vital—and vulnerable—industries. It would take less than three days for isolated power plants to run low on the small coal reserves they kept

End of the Line

on hand, and less than one day for the automotive assembly lines to grind to a halt for lack of materials.

With just one blow, Casey had already begun fulfilling his promise to plunge the country into chaos.

Farranger charged toward the SYSOP's desk. "Does engineering have those estimates yet?"

"Forty-eight hours to repair the culverts," the SYSOP replied. "A week for the bridges in West Virginia."

"We don't have that kind of time. Half the East Coast will run out of power. We'll have to reroute."

Farranger turned to one of the huge screens mounted on the rear wall of the COC, a schematic of Transcon's entire rail system. Broken track was outlined in red, and the crimson lines indicated that all coal routes leading from West Virginia to the eastern seaboard had been disabled. And of the dozen tracks surrounding the Powder River Basin, only three remained serviceable. These headed south, the opposite direction of the cut-off electrical plants. But they were the only option.

"We'll have to supply both coasts from the Midwest," he said.

The SYSOP shook his head. "It'll take two days to get Nebraska coal to the East Coast. Three if we have to run it south first."

"And half the cities between Boston and Jacksonville will shut down if we don't. Have the coal desk run the numbers on how much coal we can divert without blacking out the West Coast. And tell them to work up rationing plans while they're at it."

The SYSOP reached for the phone. "What about Detroit?"

Farranger looked at the schematic again, focusing on the largest concentration of red. Every single rail link to Detroit had been sabotaged. Nothing short of a miracle could keep the automakers afloat.

"They're on their own until we get the coal lines repaired. Give them one track for now. We'll get their first line back in service, then reroute everything over that until West Virginia's in the clear."

"Who gave you authority to reroute my trains?"

Farranger turned to see Phil Adashek storming toward him.

"Last time I checked, Farranger, you'd been put on glorified guard duty," the Axeman snapped.

"I'm filling a leadership void, Phil—" Farranger's retort was cut short by the arrival of an agitated clerk.

"Derailment," the man blurted, passing a scribbled note to the SYSOP.

"Norfolk, Virginia," the SYSOP read out loud. "Sixty-car train broke in two when a journal bearing on the eighth car blew off. Engineer dead, conductor injured."

As Farranger stood reading the note over the SYSOP's shoulder, he spotted Doug McClure coming through the front doors of the COC. The CEO hurried toward them, but his eyes never left the system map on the rear wall.

Another clerk ran up to the operations desk, nearly colliding with McClure. Farranger intercepted the piece of paper the man was waving at the SYSOP.

"Denver, Colorado," he read to the group. "Forty cars. Drawbar came off when a retaining pin exploded in the middle of the train. Main line fouled, track damaged. Both crew members dead." Farranger crumpled the note as he finished, then looked at his watch. It was 0901. One minute past Casey's original deadline. Farranger had the feeling that as bad as things were, they were about to get worse.

One glance around the COC confirmed it. Waves of clerks were coming toward them from every direction.

By 0905, the operations desk looked like a commodities trading pit. Dozens of clerks were waving handwritten slips of paper in the SYSOP's face, and reports of derailments from all over the country were piling up on his desk.

Within minutes, twenty-three trains had derailed from New York to California. The main line had been ripped apart, causing twenty million dollars in track damage. A hundred million dollars of freight now lay strewn alongside the tracks. And nineteen employees were dead.

More reports came in every minute.

Chaos. Death. The end of everything.

Farranger felt despair, but he didn't give in to it. He grabbed the SYSOP by the arm. "We have to stop the trains."

"Are you out of your mind?" Adashek shouted. "It costs us a million dollars a minute to have our main line shut down."

End of the Line

"And it's costing railroaders their lives every minute the trains keep running. How does that factor into your balance sheet?" Farranger pushed past Adashek to face the CEO. "Our people are dying out there, Doug. We have to stop this now."

"We have a million cars in our inventory," the Axeman countered with trademark coolness. "We can't let eighty billion dollars in freight rot on the main line while we inspect every one. It would take months. We might as well shut down the railroad right now and surrender."

The CEO said nothing for several moments, then finally let out a deep breath. "I'm afraid I have to agree with Phil on this one, Cal. We're already operating on a razor-thin margin. A shutdown to inspect cars could mean bankruptcy in a matter of days. Everyone suffers if that happens. Besides, I can't let a madman dictate our train schedules. For all we know, we might be playing right into his hands if we shut down."

"For God's sake, Doug," Farranger persisted. "I'm not suggesting we stop the trains for long. Just for a few hours, until we can figure this out."

A trace of shame crossed McClure's face, but before Farranger could press his point home, the Axeman intervened.

"The decision's been made, Farranger. The trains keep running. Besides," he said smugly, gesturing toward the SYSOP, "the number of derailments is already slowing."

Just as Farranger turned toward the operations desk, a solitary clerk walked up with two more notices. The SYSOP was buried in a confetti aftermath of derailment reports, but at least the flood had slowed to a trickle.

"They've slowed, but they haven't stopped." Farranger knew in his gut that this was far from over. He grabbed a handful of reports and began reading through them. All the derailments had been caused by booby-trapped cars hidden inside the trains. And in every case, the sabotaged car was on the main line when it exploded. Somehow, Casey knew exactly when and where to detonate each car so that it would hurt Transcon the most. Farranger was dumbfounded.

How is he doing it?

Even more baffling was Casey's ability to strike everywhere at once, orchestrating simultaneous derailments in nearly every state across the continental U.S. He couldn't possibly have traveled all over the country sabotaging individual cars. There simply wasn't enough time. He must have found an easier way.

Then the answer hit him. He'd been looking at the problem all wrong. It wasn't important where the cars ended up—what mattered was where they originated.

"It's not over," Farranger turned back to McClure and Adashek. "The derailments have just begun."

"And I say they'll stop any minute," Adashek argued. "We're talking about an eighty-thousand-mile network. Logistically, there are only so many locations he could've hit before running out of time, gas, and money. He couldn't have sabotaged more than two dozen cars."

"He could've rigged a hundred cars in an hour," Farranger countered. "All he had to do was go to one remote siding and hit every car in it. In a week's time, the cars would've spread all over the country."

McClure sank into the nearest chair, looking defeated. "So it's possible he's sabotaged thousands of cars." He looked up at Farranger, then Adashek. "He's beaten us. We can't take this kind of punishment much longer—trains derailing every five minutes with no end in sight. The union'll walk and so will our shippers."

"He's only beaten us when we shut down," Adashek countered. "We just have to stick it out and hope there aren't too many cars left."

"We don't have to stick it out," Farranger insisted. "Not if we can figure out how he's doing it."

"What's to figure out? He has to be using timers. He sets thirty to go off at nine o'clock just to show us what he can do, then has another one go off every five minutes until we throw in the towel."

"He's not using timers," Farranger said. "If he was, the cars could be anywhere when they detonated. They could be sitting in a yard or riding another railroad. Hell, they could be in Mexico for all he knows. Somehow, he's rigging the cars so they only detonate on our main line, where they'll do maximum damage."

End of the Line

"So how does he know?" McClure asked.

Farranger shook his head.

"Got another one," the SYSOP announced. "Bad one. In Kansas City. Eighty cars, both crew members dead."

Farranger started reading the handwritten note. "This report has two signatures," he said, suddenly looking up. "Which one of these guys is the dispatcher who took the call?"

"Both," the SYSOP explained. "The derailment happened just as the Kansas West dispatcher handed off to Kansas East."

Farranger stared at the SYSOP, thinking, then began rifling through the most recent derailment reports, the ones that had come in after the initial nine-o'clock wave.

"Maybe he has accomplices out train spotting," Adashek suggested to McClure, "and they send a detonation signal whenever they recognize a car number. That would allow him to hit cars all over the country at the same time."

"Spotters for a million cars?" McClure shook his head. "If he has accomplices, he'd have to have thousands of them."

Farranger was only half listening to the conversation as he studied the dispatches in his hands. The answer had been right under his nose.

He looked up at the SYSOP. "Stop the trains." He turned to face McClure. "I know how he's doing it, and I know how to stop him."

"How?" The CEO raised a finger to the SYSOP, holding him off.

"Casey Jones isn't setting off these explosions," Farranger said, frustrated with the delay. "We are."

McClure looked at Farranger in disbelief. "You're saying *our* people are setting off these devices?"

"Not intentionally. Our radio frequencies are setting them off. Casey Jones's devices are being triggered by the different road channels our dispatchers use to communicate with the trains. The last six derailments happened just as the trains were being handed off from one dispatcher to another." He paused, giving McClure and Adashek time to digest what he'd just said, then delivered the bottom line. "Every time we talk to our crews, we're using a detonation frequency."

Farranger grabbed the initial stack of derailment reports from the SYSOP's desk.

"The cars were armed at 0900. Any car that happened to be in the same territory as its preset detonation frequency exploded immediately. That's why we had so many reports at the same time."

"And any car that wasn't," McClure spoke up, "won't detonate until it matches up with the correct dispatching channel. So we're playing Russian roulette every time we move a train from one dispatching frequency to another."

"Except we keep playing until we lose, sending sabotaged cars all over the country until they finally hit the frequency that sets them off." Farranger picked up the stack of recent reports. "It's already happening."

McClure paled. "Our cars pass through twenty dispatching territories a week. We can't take twenty times as many derailments in the next seven days."

"Good Lord," Adashek chimed in. "If we have to inspect every car in North America, we'll be shut down for months."

"And we still wouldn't be sure we'd found them all," McClure added.

"We don't have to find them," Farranger said. "We can fix it so the cars find us. All we have to do is stop the trains and have our locomotives and yardmasters cycle through every road channel we use."

McClure looked at him as if he were crazy. "Are you suggesting that we intentionally set off more explosions?"

"They won't do any damage if the trains aren't moving."

"Why not change our frequencies?" Adashek asked.

"Because Casey Jones could still detonate the cars with a packset. It would just take him longer. We have to do it ourselves, while we know the trains are stopped. We can't let him control the time."

McClure finally nodded, then motioned for the SYSOP to carry out Farranger's instructions.

Within thirty minutes, every train on the system had been stopped. Sixty minutes after that, all the radio checks were complete and a second wave of clerks were bombarding the operations desk with incident reports.

End of the Line

The SYSOP turned to Farranger and the others with a grin. "Six hundred and thirteen additional explosions reported. None of them on moving trains. No derailments, no injuries."

McClure smiled for the first time all morning. "Put out a notice advising the other rail carriers about the problem. We still need to track down any sabotaged cars that were switched to other railroads."

"Yes, sir," the SYSOP replied. "We can use the serial numbers on the cars that have already exploded to pinpoint common sidings of origin. It should cut our search time down considerably."

"Morning, gentlemen," Megan Langford called out as she crossed the COC floor. "Sorry I'm late, but I got stuck for an hour behind a train that was stopped on a crossing. Did I miss anything?"

The four men just stared at her.

"Casey Jones jumped the gun," Farranger finally offered. He reached over the SYSOP's shoulder and grabbed a stack of notes, handing them to her. As Megan began reading, her eyes widened in disbelief.

The CEO turned to Farranger. "So where do we go from here?"

"I'm going to Spokane."

"Why Spokane?" Megan asked, looking up from the notes.

"Most of these trains were hit remotely," Farranger explained. "But Casey Jones murdered the Spokane crew in person. He killed a special agent in Dallas yesterday and then rushed halfway across the country. That's a long way to go for a random attack. I'm betting he had another reason to be there."

"And what reason is that?" Adashek asked.

"If I knew that, I wouldn't have to go to Spokane."

The Axeman's response was drowned out by at least a hundred simultaneous profanities on the operations floor. The SYSOP's clerk had entered the serial number of one of the sabotaged cars into the computer, which triggered a massive system outage. Monitors throughout the complex went momentarily blank, then displayed the same banner message scrolling across the screen: *Casey Jones is back!*

"Oh, shit," the SYSOP said. "The computer just crashed. Now we have no billing or location information on our cars. A million cars, and no idea where they are or what's inside them."

"Not to mention the fact that our dispatching terminals are linked to the mainframe," McClure added.

"Along with our e-mail, data transfer, radio communications," Adashek said. "We're screwed."

As Adashek ranted about worst-case scenarios, Megan huddled with a clerk at the computer help desk. She made a phone call, then straightened up.

"Excuse me," Megan interrupted politely.

Still, no one noticed.

"Excuse me," she repeated, this time loud enough to stop Adashek in mid-rant. "I just called Information Systems and they told me they'd reload a backup, then roll forward to a minute before the data problems began. They said the system will only be down for a couple of minutes, then everything will be restored as it was."

Farranger looked at Megan with new admiration. *A can-do woman.* The computer terminals came back to life, the system functioning normally again.

Adashek mumbled an insincere "well done" to Megan, then faded into the background. Cal smiled at Adashek's comeuppance. This was the second time in a week the Harvard man had been shown up by a lowly railroader.

Farranger and the others quickly returned their attention to assessing the extent of the morning's damage.

Megan Langford turned away from the boards to the young clerk in the computer center. She reached out a hand out in greeting. "Megan Langford, Railway Transportation Union."

"I know who you are, Sister Langford," the clerk smiled, accepting her handshake.

End of the Line

Being the only woman general chairman brought a certain amount of fame with it, but Megan was a little uncomfortable with being called "sister." This clerk had to be hard-core union; only the most fanatic members insisted on using fraternal greetings.

As Megan pulled her hand away, she realized the woman had slipped a note into her palm. She nodded, glancing over her shoulder at the men huddled around the SYSOP's desk, then quickly read the note and secreted it away inside her pocket.

The implications of what she'd read made her shudder. She glanced at the clerk, wondering if the young woman who'd stumbled onto this information even realized the significance. On any other day, Megan would have written off what she'd learned as a computer glitch, but given all that had happened, she sensed it was more than that. If she was right, time was critical, and Farranger needed to be informed immediately.

The problem was that she was a union officer operating under simple but explicit instructions: *Union first, Transcon second.*

The call from RTU President Jackson assigning her as the liaison had been as cryptic as it was unexpected. In their brief conversation, he had emphasized that Transcon management could not be trusted. Jackson had made it crystal clear that he was to be personally advised of anything she discovered *before* she reported to Transcon. She wasn't entirely sure she bought the party line, but a rookie general chairman couldn't afford to ignore an edict from the international president.

Megan was frustrated by the bureaucracy of the union and angry at herself for not having the courage to defy them. She told herself it was her duty, that it was the right thing to do.

She hoped like hell she wasn't making the biggest mistake of her life.

- 18 -

"Thank you for coming, Chairman Langford."

"My pleasure," Megan lied. This update could have been given over the phone, but International President Wade Jackson was an old-school union politician, a handshaker who had built his career on personal contacts. He had insisted on meeting with her personally.

She was somewhat overwhelmed by her surroundings. The walls of Jackson's Dallas office were decorated with pictures of labor's enduring struggle. Framed newspaper accounts detailed management's most brutal atrocities: armed Pinkerton detectives suppressing a strike at a Carnegie steel factory, Henry Ford's goon squads using force and intimidation to prevent the United Auto Workers from organizing, the Ludlow massacre of miner's wives and children in southern Colorado. The images were a graphic reminder of how far they'd come and made her proud to be part of the struggle.

Megan turned her attention to the man before her, a legend in union circles. Jackson had been elected to five consecutive four-year terms, unprecedented in the history of the union. He had forged his reputation as a ruthless opponent who preferred guerilla warfare to negotiation. His preferred strategy was to divide and conquer, attacking individual railroads with sickouts and work slowdowns until they capitulated. One by one, each regional line buckled under his relentless pressure. For almost twenty years his power over the railroads had seemed absolute.

But his influence was quickly deteriorating. As soon as Transcon began merging its way into a near monopoly over railroading, the balance of power had started to shift. Jackson's old-style tactics no longer worked. Transcon quickly became large enough to reroute traffic around rebellious workers without affecting train operations, effectively shutting out the employees until they gave in and went back to work. Jackson hadn't been able to adapt, and had continued to rely on manipulation and brute force against an adversary that couldn't be bullied. He'd been forced to surrender a quarter century of gains in the seven years it had taken to form Transcon.

"I've been hearing good things about you, Sister Langford."

Megan couldn't imagine what. She was a rookie and they both knew it. Jackson would dance around the business at hand, call her Sister Langford, and pledge solidarity forever. And he'd continue this charade right up to the moment he stuck the knife in her back and admitted that the real reason he'd called this meeting was to tell her she was no longer needed at Transcon, that a more experienced union officer was replacing her now that the situation had escalated into a national threat. Or, more accurately, now that it had escalated into a political threat for him.

Megan cut to the chase. "I don't mean to be abrupt, President Jackson, but perhaps we should get started."

"Wait." Jackson reached for a television remote control, then turned the volume up on a wall-mounted set in the corner. "I have to hear this."

Megan looked at the screen and saw Phil Adashek on CNN giving a statement.

"Our condolences go out to the crews, and apologies to our customers due to the service interruption. We have been working closely with the FBI and they believe they will have a suspect in custody in a very short time. This incident will not appreciably effect future operations. We have called on every resource available to us, and believe that we will be operating at a full capacity in less than twenty-four hours . . ."

"What a piece of work." Jackson turned the volume down, then pointed to the stock quotes rolling across the bottom of the screen. "Let's see if the market believes him."

Two beats later, the real-time market indicators showed Transcon down another quarter point, 8 percent for the day. The major indexes were also in the red, but the commodities index was skyrocketing based on anticipated shortages of raw materials.

"Guess the public ain't buying Adashek's spin." Jackson put down the remote and turned his attention to Megan, who was fidgeting in her chair.

"Am I keeping you from something more important, Sister Langford?"

"I'm anxious to get back to the operations center and catch up with Farranger."

Jackson nodded. "Cal Farranger's the one to watch, all right. He's the best railroader I've ever met. And the closest thing to a management type you can trust." Jackson paused to recharge his smile. "But I didn't invite you here to talk about Farranger. I want to discuss your career with the union."

Megan tensed, waiting for the ax to fall.

"I'm a career maker, Chairman Langford. All three of my vice presidents were elected on my recommendation, along with half of the general chairmen." He leaned forward, lowering his voice conspiratorially. "Unofficially, I claim three congressmen, too."

"I don't recall getting your support," Megan said coolly.

Jackson's eyes narrowed for an instant, but he quickly recovered and flashed another smile. "You didn't need my support. But next time might be different. You might need a friend in your corner."

"And you'll be that friend?"

"Of course. I think it's high time our organization had a woman in the international office, don't you?"

Megan was speechless. Jackson wasn't talking about removing her from the liaison post, he was talking about promoting her to the highest level in the organization. If she believed for a moment that she could take his offer at face value, she would have been thrilled. But now that the carrot was out, she knew the stick wouldn't be far behind.

"What's the catch?" she asked.

"No catch," Jackson laughed. "I'm not management out to screw you, Megan, I'm your fraternal brother who wants to help you."

His reference to "fraternal brother" set off alarms in Megan's head. There had to be a *big* catch.

End of the Line

"All I ask is that you remain loyal to the union during this crisis. Any information you discover should come to me, and only to me. I want to know everything Transcon knows, particularly how close they are to catching this Casey Jones fellow." Jackson paused. "That's not unreasonable, is it?"

Megan let out a deep breath that she hadn't realized she was holding and relaxed for the first time since entering the office. Jackson was just reminding her of the orders she'd already been given. Union first, Transcon second. Information was power, and Jackson wanted first pass at it. He just wanted to make sure Transcon officials weren't shirking responsibility, that they were doing everything possible, given the information they had, to catch the madman who was attacking all their livelihoods.

"No, that's perfectly reasonable." She returned Jackson's smile for the first time. "We all know Transcon tends to cut corners if there isn't a union watchdog at their heels."

"They certainly do, Sister Langford. And I assure you I'll be that watchdog if you'll be my eyes and ears at Transcon. And on that note, I believe you mentioned on the phone that you had stumbled across some information?"

Megan nodded. "I haven't told anyone at Transcon yet, but I'll need to inform them soon. It could be important."

Jackson's smile vanished. "I don't think you understand, Ms. Langford. Your job is to report information directly to me and no one else. My job is to evaluate that information and determine when and if to pass it on."

Megan was stunned. She had assumed her order of silence was only temporary, until she could inform her union chain of command. She had always intended to pass the information on to Transcon. But now Jackson was telling her he didn't want it reported at all.

"I don't understand," she said.

"Chairman Langford," Jackson said patiently, "how familiar are you with the Railway Labor Act?"

"Somewhat," Megan hedged. She had an inkling, but federal legislation was really the domain of the union's lawyers and lobbyists.

"In a nutshell, it makes it impossible for railroad workers to go on strike. Congress decided railroads were too vital to the nation's economy and national defense. They know a national rail strike would have devastating consequences."

"But when our contract runs out we can strike."

"For about five minutes, until Transcon gets an injunction."

"We could wildcat."

"The last time we tried that, the U.S. Army forced us back to work at the point of a bayonet. Basically, we've been denied labor's only weapon to fight oppressive management. Until now." Jackson paused for dramatic effect. "A madman is killing our members, and there isn't a federal judge or elected official in this country who'd order a man to go to work to be slaughtered. These attacks represent our ticket to staging the first truly national rail strike in U.S. history."

"You want to trade blood for money?" she asked, incredulous. Jackson didn't give a damn about the membership. He intended to use their lives as bargaining chips.

"It's tragic that our people are at risk. But think of the bigger picture—rail labor has a once-in-a-lifetime opportunity. We can get back everything Transcon's taken from us."

"Not at the expense of lives. We have to protect our members. If I can discover something useful, if I can help stop this guy . . ." Megan stumbled over her words in her desperation to make him listen to reason.

"You don't have to help," Jackson reassured her. "You're still new at this game. Nobody's expecting you to be a hero."

Nobody was expecting anything of her. That was the point. She hadn't been handpicked for promotion, she'd been selected as a stooge. Someone too green to be of any real help in catching Casey Jones. She needn't have worried about Jackson replacing her because of her rookie status.

That's why he wants me here.

"Farranger said the union was aiding and abetting this madman," Megan said, making no attempt to hide her disdain, "but I didn't believe him."

Jackson rubbed his eyes with the heels of his hands. Obviously, he now regretted that he'd taken her into his confidence. His expression changed from cordial to deadly serious in the blink of an eye. She knew that look. She had used it herself. He was going to play hardball now.

"Ms. Langford, I can break careers as easily as I make them. I'd hate to see you lose a reelection bid because I felt forced to support your opponent."

Jackson had put it bluntly. If she helped Transcon, her political career would be over before it started. To go along, she only had to keep her mouth shut. Megan smiled. She had never been good at that.

"I'd worry less about my career and more about yours," she said. "Because we're going to catch this maniac. And when we do, the membership will get rid of your sorry ass."

"I own you, Chairman Langford. Hell, I could remove you from your position right now."

"But you won't. If you do, our members will find out that Casey Jones has a willing accomplice in the international office."

Jackson seemed surprise at her defiance, but he didn't look particularly worried. Catching Casey before the strike deadline was a long shot, and they both knew it. The only thing her threat had accomplished was to make an enemy of the most powerful man in the union.

Megan stood up and walked toward the door. "You know, it's funny," she said, turning around to face him. "You said earlier that I could trust Farranger."

"Yeah, so?"

"He never told me I could trust you."

- 19 -

Though Farranger hadn't arrived until almost twenty-four hours into the clean-up effort, the collision between the Consato train and the Spokane Local was easily the worst he had ever seen. The cars closest to the point of impact were completely demolished, some ripped nearly in half. Tons of grain and plastic pellets had spilled out through the torn cars, flooding the right-of-way. The Consato locomotives lay on their sides, diesel fuel still trickling from their ruptured tanks. Of the twenty Spokane Local cars involved, only the two locomotives and the first four boxcars remained on the rails, anchored in place by a derailed gondola that looked as though it had been flattened by a trash compactor.

Farranger had been there for more than an hour, watching as the derailment clean-up crews buried the mangled cars, turning the roadbed into a graveyard. His ears were burning from exposure to the cold, his cheeks chafed from the biting wind. The early morning sun provided little relief, giving him yet another reason to regret that he hadn't arrived the previous afternoon as planned.

But the delay had been unavoidable. He'd spent the better part of the day trying to untangle the Gordian knot Casey Jones had made of their rail system. By the time he'd finally reached Spokane, the crash site had been picked clean.

Agent Kelly and his men had arrived on the scene the previous night, rudely brushing aside Transcon's asset protection team. Following them came a succession of investigators from the ICC, the Federal Railroad Administration, and the State Railroad Commission. Local homicide detectives brought up the rear of the parade, and a handful of them were still hovering anxiously

End of the Line

around the crash site, hoping to pounce on any scraps the Feds might have missed.

As if reading his mind, Agent Kelly approached, having all but packed up his team to leave.

"Go home, Farranger," Kelly said. "You won't learn anything here."

"Did you learn anything?"

"We have a rough notion of his size and weight. More importantly, I'm pretty sure we confirmed that he never worked for Transcon."

"How?"

"Sometimes," Kelly replied, "you learn more by what's not here than what is."

If the agent was trying to be cryptic, he'd succeeded. Farranger had no idea what he was talking about.

"Seriously, Farranger, if there's something you need to know, I will tell you. But personally, I think you're wasting your time here."

"It's my time to waste."

"Suit yourself." Kelly nodded to the last member of his team still packing up gear. They were finished at Spokane, and weren't about to let the grass grow under their feet. Within two minutes, Kelly and his team were gone.

Farranger was determined he would take up where they left off. He didn't know what he was looking for, but was certain he'd know it when he saw it.

He first inspected the remains of the Spokane Local's lead engine, the one Casey had personally sabotaged. Cal found nothing to help him identify Casey Jones or to determine why he had chosen this particular place for a personal assault. Instinct told him that Casey Jones hadn't selected Spokane randomly, that it was part of a greater plan.

I've got to find the connection.

Almost an hour later, Farranger was still wracking his brain. With the FBI gone, the railroad was making up for lost time by sentencing the derailed cars to a mass burial. Some of them could easily have been repaired, but the clean-up crews didn't have time to be selective. Transcon was losing thousands of dollars every minute the main line was blocked.

Gigantic earthmoving equipment had been working all morning, digging a pit thirty feet deep and half a mile long parallel to the tracks. As Farranger watched, an enormous Caterpillar maneuvered a crippled hopper toward the trench, extending its hydraulic claws under the car's belly, then flipping it end over end until the hopper teetered over the brink, crashing down to its final resting place. The symbolism unnerved him.

"Farranger."

He turned around to find Megan walking toward him. As much as he hated to admit it, he was almost glad to see her. He needed the distraction.

"Ms. Langford," he smiled. "If I didn't know better, I'd say you were stalking me."

Megan laughed. "And I'd say you were going to extraordinary lengths to ditch me again. I tried to catch up with you yesterday evening, but you'd already left by the time I got back to headquarters. So I followed you out on the red-eye." She paused to watch a gondola car being dropped into the pit. "What did I miss?"

"Just the FBI lifting about two hundred fingerprints from the cab of the locomotive."

"I'm surprised they didn't try to get footprints off the ballast," she said, then grew serious. "Look Cal, the reason I've been so anxious to track you down—"

A shriek of grating steel cut her off in midsentence, the unmistakable sound of slack rolling out.

Farranger turned to see the remaining four cars and locomotives of the Spokane Local rolling south. The clean-up crew had pushed the last gondola into the pit, and since the air brakes in the remaining cars had bled off hours ago, they had now removed the only anchor holding the cars in place.

"We've got a rollout!" Farranger shouted. Transcon had enough problems without having to sweep up after its clean-up crews. He looked south, down the tracks, relieved to see that the downgrade was mild, but it continued beyond his field of vision. Left unchecked, the cars would continue to gain speed. It wasn't an emergency situation yet, but every 50-mph rollout started at 5 mph first.

End of the Line

He brushed past Megan and ran toward the rolling cut, then slowed his pace alongside it and boarded the rear ladder of the second car. Climbing to the top rung, he reached out to turn the oversized wheel that operated the car's hand brake. The brake shoes beneath the car clamped tight, the wheels began skidding against the rail. The train slowed, but it was going to take more than one hand brake to stop it.

Farranger turned around, pressed his back against the ladder, and leaned across the gap for the brake wheel on the next car. The awkward position gave him little leverage to turn the oversized wheel, but it could have been a lot worse. At least he didn't have to jump car to car, like the brakemen had a hundred years ago.

Without warning, the rolling cut swung a hard right into Smallwood Siding, lurching the boxcar sideways. Farranger's head struck the side of the car, and the jolt nearly threw him to the rolling wheels below. He managed to regain his balance and quickly tightened the hand brake. The train finally came to a safe stop, and Farranger gingerly touched the rising lump on his temple. He now understood why so few brakemen in railroad's golden age had lived to see retirement.

The minute he dismounted, Farranger discovered why the cars had bucked. Instead of being in the straight track position required by the operating rules, the Smallwood Siding switch was lined for siding movement. Farranger's first impulse was to kill the stupid son of a bitch who'd almost gotten him thrown under a moving train. Then it dawned on him.

The stupid son of a bitch is Casey Jones.

Farranger sprinted toward the switch, hoping he might get lucky and find a trace of evidence Casey had left behind. He found just the opposite. Casey had left nothing behind, not even Transcon's permanently mounted switch lock. Farranger wondered for a moment if Kelly had taken the lock as evidence, but rejected the idea as soon as he saw the padlock's mounting. The switch lock hadn't merely been removed, it had been ripped apart, probably with a pry bar.

Farranger was stumped. It had to be Casey's work, but why? Any of Transcon's standardized switch keys would have opened the mechanism easily. Assuming he was in a hurry, why wouldn't he have chosen the simple solution?

When Farranger searched the area surrounding the switch for the jimmied lock and didn't find it, he realized Casey must have taken it with him. If so, he'd chosen a bizarre souvenir. Not only was it an exact duplicate of a thousand other switch locks, it was no longer functional. What possible use could he have for it?

Kelly's words flashed in his head.

Sometimes you learn more by what's not here than what is.

Farranger quickly made the connection. Casey had pried the lock off because he didn't have a Transcon switch key, so Kelly had logically concluded he wasn't a Transcon employee. If that was so, it still didn't explain why Casey would take a busted lock with him. Kelly's team could have removed it, of course, but Cal had watched every evidence bag get filled and didn't see anything the size of a switch lock. He was certain Casey had taken it, but why?

"Nice work, Farranger," Megan called out as she walked up to him. "I knew there was a switchman inside you somewhere."

Farranger smiled at her, then turned his attention back to the switch. "Look at what I found and tell me what you make of it. Or I guess I should say, what I *haven't* found."

"Wait," Megan said. "There's something I have to tell you first, before I lose my nerve." She hesitated, as if already reconsidering.

Farranger turned to face her. "If you know something, just say it. We're working for the same thing here. At least we should be."

"Somewhere on the system—" Megan stopped, Jackson's voice ringing in her ears. Or perhaps it was her own good sense counseling her.

Keep your mouth shut or your political career is over.

She looked at Farranger for a long moment, and finally decided to tell him. Farranger was the best hope for catching Casey Jones before more of her people died.

"Casey's hiding a car somewhere on the system. My guess is it's probably rigged with explosives." Megan paused to let her words sink in. "It could be anywhere."

-20-

A horrible thought immediately flashed in Farranger's brain. *Hydrogen cyanide.* The potent, quick-killing chemical was widely shipped by rail. A ruptured tank car in a populated area could poison hundreds of innocent people. If the missing car was full of the toxic gas, it represented a nightmare scenario.

But there were so many nightmare scenarios from which to choose. Given Casey Jones's fondness for explosives, he might be planning to detonate a tank of liquefied petroleum gas at a chemical plant, causing a deadly fire that would burn for days. Radioactive material for a dirty bomb was another potential threat, as were the trainloads of munitions shipped by the military. Farranger's mind reeled. Every lethal substance that could be mass-produced was shipped on Transcon's trains.

If Casey Jones is hiding a car, the possibilities are as terrifying as they are endless.

Rage overtook his terror-filled thoughts. He couldn't believe that he had not been informed of the situation sooner. Farranger glared at Megan. "How long have you known?"

"Since yesterday, when the computer went down," she murmured, then took a deep breath. "The car counts didn't match after the system reloaded."

"Why the hell didn't you say anything?" Farranger exploded. "You know what we haul on this railroad. When were you going to tell me, after they evacuated New York City?"

"I'm really sorry, Cal. I wanted to tell you earlier."

"The union told you to sit on this, didn't they?"

Megan didn't answer, but her expression said it all. Casey Jones was killing union members and the international office had actually ordered her to withhold vital information.

But she'd told him anyway. Megan Langford, the poster child for labor solidarity, had defied the union. Farranger felt his anger subsiding.

"The good news," she offered, "is that it isn't a tank car. It's a covered hopper."

Farranger relaxed a little. Hoppers were designed to transport bulk commodities, like grain and plastic pellets. The really dangerous cargo—hazardous material or explosive gas—was confined to tank cars.

"Do you have a car number?" he asked.

Megan handed over the slip of paper the COC clerk had given her. "GROX 293891. I've already run a car search on the computer. The current location shows 'missing offline.'"

Farranger felt the urgency rise within him, an almost physical pain. "I don't care what else is happening. We have to find that hopper."

Farranger hurried to his rental car, removed the laptop computer that the SYSOP had forced on him, placed it on the hood, and punched in the few system commands he knew. Megan couldn't stand watching him work in slow motion. She knew the computer system better than most managers, and observing Farranger's two-fingered keystrokes was as frustrating as waiting for her two-year-old nephew to tie his shoes.

"We need to know where the hopper was before it got lost," he said.

"Why do we care? Shouldn't we be more concerned with finding out where it *is*?"

"If we knew where it was, we might be able to find out where it was heading." Farranger scanned the keyboard, frowning. "I know there's a way to pull up a car history on this thing."

"It's in the billing records." Megan shrugged off his expression of surprise. "I used to be a clerk before I transferred into train service," she explained, gesturing toward the laptop. "May I?"

"Be my guest."

Megan paged through several menus until she found the billing subdirectory. "I'm not supposed to have access to this."

"I won't tell if you don't."

End of the Line

She entered the car number and scrolled down the page. "Here we go. Last known location . . ." Megan paused as the information came up on the screen. "Dallas Siding. Two days ago."

"Damn!" Farranger slammed his fist on the hood of the car. They had stood less than ten feet from that siding. But whatever deadly cargo had been there was long gone now. With a two-day head start, it could be anywhere. "What was the lading?"

Megan scrolled through several screens. "Eighty tons of ammonium nitrate."

Farranger stared at her in disbelief.

"What? It's just fertilizer, right?" she asked, confused by the look on his face.

"Until it's mixed with diesel fuel. Then it's eighty tons of high-grade explosive."

Megan's expression mixed horror and fear.

"He's going to blow up a train."

"No, he wouldn't waste something this big on a single train." Farranger paled at the magnitude of what they were up against. "He could take out a couple of city blocks."

The notion that Casey Jones was planning to kill thousands of people made Megan numb. She tried to force herself to think constructively, but the puzzle was too complex.

"It's impossible," she moaned. "Without a car number, there's no way to tell this car from any other hopper."

It came to Farranger the instant she said it. "The AEI tags! He changed the car number, but I bet he didn't change the tags." Automated Equipment Identification tags were affixed to every car in the Transcon system. There were automated trackside readers every thirty or forty miles.

Megan smiled with relief. "They can track the hopper no matter what's painted on the side."

Farranger looked down at the laptop. "You know enough about computers to get into the AEI tracking records?"

"I'll try."

Megan searched the menus for five minutes, with Farranger pacing behind her like an expectant father.

"Found it!" she finally said.

"Where?"

"It just passed by a reader in Wellington, Washington. Heading west." Megan paged through the previous stations to project its final destination. "My God, it's headed for Seattle."

"Not if we get to it first," Farranger said, already sliding into the driver's seat of his rental car.

The snow-covered Cascade Mountains provided a picturesque background for Wellington Station, an old-fashioned train depot that looked as if it had been plucked right out of a Norman Rockwell painting. It stood at the foot of the mountain, its roof sagging under three feet of snow. The surrounding area was thickly forested, broken only by a narrow path cleared to accommodate Transcon's tracks.

As Farranger's rental car slid across the icy parking lot near the depot, his hopes of finding the hopper gave way to disappointment. Wellington had no yard, no storage tracks, not even a promising branch line that might lead to unseen industry tracks. And there wasn't a single freight car in sight.

"Is that what I think it is?" Megan pointed to the solitary train docked in front of the depot.

"The Transtour Zephyr," Farranger said, looking at it in admiration. "A rail buff's dream and Transcon's only remaining passenger train. Of course, the Axeman's putting it on the chopping block as soon as the contract runs out with the state of Washington."

The Zephyr was an excursion train, a throwback from the golden era of rail travel. Its cars were an eclectic collection of antique passenger equipment that spanned three generations. The only anachronism was a modern diesel engine that pulled the train over the steep grades of the Cascade Mountains.

Megan admired the ornate silver exterior of the restored passenger train. In her eight years of train service, she'd never seen anything like it. *A five-star hotel on wheels.*

End of the Line

They got out of the rental car and walked toward the tracks, giving the crowd of people boarding the Zephyr a wide berth. There wasn't any freight equipment at the station now, but that didn't mean the hopper hadn't been there, Farranger realized. He'd know more once he found the AEI trackside reader.

"There," he said, spotting a small metal box mounted just outside the rail. "That's our reader."

"So where's the hopper car?" Megan asked.

Farranger reached into his pocket and pulled out a local train lineup and an oversized track chart of the Washington division. He traced his fingers across the main line on the map, studying the sidings to the west.

"The hopper passed this detector," he said, "but it hasn't passed the next one, which is about fifty miles down the line on the other side of the Cascades. So it's somewhere in these mountains."

"On a train?"

Farranger scanned the train schedule and shook his head. "There hasn't been a westbound in eleven hours. It must be sitting in a siding. And there's only four on the mountain, so it shouldn't take too long to check them out." He glanced at the surrounding trees. "They haul mostly timber up here, so a hopper ought to stick out like a sore thumb. All we have to do is drive along the right-of-way until we spot it."

"Uh . . . Farranger." Megan tapped his arm and pointed westward down the tracks. "We're not driving over that."

Farranger looked down the roadbed to see several feet of snow on the tracks and on either side of the rails. In the distance, on-track machinery was heading toward them, throwing a plume of white into the air. The equipment was an unusual mix of technologies, a modern jet engine mounted on a fifty-year-old flatcar. Pushed from behind by a locomotive, the jet engine blasted snow off the rails and onto the right-of-way. The tracks were cleared in its wake, but it left an additional two feet of snow piled up on both sides of the roadbed.

Megan was right. No way could they drive over that.

"Well, Ms. Langford," he said, gesturing toward the Zephyr. "I guess it's about time we ride in style."

Kem Parton

Through the window of the Zephyr's lounge car, Casey Jones watched as Farranger and Megan flashed their Transcon IDs and obtained tickets from the stationmaster. He loved it when a plan came together.

"Can I take that for you?" A porter pointed to Casey's single piece of luggage, a beautifully engraved box designed to hold a custom-made pool cue.

"No thanks," Casey said, sliding the case closer to him. "I make my living with this thing, and I hate to let it out of my sight."

"I used to shoot a pretty good game myself," the porter said, admiring the craftsmanship of the case. "Mind if I have a look?"

"Yeah," Casey said, stone-faced. "I mind."

After the offended porter stalked away, Casey turned to look at the Cascade Mountains through the opposite window. Sheer faces of rock had collided together in sharp angles near the top. A thick layer of snow covered the entire range, held precariously in place by a combination of timber and rock—a natural dam with a hair trigger.

He leaned back in his seat and took in the interior. The Zephyr was nothing less than a work of art. He was particularly fond of the lounge car, a century-old Pullman that dated back to a time when engineers were treated like celebrities. The most famous of them all, the original Casey Jones, might have pulled this very car behind his famous Cannonball. Casey smiled at the thought. The Zephyr touched his soul like no other train could.

In a way, he envied Farranger and the other passengers.

They were headed for an icy grave, but they were going there in style.

-21-

"All aboard," the conductor bellowed.

Farranger and Megan sprinted toward the observation car at the rear of the train, stopping just short of the platform to take in the sheer magnificence of the antique car. Shaped like a double-decker bus, it towered over the sleek passenger cars that made up the rest of the Zephyr. Floor-to-ceiling windows and a glass-domed roof made it look like a reverse greenhouse, providing the passengers inside with a full panorama of the passing landscape.

They stepped into the car and maneuvered through the crowd of tourists who'd already claimed the premium sightseeing positions. Passing through a set of sliding-glass doors, they entered the next car forward, a circa 1915 Pullman lounge with decor that was plush to the point of gaudy. The walls had been papered with red velvet, the mahogany chairs upholstered in red, and red felt covered the tabletops. Yellow-fringed lampshades hung from the electric lights overhead, disguising them as antique lanterns.

"They don't make them like this anymore," Farranger commented.

"Thank God," Megan replied. "It looks like a French whorehouse."

"I'll have to take your word on that," he laughed. Farranger looked around for an empty seat, but the lounge car was packed. "Let's go to the dining car. I need a table to lay out the track charts."

They walked through three coaches, which contained the majority of the Zephyr's passengers. Each car had two rows of 1920s-style love seats that faced each other to allow travelers the ease of conversation.

Another set of glass doors opened into the dining car, a restored Pullman that was opulent by any standard. The inlaid-marble tabletops had been set with fine china and crystal bearing Transcon's logo. Gaslight fixtures supplemented the winter sunlight streaming in through the windows, and the walls were decorated with paintings from the railroad's extensive collection of nineteenth-century Western art. The adventurous portrayals of the untamed had been designed to entice Eastern travelers to "go west," preferably by rail. Considered little more than travel brochures when they were originally created, the paintings were now valued at a hundred thousand dollars each.

Farranger grabbed a table at a starboard-side window and spread out the track chart.

"There are four sidings," he said, tracing the rail line on the map. "The first three are on this side of the train."

"Shouldn't be too hard to spot a hopper with a freshly painted car number," Megan remarked.

"If Seattle's his target, Casey Jones'll be waiting for the hopper there. If we spot it before then, the car can be disarmed and he won't be any the wiser."

"That's a lot of ifs."

"Yeah, well here's another one. If we're lucky, we can stake out the hopper in Seattle once it's disarmed and use it to catch him. Even if he doesn't show himself, we can pinpoint his position when he uses the detonation frequency."

Farranger checked his watch, then looked out the window. For the first time, he felt he had the upper hand over Casey Jones. He was anxious to get moving. But the first siding was still eighteen miles away.

"Let's get something to drink," he suggested, looking for a distraction.

Megan reached out and touched his arm. "Don't worry, Cal. We'll find the car. I have complete faith in you."

Her unexpected words of encouragement filled Farranger with optimism. He was sure it would pass as quickly as the mileposts along the track.

End of the Line

The fourth coach ahead of the dining car was empty, serving primarily as an overflow car to accommodate the increased tourist trade during the summer months. Less luxurious than its 1920s counterparts, the coach emphasized form over function. The seats were arranged airline-style, comfort taking a backseat to capacity.

The design had been one of Amtrak's attempts at cost control, and the results were predictable—no one wanted to ride in it. Looking at it made Casey feel somewhat insignificant. His campaign to destroy the railroad was nothing compared to the government's efforts.

He made his way to the front of coach four, cue-stick case in hand, pausing for a last look out the window to check his location. The Zephyr was speeding through the Cascade mountains at 60 mph. Snow-covered trees dotted the cliffs above and below him.

The perfect setting for a historic journey.

According to his own head count, there were more than two hundred passengers and crew aboard. Enough to break the regional fatality record for a single train.

Casey opened the coach's sliding-glass door to reveal a second, more formidable barrier leading to the baggage car. Originally commissioned as an express-mail car, the sides and doors had been constructed with two-inch-thick armor plating designed to keep out a century of would-be bank robbers.

Removing a cab key from his pocket, Casey let himself into the baggage car, then snapped the key off in the lock and closed the door behind him. He sealed the compartment by turning a large wheel, securing the door tighter than a bank vault. No one would be able to follow him without a blowtorch.

He moved to the only flat surface inside, a desk formerly used by postal clerks to sort mail. He placed his case on the desk and opened it. Lying inside was a metal pry bar separated into two pieces. He pulled them out and screwed them together.

Casey felt reasonably certain that he was the only person ever to commission his own custom-made pry bar. It was his own personal fashion statement, the sophisticated terrorist's must-have accessory. He felt sure it would be all the rage if they ever held a convention.

Exiting the forward compartment of the baggage car, he crept silently across the locomotive walkway behind the engineer's seat. Readying his pry, he opened the door of the cab and stepped through it.

"Hello, boys," he greeted the two surprised crewmen. "Ready to make history?"

Farranger started to extend a toast toward Megan, then hesitated, searching his mind for some common ground, something that would transcend the union/management conflict that always seemed to be between them.

"To Sims," he finally proposed.

"To Sims." Megan set her glass on the table and leaned back comfortably in her chair. "So what's your story, Farranger?"

"Not much to tell. I'm a fourth-generation railroader. I worked in the craft for ten years, then went into management. I was the first Farranger to do that, so I'm the black sheep in the family." Farranger paused, recalling his early years as a superintendent. "Management was different on the California Western. We were always railroaders first. Now I spend my time filling out reports, watching shippers go bankrupt because their business isn't 'high margin' enough, and seeing good men get the ax."

"Ever consider a life outside the industry?" Megan couldn't help but think of the Axeman's veiled threat to fire Farranger once Casey Jones was caught.

"I've tried," he shrugged. "Spent some time in my twenties roughnecking in Texas, and I worked on a tramp steamer to Brazil. I got down there and guess what I wound up doing?"

"Railroading."

End of the Line

"I had been running away from it, but by then I was forced to conclude it was all I ever really wanted to know. My dad worked the Milwaukee yards. When I was a kid, I used to collect timetables like other kids collect baseball cards."

"So while the other boys wanted to be superheroes—"

"I was the only one who knew that Superman really wasn't more powerful than a locomotive."

Megan laughed. "You know what you are, don't you?"

"What?"

"A foamer."

Farranger wanted to act offended, but he couldn't help laughing.

"So tell me, Cal, if you like railroading so much, how come you're in management instead of working for a living in train service?"

"You're a union rep lecturing me about working for a living?" Cal smiled hopefully, but Megan's reaction told him his union bashing fell flat.

"Seriously."

"Seriously?"

Megan nodded to reaffirm her question.

"All right, seriously then." Farranger sighed as if he didn't know where to begin. "I used to be an engineer. Was one of the best, or at least I thought I was. Worked a road switcher out of San Bern. My best friend, a guy named Frank Facine, was my conductor. We knew all the tricks. No shortcut was too dangerous to get the work done quickly so we could get an early quit."

"This story doesn't have a happy ending, does it?"

Farranger shook his head slowly.

"We were spotting a half dozen cars of fruit in an industry track, my conductor riding the point. In fact, he was standing on the knuckle riding the cars to make a joint with a dozen or so cars that were already in the track."

"Riding the knuckle?" Megan interrupted. "That's a damn foolish way to make a joint."

"We'd done it a thousand times before. Except this time I got a kicker in the air line. It threw Frank off the knuckle, right into the cut of cars we were coupling into. The slack ran out and made the coupling though his hip."

Megan returned a squeamish grimace but said nothing.

"Ever see a man get pinched?"

Megan shook her head.

"The absolute worst way to die. Frank was in awful pain, his legs dangling above the tracks with the joint made right through his midsection. Something about the pressure between one hundred tons of freight, you bleed to death very slowly. In some cases a man can live for hours, usually in shock, but he can still talk like we're talking now."

"He say anything?" Megan had heard that those who survived a coupling could be lucid for hours, though she'd never seen it herself.

"That he loved his wife and kids. Said he didn't hold me responsible." Farranger drifted off.

"You're weren't responsible, Cal. Engineers are in charge of the engine, conductors are in charge of the train. It isn't your fault your conductor decided to violate a cardinal rule."

Farranger nodded at Megan's reassurance, but didn't buy it. They were a team, and he'd known exactly what his conductor was doing. Engineers were supposed to take their groundman's switching commands, but not blindly.

"I had called for medical assistance on the radio, but we both knew there was nothing they could do."

"So what happened?"

"Frank was in pain, but he had one last request. He wanted me to pull the pin. Frank was a hurry-up guy to the end. He didn't want to wait for his life to slowly drain away. He wanted it over quick."

"So did you?"

"Yeah," Farranger replied dully. "I pulled the pin and watched him split in half before my eyes."

Megan cringed at the visual. "Why are you telling me all this?"

"You asked why I don't work in train service," Farranger replied. "Now you know. I haven't run an engine since the day it happened. Don't think I ever will. I couldn't quite tear myself away from the railroad completely, though."

"You miss being an engineer?"

"Every day."

End of the Line

Megan felt empathy for Farranger. And something else. It was as if she'd just peeled another layer away from his gruff exterior, revealing someone who was becoming increasingly human. Somehow she'd never expected to find anything vulnerable in management. It wasn't enough to make her change her core beliefs, but she'd just found her first exception to a rule that she'd formally applied universally.

"Siding," he suddenly said, looking out the window.

Megan turned and peered out, her forehead almost touching the glass. They exchanged looks of disappointment when they saw a train with thirty cars of freshly cut timber in the siding. False alarm.

"It is beautiful up here," she said, her eyes lingering on the scenery. "Kind of a shame they had to run tracks through it."

"They almost didn't. They looked for a path over the mountains for years but never found one."

"So how'd they do it?"

"They didn't. They blasted right through them." Farranger pointed to a slight curve in the tracks ahead. "Stampede Tunnel. Two miles long, right through the mountain."

Megan looked out the window again and saw the tunnel entrance less than two miles away. "Must've taken years."

"It did. And right after they finished construction, they abandoned the line for nearly a decade."

"Why?"

"Nobody wanted to ride on the Stampede Pass. Not long after the pass opened, some ninety years ago, a train coming out of the tunnel was hit by an avalanche. It ripped the cars apart and buried them under forty feet of snow. Killed over a hundred people. It took rescue workers three days to dig out the bodies. Stampede Pass became known as Death Mountain."

"And that's where we're headed? You sure know how to show a girl a good time."

Their conversation was cut short by an approaching porter. "I have a package for you, sir," he said, handing Farranger a small gift-wrapped box. "Compliments of one of the passengers."

Farranger looked around the dining car, certain the porter had made a mistake. But then he looked more closely at the package and saw his name written on the gift tag.

"Well, open it," Megan urged.

Farranger smiled, suspecting that she was somehow the culprit. He ripped off the outer wrapping and removed the top. The smile disappeared from his face.

"What is it?" she asked.

He held up two brick-shaped objects tied together with a red ribbon. "AEI tags."

Megan paled. They'd been outwitted.

They weren't tracking the hopper car, Casey Jones was tracking them. Suddenly, Farranger didn't feel so lucky that he just happened to be in Washington.

The train lurched forward slightly and began to decelerate, the jolt strong enough to knock over several glasses in the dining car. Megan glanced out the window. At the current rate of deceleration, it looked as though the Zephyr would stop just short of the tunnel entrance.

"The engineer's stopping the train." Megan sighed in relief.

Farranger considered the possibility but rejected it almost immediately. "I don't think so. I think Casey's slowing the train so he can get off." He looked out the window. The Stampede Tunnel lay directly ahead.

"Why would he stop?" Megan asked. "We're in the middle of nowhere."

Farranger jumped up and grabbed Megan's hand, running toward the next car.

"Because Seattle isn't Casey Jones's target. The Zephyr is."

- 22 -

Farranger burst through the forward coach doors and ran down the aisle toward the engine. Megan raced after him, struggling to keep up. She finally grabbed him, forcing him to stop and turn around.

"A target for what?" Her tone was tense with fear.

He hesitated, then looked her squarely in the eyes and lowered his voice. "For another Death Mountain avalanche."

Megan shook her head, staring at him in disbelief and horror.

Farranger grabbed her firmly by both arms. "Casey went to a lot of trouble to lure us to Stampede Pass. I think he's planning to recreate the highest-fatality avalanche in U.S. history." He took a deep breath, as if gathering the courage to say his next words. "And if we don't stop this train before it exits the tunnel, he's going to succeed."

Farranger hoped like hell he was wrong, but even though the train was decelerating rapidly, he could hear the diesel engine still roaring under full throttle, straining against the competing forces of the braking cars. The fact that Casey had set both the brakes and the throttle could mean only one thing: he was planning a running release. He'd slow just enough to detrain, then throw off the brakes. Already under full power, the locomotive would accelerate twice as fast as an idle engine, making it impossible for anyone else to detrain as the Zephyr sped toward his trap.

An instant later, the train lurched forward with a sudden burst of speed, throwing Farranger and Megan off balance.

Casey had gotten off.

Farranger lunged between a row of seats for the emergency brake cord. He gave it several hard yanks, but nothing happened. The cable was in perfect working order, snapping back in place after each pull. Casey hadn't bothered to cut the line; he didn't have to. He'd made certain that no one was left alive in the locomotive cab to respond to a call for an emergency stop.

"We've got to shut down the engine."

They raced down the center aisle to the express-car door, only to find it locked. Farranger wrestled with it, then gave up and tried three times to force it open with his shoulder. The steel plating didn't yield.

Farranger backed away from the armored door, aware that his futile attempts were wasting what little time they had left. The Zephyr was about to enter the two-mile tunnel.

"I have to get to the observation car." He motioned Megan toward a tour-guide intercom mounted on the wall. "Get on the intercom and tell everyone to go to the Pullman lounge. It'll be the last car out of the tunnel, so it's our best chance."

Megan knew he was distorting the facts. The observation car would be the last one out of the tunnel, and the design made it a death trap. If an avalanche did hit them, the last place you'd want to be was in a glass car.

But that's exactly where Farranger was headed.

Before she had a chance to object, darkness engulfed the coach. The Zephyr was entering the tunnel.

"You've got two minutes," Farranger said, hurrying back down the center aisle.

"What are you going to do?"

"Find another way to stop the train," he hollered as he opened the dining car's vestibule door.

Farranger raced through the dining car. Reaching the first of the Zephyr's coach cars, he heard Megan's voice blaring over the train's internal speaker system.

"Attention, passengers and crew. This is an emergency announcement. Please remain calm and proceed in an orderly fashion to the rear lounge car immediately."

No one moved. Most of the passengers looked concerned, but not concerned enough to give up their prized window seats. Farranger was amazed.

"Now!" he shouted. A few people started to collect their possessions but showed no sense of urgency. He mentally pleaded with Megan to step up her tone.

End of the Line

"Attention, all passengers and crew," she repeated, her voice strained as she enunciated each word. "This is an emergency. The train is heading straight into an avalanche that will hit when we exit the tunnel. You now have less than two minutes to get to the lounge car."

Panic erupted. The passengers shoved their way into the center aisle, running roughshod over anyone moving too slowly. Farranger had no choice but to join the fray, elbowing his way through the crush of human bodies until he reached the Pullman lounge. He finally made it to the rear, only to collide with a wall of passengers from the observation car pushing in the opposite direction. He forced his way through them, using people as leverage to propel himself into the observation car.

He sprinted the final ten yards through the empty car, his eyes on the glass door at the rear of the train. He could see the tunnel entrance; the Zephyr was already past the halfway point, racing toward the other end at well over 60 mph.

They would be exiting in less than a minute.

Farranger had no chance of stopping the entire train in time; his only hope was to stop the rear before the avalanche hit the head end.

He stepped out on the boarding platform, looking for access to the angle cock beneath the car. He climbed over the waist-high iron bars surrounding the platform and found a foothold on the car's knuckle. Holding on to the iron bars, he crouched down, then reached beneath the platform and opened the angle cock. A loud burst of air rushed out. The composite brake shoes clamped down, the wheels locked in place, and a deafening metallic screech filled the tunnel. Each car jolted against its neighbor as the slack ran in.

Farranger was slammed headlong into the platform gate. His feet slipped off the knuckle, bouncing violently over the succession of ties as he struggled to keep his grip on the iron grating.

The Zephyr slowed rapidly, then jolted to a halt. Farranger hung dazed from the platform railing for a moment, and when he regained his senses he realized the awful truth. He'd stopped the train too late. Only the rear platform of the observation car was still inside the tunnel.

The rest of the train was completely exposed.

He scrambled over the railing and opened the door of the observation car, intending to evacuate the train, but passengers were already forcing their way through the sliding door of the lounge car, which had been knocked askew and had jammed, leaving only an eight-inch opening. The few who had managed to squeeze their way through were coming toward him, running blindly in their panic.

Before Farranger had a chance to think, the stone archway at the mouth of the tunnel exploded in a deafening blast, sending snow, granite, and ice plummeting toward the observation car as if a dam had burst.

The glass dome and roof buckled easily, crushing the upper level of the car. The first-floor ceiling collapsed under the weight to half its normal height. Boulders ripped through the aluminum hull like it was paper, paving the way for tons of snow, glass shards, and earth to enter the lower cabin. The sides of the car crumpled inward until the interior steel supports snapped, imploding the windows and sending a river of snow into the compartment.

Farranger watched helplessly as rock and ice pelted the people trapped inside, then turned away in horror when a strip of sheet metal fell from the ceiling and decapitated a man before his eyes. The other passengers were buried alive, their cries of terror silenced under a mountain of snow.

The front of the compartment filled within seconds, blasting a glacier of ice toward the back of the cabin. Furnishings were torn from their floor mountings and carried along with the mass of debris, ice, and bodies roaring toward Farranger.

Megan ran to a cliffside window of the dining car when she heard the explosion. The Zephyr was hugging a gentle curve around the mountain, giving her a clear view of the blast that had crushed the observation car flat against the rail, then buried it under a thick blanket of white. The torrent of snow plugged the mouth of the tunnel and coursed outward over the rear of the

End of the Line

train. By the time the billow of white powder settled, the lounge car and most of the third coach had also been swallowed.

Megan's legs went weak at the thought of Farranger crushed inside the observation car, and she put a hand up against the cold glass to steady herself. She closed her eyes, fighting back tears and a rising panic. There was still a chance he was alive. No point in assuming the worst, she told herself.

She pulled the packset off her belt. "Langford to Farranger. Over."

Nothing.

She cranked up the volume and tried again. "Langford to Farranger. Come in." She pressed harder on the transmit button, her voice dropping to a whisper. "Please."

Loud hissing static came back in response.

The Zephyr was still in mortal danger. Megan remembered Farranger's prediction of how Casey would first disable the train, then send an avalanche down upon it to duplicate the first Death Mountain catastrophe. If Farranger was right, it would be only a matter of seconds.

Megan had just raised the packset to try again, when a clap of thunder rocked the dining car with the force of an earthquake. To her left, at the top of a mile-long ridge, she saw six evenly spaced explosions going off just below the summit, sending white geysers several hundred feet into the air. Huge wedges of packed snow and ice broke free from the peaks and plunged down the sharp slope of the mountain. The force gathered momentum, lifting a twenty-foot layer of fresh snow from the ground and rolling it over like a giant wave.

The avalanche was at least a mile long and nearly forty feet high, uprooting thirty-foot trees and snapping them like twigs as it raced down the mountain.

Megan's heart pumped wildly as fear overcame her. The explosion at the mouth of the tunnel had been nothing more than a firecracker, set only to block their escape. But this was a power greater than anything she had ever imagined. There was nowhere to hide. The avalanche would be on them in seconds.

Then she remembered the lounge car. Already buried, it might provide protection when the wall of snow hit. It was her only hope.

She raced through the first two coaches, the vibration under her feet increasing in intensity as the avalanche closed in. A glimpse out the window confirmed it. The wave of snow towered over the Zephyr, obscuring the mountain behind it. She wasn't going to make it.

Megan yanked open the door to the third coach and plunged into total darkness. The windows were pasted with snow, obliterating all light. She groped her way forward, toward the sound of voices ahead in the lounge car. She had just made it past the halfway point when the wall of snow slammed into the Zephyr broadside.

Megan was thrown to the floor. As the avalanche pounded the roof, thin strips of tin plating peeled off the ceiling. Above the roar, she could hear glass shattering and the crack of metal as knuckles snapped off at the joints.

The full force of the wave hit the engine and cars at the front of the train, crumpling their steel frames on impact before sweeping them over the cliff.

Megan scrambled to her feet in the partially buried coach, running toward an arm reaching out to her from inside the lounge car. Just as they locked hands, the roof of the coach sheared off. She dove inside the lounge car a split second before the coach filled with snow and tumbled over the cliff. Snow blasted through the lounge door, thrusting her farther into the car and packing the forward vestibule with a wall of ice.

The lounge car shook violently as the avalanche continued thundering overhead. Windows on the mountain side imploded, raining glass and snow over the terrified passengers. Megan found herself praying as the tide rose over her waist, certain they were going to be buried alive, but the flooding compartment finally reached an uneasy equilibrium, the flow stopping at chest level. Tears of relief sprang to her eyes.

As the devastating wave of snow and ice moved farther down the mountain, the murderous roar subsided, only to be replaced by something even more frightening: the silence of their icy tomb.

In the dim lighting provided by a single battery-powered emergency fixture, Megan saw terror reflected in the passengers' faces, yet they were all eerily quiet except for a few muffled sobs.

End of the Line

Megan surveyed the damage. Tons of snow had forced the roof downward, crushing the cabin like a stubbed cigarette butt. The lowest point of the ceiling was just inches above the heads of the taller passengers. Megan stared at it uneasily, terrified it was going to give way any minute.

Snow was starting to soak through her clothes, and the lounge was packed so tightly she couldn't take a deep breath. The air was cold and dank, chilling her lungs as she and the other two hundred passengers gasped for the limited oxygen. In just a few hours, they'd all be frozen—if they didn't suffocate first.

The silence soon gave way to panic. Passengers began calling for help and urging others to dig their way out. Megan knew it was useless. Their cries were muffled under a layer of snow that had already compacted into an impenetrable barricade of ice.

If Farranger were here, she thought, things would be different. But he had sacrificed his life to give them a chance, and Megan didn't intend to squander it. She still had her packset. If she could communicate with the outside world, they might still have a chance.

Megan dug a hand into the snow, wincing at the slivers of glass slicing into her skin as she felt for the radio attached to her belt. Her fingers closed around the device, and she brought it up slowly, careful not to snap off the fragile antenna.

"Emergency! Emergency! Emergency!" she radioed. "Any station, respond. Over."

She released the transmit button but heard only static. She repeated the call several times without any success.

All the passengers were watching her, a glimmer of hope illuminating their faces. Megan wanted desperately to reassure them, but even if someone had heard her call it would take hours to get rescue equipment in place, and even longer to drill through 120 feet of ice. She'd been wrong—even Farranger couldn't have helped them.

Megan knew that a rescue team would eventually arrive. But knowing that gave her no comfort.

By then, it would be too late.

-23-

Farranger gasped for air, choking as snow rushed inside his mouth and nose. He saw an instant of total darkness before a stinging sensation forced his eyelids shut. He could feel his arms and legs, burning cold, but had no power to move them. He was being buried alive.

As the bitter cold of his icy grave seeped through his clothes, he panicked, knowing his body temperature was dropping fast. He took several short breaths but swallowed more snow than air. He was going to suffocate. He fought to calm himself, realizing his only hope for survival was to think his way out.

He forced his lips closed around the mouthful of snow that was suffocating him, willing himself to swallow the icy water as it melted. Then he took slow methodical breaths, filtering snow through his teeth.

Clinching his fists open and closed, Farranger managed to compact the snow around his hands, giving him a little room to move his arms. He dug toward his face, trying to provide himself a small buffer of air. Breathing through the icy mask became a conscious effort. He dug in short intervals, pausing to fill his oxygen-starved lungs with recycled air.

He felt his consciousness slipping away and bit down on his lip to stay alert. He clawed madly at the compacted snow now, his lungs nearly bursting by the time he finally broke through. Air rushed into his mouth from the small reservoir he'd created. He gulped several involuntary breaths, then regained control. Fresh air was a valuable commodity, and he'd have to ration his supply.

Farranger shook off the dizziness but realized he was completely disoriented. He couldn't tell up from down. He had to dig, but in which direction? He could be less than two feet from

End of the Line

the surface, digging the wrong way, wasting precious minutes he didn't have. His heart began to pound. Already half frozen, he didn't have time for trial and error.

He listened for sounds from the surface, but all he could hear was the faint ticking of his wristwatch.

And with that sound came his first ray of hope. Farranger remembered the old railroad adage that an accurate timepiece can save your life. His watch might just save his today. He carefully removed it, then fumbling over the mechanism with frozen fingers, he managed to depress a button on the side of the face. A tiny light glowed white, piercing the darkness. A few inches of visibility was all he needed.

He held the watch in front of him, then released it. It fell sideways at a sharp angle to what he'd previously thought was up. He might be disoriented, but gravity couldn't be fooled.

Methodically carving his way through the snow to his right, Farranger fought the temptation to start burrowing in a frenzy. Working himself into a sweat would present a serious danger. Perspiration would freeze on his skin, causing almost instant frostbite.

He chipped away at the snow, scraping his fingers raw as he eased his body forward just inches at a time in the tiny cavern he was creating.

But despite his efforts to pace himself, Farranger tired quickly in the oxygen-poor environment. His movements grew sluggish, pawing at the ice above him without conviction before stopping altogether. What was the point? Megan and the other passengers were already dead. It would only be a matter of time before he joined them. He could feel himself submitting, falling into a sleep from which he knew he'd never wake up.

"Emergency! Emergency! Emergency!"

A surge of adrenaline rushed through Farranger at the sound of Megan's voice. *She's alive!* He reached for his packset, but finding it wasn't on his belt, he realized it must have been thrown clear when he was blown off the observation car. The sound of Megan's call was audible, though, so the radio had to be on the surface. And close by.

Farranger plowed at the snow above him with renewed vigor. Ice shavings fell on his face, a thin film of frost coating his skin as it met the sweat of his exertion. The white powder was less compacted now, heaping down on him in large clumps. He moved armloads at a time, then snaked his body forward through the gap.

Sensing that his deliverance was at hand, Farranger heaved himself upward, punching his fists through to the open air of the tunnel. As his face finally broke the surface to freedom, he gulped air until he became light-headed, then struggled to his feet and tried to get his bearings.

He was in the tunnel, but the exit was blocked floor-to-ceiling with ice. The only light was provided by the end-of-train device mounted on the rear knuckle of the observation car. The battery-operated marker was blinking red, providing a periodic glimpse of the darkened tunnel. Except for twisted bits of metal framing that littered the snow on the tunnel floor, the rest of the car was completely buried.

"Emergency! Emergency! Emergency!"

Farranger dug through the snow and debris until he found his radio.

"Megan, are you all right? Over."

"Cal?" The pitch of her voice rose in astonishment. "Where are you?"

"I'm in the tunnel. What's your situation?"

"We made it to the lounge car, but the rest of the train is gone."

"Can you dig your way out?"

"No way. It's half filled with packed snow. The doors are jammed, and the roof sounds like it's about to buckle. But we're still on the rails if you can get to us."

Farranger backed away from the tunnel mouth. A full car-length separated him from the lounge, all of it packed with snow. It would take him a week to dig through. He'd have to find help.

"Megan, the tunnel walls are too thick. Nobody will hear a radio call from in here. I'm going to have to get to the microwave repeater at the other end."

"Please hurry, Cal. I don't know how long we can last."

End of the Line

He wanted desperately to offer her some words of encouragement but had very little hope to offer. "Megan, I'm sorry. If I'd stopped the train two car-lengths sooner—"

"And if you'd stopped us two cars later, we'd all be dead. Now, get going."

Farranger hesitated. He knew it was his fault, despite Megan's attempt to let him off the hook. He depressed the transmit button a final time. "Farranger out," he said, then stowed his packset and set off for the long run through the tunnel.

He moved between the rails, the safest path through the darkness surrounding him. The faint glint of light at the other end seemed like an eternity away, and it occurred to him that he might not be able to go the distance. He was already exhausted, and even if he could hold up, Casey was still out there.

A lot could happen in two miles.

Casey paced in front of the tunnel entrance, cursing Farranger with every step. The poetic death he'd planned for the passengers was now in a shambles, a difficult turn of events to accept. He'd played by the rules, worked tirelessly to devise a brilliant plan, and had executed it perfectly. But still he'd failed. It was enough to make him lose faith in the American dream.

Months of planning had been wasted. Instead of being swept over the mountain in a blazing moment of glory, the passengers would slowly freeze to death. Then, as the ultimate insult, some overly efficient coroner would probably list the cause of their deaths as hypothermia. Good-bye, Guinness.

Casey knew what he had to do. He'd have to kill Farranger and finish off the Zephyr with panache. The task would be daunting, but on the upside, the passengers' untimely survival meant he would now be able to taunt his dying victims.

Casey removed his packset, cleared his throat loudly into the open microphone, and began chanting, *"There once was a train called the Zephyr—"* then stopped mid-stanza.

For the life of him, he couldn't think of a rhyme for *Zephyr*. Casey made a mental note: next time he went on a record-breaking killing spree, he'd buy a rhyming dictionary first. He started again from the top.

> *"There once was a man named Jones,*
> *Who filled the Zephyr with snow to its domes.*
> *Men were freezing inside,*
> *Casey laughed while they cried*
> *The sweet songs of their last dying moans."*

Casey released the talk button, disappointed in his impromptu verse. It hadn't really captured the essence of fear that he was shooting for. He should have gone with a haiku.

"Not my best work," he admitted to his audience. "But don't worry, folks. I'm not about to quit my day job."

Farranger stopped stock-still. Packset range was only about two miles in a direct line of sight. The madman who called himself Casey Jones was either in the tunnel or just outside. The pitch-black walls around him provided the perfect place for an ambush. He was at Casey's mercy if he decided to attack.

"I hear your girlfriend is in a bad way, Farranger," Casey said over the radio. "Buried to her waist in snow. I think it's kind of fitting, don't you? I mean, dying as she lived, with ice between her legs."

Farranger ignored him and again started running through the darkened tunnel. He had other things to worry about. His clothes were soaked and frozen, cold stinging his aching limbs with each stride over the uneven ties, and he was already gasping from the thin mountain air. He wasn't about to waste precious breath talking to Casey.

"Won't talk to me, eh, Farranger? Maybe Chairman Langford in the lounge car will be more sociable. What do you say, Ms. Langford? Pleasant conversation is an important part of the whole passenger-train experience. Besides, it might help pass the time it takes for hypothermia to set in."

Farranger listened for Megan's response, but only the sound of static echoed in the tunnel.

"No? How about a song, then? If you're dying and you know it, clap your hands. If you're dying and you know it, clap your hands . . . Everybody join in. If you're dying and you know it, then your face will surely show it, if you're dying and you know it, clap your hands."

Farranger was tempted to turn off the radio, but he couldn't afford to. As long as Casey was talking, he couldn't be lurking in the shadows nearby.

"That concludes the musical part of our program," Casey went on. "For my next act, I plan to destroy what's left of the Zephyr. Unlike the slow death that Farranger has to offer you, mine will be quick and relatively painless."

Farranger was sure Casey was bluffing, trying to demoralize the already frightened passengers. A second attack on the dying Zephyr hardly seemed necessary. But then again, Casey Jones wasn't one to make idle threats. If there was a way to get at the Zephyr, he would find it.

"I don't understand your interference, Farranger," Casey said. "Transcon is an abomination against railroading. It's not worth dying for."

"It's not worth killing for, either," Farranger replied angrily.

"So you *can* talk! I was beginning to think you didn't like me. Call me sentimental, but it means a lot to be able to share my accomplishments with another railroader who can appreciate them. You can be my Tonto, or better yet, my Sim Webb."

"Who?" Cal was determined to keep him talking.

"My point exactly," Casey answered. "Sim Webb was Casey Jones's fireman. He survived, but nobody remembers his name. You're just like him. Seeing as how you'll be dead soon, it isn't a perfect metaphor, but you get my drift. While you fade into oblivion, I'll be making railroad history. Just like the original Casey Jones."

"The real Casey Jones was a hero," Farranger said. "He sacrificed his life to save a trainload of passengers."

"Passengers who never would've been in jeopardy in the first place if he hadn't been speeding and missed a signal. People don't remember the cause, Farranger, only the effect. History will record mine as a mission of mercy, just like the Zephyr. Isn't the quick death I plan for the railroad much kinder than letting the corporate suits slowly bleed it dry? No, my friend. Transcon is the villain here. I'm the hero."

"You're a lunatic," Farranger said in disgust.

"*Lunatic* is such a strong word. I prefer *sanity-challenged*. Really, Farranger, you should try to be more sensitive. If you're this testy over losing the Zephyr, I'd hate to see what you're like by the end of the week."

Farranger knew Casey was alluding to the ammonium nitrate car. "As long as you're going to kill me anyway," he said, ignoring the comment, "why don't you tell me where the car is?"

"Straight to the point," Casey cackled. "I like that in a victim. Don't worry about the car, Farranger. It's in the safest place."

There was some kind of hidden clue in Casey's oddly worded response, but Farranger didn't have time to decipher it. He could see the mouth of the tunnel coming into view ahead. He was nearly there. Casey was nowhere in sight, but that didn't mean he wasn't lurking just outside.

"I've enjoyed chatting with you, Farranger, but it's time for me to sign off. I'm a busy man—things to do, places to go, people to kill."

The radio went silent.

Now, Farranger thought, it was time to worry. Casey could be anywhere.

His senses on high alert, Farranger emerged from the tunnel, still running between the rails as the sunlight hit him. He slowed to a walk, trying to catch his breath from the two-mile run. Still no trace of Casey.

Farranger raised his packset. "Emergency! Emergency! Emergency! Any station respond. Over."

Several seconds passed, but there was no reply.

He started to make the call again, then saw the microwave tower at the edge of the right-of-way. The cabling had been cut; open threads of copper wire protruded from the black insulation. Without the microwave antenna to relay his four-watt transmission, the signal would barely reach past the roadbed. His radio was useless.

It had already taken him fifteen minutes to run the length of the tunnel, and he was running out of time. Megan and the others couldn't last much longer. His only remaining hope was another two miles down the line. He had to get to the siding where he'd seen the timber train. Using the more powerful radio on the locomotive, he might be able to transmit through the next repeater down the line.

Farranger looked down the roadway, mentally reconstructing the track layout. There was a hard curve ahead, the tracks disappearing around a mountain of rock. Two mileposts farther east was the siding that held the thirty-car train.

Farranger jogged beside the tracks. It was a downhill leg, but the frigid wind made the trek almost unbearable. He pressed forward, ignoring the stabbing pains in his chest, trying to push the thought of Casey lying in ambush out of his mind. He had to focus on reaching the locomotive radio.

Farranger trudged over the mixture of snow and ballast, sinking ankle-deep with each step, his legs cramping through his frozen clothes. He feared that before long, his muscles would tighten so much he wouldn't be able to move them at all, and all hope for the Zephyr would be lost. A feeling of defeat suddenly overwhelmed him. Failure was only minutes away.

But then he saw his salvation. Coming around the curve, crawling uphill at 10 mph with its whistle blaring, was the timber train. Rejoicing at the sight, Farranger waved his arms to get the engineer's attention. He'd assumed that the timber train was unmanned, but now he realized the crew must have been directed into the siding to let the passenger train by.

Farranger gave a switchman's hand sign, letting the engineer know that he intended to board while the train was still in motion. He couldn't afford to wait ten minutes for the brakes to set and recharge.

The engineer acknowledged him with five short blasts of the locomotive's whistle.

Farranger ran the remaining few yards to the train, then reversed direction to pace the engine. He boarded on the conductor's side of the engine on the forward stairwell. Edging around the catwalk to a small platform at the front of the engine, he yanked the nose door open.

"I need your radio," he gasped as the trainman met him in the doorway. "There's a passenger train in trouble ahead."

Casey Jones stepped out of the shadows, holding his pry bar like a battering ram. "You think they're in trouble now, wait till I run this train up their ass."

Farranger got his first clear look at the madman who had taken a railroad legend's name. It was only a glimpse, a twisted smirk below blocky wayfarer sunglasses. Before Farranger could react, Casey slammed the pry bar into his ribs. Farranger doubled over and staggered backward. His left foot slipped off the front of the engine but found refuge on the three-foot drawbar shooting out from below the platform. The only thing separating him from the tracks below was a piece of metal the width of a balance beam.

Farranger peered over the attached knuckle, transfixed by the near-hypnotic passage of ties rolling under the engine.

Casey moved quickly, jamming the blunt end of the pry into his back. Farranger dropped face-first to the knuckle, clutching it tightly as his legs straddled the drawbar. A second strike to his ribcage threw him off his perch. As he slid upside down under the drawbar, he wrapped his arms and legs around it in a death grip.

Farranger was in agony, the succession of painful blows now overtaking his adrenaline. But despite the pain, he tightened his grip around the square metal pole. One false move and he'd be ground to a pulp beneath the engine.

Casey hovered over him, pry bar in hand.

"Ever see someone run over by a train, Farranger? You'll be cut into more pieces than a med-school cadaver. It slices, it dices, it makes julienne fries." Casey stepped to the conductor's side of the platform, shifting his pry as if lining up a putt. "Fore!" He swung the pry bar full force, striking Farranger's legs.

Farranger's feet slipped off the drawbar, skipping across the tracks before the forward movement of the train dragged them under the rolling engine. It took every last ounce of his strength to hold on as the force below pulled him taut at a forty-five-degree angle.

End of the Line

Casey leaned over the drawbar to examine his helpless enemy. He wedged the pointed end of the pry bar under Farranger's fingers but exerted no pressure.

"End of the line, Farranger. Tell me something: how does it feel to know you're about to die out here in the cold while your boss Adashek is back in Dallas riding the CBO&E gravy train?"

Farranger had no idea what Casey was taking about. He couldn't speak psychopath, and it didn't look as though Casey intended to translate. And at that moment, he no longer cared. He was consumed by a hatred he hadn't thought himself capable of; his only thought was to destroy the monster standing over him.

Farranger stared into his enemy's eyes. "You'd better hope this kills me."

"I have my fingers crossed." Casey smiled, then with one savage move, jammed the pry under Farranger's grip, slicing it across the metal and ripping his fingers from the drawbar.

Farranger dropped to the tracks below.

-24-

Farranger slammed against the tracks, dead center between the rails. Two hundred tons of locomotive thundered overhead, passing just inches above his face. Beside him, the wheels sliced across the rails, twin sets of guillotines alternately compressing and releasing the ties beneath him like a rolling wave, lifting him closer to the crushing force of the steel carriage each time the ties rebounded.

He pressed his body against the wooden ties, trying to make himself as flat as possible. He'd heard tales of men who had survived being run over by a train by lying in the shallow depression between the rails, a stunt made famous by young Navajo trackmen pitting their courage against the iron horse. But even if the stories were true, it gave him little comfort. In all his years on the railroad, he hadn't seen many old Navajo trackmen.

Four seconds later, he saw a brief flash of sunlight, then the first timber car rolled overhead. The two-foot clearance below the flat car seemed spacious compared to the tight quarters beneath the engine. Farranger sighed in relief. He had survived. But it wasn't time to relax yet—he was still trapped, a captive beneath a moving train in what rail folklore called the Navajo Limbo.

"Well, Ms. Langford, looks like it's just you and me—" Casey stopped midsentence as he heard his voice echoing in Farranger's packset. "Then again," he went on, clicking his transmit button on and off several times, "maybe not."

Farranger fumbled blindly for the volume knob on his radio and turned it down, but it was too late to play dead. If his radio hadn't been crushed, Farranger probably hadn't either—and his radio had been turned up full blast, a clear beacon for Casey to

End of the Line

home in on. And Farranger knew Casey wouldn't take his death for granted; he'd want a body.

"You're dead, Farranger!" Casey shouted. Farranger's packset was silent, but it didn't matter. Casey was yelling so loudly, Farranger could hear him over the din of the rolling train.

A chill ran down Farranger's back. Trapped between the rails, he was easy prey. His only hope was to escape from under his rolling prison before Casey fixed his position.

Farranger timed the passing between two sets of axles as they rolled by his head. The escape window was less than two seconds. If he misjudged a fraction of a second in either direction, he'd be sliced in half. Even Navajo trackmen had more sense than to try slipping between the wheels of a moving car. Then again, they didn't have to deal with a nutcase waiting to skewer them with a pry bar.

Farranger flipped the volume on his radio back to full, then removed his packset and placed it on the ties beside him.

"Knock, knock." Casey's voice bellowed again from Farranger's radio.

Glancing toward the engine, Farranger could see Casey's legs flash between the wheels on the cliff side of the train. He was just three cars away. It was now or never.

Farranger took a deep breath, then heaved himself toward the outside of the tracks. The clearance between the top of the rail and the car's undercarriage was too low for a clean getaway. His shoulder caught the bottom of the flat, halting his roll. He stopped short, straddling the five-inch ribbon of steel facedown. The wheels screeched behind him, their weight pressing the rail downward as they bore down on him. Shoving hard against the ties, Farranger flipped over on his back just outside the rail, inches ahead of the flanged wheels of the timber flat. His heart was pounding. If he'd been a second slower, he'd have saved Casey a lot of trouble.

"I said . . . knock, knock."

Farranger clambered to his feet on the mountain side of the train, silently running down the right-of-way in the opposite direction of the moving cars.

He put three car-lengths between himself and his packset, then climbed aboard a passing timber car and grabbed the switchman's handhold near the base of the flat. The force of the moving target nearly pulled his arm out of its socket. Farranger suppressed a scream. He couldn't afford to reveal his position.

"Who's there?" the packset hissed.

Farranger scrambled up the side of the car, raising his head over the timber just enough to spot his enemy. Casey was two cars ahead, walking toward him.

"Casey," he answered himself.

Farranger climbed to the top of the pile of banded logs and crouched low. He could feel the train accelerating as it approached the flat grade near the tunnel. To save the Zephyr, he'd have to make quick work of Casey, then stop the train before it reached ramming speed.

"Casey who?"

As Farranger watched, Casey stopped dead in his tracks, his head snapping toward the decoy packset. Then he charged toward the rail, raising the pry bar like a javelin, trying to draw a bead on anything moving between the rails.

"Case he's alive, he won't be for long," he said, laughing maniacally.

Farranger held still until the timber flat moved into position. Casey had taken the bait.

Time to spring the trap.

Farranger leapt from his perch to the right-of-way, propelled forward by the train. He plowed into Casey, dislodging his pry bar and sending both of them sprawling. They landed hard against the snowy right-of-way.

Casey recovered first. He rushed toward Farranger, throwing a clumsy roundhouse punch aimed at his head. Farranger dodged the blow easily, then stepped inside the punch. He pinned Casey's arm, locking it between his forearm and armpit, then arched him backward until his face was a clear target. He jammed the palm of his hand into Casey's nose, breaking it.

Casey clawed at Farranger's face like a wild animal. Farranger held firm and landed as many body blows as he could. Casey was stronger, but Farranger had the advantage of leverage.

End of the Line

Suddenly, Casey's weight shifted. He grabbed Farranger in a bear hug and lifted him off the ground in a blind rage, throwing them both into the side of the moving timber train.

Farranger bore the brunt of the collision as they slammed into the rolling flat. The glancing blow from the three-thousand-ton train hammered into him, yanking Casey from his grip and tossing Farranger in a spinning arc to the right-of-way.

He landed hard, spitting blood. He willed himself to his feet, only to find that the balance of power had shifted.

Casey had recovered his pry bar and was twirling it like a baton as he advanced, backing Farranger toward the tunnel entrance. Farranger was cornered, hemmed in by the steep cliff on one side and the train on the other. The tunnel was only a few yards behind, but the narrow entrance was completely blocked by the timber train, leaving him no room to squeeze inside.

Farranger frantically searched the right-of-way for a weapon, any blunt object he might use to defend himself. At the edge of the cliff, he spotted some wooden crossties that summer track gangs had left behind for spring repairs. Several were wrapped in chains with S-connectors that allowed cranes to lift them into position over the tracks. Farranger briefly considered using the chains as a weapon, but they were wrapped so tightly around the crossties that he'd never be able to free them in time. He was on his own against an armed and deadly opponent.

He continued backing away from Casey until his back was pressed against the frozen slab of rock surrounding the tunnel.

Trapped.

Casey closed to within striking distance, then glanced toward the cliff. "Steep drop, eh, Farranger? Still, a fella might survive the fall if he's properly motivated." He moved his hands closer together, holding the pry bar like a baseball bat. He swung the pry bar, bashing Farranger just below the shoulder. It was a glancing blow, but one that sent him staggering toward the cliff. Before Farranger could recover, Casey swept his legs out from under him, throwing him to the ground at the edge of the steep drop.

Farranger landed facedown on a single tie lying there, the chain attached to it slashing his forehead open. The momentum of his fall nearly shoved the tie over the brink. It slid sideways, scraping handfuls of ballast and white powder over the edge. As he watched the debris tumbling down the slope, Farranger wondered how many seconds would pass before he followed.

"Go ahead, Farranger, take a dive." Casey gestured toward the cliff, laughing. "I recommend a triple back somersault with a twist. I'll give you high marks for difficulty and artistic impression." Using the pry bar, Casey rolled Farranger over on his back, pressing a heavy boot on his chest.

Farranger watched, as if caught in slow motion, as Casey raised the pry over his head and prepared to land the fatal blow.

"I know you don't understand now, Farranger." Casey shifted his grip on the pry to the sharpened end. "But I think you'll get the point shortly." He aimed the sharp end of the thirty-pound bar directly at Farranger's head.

Farranger jerked his head to the right. The pry missed him by inches, burying itself in the tie. He heard wood cracking behind him as Casey tried to unwedge the pry bar for a second strike. He wouldn't miss a second time.

The tie shifted sideways, one end slipping over the cliff. As Casey worked to free his weapon, it rocked back and forth over the edge of the steep precipice. Then Farranger saw it—the S-connector at the end of the chain.

Just as Casey freed the pry and lifted it over his head for a second strike, Farranger grabbed the connector and hooked it through one of the laces in Casey's work boots. Bracing his feet against the snow-covered ground, Farranger shoved the crosstie over the cliff just as Casey began his downward thrust.

The pull of the two-hundred-pound tie pulled Casey's leg tight, then yanked him off his feet. The pry bar missed, rattling harmlessly against the tie. Casey's hands grabbed for purchase on the ground in a desperate attempt to prevent his fall over the edge.

Farranger got to his feet as his enemy fought a losing battle with gravity. Casey's fingers clawed through the snow and were digging into the hard ground beneath, offsetting the force of the tie pulling him over the edge. Farranger's expression turned soulless as he pressed his boot over his enemy's hand.

"The Canyon Demonio crew and Sims were good men." Farranger shifted his weight to crush Casey's knuckles. "Please give them my regards when you see them."

End of the Line

Farranger stared at his opponent until Casey's expression acknowledged he understood his fate.

"Relax, Casey." Farranger twisted his foot until Casey released his grip. "It's all downhill from here."

"You're still dead, Farranger," Casey yelled, looking him straight in the eye as he slipped over the edge of the cliff. "You just don't know it yet."

The tie rocketed over the steep pass, sledding between trees in a high-speed luge run over the virgin white powder. Tethered to the heavy wooden beam, Casey's body bounced over moguls of snow and protruding rock, hitting every obstacle nature could place before him. He was still fighting ferociously to gain control, grasping for anything that might slow his descent.

"The mighty Casey just struck out," Farranger whispered under his breath. Casey Jones ricocheted off one snow-covered rock to the next like a giant pinball, each painful impact diverting his path without slowing his downward momentum. Farranger wondered how much more punishment one psychopath could take.

Farranger had no doubt he'd gotten the best of it. Though cold and exhausted, his victorious battle with Casey had left him strangely invigorated. He had a few pry-bar-shaped bruises he'd no doubt feel tomorrow, but no permanent damage was done. His twenty-year lucky streak was intact.

Casey was not so lucky. Farranger doubted he'd survive the run down the mountain, but he couldn't hang around to find out. He had a train to catch.

He turned toward the timber train. It was already ten car-lengths inside the tunnel and picking up speed. In the juncture between the cars, he could see that the air hoses were disconnected, dangling uselessly over the tracks. The only working brakes were on the locomotive, and it was already inside the tunnel. He'd have to find a way to the engine. And even if he reached it in time, he had only one set of brakes to stop the momentum of thirty cars.

For the Zephyr's sake, he hoped it would be enough.

Farranger ran alongside the flatcars. The train was traveling at 20 mph, and he'd never attempted to board a car moving that fast. The switchman's handholds at the base of the flat were too low to grab at a full sprint. They were made for riding, not boarding. He needed to find something above him to pull himself up with.

Half the train was in the tunnel, and Farranger was running out of options. He lunged for the thick banding cables that held the logs in place. The flat metal strips sliced into his hands, but he managed to hold on. The force of the train jerked him off his feet, dragging them over the ties just outside the rail. Farranger climbed the banding cables hand over hand, until he was able to maintain a foothold at the base of the flat.

As the train accelerated, he stepped from car to car, using the huge logs as his walking path. The tunnel was brightly illuminated by the locomotive headlight, allowing him to see the yellow-white reflection of the snow-packed Zephyr ahead. It was close, less than a mile away. Farranger stepped up his pace, barely able to keep his footing on the wet timber, but he didn't have time for caution. The engine had already passed the halfway point in the tunnel.

Leaping from the head car to the locomotive, Farranger raced across the catwalk, expending his last bit of energy in a sprint to the cab. Inside, the view from the forward window showed the snow-plugged tunnel exit in front of him, quickly closing in at 40 mph. In the middle of the white mass, a red blinking end-of-train device marked the bull's-eye of a target he couldn't avoid.

Farranger jerked the throttle to idle, then thrust the locomotive brake lever to full. The brake shoes jammed against the steel wheels on the locomotive, locking them in place. The engine skidded over the rails, the train slack smashing against it from behind in a series of thundering crashes.

Farranger glanced at the speedometer. The speed was dropping, but he'd never stop short of the Zephyr.

"Megan, brace yourself!" he yelled into the locomotive radio.

"Are you bringing help?" Megan's weakening voice was barely audible over the train noise in the tunnel.

"Not exactly."

Farranger took the engineer's seat and prepared for impact. Barreling through the snow at the end of the tunnel, the train lost momentum as it cut through the frozen blockade. But it wasn't enough. The locomotive slammed into the rear of the Zephyr at

10 mph, nearly three times the maximum recommended coupling speed. The jolt threw Farranger out of his seat and into the control console, then flung him down to the floor.

Battered and exhausted, he managed to stand up and look out the forward cab window. To his surprise, the rear end of the Zephyr was firmly attached to the front of his locomotive.

The joint had been made.

"I'll be damned," he mouthed subconsciously, somewhat amazed his locomotive had coupled to the crippled train. It hadn't even occurred to him that the observation car might have a working knuckle. Maybe his luck was beginning to change.

Farranger was quick to act upon his unexpected good fortune. He released the brakes, put the reverser into the reverse position, then advanced the throttle. The Zephyr quivered. The snow surrounding the tunnel exit began to work its way free as he backed up the train.

The observation car emerged from the mountain of snow and ice first, compacted to a fraction of its former size. Behind it, the lounge car scraped off a load of snow against the roof of the tunnel, then slowly came into view.

The lone engine strained against the heavy load in full throttle, belching out enough diesel exhaust to fill the enclosed tunnel. The fumes were so thick the headlight could barely penetrate them. But a brief glimpse of the crushed lounger told Farranger all he needed to know. Not everybody had made it.

He throttled up to 10 mph, then immediately backed off when the lounger began shaking violently, yawing sideways on flanged wheels that no longer matched the rail gauge. The car was truck-hunting for its own gauge, a condition he'd made worse by adding power. Farranger slowed to a compromise speed of 8 mph. Any faster and the lounge car would derail. Any slower, his exhaust would asphyxiate the passengers inside the enclosed tunnel. The pace was frustratingly slow, but it would get them safely to the tunnel entrance.

After a squealing, screeching, metal-grinding fifteen minutes, Farranger managed to ease the ruined cars out of the smoke-filled tunnel into the sunlight. The open air threw everything into high relief—the damage done to the train, the barely audible screams and moans from the snow-packed lounge car, and his own bruised and battered exhaustion.

He limped down off the locomotive. Open air didn't mean rescue, since they still had to make it down the mountain to reach the next radio repeater, then call for assistance. But most of the Zephyr passengers had survived, Farranger thought with grim relief. He wondered how many they had lost.

And underneath it all, thrumming in Farranger's shock-weary brain, a single thought. *Megan. Megan was alive.* He didn't have the energy to wonder when he had grown to depend on her. He merely accepted it as a change in his life.

The lounge car looked as though a steamroller had passed over it—a juggernaut of ice and snow that had mangled the steel framing into a lopsided rectangle. He dashed alongside the car, stopping at the sound of muffled voices.

"Here! We're in here!"

Reaching up, Farranger wrenched at a ripped-apart section of sheet metal, tearing it open further with numbed hands.

A very happy and very scared human face appeared in the gap.

The first passengers emerged, relief and horror mixing in their expressions. Farranger did what he could to help them down onto the track bed. Several had broken bones and most exhibited cuts, bruises, and the early stages of frostbite. But he gasped in relief at the sheer numbers of them. Casey's try at the record books had failed.

Where was she? As one after another survivor emerged from the wreck, Farranger had to bite back his panic. *She's still in there, she's buried, she died in a heroic effort to save others . . .*

When no more human faces appeared at the torn hole in the side of the lounge car, Farranger sagged back with weariness and despair.

"Did you see a woman, a girl, golden hair . . . ?" The passengers stared back him blankly, wrapped up in dramas of their own.

"Cal." The soft voice called his name from somewhere behind him. Farranger grunted with pain as he swung his battered body around. Megan stood there, pretty battered herself, a lopsided smile on her face.

End of the Line

Farranger didn't stop to think. He went to her. Their short and clumsy embrace helped knock off stray bits of ice and snow that still clung to their clothes.

"The bastard," Farranger whispered. "Thank God, he didn't get you."

"I'm kind of glad to see you, too, Farranger," Megan whispered in a shivering voice, "though it might just be the hypothermia talking."

Megan pulled away abruptly, and Cal sensed not everything had thawed. He cupped his hands, exhaled hot air into them, pretending his best that their embrace had never happened. Megan needed no prompting to play along.

"Took your sweet time getting us out." Megan shook her head in mock disgust. "I'll tell you what, Farranger, next time you stay in the frozen car and I'll stop the train."

Cal nodded in silent agreement, making a mental note that they were once again on a last-name basis. God forbid anyone should get too close to Megan Langford.

"He's dead, right?" Megan asked.

"I sincerely hope so," Farranger replied coolly, no trace of remorse in his voice.

"If he isn't," Megan shot back, "he's definitely scratching you off his Christmas card list."

Farranger forced a smile, but inside he found it hard to see the humor. If Casey survived, he'd be holding a ferocious grudge against him. Not that Cal could really blame him. It was hard not to take being thrown off a mountain personally.

A chill ran down his half-frozen back. Casey was already killing people for sport—what would do if he was pissed off?

PART TWO

- 25 -

Dawn was still two hours away, and there was no moon to speak of. Save for a dim signal light that was holding a standing freight train at bay, the right-of-way was pitch-black. His eyes puffy and bruised, a near-crippled Casey Jones peered beyond the roadbed, but figured he wasn't missing much in the way of scenery. Transcon's Montana branch was in the middle of nowhere, separated from the rest of civilization by snow-covered plains stretching for miles in every direction.

He'd selected the site months ago, long before his ride down Death Mountain. He reasoned that its isolation would make it the perfect place for his little test run. Strategically, he knew the location was as unimportant to Transcon as it was to him. He doubted anyone would miss this remote stretch of track or the short siding lying just a mile ahead of the train. It was, by any definition, an ugly wasteland.

And it was about to get a lot uglier.

Casey hobbled alongside the standing train, unsure which of his two battered legs to favor. The brutal fall over the cliff at Stampede Pass had transformed him into raw flesh and one continuous contusion. The left half of his face was an open wound that made him look as though he'd used a belt sander for a pillow.

Thanks to Farranger, Casey had not only hit every goddamned rock and branch down the two-thousand-foot slope, he'd lost valuable targets in Washington and Cajon. The man was no longer a simple nuisance; he was a certified pain in the ass. He'd earned himself the top position on Casey's death list, which was no small feat, considering the current list was the size of a phone book.

Farranger hadn't been part of his original plan, but Casey was a big-tent kind of killer; there was room for everyone in his grand finale. He felt confident that Farranger would accept his invitation. He was just smart enough to find the trail Casey had left, and just dumb enough to follow it.

When Casey chuckled at the thought, sharp pains shot through his chest and he cursed himself for overexerting his newly disabled body. The half-mile walk from his truck had been like a marathon, his stamina ebbing with each painful step. Crunching down handfuls of Vicodin and white crosses was the only the way he was keeping himself going.

Still, he knew he'd been lucky. His bloody tumble down the mountain had deposited him unconscious less than a quarter of a mile from a secondary highway. And his sleep might very likely have ended up a death nap were it not the pecking of a bird on his open wounds. He distinctly remembered thinking to himself that it couldn't get any worse. But then it started to snow.

His trek to the highway had been nearly unbearable, taking almost half an hour, but his efforts were immediately rewarded. His condition had attracted the attention of a local soccer mom suffering from a misplaced sense of Samaritanism, who was driving by in a minivan.

To her terminal misfortune.

From there, it was only a short carjack to his truck, where he left the dead woman and one of Detroit's worst ideas behind.

Casey resisted the temptation to applaud the ingenuity of his escape. Truth was, he'd been incredibly fortunate, a hapless benefactor of the railroad gods that were watching over him. But it was far too early to offer a prayer of thanks.

He still had a few commandments to break.

He moved carefully over the icy ballast, using a pry bar for a walking stick as he felt his way along the boxcars. The tool felt awkward, not balanced like the custom pry he'd lost during the fall. But he reminded himself that his second-rate crutch would still make a first-rate weapon. Whatever he lacked in accuracy, he'd make up for in brute force.

With painkillers and amphetamine coursing through his veins, he edged toward the head end of the train, nearing the three-engine consist. The crew had turned off the headlights, but he

End of the Line

could make out the lead locomotive under the soft red light of a nearby signal tower. The stop signal had been one of his simpler tricks, requiring only that he lay an iron bar across the tracks to shunt the circuit. By simulating a phantom train in the next block, he'd held the crew in place for almost eight minutes. In nine, they'd be dead.

Casey stepped inside the locomotive through the nose door and quickly sized up the crew. The conductor was a woman and could be easily dispensed with. The hoghead was another matter, though, a bull of a man who looked like he belonged on the professional wrestling circuit.

"Damn!" Casey said, impressed. "Looks like I'd better kill you first."

Before the man had even turned completely around, Casey jammed the blunt end of the bar into his face, breaking his cheekbone. A second strike snapped his neck. The man slumped dead in his seat.

"Ah, the sweet spot," Casey reflected.

He turned away from the engineer just in time to see the conductor escaping through the interior nose door. He leveled a wild swing at the woman but missed her head by a full two inches. She disappeared into the toilet compartment, then Casey heard the exterior nose door slam open.

"Women," he muttered. Chasing her wasn't an option. He could barely walk, much less run someone down.

Luckily, he didn't have to.

He pushed the dead man off the engineer's seat and positioned himself behind the control console, flicked on the locomotive headlight, and scanned the featureless Montana landscape around him. The entire area was flat and covered with at least four feet of snow. The roadbed had been plowed and salted for foot traffic, but walking through the tundra alongside the right-of-way would be nearly impossible.

The terrified conductor came into view. She was taking a predictable escape path, running between the rails away from the engine. Casey smiled in anticipation as she headed for the only cover in the barren landscape, a siding full of cars about a mile ahead.

The nearest car was a black tanker of liquefied natural gas. A large circle of thin white frost was forming on its side, rapidly spreading outward from the small puncture he'd made in its hull. The invisible gas inside the tank was depressurizing as it escaped, allowing Casey to approximate its position by tracking the billowing fog of condensation.

He turned his attention back to the conductor, who was running directly toward the tank. Bludgeoning the engineer had been fun, but the woman's death would serve a more useful purpose. She would be the human guinea pig in his little experiment to determine the kill radius of the tank car. He hadn't anticipated a volunteer, but her presence would give his field test the one element it was missing: a woman's touch.

Rummaging through the conductor's overnight grip, Casey found a fusee. He struck the flare against the floor, unleashing a bright red flame as the cap broke off. He leaned out the engineer's window and lobbed it in the direction of the tanker. It landed thirty yards from the locomotive.

The approaching fog was already halfway between the tank car and his locomotive. By Casey's estimation, the gas would hit the fusee in less than two minutes. NORAD would be alerted in three. He could almost picture the top military brass scratching their collective heads, frantically trying to connect the impending explosion with a ballistic missile launch.

The conductor was running at a full sprint, no doubt motivated by his little game of engineer piñata. She didn't even bother to look back until she entered the shroud of condensed air.

"Thatta girl," Casey said, as she slowed to think through her situation. "Now, why do you suppose I'm not following you?"

He could almost read the woman's mind as she peered through the cloud of gas to the leaking tank car, then looked back at the burning fusee. She started running again a moment later, this time in the opposite direction. She was smart enough to know that she'd never outrun the gas by trying to escape through the snowy plains, so she was taking the only path that gave her a chance, the one that led straight back to Casey.

"I'm a chick magnet," he laughed as she ran toward him. In less than a minute she would, quite literally, be toast. What he wouldn't give for a bag of marshmallows and a forty-foot stick.

End of the Line

Though he knew the conductor couldn't see him, Casey extended his free arm toward her and gave her a thumbs-up, then slowly turned it downward as if denying mercy to a beaten gladiator. And why not? The railroad was his empire, his to command as he saw fit. Like the great Caesars of the past, he would vanquish the uncivilized hordes at Transcon and liberate oppressed railroaders throughout his realm.

That would be the easy part.

Becoming immortal, now that would be a lot trickier. There was room for only one railroad legend, and Casey had missed that train by nearly a century, preempted by his old childhood hero. His love-hate relationship with his namesake was rapidly distilling to pure hate. He'd never get the fame he deserved as long as that overrated Illinois Central engineer was hogging the historical spotlight.

And the only way to kill a legend was to replace it with a bigger one. If the original Casey Jones could become famous for saving a few lives, then as a latter-day Casey, he would make splashier headlines by killing a thousand times more.

Soon, when people spoke of Casey Jones, they'd be referring to him.

"Train GFHV102, this is DS41. Show you stopped at milepost 1297. Over."

Casey snapped out of his reverie at the sound of the locomotive's radio. He grabbed the interior handset, keeping his eyes on the approaching gas, which was now only a few yards away from the torch. The exhausted conductor was coming up on the inside rail, pushing her body to the limit. Casey had to smile at her determination. She was about to break out of the cloud and cross past the fusee into the safe zone. It looked as though she might make it after all.

He depressed the transmit button and held the handset out the window so the dispatcher could experience the upcoming events firsthand. He reached for the headlight switch, waited until the conductor was only a few feet from safety, then threw a blanket of darkness over the right-of-way. *Nothing like darkness,* he thought, *to bring out the beauty of a fireworks show.*

The uneven height of the crossties, a minor obstacle in daylight, had become high hurdles for the conductor. The light of the flare provided just enough light for Casey to see her shadowy form tripping toward the tracks.

As the fog approached the fusee, he braced himself against the control console. The condensed air passed over the flare but didn't ignite. A moment later, though, the gas pushing the column of air in front of it did. The mist instantaneously transformed into an inferno, and a fireball with a half-mile radius lit up the night sky. A central pillar of flame twenty stories high shot up from ground zero. The heat was so intense, Casey could feel it through the locomotive glass.

The shock wave hit the cab a half second later. The windows shattered with a sonic boom. Casey was thrown backward but regained his footing just in time to see the burning vapors forming a much-anticipated mushroom cloud. The fire pulled in loose debris as the burning fuel fed its voracious appetite for oxygen. The vacuum pulled Casey toward the front of the cab, momentarily sucking the air out of his lungs before the pressure finally subsided.

The conductor was thoroughly doused in burning gas now, frantically running in circles at the outer edge of the flames. Her screams pierced the night air and rippled over the open radio. Casey watched the show with voyeuristic pleasure, clapping his approval as the human torch finally collapsed in the snow.

"Bravo!" he shouted. Another closed-casket funeral, courtesy of Casey Jones.

But the show wasn't over. Huge chunks of flaming metal began hailing down around him, pelting the snow with the airborne remains of the railcars in the siding. Casey flinched, pulling the radio handset back inside the cab as the burning shrapnel struck the locomotive.

"Tell Farranger this crew was for him," he said into the radio, then let the handset fall to the floor.

He was certain the epitaph would weigh heavy on Farranger's conscious. The guy was just arrogant enough to believe that Casey had murdered the crew in his honor.

End of the Line

Actually, he'd killed them more for his own pleasure than to even a score. He realized that he had developed a taste for murder, an insatiable appetite that was becoming increasingly difficult to squelch. What had started out as a pleasant diversion between derailing trains had now evolved into a bonafide addiction, the kind of single-minded obsession that threatened his self-image as a well-rounded terrorist. If not for the fact that he was going to be dead soon, he'd have to consider enrolling in a twelve-step program. After all, it wasn't as though they had a patch for this sort of thing.

Casey detrained, shrugging off any lingering doubts he might have had about his budding psychosis. It was time to concentrate on escape. He headed for his truck, guided by the light of the diminishing fireball and the small subsidiary fires dotting the landscape. Unconsumed gas was stuck to every surface like napalm, slowly burning itself out, the flames now just a few inches off the ground.

Casey got in his truck and surveyed the damage one last time. The siding and the cars had been destroyed, and those cars that didn't vaporize instantly had become deadly missiles, flinging fiery shrapnel for miles. The remaining debris was tiny but looked like a meteor shower flaming out on reentry. The overall effect convinced Casey that he'd broken new ground in the field of functional art. Not only was it beautiful, it had a kill radius of nearly half a mile.

He sped along the access road beside the right-of-way, confident that his tank-car experiment had been an unqualified success. The destruction had far exceeded his expectations, the only glitch being the unconsumed gas. He wasn't getting complete combustion, but he'd already anticipated that problem. By using the hopper as a detonator, he'd be able to completely atomize the gas before ignition, thus doubling the efficiency of the reaction. He'd further increase the dosage of his explosive cocktail by adding another twenty or thirty tank cars of liquefied natural gas to the mix. It would be his dream train, giving him approximately twice the firepower used against Dresden.

He'd have a city killer.

Kem Parton

As Casey checked his damaged face in the rearview mirror, wincing as he ripped a loose piece of skin off his left cheek, it occurred to him that his grotesque features were probably a blessing in disguise. He doubted if anyone would be able to muster the courage to look at him, much less identify him.

The anonymity would be useful, but also short-lived. The whole world would know his name in just a few hours.

-26-

The COC morning shift was bustling with activity, but Farranger barely noticed. He and Megan were huddled behind the SYSOP's workstation, listening to the static-filled recorded radio transmission for the third time.

"Tell Farranger this crew was for him."

Farranger shook his head in despair, then signaled the SYSOP to end the transmission.

"It's not your fault, Cal," Megan said.

Farranger's heart turned to lead. People kept telling him that. He looked up at her, wondering just which one of his screwups she was referring to. He hadn't been able to protect the Montana train crew any more than he'd been able to protect the rest of the system. And Megan was a perfect example—he'd led her directly into one of Casey's traps, a fatal mistake that had cost thirty Zephyr passengers their lives.

Incredibly, the ordeal at Stampede Pass had only seemed to increase Megan's resolve to find Casey. Against medical advice, she had insisted on accompanying him to Dallas to help search for the hopper. And she had spent the better part of the morning marshaling local union representatives across the system to aid in the hunt.

"You should get some rest," Farranger offered, noticing how weary she looked.

"And you should be in a hospital," she countered.

"Doctor gave me a clean bill of health," Farranger grunted with a certain amount of pride. The boast was a facade. He was beginning to feel cursed, like some kind of modern-day Typhoid Mary. Everywhere he went, people around him died while he walked away with barely a scratch. Everyone he cared about had died, and it had been because of him. Only Megan remained, and he vowed he'd do everything to protect her.

But first Farranger had to somehow close the book on Casey Jones.

The Washington State police had followed a trail of blood that led halfway down Death Mountain, and the forensic specialist who'd examined Casey's route had found it incredible that the man had survived the fall. By his estimation, Casey was nursing several broken bones and had to be "a few quarts low" on blood. Based on this assessment, the state police had searched the surrounding area for hours, anticipating the easy capture of a half-dead fugitive.

But they didn't know Casey. Their search had barely begun when he lit up the night sky in Montana three hundred miles away.

"Lubbock and Abilene reporting," the SYSOP suddenly announced. "Search complete, no hopper."

Farranger nodded, the latest negative report in fifteen hours of fruitless searching. "Two more backwater stations with only a handful of cars," he noted dryly. "That only leaves 999,000 cars to check." Farranger shook his head, thoroughly frustrated by the lack of progress. None of the major yards had reported, except to say that it would take weeks to physically inspect the tens of thousands of cars that passed through their terminal on a daily basis. Farranger was sure they didn't have that long. According to Casey, the "grand finale" would come in hours, not weeks.

He turned away from the SYSOP, trying to spot Agent Kelly in one of the upper-level executive offices that surrounded the operations floor. He knew Kelly was in the CEO's second-floor office at that very moment, no doubt listening to McClure cite reasons why Farranger shouldn't be charged with obstruction of justice. It wouldn't be an easy sell. Farranger had waited half a day before reporting the missing hopper to the FBI, and the Bureau wasn't known to have a great sense of humor.

He briefly imagined himself being hauled out of the COC in handcuffs, then quickly dismissed the thought. He didn't have time to worry about whether or not Transcon's CEO could smooth things over with the Feds.

"Put Bloomberg back on the screen," he said. "Let's see if they have video on the Montana explosion."

The SYSOP depressed a button on his console, and the center screen on the COC wall came to life. Bloomberg Financial News was repeating its top story on the massive explosion for the umpteenth time. They had been reporting the story for two hours, but now there were pictures.

Amateur video from Charlo, Montana, nearly twenty miles away from the blast, had captured a massive fireball lighting up the night sky. The distinctive mushroom shape was darkly reminiscent of Cold War nightmares and seemed to confirm earlier eyewitness accounts of a nuclear detonation. Farranger knew better. The cause of the explosion had already been identified as a single tank of liquefied petroleum gas, but the fact that the source wasn't nuclear offered little comfort. Weapons-grade plutonium was relatively hard to come by, but tank cars were not. Transcon had tens of thousands of them running unprotected across the system.

Live aerial shots of the aftermath made a persuasive argument for the nuclear theory, though. A half-mile black crater had been burned into a blanket of snow, with numerous fires still licking its outer radius. A lone freight train, its engine charred black, was the only man-made object that remained intact. The tracks in front of it were on fire, creating a path of flaming ties that led to the center of the detonation, a siding that no longer existed. On either side of the scorched roadbed, broken rail kinked up in twenty-foot-high coils. Burning chunks of railcars, some the size of a Buick, dotted the perimeter up to six miles beyond the blast.

On the video screen beneath all the destruction, a stock ticker showed red across the board, Transcon leading the way down by making a fifty-two-week low.

A sense of hopelessness filled Farranger as he stared at the devastated scene. How the hell was he supposed to protect the railroad from something like this?

He couldn't. And Casey knew it. Destroying this worthless stretch of railroad was his way of underscoring that point. Casey was sending a message, proving he could attack at will and daring anyone to try and stop him.

Farranger was certain there'd be no second warning. Casey's next assault would be his grand finale, an attack specifically designed to inflict maximum damage and fatalities. And if they didn't find the hopper in time, he'd have the means to make this threat a reality. As bad as the liquefied natural gas explosion had been, it would be nothing compared to the devastation produced by eighty tons of ammonium nitrate exploding in a populated area.

"Christ, this is even worse than they said it was!"

Farranger looked up at the sound of Kelly's voice. The agent was walking toward him with the CEO in tow.

"This missing car of yours, Farranger," Kelly said, pointing to the screen. "Is that it?"

"No, we're looking for a covered hopper, a car that normally carries dry-bulk cargo, like grain or plastic pellets."

"Lucky for you, Farranger," the agent smiled, then turned to the screen as if the matter was settled.

Farranger was caught completely off guard by Kelly's relaxed tone. He'd fully expected to be read the riot act for withholding information about the hopper. For a moment, he credited the agent's demeanor to McClure's diplomacy, then realized it had to be more than that. Kelly knew something, something that had convinced him to dismiss Farranger's information as unimportant. Whatever it was, Farranger was in no position to press the issue.

"Did you talk to Adashek?" he asked instead.

"Ran into him this morning as he was leaving Love Field," Kelly replied. "He was flying out to Chicago to meet with some of your bigger customers to assure them that Transcon can meet their delivery schedules." Kelly paused, looking up at the screen again. "Of course, that was before you started getting one-kilometer potholes. I think it's going to be a much harder sell now."

"Did you ask him about what Casey said?"

"You mean his alleged comment to you about 'Adashek riding the CBO&E gravy train?' No such animal. We checked with every known historical archive. The closest we could find was the Chicago, Burlington, and Quincy, the CB&Q and the Baltimore and Ohio, the B&O. There's never been a railroad with the initials CBO&E."

End of the Line

"And even if there was," McClure interjected, "Adashek didn't work for it. I hired him away from a Wall Street firm that specialized in mergers and acquisitions."

"But what did Adashek say?" Farranger persisted.

"He said he didn't know anything about Casey Jones or this nonexistent railroad of yours," Kelly said. "But he sure had a few choice things to say about you. Not exactly what I'd call a stellar performance evaluation. According to your pal Adashek, you're making the whole thing up. He said he tried to fire you last week for insubordination, and he claims this is your way of getting even with him."

"Is that what you think?" Farranger asked, hoping the agent's easy manner meant he put little stock in the accusation.

"I could care less about your corporate politics. Even less about listening to paranoid conspiracy theories from some overpaid suit."

"Does it mean anything to you that Casey Jones singled out Adashek by name?"

"He was probably feeding you a red herring, Farranger. Psychopaths have been known to do that from time to time."

Farranger had to admit that an offhanded remark from a homicidal madman wasn't exactly a hot lead. But he wasn't ready to dismiss Casey's remarks as irrelevant. There had to be some kind of personal link, if only in Casey's mind. If the CBO&E wasn't a railroad connection between the two men, what else could it be?

His train of thought was derailed by a muffled beeping sound. Listening closer, Farranger could make out a single-tone digital melody. The tune was vaguely familiar, but he couldn't quite place it, and it took him a minute to realize the sound was coming from inside his own jacket.

He pulled the ringing handset out of his pocket, then hesitated before answering, knowing it had belonged to the dead crewman at Canyon Demonio. He'd had every intention of delivering it immediately to the man's next of kin, but then he'd gotten sidetracked by a runaway train. Now he'd have to face the unpleasant task of telling the caller that the owner of the phone was dead.

He flipped open the phone, wondering if there was any good way to deliver the bad news.

"You paged me," a voice said over the open line.

Farranger was dumbfounded, recognizing the voice. "Adashek? Why are you calling this number?"

He heard only an awkward silence before the line went dead.

Why would Adashek be calling a dead engineer?

A heartbeat later, the answer came to him as clearly as the tune on the cell phone's ringer.

The Ballad of Casey Jones.

"That was Phil Adashek," he told the group. "Casey's partner."

"What?" McClure said, incredulous. "You can't be serious."

"This phone," Farranger explained, holding out the cellular, "was found at the Canyon Demonio wreck. I've been carrying it around all week thinking it was part of the crew's personal effects, but it's not. This phone belongs to Casey. It's the only explanation that makes any sense."

"Even if it *is* Casey's phone," McClure said, obviously skeptical that there could be a traitor in his inner circle, "how does that put Adashek and Casey together?"

"Adashek didn't know I had the phone. He thought he was calling Casey," Farranger guessed. "He hung up when he recognized my voice."

"Let's not get ahead of ourselves," Kelly spoke up. "Did the caller *say* he was Adashek?"

"It was him. Casey had apparently paged him."

"Don't let your imagination get ahead of the facts," Kelly said. "Right now all we have are two conversations that only you heard: one from a psychopath on a train, and the other from some unidentified caller. And coincidentally, both incriminate the man who tried to fire you last week. Are you sure this isn't just wishful thinking on your part, Farranger?"

"You think I'm making this up?"

"I'll check out the phone." Kelly took the cellular from Farranger. "But what possible motive could Adashek have for aiding someone bent on destroying Transcon?"

"They found it!" the SYSOP interrupted, tapping his headset to indicate an incoming transmission. "They found the hopper!"

-27-

The Bloomberg Financial News vanished from one of the theater screens in the COC, replaced by a grainy video image of a dull gray hopper. A switch stand identified the track as Rip 1 at Kansas City Yard.

"We have visual on the car," the SYSOP informed the group crowding his workstation, then looked directly at Agent Kelly to acknowledge his report. Disarming the hopper was an FBI operation.

Farranger had to give the agent his due. Though Kelly had downplayed the hopper's potential, he'd still taken the threat seriously, putting together a crack response team in record time. In less than an hour, they'd evacuated the yard and set up an impenetrable curtain of security around the hopper.

"Doesn't look like it's leaking much to me." Kelly pointed to the small puddle beneath the hopper's center dump gate.

"It shouldn't be leaking at all," Megan said. "Hoppers don't carry liquid cargo."

Farranger studied the video image, more concerned with what he saw stenciled on its hull. The serial number wasn't just bogus, it was obsolete—a relic from the long-defunct Kansas City Southern Railroad fleet.

It was also Casey's signature.

"KCS 382." Farranger pointed to the serial number. "That translates as 'Casey's 382'—the famous engine number of the real Casey Jones."

Farranger allowed himself to relax a little, now that there was no longer any uncertainty about the car's identity. He looked at the deputy director, watching for a reaction to their discovery, but the agent remained stoic, unfazed by Casey's psychotic attempt at irony. Though he reexamined the video image with renewed interest, he didn't seem overly concerned to learn that Casey had left his calling card.

"They've secured the perimeter," the SYSOP relayed, tapping his radio headset to confirm that he had contact with the on-site team. "One mile in all directions."

"Tell them to start jamming," Kelly ordered. "Full RF spectrum."

"You're sure this will keep Casey from detonating the car?" McClure asked, his fingers nervously drumming the SYSOP's desk.

"He *could* overpower the signal with a handheld transmitter at close range," Kelly admitted. "But to do that, he'd have to sneak through a net of armed federal agents. I've got all entrances to the yard covered, a dozen motion sensors in strategic locations to detect intruders, and snipers at every compass point. Nobody's that good."

"They're ready to go in, Mr. Kelly," the SYSOP said.

"Tell them to send in the point man."

The SYSOP repeated the order. A moment later, a heavily armored field agent walked into view on the video screen, a yellow FBI logo emblazoned on his back. He walked alongside the hopper, swiping his palm across the skin of the hull. He stopped to examine his hand, then flashed a thumbs-down sign at the camera.

Kelly translated the field agent's sign language. "No condensation on the hull."

"Meaning what?" McClure asked.

"Meaning we just ruled out Farranger's cockamamy theory about a diesel-nitrate explosive. If there were a few thousand gallons of diesel fuel inside that car, the hull would be sweating."

Farranger looked at the car again. Though he hated to admit it, the agent was right. It was unseasonably warm in Kansas City, and if the hopper was holding liquid cargo, the skin of the single-hull car would practically bleed condensation.

"And for future reference, Ms. Langford," Kelly went on, "diesel nitrate makes a dark sludge, not a clear liquid like your carman found."

End of the Line

Farranger saw Megan bristle at the condescending remark, but again had to admit he was right.

"If this isn't the right car," Farranger said, increasingly sure that it wasn't, "then we're back to square one, searching a million-car fleet for a bomb that might be anywhere."

"If a bomb exists at all," McClure interjected, his tone bright with optimism.

"Oh, it exists, all right," Kelly replied. "We found it two days ago."

"Two days ago?" Farranger's tone rose in anger. "And you didn't tell us until now?"

"This is an ongoing investigation," Kelly explained without blinking an eye. "There are certain details we don't make public. Our perp reads the newspapers, too, and doesn't need a daily status report."

Farranger had no doubt that Kelly's security concerns took a backseat to protecting his turf, but he was certainly in no position to criticize anyone for withholding information.

"So where's the hopper?" he finally asked.

"Who said anything about a hopper?"

The agent seemed to be talking in riddles, and Farranger was getting impatient. Then it hit him.

"The tanker truck?"

"Bravo, Farranger."

"I don't understand," Megan said. "What about the tanker truck?"

"Not that any of you have a legitimate need to know," Kelly said, "but since Farranger already knows just enough to be dangerous, I'll fill you in. Our lab guys found traces of ammonium nitrate and a partially built detonator inside the diesel truck while we were investigating the special agent's death. Casey wasn't filling the hopper with diesel, he was using ammonium nitrate from the hopper to fill up the tanker truck."

"So Casey was making a truck bomb," Megan concluded. "Like the one they used on the Oklahoma City Federal Building?"

"A lot more powerful. He was only five miles away from here, the nerve center for your entire railroad."

McClure's eyes slowly scanned the massive operations floor, as if trying to calculate the damage a bomb would do. "We'd have lost everything: computers, communications, our dispatching capability. He'd have shut down the entire system for weeks. And in the shape we're in now, the banks would have called our loans in before we ever had a chance to get it started again."

"Not to mention the thousands of employees he'd kill," Megan added, irritated by McClure's misplaced priorities.

"Fortunately, thanks to the special agent who showed up, that didn't happen," Kelly said. "Casey killed the agent, but he had no way of knowing whether or not Officer Dumars had called in an intruder report. He couldn't risk further exposure, so he aborted his plan."

Farranger was too stunned to speak. In an instant, the agent had turned his theory about the hopper upside down. He couldn't refute the cold logic of Kelly's explanation, but something about the hopper still didn't feel right. Casey had taken extraordinary measures to make the car disappear. There had to be a reason.

"It doesn't make sense," he finally said. "If he was planning a truck bomb, why go through all the effort of hiding the hopper?"

"You mean the missing electronic tags, the bogus car number, and the computer high jinks?" Kelly asked. "I have a theory, but you might not want to hear it."

"Go ahead," Farranger said, certain his own theory about the car was already as far off the mark as possible.

"I think he was playing a game with you, Farranger. Once the special agent interrupted his original plan, Casey decided to improvise. He'd already tried to kill you once, in the parking lot, for your interference in California. What better way to even the score than by letting you chase the missing tags all the way to the Zephyr?"

Farranger said nothing. He didn't have to. Kelly's theoretical question was intended to send a very real message—Farranger should stick to guarding trains and leave the investigation to the professionals.

"Checking for tamper devices." The SYSOP broke the silence, directing Kelly's attention to the renewed activity on the video link.

End of the Line

Kelly pointed to the field agent, who was now beneath the car making a visual inspection of the center dump gate. "They'll open her up once they make sure there are no booby traps."

Farranger watched along with the others, but his thoughts were elsewhere. Casey Jones had played him for a fool. Not only had he stumbled into a trap, he'd nearly taken Megan along with him. What the hell had he been thinking?

"It's clean," the SYSOP relayed to Kelly. "They want permission to enter."

Kelly nodded, and the SYSOP passed the okay on to the scene leader.

Farranger held his breath as the field agent probed the two-foot-diameter dump gate with a crowbar-like device. Though the man was a thousand miles away, Farranger braced himself for an explosion, flinching involuntarily when the bolt gave way and the metal cover swung downward.

But there was no explosion, no rush of ammonium nitrate through the open gate. A trickle of clear liquid dribbled out for a few seconds, then nothing.

"He says the hopper looks empty," the SYSOP reported as the field agent kneeled to look inside. "Might be some water trapped inside . . . definitely not fuel."

"Somebody might have run it through a locomotive washrack by mistake," McClure guessed.

The field agent turned toward the camera and shrugged his shoulders. Kelly shook his head in disgust, then motioned for the SYSOP to cut the video signal. A moment later, the screen went dark.

"Well, Sherlock?" Kelly's eyes shifted from the monitor to Farranger. "Are you satisfied?"

Farranger nodded, though he was far from satisfied. Even if Kelly's theory about the tanker truck was correct, the hopper shouldn't be empty. A diesel tanker was about half the size of an eighty-ton railcar. If Casey had used this hopper to fill the tanker, there should still be forty tons of nitrate left inside. Something wasn't adding up.

"Just got an update from the response-team leader about the leak," the SYSOP said, then depressed a button to reenergize the video link. He held both hands over the headset to block outside noise, then his eyes widened as the transmission came through. "It sounds like he's saying the liquid is—"

"Vodka," Farranger finished a split second after the video image reappeared on the screen. The field agent was holding a broken bottle of Smirnoff's up to the camera.

"Have him look inside the car," Farranger ordered, without bothering to wait for Kelly's approval. A moment later, the field agent disappeared inside the manhole-sized opening, entering the belly of the hopper.

"Five-gallon drum of water . . ." the SYSOP reported. "Sleeping bag, blankets, ice chest filled with cold cuts . . ."

The group listened in growing astonishment as the SYSOP rattled off an inventory that sounded like a grocery list for an extended camping trip. A smile came to Farranger's face as the purpose of the hidden cache became clear. Someone was planning on living inside the car.

Someone like Casey Jones.

Kelly caught on at the same instant. "Casey's getaway car," he said.

"Not quite as plush as a Pullman sleeper," Farranger noted. "But it has certain advantages over other forms of transportation."

"Like not being checked when crossing an international border." Kelly nodded in agreement. "Nobody would think to look for a passenger inside a sealed freight car. Five will get you ten this car is headed for Canada or Mexico."

"Let's find out." Farranger reached over the SYSOP's shoulder and punched the newly acquired serial number written on the hopper's hull. The number might be bogus, but if Casey wanted to send the car anywhere, he'd eventually have to add the hopper to their computer inventory. A second after hitting the enter key, Farranger was rewarded with a complete billing history and scheduled itinerary.

"This car was added to our inventory less than an hour ago," he said, interpreting the billing shorthand on the screen. "It's shown as a load of ammonium nitrate scheduled to leave Kansas City this evening. It's also scheduled to switch trains at Chicago, La Crosse, Saint Paul, and Fargo . . ."

End of the Line

Farranger paused to consider the hopper's lading. The car was empty, but for some reason, Casey had billed it as a load. If he had picked the lading at random, he couldn't have made a worse selection. A loaded car of ammonium nitrate was exactly what they'd been looking for.

"The final destination?" Kelly asked, prompting Farranger to page down to the next screen.

"Winnipeg, Canada."

"I knew it!" Kelly said, triumphant. "We've got him now. All we have to do is stake out the car and wait for him to show."

"Farranger, you said the billing was entered just an hour ago," McClure said. "How is that possible? Just yesterday, we changed all of the passwords and installed a firewall that was supposedly unbreakable."

"Let's find out where he got in," the SYSOP volunteered, then queried the last user ID that had altered the billing record. A pop-up window appeared in the center of the screen.

USER: Phillip Adashek. Terminal Location: remote laptop.

"Adashek," Farranger read out loud, feeling a touch of vindication. After hanging out on a limb all morning, it was good to be back on solid ground. He'd found a smoking gun in Adashek's hand.

The CEO peered over the SYSOP's shoulder to see the screen for himself. "It can't be," McClure muttered.

Kelly assumed his voice of reason. "All this proves is that someone using Adashek's ID set up the routing for this car."

"But everything fits—"

"A little too well, Farranger," Kelly said, refusing to give an inch of ground. "I think Casey is the one pointing the finger at Adashek. He's leaving a bogus trail of clues for you to follow, just like he did with the tags on the hopper."

"What makes you so sure Adashek isn't involved?" Farranger asked.

"Where's the motive? The last thing he'd want is anyone attacking his meal ticket."

"He's right." McClure pointed to the overhead screen, which was displaying the Bloomberg Financial News. A rolling stock ticker was giving real-time quotes beneath one of the talking heads. "As a company insider, Adashek has most of his net worth tied up in Transcon. Helping Casey destroy it would be financial suicide."

The Bloomberg screen supported McClure's argument. Transcon's stock had dropped nearly 50 percent in a week, and there was no end in sight. Insiders like Adashek and McClure, men with large equity stakes in the company, were being wiped out. Many of Transcon's customers were faring even worse.

The bleakest economic news was being shown on a graphic insert at the corner of the screen. The scarcity of rail-transported commodities had sent the Chicago Board of Options index skyrocketing to hundred-year highs, driving the price of raw materials above the cost of production. The resulting inflation was choking entire industries out of existence, taking tens of thousands of manufacturing jobs with them.

Farranger was no economist, but it was obvious that the country was on the verge of a complete financial breakdown. The only winners in the economic melee were a handful of bearish speculators who'd bet on a meltdown that no one could have foreseen.

No one except Casey, he thought.

He edged closer to the screen, focusing on the options index, which was ticking upward every few seconds. He'd seen it a dozen times in the COC, but now, for the first time, he noticed the significance of it. The answer had been right under his nose.

Adashek wasn't going down the drain with Transcon, he was using their misfortune to become rich.

Farranger looked up at Kelly. The agent wanted a motive. Now he had millions of them.

"Adashek is riding the CBO&E gravy train," Farranger said. "Just like Casey said."

"We've been through this, Farranger. There's no such railroad—"

"Casey wasn't talking about a railroad. He was talking about the Chicago Board of Options Exchange. The CBO&E." Farranger pointed to the commodities index on the Bloomberg screen.

Kelly stared briefly at the screen, then grinned at Farranger. "I take back half the bad things I've been thinking about you, Farranger."

End of the Line

"I think it's time we find out what Casey already knows," Farranger replied. "Mr. Kelly, do you have any friends at the Securities and Exchange Commission?"

- 28 -

Farranger stood over the SYSOP's shoulder, staring at a computer monitor displaying a detailed listing of shipping records for all the cars in Dallas Siding. According to the screen, all the loaded ammonium nitrate cars there had been dumped at a local fertilizer plant the day before Casey's arrival.

"Computers don't lie." The SYSOP pointed to the monitor as if to punctuate the statement.

"So you keep telling me," Farranger said dryly. The man had repeated the cliché four times in the last hour, and Farranger was growing weary of it.

He turned away to scan the upper level of the COC, keeping an eye out for Agent Kelly. He expected him to return any minute, and Farranger wanted to be in the CEO's office with McClure and Megan when Kelly presented his findings. He had little doubt that Kelly's trip to the SEC had produced a mountain of evidence linking Adashek to Casey Jones. Proving the Axeman's involvement would be a huge break, but it was less important to Farranger than solving the riddle that Casey had left for them: if the getaway hopper was empty, what had happened to the ammonium nitrate that was supposed to be inside?

"So much for your explosive hopper theory," the SYSOP went on. "If the cars were empty when he got there, Casey couldn't have rigged one as a bomb."

"But if all the hoppers were empty, then where did the nitrate in the diesel tanker come from?"

That was the million-dollar question, the one neither the SYSOP nor the computer could answer. All Farranger knew for sure was that Casey had billed his empty getaway hopper as a load of ammonium nitrate. Choosing that particular cargo might have been a random selection, but Farranger couldn't shake the idea that there had been more to it. He had the distinct feeling that they were missing eighty tons of ammonium nitrate, and that he was the only one looking for it.

"Do me a favor," he said, just as he spotted Kelly walking through the upper-level corridor surrounding the open COC floor like a horseshoe. "Get a hold of the plant manager and the train crew that works the siding. I want visual confirmation that each car was dumped."

"It's a waste of time," the SYSOP objected.

"You've got something better to do?"

When Farranger glanced up at the corridor again and saw that Kelly was approaching the CEO's office, he hurried across the COC floor, a more direct route to McClure's office. He was anxious to hear what the agent had discovered. He only hoped that Kelly's investigation had been more successful than his.

The CEO's executive suite was immense, a far cry from the storage locker that had been Farranger's office in San Bernardino. Meticulously decorated with Italian sculptures and original oil paintings, the room looked more like a museum exhibit than a work environment. The walls were adorned with tributes to the empire builders of the past: Cornelius Vanderbilt, Jay Gould, Cyrus K. Holiday, James J. Hill, and others who'd left their mark on an industry steeped in tradition. McClure stood atop them all, having built the greatest rail empire the nation had ever seen. He was a visionary, and Cal was certain his portrait would wind up similarly enshrined in some executive suite a hundred years hence.

A twelve-seat conference table stood in the center of the room, its four-foot width a no-man's-land between Transcon's CEO and union leader Megan Langford.

Cal walked the par three to the conference table and slipped into an open chair. He'd walked in on an intense strategy session. The topic of discussion wasn't Casey or Adashek, but the union's upcoming strike vote. From what he could gather, the two natural adversaries were in general agreement: both McClure and Megan wanted to avoid a crippling strike. But he knew their alliance was a fragile one, based less on mutual trust than on self-interest, and he had no doubt the uneasy truce wouldn't last once the crisis was over.

He had barely settled into his seat when Kelly burst into the room so briskly that he generated a small breeze. Waving a one-inch stack of documents over his head, he made a beeline for the conference table.

"I take it you found something." Farranger nodded toward the papers in Kelly's hand.

"Turns out Adashek was quite an active trader." Kelly lobbed the documents across the table to Farranger. "He's built up a sixty-million-dollar nest egg by trading options."

Farranger thumbed through the pile of papers in front of him, which contained faxed transaction records from Adashek's personal brokerage account. The sheer volume of trading activity was mind-boggling.

"But that doesn't mean he's connected to Casey," McClure argued. "In his day, Adashek was one of the most aggressive traders on Wall Street."

"He's gotten *real* aggressive in the last week," Kelly replied. "He's been trading for years, but ninety percent of his money was made *after* Casey Jones made his first appearance at Canyon Demonio."

Farranger had suspected as much. "According to this," he said, spotting a name he recognized on one of the more recent transactions, "Adashek took a highly leveraged option position on Consato only a few minutes before Casey derailed their train in Spokane. He made four million in one hour."

McClure shook his head in disbelief.

"There are at least two dozen other examples where Adashek managed to place a trade just a few minutes before disaster," Kelly added. "Together, Adashek and his wreck-happy partner are getting rich betting on long shots that are guaranteed to come in."

"But Adashek's already a wealthy man," McClure persisted. "Why risk everything to join forces with a psychopath?"

End of the Line

"He was vulnerable." Kelly pointed to the brokerage receipts Farranger was flipping through. "Based on what we've just found, it looks like he'd been engaged in illegal trading for almost a decade before Casey brought him into the big league. Over the years, he's shown a remarkable knack for making a profit off companies that fail."

Kelly had said nothing about blackmail, but the conclusion was written all over his face. Casey must have some kind of leverage over Adashek.

Farranger began studying the account transactions closer, looking for the fulcrum that Casey had wedged under the Axeman. He was looking for something specific and a lot closer to home. If he was right, he'd find the answer in his own backyard.

"But the SEC requires that company insiders file all transactions," McClure went on, still unwilling to accept what he was hearing. "If Adashek was trading Transcon stock, or any of our merger partners, he would've been found out instantly."

"He was smarter than that." Farranger pushed the papers across the table to McClure in disgust. "He didn't trade railroad stocks, he traded on our customers. Some of the companies on this list have been loyal customers of the California Western for years. When Adashek took over, the first thing he did was stop service to these industries. He drove them out of business by cutting off their rail access, then shorted their stock down to zero."

McClure slumped lower in his chair as he reviewed the transaction log. "Adashek's getting rich using my railroad to bankrupt shippers."

"So Casey stumbles on Adashek's game," Kelly theorized, "and threatens to expose him unless he pulls some strings at Transcon. Faced with thousands of counts of securities fraud, Adashek does the one thing he's trained for."

"He makes a deal," Megan guessed. "In addition to being the inside man, he provides the bankroll to fund Casey's stock tips. Together, they reap millions from Transcon's misery."

"Then they skip the country," Kelly finished. "Adashek booked a flight this morning from Chicago to Buenos Aires that leaves at midnight tomorrow. Lucky for us, he used a credit card. He doesn't think we're on to him."

203

"Why should he?" Farranger said. "He was interviewed by the FBI's lead investigator this morning, but the only topic of conversation was the question of when I'm going to be fired."

Kelly's face turned red, but he ignored the comment. "Anyway, he's also closed out his brokerage account. He wired thirty million to a Swiss account and another thirty million to a bank in the Caymans. He also withdrew a million in cash."

"An even split between Casey and Adashek," McClure said. "But why all the cash? A million dollars is a lot of pocket money to carry around."

"I'd say it's traveling expenses for Casey," Kelly explained. "Since Adashek doesn't know we're on to him, he can hop a plane any time he wants, but Casey doesn't have that luxury. Even if he managed to smuggle himself to Canada inside the hopper, he wouldn't be safe. He'd have to buy his way into a country that has no extradition treaty with the United States. I think that's what the cash is for. A million dollars cuts through a lot of red tape."

Though it sounded logical, Farranger just couldn't buy it. He'd met Casey, looked into his soulless eyes. Casey wasn't interested in building nest eggs for the future. He was a man mired in the past, obsessed with rewriting the original Casey Jones legend in Transcon's blood.

"So now we go after them?" Megan asked.

"We don't have to," Kelly replied. "We're in the enviable position of letting them come to us. We'll pick up Adashek at the airport, if not before."

"And Casey?"

"We'll let his getaway hopper travel on its planned route from Kansas City tonight, and we'll have men on the train waiting to arrest him when he tries to board. Any questions?"

"Just one." Farranger shifted in his seat, uneasy with Kelly's unbridled optimism. They were still a long way from catching Casey, but the agent was acting as though they already had him in handcuffs. "What happened to the eighty tons of ammonium nitrate that was supposed to be in Casey's getaway car?"

Kelly looked startled. For the first time all afternoon, he didn't have an answer ready. He apparently hadn't given the missing lading a second thought. "Well . . . it must have . . ."

End of the Line

McClure came to his rescue. "Casey had to bill the empty car as a load," he said matter-of-factly. "Otherwise, he'd run the risk of the car being filled with lading while he was still inside."

"But why go to all that trouble to hide the car, then turn around and leave a string of clues for us to follow?" Farranger asked. "I mean, he painted his name on the car, for Christ's sake."

"It fits with our psychological profile," Kelly replied. "Psychotics with delusions of grandeur often leave clues, either consciously or unconsciously. They want to get caught so everyone will see the extent of their accomplishments." Kelly paused, turning to face Farranger for the first time since the mention of his firing. "Sometimes, Farranger, the most obvious answer is the correct one. Sometimes the butler really did do it."

Farranger bristled, but had nothing concrete with which to refute the FBI agent's arguments. In the back of his mind, he still thought there was more to the hopper than met the eye. But before he could convince Kelly and the others, he'd need to gather facts—maybe even take a trip to Dallas Siding and poke around.

"We have nothing to lose, Farranger," Kelly went on. "Even if he doesn't show, the only thing we're out is man-hours. A small price to pay for a chance to end this once and for all."

"The price might be higher than you think. What if Casey discovers your stakeout and decides to target your train?"

"Then it's a good thing you'll be making sure nothing goes wrong by taking charge of the railroad side of this operation."

Kelly glanced at McClure, who nodded in agreement, then said, "Farranger will handle it personally."

"You make the travel arrangements, Farranger," Kelly continued. "I'll take care of Casey."

Farranger was chafing at the new assignment but held his tongue. Not only would it be an operational nightmare, it would consume what little time he had left to investigate on his own.

"It's settled then," Kelly declared. "You start making preparations. I'll take the first flight out and contact you later."

"Where are you going?" Farranger asked.

"Kansas City," the agent grinned. "I'm going to be on the train when the hopper leaves at midnight tonight. You don't think I'm going to let someone else make the collar, do you?"

When McClure and Megan chuckled, Farranger felt like the odd man out. The other railroaders shared none of his doubts; they were practically celebrating Casey's capture in advance.

"We don't want to get overly confident." McClure sobered as he turned to look squarely at Megan. "We still have one major threat facing Transcon's survival."

"The union meeting in Chicago tomorrow? And whether Jackson has enough votes to get a strike?"

McClure nodded solemnly. "If Jackson gets a strike, it's all over. Transcon will be out of business in a week, whether we catch Casey or not."

"Jackson probably has enough votes to get a strike now," Megan said. "But things might be different once they find out we're closing in on Casey—"

"They can't know anything," Kelly interrupted. "And neither can anyone else who isn't directly involved with our stakeout. If Casey catches wind we're on to him, he won't come within a hundred miles of the hopper."

Farranger realized that the precaution was a necessary one, but McClure had to be thoroughly frustrated. The one piece of potentially good news he'd gotten couldn't be shared with the group that needed to hear it the most.

Sure enough, McClure started to protest, but Kelly waved him off as he reached in his pocket to answer his cell phone, making it obvious that he cared little about the CEO's union problems.

"How about this, Ms. Langford," McClure finally said. "I'm going to be in Chicago tomorrow anyway for our annual meeting with the board of directors. Would it make a difference if I made a plea to the union in person?"

"I don't know," Megan said, then smiled. "But the brotherhood always appreciates a good groveling. You might make a difference if the vote is close."

Farranger was amazed at how quickly McClure and Megan had reverted back to their traditional roles. The war wasn't over yet, but the two reluctant allies were already planning the peace settlement. Farranger had little to add to their strategy session. The more they talked, the more invisible he became, fading into the background of a crisis they were assuming was all but wrapped up.

End of the Line

"I guess I'll get started on the train." Farranger stood up. The two railroaders barely broke their caucus to acknowledge his departure, and Kelly paid him even less attention. The deputy director was still on the phone, issuing orders to set up his part of the stakeout.

Farranger left feeling the same way he had before the crisis started—like a fifth wheel that had outlived its usefulness. His only remaining task was to set up the train for Kelly. Probably an exercise in futility, but one that would require enormous logistical planning. He'd have to organize the entire railroad around this one train.

He checked his watch, then picked up his pace, heading to the COC. The hopper was scheduled for a midnight departure from Kansas City, which meant a lot of preparation and little time to prepare. Kelly's men would have to ride on the engines or inside boxcars near the hopper. Both options were problematic because Casey had the hopper slated to run on a half-dozen different trains. The agents riding on the locomotives would have to detrain and board different engines each time the hopper was switched to a new train. But if Casey was watching the terminal, a dozen agents scurrying from one set of locomotives to another would be a dead giveaway. Farranger would have to find secluded spots a few miles before each terminal where the agents could detrain, then taxi them to the yard. When the hopper arrived, they'd already be hidden on a new set of locomotives as they exited the roundhouse.

Farranger figured the engine swap was doable, but if Kelly actually wanted his men riding inside freight cars he was probably out of luck. If all the trains were mixed freight, it would be easy to keep the surveillance cars married to the hopper as it was handed off from one train to another. But Casey's hopper was scheduled to run at least once on a unit train, where each car on the manifest was identical to the hopper. A stray boxcar would stick out like a sore thumb. Putting men inside a covered hopper wasn't even an option. The openings were too small for getting in and out of quickly. They would have to egress one at a time and be completely exposed in the process. And if Casey derailed the train, everyone inside would be dead.

There were other problems, each made worse by the short notice. The sidings for meeting other trains along the thousand miles of track would have to be selected in advance, or else the train might get too far ahead or too far behind Casey's itinerary and raise suspicion. Farranger would have to personally brief any of a hundred people who might handle the car to prevent it from being sidetracked. Because Casey was monitoring their radio communications, these conversations would have to take place in person or on the phone. One slipup over an open channel and the entire operation would be compromised.

When he considered all the problems they faced, Farranger could almost hear Casey laughing at him. Personally, Farranger thought there was little chance that Casey would show, but he was determined to set things up as best he could. After all, there was always the possibility that Kelly was right.

Farranger headed for the SYSOP's station. He still had unanswered questions, but they took a backseat to his primary duties. Besides, all he really had to go on were vague doubts, a few inconsistencies, and some minor details that didn't quite fall into place.

That, and the overwhelming sense that they were playing right into Casey's hands.

-29-

The predawn sky hadn't done anything to change Dallas Siding's flat, barren, unremarkable stretch of railroad surrounded by even less remarkable scenery. Barbed wire cordoned off the right-of-way, keeping a handful of grazing longhorns from straying across the tracks. It looked like any of a thousand other sidings Farranger had seen, the only difference being that this siding was now a crime scene.

Its only standing structure was the silver signal shanty in which he'd found Dumars's impaled body. Farranger had seen some brutal things in his career but none more horrifying than the sight of the crucified agent. He could still see it—the blood, the spiked limbs, the agent's pale and contorted face. Looking at that shack again brought those unsettling memories back into vivid focus, a chilling reminder of why he hadn't wanted to come back.

But he'd had to. He still had a lot of questions about the hopper, and the answers that Kelly was spouting just didn't jibe with his instincts. He'd tried all night to ignore the nagging intuition, immersing himself in the thousand details required to set up Kelly's rolling stakeout. But the agent's train had departed Kansas City at midnight, taking with it the last of Farranger's remaining tasks, and leaving him with only his doubts.

He looked around the empty siding. The tanker truck had been removed, but its tracks were still visible, cutting parallel trenches into the ballast eight feet from the outside rail. He crouched down near the tracks and carefully sifted through the crushed rock. Studying the scene through the eyes of an investigator, he could understand how Kelly had reconstructed the events of four days ago. But Farranger wasn't an investigator, he was a railroader.

And through the eyes of a railroader, the pristine white ballast said Kelly's explanation didn't wash.

When a car horn sounded, Farranger looked up to see a Geo Metro speeding along the roadbed, throwing a hail of gravel in its wake. He smiled to himself and shook his head as Megan barreled over the road crossing doing at least 40 mph, then stopped on a dime just a few feet in front of him. Thankfully, she didn't work as an engineer. No telling what she'd do with a few thousand horsepower at her disposal.

"They told me you were out here looking for something," she said as she stepped out of the car. "But I told them you had more sense." She looked around the nearly vacant murder scene. "Find what you're looking for? A second gunman in the grassy knoll?"

"A second hopper maybe."

Megan frowned, annoyed by Farranger's single-minded focus on railroading. Her flight to Chicago was leaving in less than an hour, and she'd come to say good-bye. Maybe more. The last thing she wanted to talk about was hoppers.

"Look at this." Farranger pointed to the area between the rail and the tire tracks. "Here's where Casey supposedly transferred ammonium nitrate from one of the hoppers to the diesel tanker."

"Casey *did* move the ammonium nitrate." Megan was getting even more irritable. Farranger was couching an undeniable fact as hypothetical. The FBI had found traces of ammonium nitrate inside the truck. There couldn't possibly be any doubt about how it got there.

"A neat trick," Farranger went on, "moving all that nitrate without spilling any."

Megan looked down at the dusty white ballast. The black granules of ammonium nitrate should have stood out like a sore thumb, but there was no interruption in the sea of white. She certainly didn't have any explanation, but she was almost afraid to hear Farranger's. "Then how did the nitrate get in the truck?"

"You can get ammonium nitrate at any farm supply store. I think Casey seeded the tanker to make it look like he was planning a mobile truck bomb."

"He *was* planning a truck bomb," Megan corrected. "All you've managed to prove is that he cleaned up after himself."

End of the Line

"Well, he didn't do a very good job. He left a tanker truck and a dead special agent behind. Then he signed his name on a tagless car to make sure the hopper would be easy to find."

"You think finding that car was easy? One unmarked hopper in a million?" Megan was incredulous. "We were incredibly lucky to find it as soon as we did. It could've taken weeks."

"Only because you made it hard," Farranger snapped, immediately regretting it. Keeping the information about the hopper to herself hadn't been Megan's finest hour, but he shouldn't have thrown it back in her face. More than anyone else, he needed Megan Langford to believe him.

"Casey couldn't count on your silence, Megan," he said, his tone softening. "He had to assume we'd act as soon as we found out the car was missing in the computer."

Megan had defied her own union by bringing Farranger the hopper, the one clue that might ultimately lead to Casey's capture, but she knew Farranger was right. If she'd revealed the information at once, they would have tracked down the car in a few minutes instead of a few days.

"Okay, let's say it was a setup, and Kelly's out chasing some elaborate decoy," she conceded. "Where does that leave us?"

"With eighty tons of ammonium nitrate we can't account for. Casey's so-called getaway car was empty. What happened to the ammonium nitrate that was supposed to be inside?"

"It never existed," she said, exasperated. "Casey billed the hopper as a load so we wouldn't fill the car while he was riding inside."

"But why nitrates? If he was going to make something up, why not make the lading plastic pellets or grain, something less suspicious? Why pick the one type of freight that would be sure to draw attention to the hopper?"

"You're the one who said Casey wanted us to find the car."

"He wanted us to find a decoy. I think the ammonium nitrate is still out there somewhere."

"A second hopper?" Megan asked, skeptical. "There was one car missing in the computer and we found it. There's no way Casey could've altered another record without us knowing about it."

"Maybe he figured out a way around the computer."

"There is no way around the computer." Megan could tell from Farranger's expression that he didn't share her confidence in Transcon's mainframe. But she was utterly certain. Planting a decoy was one thing, but hiding a second car simply wasn't possible. There was no way to fool the computer without leaving a trail. If there was another car, they'd know about it. She glanced at the empty siding track. "Did you check out the other cars in the siding?"

"Yes," Farranger admitted. "Every load of ammonium nitrate was dumped at a fertilizer plant the day before Casey arrived. The plant manager and the train crew saw the cars being emptied with their own eyes."

"So even if Casey managed to trick the computer and hide a second car, it wouldn't have done him any good," Megan concluded, as if she'd won the debate. "The nitrate he needed would've already been part of somebody's lawn by the time he arrived at the siding."

Farranger had anticipated her response, but couldn't argue with her logic. She'd pinpointed the one problem he couldn't get around. Casey couldn't make a bomb out of an empty hopper. Still, Farranger was convinced that Casey had somehow managed the impossible. The whole point of creating a decoy was to draw attention away from something else. And he was certain that something else was the eighty tons of missing ammonium nitrate.

"Please believe me, Megan," he pleaded. "There *is* another car out there somewhere. I can feel it."

"You have anything to back up that feeling?"

Farranger shook his head. All he had was speculation and conjecture. He was grasping at straws, and they both knew it.

A series of short and long blasts from a locomotive horn turned their attention to an underpowered freight train that was signaling its intent to enter the siding.

"I can't get caught on the wrong side of this dog." Megan checked her watch, a visible confirmation that her time had value and Farranger's allotment was running out.

"I guess this is good-bye, Farranger." Megan gave a friendly salute, but her voice added a tone of finality to their parting. She began walking toward her car without waiting for a response.

End of the Line

Megan stepped inside her Geo without looking back. She revved the three-cylinder engine until it redlined, then popped the clutch for a ballast-spitting start that sent the compact car fishtailing over the right-of-way. She beat the train to the road crossing, passing under the warning gates just as they began to lower.

Farranger watched her car disappear behind the oncoming train, finally turning away when the train crew signaled him with another series of blasts on the locomotive's horn. They were asking him to man the siding switch, a standard request designed to save the crew some shoe leather. If the conductor dropped off at the switch, he'd have to wait for the entire sixty-car freight train to roll into the siding before he could line it for straight track movement. If Farranger lined the switch, he could save the conductor a mile walk back to the head end.

He double-timed to the siding switch as the engines pulled within half a train-length of the turnout, grabbed his key ring, then shoved the brass fitting into the lock that protected the siding switch. He turned the key, but the latch didn't spring. After a frustrating half minute of trying, he finally gave up and pulled out the key.

Then he saw the problem. In his rush to beat the train to the switch, he'd tried to open the Transcon lock with the California Western key that he'd saved as a keepsake. He must be getting old. He'd made the same bonehead move at Baker Siding and nearly killed a crew because he was overly nostalgic for his old railroad. He quickly inserted the right key, and the lock opened easily. Waving the conductor forward, he lined the switch for siding movement, then backed away from the rail as the train entered the turnout.

As it rolled past, Farranger compared the two brass keys. They were remarkably close in size and shape, and the cut of their teeth was similar. Aside from the railroad name engraved on the handle, he could scarcely tell them apart.

He took the California Western key off his ring. It was useless now, a relic from a forgotten railroad. He tossed it between the rails, the trainman's common repository for all railroad trash. The gesture seemed symbolic to him, though, the formal shedding of his last tie to a dead railroad.

He walked away from the switch, determined to leave the key and the California Western behind him. He refused to end up like Casey, clinging to the past, waiting for some resurrection of the good old days that would never come.

But then Farranger stopped suddenly, realizing that it was Casey's allegiance to the past that had betrayed him. Farranger's old railroad ways had caused him to make a rookie's error, one so obvious that he'd completely overlooked it until now. Casey had made the same mistake in Spokane, but with one crucial difference.

Casey had taken his mistake with him.

-30-

Farranger kept his eyes on the rear wall of the COC as he walked toward the SYSOP's station. All seven screens were linked, each displaying a portion of Transcon's massive coast-to-coast rail system. The computer-generated track chart was showing a spiderweb of black lines, with Kelly's intended route from Kansas City to Winnipeg highlighted in green. A locomotive icon tracked his current position in real time, automatically updating each time the train passed a trackside detector.

The display told Farranger little he didn't already know. He'd received a phone update only twenty minutes ago, while he was still at Dallas Siding. The SYSOP's report had been routine, but the task Farranger had assigned him in return wasn't. He'd sent the entire COC crew on a scavenger hunt, one that might actually tell them something about the elusive Mr. Jones.

"So far, no Casey," the SYSOP said, seeing Farranger. "Next stop is Chicago at 5:00 P.M."

Farranger nodded, turning his attention to a stack of weathered timetables lying on the SYSOP's workstation. "Did you find the hardware I asked for?" he said as he leafed through the pile of manuals, then scanned the workstation for the missing items.

"We took up a collection from the senior dispatchers." The SYSOP opened a desk drawer to reveal a switch lock and a dozen brass keys. "Managed to scrounge up everything you wanted."

Farranger scooped up the keys, taking a quick inventory to ensure that each of Transcon's former railroads was represented. He removed the California Western key from the group, then culled out seven others that were either too large or too small to fit the lock. He inserted the first of the remaining four keys into the lock and turned, but the key was too small to spring the mechanism.

"Why the sudden interest in switch keys?"

"When Casey derailed the Consato train at Spokane," Farranger explained as he inserted the second key, "he tore off a switch lock at the siding."

"Must not have had a key," the SYSOP offered, though his interest seemed to wane when the second key failed to spring the lock.

"I think he did have a key." Farranger gestured toward the collection in front of him. "Just not the right one."

"So you figure Casey's a railroader. And if he worked on one of the old lines, his key wouldn't work in the new locks." When Farranger tried the third key, which was too wide for the lock's narrow keyhole, the SYSOP went on. "Only problem is, you haven't narrowed it down any. He could be from any of the former lines. None of these keys work."

"I'm not looking for a key that works," Farranger said as he grabbed the final key, one emblazoned with the logo of the Chicago and Memphis Railroad. "I'm looking for one that explains why Casey had to take a broken switch lock from an accident site."

"Souvenir?" the SYSOP suggested. "Can't think of any other reason to take a busted switch lock."

"I think he had a very good reason." Farranger took a deep breath, then inserted the C&M key. He jiggled the brass fitting inside the lock for a few seconds, then tried to remove it. But unlike the others, the C&M key wouldn't budge.

"Sorry," the SYSOP said.

"Don't be." Farranger flashed the man a victorious smile, then tossed him the frozen mechanism. "Casey just gave us his address."

"I don't get it."

"He couldn't leave the lock behind if his key was stuck inside. It'd be like leaving a calling card from his former railroad."

The SYSOP let loose a low whistle, shaking his head as he studied the C&M logo stamped on the brass handle. "So Casey is off the old C&M."

"You don't sound surprised."

End of the Line

"I guess I'm not. The C&M was Transcon's first takeover and by far the most brutal."

"They were all brutal." Farranger recalled his own experience on the California Western.

"Not like this one. The boys on the C&M were rough customers, a clannish bunch with an almost fanatic devotion to their railroad. The C&M used every dirty trick in the book to fight the takeover. From what I heard, some of Transcon's accidents around that time weren't exactly accidents, if you know what I mean. It was like David versus Goliath."

The SYSOP picked up the C&M timetable from the stack, flipped through it until he found a map of the rail network, then handed it to Farranger. "Except this David didn't even have a sling. The C&M was a two-bit regional carrier. They were no match for Transcon. Needless to say, Adashek was pissed. He fired damn near everybody. Sacked every member of the management team, then did his best to blackball them in the industry. Nobody would touch an ex-C&M guy for fear of pissing off Transcon. They became pariahs over night, unable to get a job doing the one thing they were trained for."

Farranger was studying the C&M map as he listened. The trackage was every bit as modest as the California Western. A single main line left Chicago, then branched out to serve gulf-coast ports in Texas and Louisiana. By any measure, the C&M had been a minor-league player in an industry dominated by giants. But at the same time, this small railroad had produced one very large problem.

Farranger closed the timetable and glanced at the front cover, which listed the former C&M's senior operating team. The name of the Chicago superintendent, Keith Jones, leapt off the page.

"Keith Jones," he read out loud triumphantly. "It's got to be him. What do you bet his middle name begins with a *C?* K. C. Jones."

The SYSOP studied the timetable. "Well, Keith Jones certainly was crazy enough to be our man. He used to run the C&M's Chicago operation. I guess you could say he was the leader of the resistance. Whenever the C&M boys were up to no good, you could bet Jones was behind it. Talk was, he used to derail trains on other railroads so he'd have the best safety record in town.

They never proved anything, but there wasn't a trainman in Chicago whose sphincter didn't pucker when they heard his name. Problem is, he's been dead for seven years."

Farranger's hopes deflated as quickly as they'd risen.

"Jones was number one on Adashek's hit list," the SYSOP went on. "The Axeman flew to Chicago just so he could fire him personally. He had the special agents escort him off his own railroad, like he was some kind of criminal, which I guess he was. Needless to say, Jones couldn't handle the humiliation. He took a header in front of a train the week after Adashek gave him the ax. I remember seeing the picture in the *Sun Times*. Not pretty."

"Know anyone else on the C&M who'd want to carry on the fight for their leader?"

"I didn't *know* any of them. Only knew Jones by reputation. I worked yardmaster on the Santa Fe in Chicago, and the C&M guys used to come into our yard for interchange. They talked about Jones like he was God, but I doubt he had much of a following. I always sensed more fear than respect, like they were afraid of what might happen if they said anything bad about him. People who got on Jones's bad side seemed to wind up under the wheels of a train."

The description sounded too much like Casey for Farranger to believe it was a coincidence. He paged through the C&M timetable, practically tearing the pages apart until he found a photo gallery of the railroad's management team. A shudder ran through him when he found Keith Jones's picture.

The face belonged to Casey. Printed below was the man's full name: Keith Christian Jones.

Farranger placed the timetable in front of the SYSOP, a finger on the photograph. "He was very much alive when I saw him two days ago."

The SYSOP stared at the picture, incredulous. "But why would he fake his own death?"

"You said it yourself. He'd be a prime suspect if anyone thought he was alive. So he uses a little misdirection and pulls off the ultimate disappearing act."

"Misdirection?" The SYSOP looked skeptical.

End of the Line

"In one hand, he shows us what we want to see," Farranger explained, noting a pattern in Casey's ruses, "then hides what he doesn't want us to see in the other."

"Like putting a bloody corpse on the rails, so we don't go looking for the real Keith Jones."

"He pulled the same kind of shell game on me," Farranger said, remembering the trick that had led him to the Zypher. "He left a bright trail of AEI tags for me to follow to Washington, while the car I was really looking for was halfway across the country."

Casey had also used the same kind of trick at Dallas Siding, Farranger realized. He'd blinded them with misdirection, shining so much light on the getaway hopper that they hadn't bothered to look beyond the obvious.

"Ever hear the story of the drunk who lost his wallet in the alley but looked for it in the street because the light was better?" he asked.

"What the hell does that mean?"

"It means we need to start looking in the shadows." Farranger was sure the missing nitrate was where it had always been, inside one of the other hoppers that had been at the siding. "Let's see if we can't find a second hopper. Pull up a car list on Dallas Siding from four days ago."

"What for? Every car in that siding was accounted for. All the loads that came in were dumped at the fertilizer plant."

"Humor me. I'm playing a hunch."

A few keystrokes later, the computer screen was filled with information.

"Fifty cars," the SYSOP reported. "Twenty of them were loads of ammonium nitrate, the same number the crew said they took to the fertilizer plant."

"Now pull up the billing records for the shipper. Let's see how many cars we charged them for."

"I'd say we billed them for twenty."

"And I'm betting we didn't."

The SYSOP turned back to his computer and typed in a billing query. The answer came back a moment later; the plant had only been billed for nineteen cars.

"I don't understand." The SYSOP stared at the screen. "If they took twenty cars to the plant, how come we only charged them for nineteen?"

"Because we only bill for the freight we deliver," Farranger replied. "The crew dumped all the loads, but one of the cars they took from the siding was already empty."

"But they all showed as loads in the computer. Casey only altered one car record, the hopper on Kelly's train. He couldn't have made another change in the computer without us knowing about it."

"The change wasn't in the computer. Casey wasn't trying to fool Transcon's infallible machine, just the people who use it."

"I don't follow."

"Suppose Casey sets his sights on two hoppers, one loaded with ammonium nitrate, the other empty. Long before they arrive in Dallas, he swaps their serial numbers and AEI tags so each hopper assumes the other's identity in the computer. The hoppers arrive at Dallas Siding along with fifty other cars. A local crew takes the loaded cars, dumps them at the fertilizer plant, then returns the empties to the siding. Except they didn't dump all the loads, because Casey's car showed as an empty on the computer. It stayed in the siding, fully loaded, waiting for Casey to arrive."

"But wouldn't that mean the crew would've tried to dump an empty car at the plant?" the SYSOP argued.

"You were a yardmaster. You know the railroad diverts loads all the time, rerouting routine shipments to priority customers that are critically short of the same material. The crew wouldn't have given it a second thought."

The SYSOP nodded, but still didn't look entirely convinced. They both knew, though, that it was the way the railroad worked. And so did Casey. The borrow-from-Peter-to-pay-Paul strategy was so common it drew little attention from switch crews that often wound up with empty cars.

"So Casey arrives at the siding," Farranger continued, thinking out loud, "and fills the loaded nitrate car with diesel to create an eighty-ton bomb. The car leaves the siding, traveling on the legitimate billing of the empty car. He didn't have to alter anything in the computer."

"And the empty?"

End of the Line

"He removes the tags, gives it a phony car number, then fills the inside with groceries to make it look like his getaway car. Just in case we don't spot the hopper at the mandatory thousand-mile inspection, he makes sure the computer alerts us that he's removed a single car from our inventory."

"But why alert us at all?" the SYSOP asked. "If he left the billing alone, the car would travel on the intended route of the loaded car, and we'd be none the wiser."

"Because he wanted us to find his getaway car. It's a decoy to tie up all our resources on a wild-goose chase. Kelly has his entire task force either riding the train or watching fifteen hundred miles of track. They're staking out the one route that Casey has personally selected for their search, looking in exactly the wrong place—because 'the light is better.' In the meantime, no one's looking for the real hopper, and Casey's free to roam the rest of the system."

"Sounds like guesswork to me. An interesting theory, but you're going to need a helluva lot more evidence to convince Kelly his whole operation is a waste of time."

Farranger knew the SYSOP was right. Kelly dealt exclusively with facts, so Farranger needed something concrete to prove his case. He needed to find the missing car.

But four days had passed since the cars had left the siding. Even if he was right, Casey almost certainly would have covered his tracks by swapping the car number on the hopper again, changing identities with any of a thousand cars at any of a hundred locations down the line. It was a daisy chain with a million permutations, none of which would show in the computer. The only way to find the car was to search every hopper on the system, exactly the same problem they had faced when they first started.

"Maybe we can't track the car," Farranger said, moving to a more productive line of reasoning. "But we might be able to find the destination."

He studied the system map for a likely target, but Casey hadn't left him much to work with. Damaged track, indicated by red lines on the schematic, already outnumbered the intact routes by a wide margin. The once mighty network was in shambles, reduced to a patchwork of out-of-service lines and detour routes.

"Don't bother looking for a travel radius," the SYSOP said. "A car from Dallas Siding could have reached any spot in the country by now, assuming it wasn't on one of the lines Casey took out."

His words drove home the one assumption they could make. Casey was a psychopath, but he was also a shipper who needed the hopper to reach its intended destination. He couldn't risk derailing his own car in the minefield he'd created. He needed at least one safe route to move the hopper.

"Delete all the routes out of Dallas Siding that have been sabotaged," Farranger said. "Casey had to leave himself a back door, one that only he knew about."

The SYSOP nodded and began manually deleting the rail lines that had fallen victim to Casey's attacks.

One red line after another disappeared from the rail-network schematic on the screen. When the SYSOP finished, the only remaining line connected to Dallas was the Texas branch of the former C&M railroad. The unmolested track stopped abruptly at Chicago, considerably short of the Canadian destination that marked the end of Casey's supposed escape route. Farranger was sure it was the end of the line, in more ways than one.

"Overlay the route of Kelly's train," he said.

The SYSOP complied, plotting the intended route. Kelly's train stayed on C&M's trackage until the scheduled arrival in Chicago at 5:00 P.M., then veered off to the northwest on Transcon's other lines. Farranger mentally erased the second half of Kelly's route, certain the train was never intended to leave Chicago. The getaway car wasn't just a red herring, it was a trap.

And if he was right, Kelly wasn't the only target.

"The union meeting in Chicago," he said, keeping his eyes on the screen. "What time is it scheduled to start?"

"McClure said the reception starts at five o'clock."

The timing couldn't be a coincidence. Kelly, McClure, and the union would all be in Chicago at the same time, allowing Casey to get them all in one bold stroke. And Adashek would be there, too. Given the Axeman's brutal treatment of Keith Jones, Farranger figured Adashek was overdue for a double-cross. For Casey, this wasn't about money, it was about revenge. Casey had to be planning to use his grand finale to terminate his partnership with Adashek.

End of the Line

"We need to get Kelly on the horn now," he said.

"He doesn't want to break radio silence."

"Casey left a clear path for the hopper to Chicago." Farranger pointed to the conspicuously intact C&M branch line. "Kelly's train is going to arrive there at five o'clock, which just happens to be the same time the union meeting is scheduled to start. Casey's going to get them both at the same time."

The SYSOP looked unconvinced but handed Farranger a headset.

"Farranger to Kelly. Over." Farranger heard his transmission go out in a scrambled time delay.

"Kind of busy right now, Farranger. I'm waiting for your boy to show up."

"He's not coming," Farranger replied. "It's a trap. Casey has another hopper, and he's going to detonate it when your train reaches Chicago."

"Another car? What the hell are you talking about?"

"I think it's in Chicago right now." Farranger wished he could be more definite. "Or it will be at five o'clock."

"You think!" Kelly shouted. "So you don't even know if there is a car?"

"I know the target. Everything points to Chicago. We have to abort your train and evacuate the right-of-way in the city."

"We're not aborting anything," Kelly said. "And you're not going to do anything on the right-of-way that would tip Casey off that we're waiting for him. I'm glad you have a hobby, Farranger, but I'm perfectly capable of handling this operation without your help. I've got half the bureau watching this train. I couldn't be in better hands."

"Listen to what I'm telling you. He's going to get everyone at once: your train, the union, McClure, even Adashek. You'll all be in Chicago at the same time."

"Why would Casey grease his own partner? He's the one with the keys to the money boxes."

"It's not about money. Casey wants revenge on Adashek for destroying his railroad. He's playing him like everyone else."

"Adashek's not being played, and neither am I. The union meeting is somewhere downtown, miles away from where this train will be. Unless this magic car of yours has a nuclear bomb inside, he couldn't get all of us even if he wanted to."

Kelly had a point. A single hopper wouldn't be powerful enough to accomplish Casey's mission. Maybe, Farranger thought, the hopper was only part of Casey's grand finale.

"We might be dealing with more than just the hopper," he said. "He could explode the car next to a chemical plant, or on a track filled with poison-gas cars. There's no telling what the kill radius might be."

"Are you just making this shit up as you go along?" Kelly snapped. "Listen, Farranger. As of this moment, this train is our best chance to catch the bad guy. If you can't prove otherwise, this conversation is over."

"I have a positive ID on our man," Farranger said, trying to convince Kelly to listen. "He's a Chicago railroader named Keith Christian Jones."

The brief silence that followed renewed Farranger's confidence. But both were shattered a second later.

"I'll give him your regards when he's in custody. Kelly out."

"He's off-line." The SYSOP tried the call button several times without success. "He's shut off his receiver."

"He didn't believe me," Farranger sighed.

"I'm not sure *I* believe you," the SYSOP said. "What the hell did you expect—that the FBI would abort a major operation on a hunch, blow their only chance to catch Casey? All because a car that may or may not exist is hidden somewhere in a hundred square miles of the most dense trackage in the world?"

"It exists," Farranger insisted. "And we have to find it before five o'clock."

"Fat chance. Chicago has more track than most countries. If the car does exist, it would take a battalion of men a week to find it."

The SYSOP was right. Chicago wasn't some rinky-dink operation like San Bernardino. There were thousands of miles of tracks that connected as many industries. The chances of finding a single hopper among the tens of thousands of other cars in Chicago was exactly zero.

End of the Line

"Then we have to get our people out." Farranger checked his watch: 9:00 A.M. "The union reps will start checking into the Swan Hotel this morning, if they haven't already. We need to warn them that they're a target."

"While we're at it, why don't we evacuate eight million people from Chicago and start a real panic," the SYSOP grunted, then looked up at Farranger and softened his tone. "Sorry, Farranger, but McClure doesn't want anyone at Transcon interfering with the union meeting, and that includes you. Besides, I know Jackson, and he'd never believe you. It would look like a management trick to disrupt their meeting."

Farranger knew Jackson, too, and he had to agree. If he couldn't convince Kelly or the SYSOP, there was little chance Jackson would believe him. He was on his own. There was only one person who might believe him. And she was a target, too.

"I'm going to Chicago," he said.

"I told you," the SYSOP sighed, "even if there is a bomb out there, you'll never find it."

"I'm not going there to look for the car. I'm going to get Megan Langford out."

-31-

Chicago was a short flight away from DFW. Aside from his steel-toed boots setting off the metal detector, the trip had been uneventful. Farranger made O'Hare by noon and the Swan Hotel by twelve thirty.

The lobby of the Swan Hotel, only a half-mile stagger from Chicago's famed Union Station, was packed when Farranger arrived. Hundreds of union representatives, anxious to make the most of their trip to the big city, had already begun a drinking binge that would go on for two days.

The union's collective bender had started long before their arrival in the Windy City. Since local representatives could travel for free with their rail passes, labor leaders from all over the country had made the annual pilgrimage by train, letting Amtrak serve as their designated driver. The free ride left them extra pocket money for important things like beer and hookers, both of which were in abundant supply.

Farranger tried to find a familiar face in the sea of drunks, making a token search for McClure. He didn't expect to see him, though. The drunken revelry was a bit lowbrow for the CEO, who would probably delay his appearance until the formal reception. Farranger didn't see Megan either.

He spotted Jackson instead.

Ever the consummate politician, Jackson was flashing his sincerest smile as he made a circle around the lobby, leaving a trail of rhetoric and backslapping in his wake. Watching the union president work the crowd, Farranger knew it would be nearly impossible to convince him to evacuate the hotel. This was Jackson's show, and he'd never leave before the final curtain.

End of the Line

Farranger made brief eye contact with him, then caught a glimpse of Megan. She was standing apart from the crowd with her arms crossed—an unmistakable message to the drunken conventioneers that she wasn't to be mistaken for one of the girls on duty.

"Megan," he called out, pushing his way toward her.

"Cal?" Megan's eyes widened in surprise.

"We have to get everyone out of here." Farranger grabbed her by the shoulders and pulled her toward him. "There *is* a second hopper, and I think Casey's going to detonate it somewhere in Chicago at 5:00 P.M."

"Cal, we've been through this," she sighed. "The computer—"

"He didn't make the switch in the computer. He swapped the numbers on the cars themselves, a loaded hopper for an empty one. The crew never dumped the loaded one at the plant because it was billed as an empty car."

Megan had to admit that it was possible Casey had tricked them. That didn't mean the car existed. But if it did, Transcon's massive Chicago operation would be the perfect target.

"So where's this phantom car now?" she asked, trying to hide her growing concern.

"Somewhere in Chicago. I . . . don't know exactly where."

"There's about a million miles of track in this town." Megan pulled the color brochure out of her jacket pocket that had been sent out to direct union representatives to the Swan. She turned to the back, which showed a detailed map of all the significant railroad facilities in the Chicago area, then handed it to Farranger. "If this car really does exist, how do you propose we find it?"

"We don't."

Before she could respond, Jackson's voice bellowed sarcasm from behind them. "There he is, boys. The man Transcon sent to protect us."

Farranger turned to face him. As if on cue, the crowd went silent, the rowdy group turning in unison to hear their national leader speak.

"Can he protect us?" Jackson shouted.

Kem Parton

A handful of disciples and loyal supporters vocalized their approval with various anti-Transcon slogans that merged into white noise.

"Look, I'm not trying to start any trouble, but you have to get your people out of here," Farranger said to Jackson. "You're all in danger."

"Danger!" Jackson laughed. "You hear that? Transcon's trying to scare us off. Are we afraid?"

The crowd grew louder, their voices unified in a resounding "No!"

"Listen to me," Farranger pleaded, lowering his voice so that only Jackson could hear him. "I came here to warn you, not to scare you off."

"Warn us about what? Calling a strike that will force Transcon to return everything they've stolen from us?"

"I don't care about your politics. Casey's rigged an eighty-ton hopper filled with explosive—"

"A hopper?" Jackson said, smirking. "The nearest tracks are half a mile away at Union Station. Last time I checked, Metro doesn't use hoppers in passenger service. Besides, Mr. Casey Jones wouldn't hit us." Jackson made a sweeping gesture toward the delegates in the lobby. "Who else is going to vote for the strike he so desperately wants?"

Jackson's flip attitude told Farranger there was more to the prediction than braggadocio. He was acting too sure of himself, too unconcerned for his own personal safety. He knew something, and Farranger had a pretty good idea what it was.

"You used to work on the old C&M, didn't you?" he asked, the accusation evident in his tone.

"Bravo, Farranger! I'll bet you're going to ask me next if I knew a superintendent named Keith Jones who's a lot less dead than people think."

"You knew it was Jones, but you stood by and did nothing while he killed your people?" Farranger was dumbfounded.

"I didn't *know* anything." Jackson suddenly looked nervous, as if he'd just realized that his candor might have cost him the support of the few sober delegates nearby. "But I can't say I'm surprised, not after what Transcon did to him. And as far as not protecting my people, nothing could be further from the truth.

I'm the only one who's doing anything at all. Once the strike vote is taken, I'm going to send them back home, where it's safe."

"If they live long enough to cast their ballots," Farranger said. "If you knew Jones, then you know what he's capable of."

"Which is precisely why I know I'm not a target. Keith Jones always took care of his own. Haven't you noticed that he's never touched anyone or anything connected to the former Chicago and Memphis Railroad?"

Farranger had noticed, which was how he'd been able to trace the hopper to Chicago. But he didn't share Jackson's faith that Casey would continue to abide by some self-imposed limits. "You're willing to gamble the lives of everyone in this hotel on his soft spot?"

"The gamble would be to leave the sanctuary of this hotel," Jackson countered. "Jones might well be planning some kind of demonstration to convince our membership that a strike is their only protection. But if that does occur, I assure you we're not the target. We're the target audience."

Farranger was stunned by Jackson's Machiavellian logic. Far from being afraid of Casey Jones, Jackson was actually rooting for him. "You're putting your trust in a psycho. Someone who derails trains and kills crews for fun."

"Only on other railroads. Did the same thing back when he was a superintendent. Took care of his own. That way, the C&M became the best by default. He always bragged that his yard at Lanham was the safest place in town."

The safest place. Casey's warning about the hopper's location came full circle in an instant. One glance at Megan, and Farranger could see that she'd just made the same connection.

The car was at Lanham Yard.

Casey's safest place.

"We can be there in twenty minutes." Megan looked Farranger directly in the eyes, making it clear that she was including herself in the hunt.

Farranger took the hint. He grabbed her around the shoulders and started through the crowd, brushing past Jackson without another word.

"If you leave now," Jackson called after Megan, "you'll no longer have a place in this organization. I'll see to it myself."

Megan didn't acknowledge the threat. Jackson had the power to ruin her, she knew, and he was more than willing to use it. An entire career of fighting to earn the respect of the membership would be lost overnight. And it wouldn't end if she left office and returned to the craft. Jackson's cronies would still make her life a living hell. She'd be hazed out of the industry.

Yet despite all the reasons not to side with Farranger, she didn't even break stride.

Farranger drove across a narrow signal bridge, slowing his Ford Taurus rental as he caught his first glimpse of Lanham Yard three miles away. The facility was enormous, at least a hundred tracks and thousands of cars. The two main lines passing beneath the bridge cut the yard exactly in half. Even if he and Megan split up, it would take a good five hours to scour the mammoth installation. Time they didn't have. The hopper's 5:00 P.M. detonation was due in less than three hours. If they didn't find the car by then, it would find them.

Three miles of urban sprawl preceded the south entrance of the yard. A caravan of commercial trucks and dilapidated factory buildings lined the street, momentarily obscuring the tracks from view. When Farranger and Megan finally reached one of the gated yard entrances, they were greeted by a propaganda billboard: WELCOME TO LANHAM . . . THE SAFEST PLACE TO RAILROAD IN CHICAGO.

"I don't have a good feeling about this," she said, reading the sign.

"Neither do I. But we've got to find the car. We're the only ones still looking."

"What if Casey's watching us and decides to blow it up?"

Farranger looked around at the decrepit brick factories and abandoned warehouses surrounding the facility. "The yard's pretty isolated. If Casey's going to detonate the hopper, better to do it here, where nobody gets hurt."

"Yeah," Megan replied. "Nobody but us."

- 32 -

Casey hobbled alongside track 411, inspecting the train that would bring him immortality. The lading was nearly perfect, custom-built per his specifications. All but seven of the forty cars were tanks loaded with liquefied natural gas. The others were a harmless mixture of empty flats and intermodal container wells. He hated having any nonexplosive cars on his train, but he refused to let a few spoilsports detract from the beauty of his ultimate killing machine. He already had enough explosive power to level ten city blocks. Anything more would just be showing off.

He accelerated his inspection, stopping only to uncouple the air hoses between each car. An intact air line had been his undoing at Cajon Pass, and he wasn't about to make the same mistake twice. A continuous process of improvement was the cornerstone of quality, he reminded himself. Besides, you never knew when some smart-ass with a shotgun might come along and ruin another perfectly good derailment.

He stopped beside the car coupled to the engine at the north end of the track, admiring the Rambler's graffiti on the hull. Even though the artwork was amateurish, it evoked a profound emotional response, rekindling memories of Agent Dumars's execution. The pleasure was so intense that it nearly brought him to tears.

But it was unbecoming for a legend to become misty-eyed. Casey returned to the business at hand. He stepped between the hopper and the locomotive, then crawled under the knuckle connecting them and poked the dowel in the center upward. A metal rod the size of a track-relay baton popped up.

Casey removed the dowel and examined his handiwork. The hopper was bunched tightly against the engine, keeping the two halves of the sabotaged knuckle temporarily intact. The train would stay together as long as his brave little engine was shoving.

He backed away from the knuckle to take stock of the engine. The cab of the locomotive was facing the hopper, ready to shove the forty-car train from the rear. The General Electric C44-9W Comfort Cab was one of his favorite models, a single locomotive harnessing 392,000 pounds of brute strength that delivered four thousand horsepower to its six traction motors. Just thinking about the raw power of this two-hundred-ton monstrosity sent a tingle of excitement coursing through Casey's body, like Viagra for his soul.

Casey climbed aboard and entered the cab through the nose door. Pulling an overstuffed backpack out from under the engineer's chair, he rummaged through it until he found a large bronze key. Inserting the reverser in the center panel, he rotated the drum to the right until it clunked into the forward position. The engine rocked slightly, but the brakes held firm.

He advanced the throttle to Run Eight, reveling in the feel of four thousand horses straining to be unleashed. The engine responded immediately, belching a cloud of damn-the-environment diesel exhaust into the air. The sheer power of the fuel-guzzling behemoth made Casey proud to be an American.

He gazed out the front window of the cab, admiring the rest of his train. Everything was in place. He had only to release the locomotive brakes and the engine would deliver his rolling Armageddon south to Union Station.

In less than an hour, Chicago would truly become the Windy City.

Megan was beginning to think she was wasting her time. Eleven tracks, and she had found nothing. A rough conversion of car-lengths told her she had walked almost five miles. Her back was

End of the Line

aching from stooping down beside dozens of hoppers to examine their dump gates for signs of leakage.

As she walked alongside track 411, her expectations fell even lower. There was only one hopper on the entire track. She decided to check this last car, then radio Farranger and see if he was ready to call it quits. Checking every car in Lanham Yard was turning out to be an exercise in futility.

She was almost on top of the hopper before she noticed that the hull seemed to be sweating. Touching the side bulkhead confirmed it. A fine mist of condensation had formed on the hopper's skin. She felt a tinge of excitement. Maybe she wasn't wasting her time after all. Bending down to the rail, She reached under the car and swiped her hand along the seam of the dump gates. It was slick, leaving a thin film of black paste on her fingers. She hurried over to the small space between the engine and the hopper to run the final test on her discovery.

After mashing the paste into a sticky black ball, Megan carefully placed it on the rail. She scrounged the yard, quickly finding a discarded brake shoe to complete her crude field test on the unknown substance. Using both hands, she slammed the ceramic brake shoe hard on the small pellet. The black glob exploded like a firecracker.

She had found the car.

"It's only got an eighty-ton capacity."

Megan turned on her heels and saw a man in wayfarer sunglasses jumping off the locomotive platform behind her, cornering her in the narrow gap between the hopper and the engine.

"But you know what they say, Ms. Langford. It's not the size of the hopper that counts, it's how you use it."

The walls of Megan's prison closed in as the man approached her. Half of his face was raw and bloody, the other half covered with dark bruises. There couldn't be any question who he was. He didn't just look like a monster, he was a monster. She knew she was as good as dead. Her only hope was Farranger, but he was on the other side of the yard.

She immediately thought of her packset, but she knew Casey would be on her before she ever got it out of her pocket. The only possible way to get a distress call out would be to let him do the talking.

"Think you're a clever girl?" Casey went on. "Think you found the bomb?"

Casey advanced to arm's length, backing Megan against the knuckle between the hopper and the engine. She slid her hands inside her jacket pocket, probing blindly for her packset. If she could just get it turned on and depress the transmit button, then keep him talking, Farranger would hear it. He was on the same frequency.

"Well, I hate to disappoint you, Ms. Langford, but you only found the detonator." Casey swept a hand toward the train. "Liquefied natural gas. Enough to create an explosion the size of Hiroshima. It just goes to show you, even a mushroom-shaped cloud has a silver lining."

"You're insane," Megan said, raising her voice to cover the beep of the radio as she turned it on. "You'll kill thousands of innocent people."

"Hundreds of thousands, I should think. A little fringe benefit the military refers to as collateral damage. I'll also be destroying Oprah, the Cubs, and that ugly Picasso in front of the Civic Center. If you look at it that way, humanity will be coming out ahead."

"What would you know about humanity?" Megan carefully depressed the transmit button as she spoke, hoping he couldn't hear the faint burst of static.

But she could tell from the look on his face that he had.

Casey grabbed her by the shoulders, spun her around, then wrenched her right arm behind her. When she cried out in pain he increased the pressure.

"That's good," he hissed into her ear. "The union's having its arm twisted for a change." Casey steered Megan toward the hopper, then flung her against the side of the car. Her head slammed against the steel hull with a dull thud, and she crumpled to the ground at his feet.

Casey knelt over her body, almost afraid to check her vital signs for fear the hopper had claimed its first victim. He might be getting a little too proficient at this murder gig for his own good. He hoped like hell he hadn't overachieved. He needed live bait.

End of the Line

To his relief, he found a pulse. He picked Megan up and threw her over his shoulder, carried her to an empty flat eleven cars back from the engine, then dropped her facedown across the wooden deck at the north end of the car, her arms and head hanging over the edge. He quickly patted down her body until he found what he was looking for, a rectangular bulge in her jacket pocket.

"Why, Ms. Langford," he said as he reached over and pulled it out. "Is that a packset in your pocket, or are you just glad to see me?"

He removed his own radio, matched its frequency to hers, then slipped the packset back into her jacket. If Megan the union maid was here, Farranger had to be close by. Casey had all but written off killing him, but now fate had delivered him unexpected good fortune.

Casey climbed onto the flat and examined the chipped wooden planks running the length of the car, debating how best to secure Langford. Then a delightful thought crossed his mind; he'd give her the Von Helsing treatment. He pulled a wooden mallet and four-inch nail from his backpack, then rolled Megan onto her back.

Straddling her chest, he extended her right arm on the decking, then positioned the nail in the center of her palm.

Time for a wake-up call.

Casey swung the mallet, striking the nail dead center. It penetrated the union rep's hand cleanly, solidly embedding itself in the wood underneath.

Megan regained consciousness with a scream, with Casey still sitting on top of her. He examined the crucified hand, which was bleeding profusely.

"You know what they say to do about a flesh wound, don't you?" Casey raised the mallet again and drove the hilt of the nail flush against Megan's palm. "Direct pressure. You might want to get a tetanus shot, though. No telling where that nail's been."

Casey jumped off the flat, then turned to face her, his tone icy. "It's Judgment Day, Ms. Langford. And I'm the angel of death. My sentence will be executed at precisely five o'clock. The hopper will detonate, atomizing the gas inside the tanks. The cloud of petroleum mist that will then cover the city is going to ignite an instant later. The fireball should be several miles across."

Casey paused to let his words sink in. It was vital that someone understand the magnitude of his achievement. There would be no one to tell later.

"Then comes the really cool part. The fireball will consume every molecule of oxygen until it burns itself out. Half a million people will suffocate in the first ten minutes—the so-called Dresden effect—and hundreds of buildings will burst into flames. The explosion will rupture water lines and knock out electrical power, leaving no way to fight the fires that will spread unchecked in every direction. When my great Chicago fire is finished, Mrs. O'Leary's cow will look like a second-rate arsonist."

"You won't get away with this," Megan gasped. "Farranger will stop you."

"Why don't you just give your boyfriend a call?" Casey said with a laugh, looking pointedly at her bloodied palm before turning abruptly and walking away. "Tell him you need a hand."

By the time he reached the locomotive cab, Megan's distress call to Farranger was already blaring over his radio. Her timing was perfect.

Casey opened the throttle and flipped off the locomotive brake valve, feeling a rush of excitement as the train came to life. The engine shuddered forward, ramming the cars with a jolt that removed the remaining slack, then, overcoming the standing inertia, the entire train began to move.

Casey clambered off the locomotive on the conductor's side and crossed four yard tracks to the two main lines that split the enormous freight yard in half. He proceeded a dozen paces beyond to an open-air commuter platform adjacent to the east main, where he waited two minutes for a southbound commuter. A single engine was shoving the two-car train from behind, the cab facing the opposite direction. To a layman, it would look as if the train were running backward, but it was a common Metro practice. Crews endured the awkward engine placement so they could face forward on the return run from Union Station.

In this case, they need not have bothered, Casey thought. There would be no Union Station from which to depart.

End of the Line

The doors opened automatically, and he stepped inside the nearly empty commuter. The Metro accelerated, quickly overtaking the slower tank train coming out of yard track 411 on the adjacent West Main.

"I think I can, I think I can," Casey whispered.

Watching the departure of the deadly freight was a bittersweet moment for him. It would be the end for Transcon, but it would be the end for him, too. He took a last look as his five-thousand-ton gladiator rolled into the arena, then put a hand to his forehead. "Those who are about to die salute you," he said.

Without taking his eyes off the tanks, Casey reached for his packset and flicked it on, listening with amusement as Langford described her situation to Farranger. As soon as the airwaves cleared, he put his mouth to the microphone and pushed the transmit button.

"The yards are lovely, dark and deep,
But I have promises to keep.
And miles to go before I sleep,
And miles to go before I sleep."

Fifteen miles, to be exact.

-33-

Farranger's Taurus sped across the east yard, kicking up gravel as it fishtailed over the soft ballast. Megan was less than half a mile away, but the most direct path to her was blocked by the yard's two thousand railcars on his right, forming a mile-long wall of steel. He couldn't even see the main line, much less Megan's train.

He floored the Taurus, accelerating to five times the posted speed limit. To reach her, he'd have to retrace his route across the signal overpass, then drive down the access road to the right-of-way. It was a three-mile detour that would take him through the heart of the congested factory district surrounding Lanham Yard, but he still had time to make up the distance. Megan's train was powered by a single unit that was shoving uphill. He had a chance to catch the tanks before they reached runaway speed.

As he turned toward the main exit, a two-lane gate through a chain-link security fence, Farranger saw the silhouette of a Transcon police cruiser parked along the fence line. *Damn,* he thought. He prayed the special agents wouldn't give chase, but he'd personally instructed the security team to be on full alert and to assume that anything the least bit suspicious was a threat.

They'd taken his orders seriously. Lights flashing and siren wailing, the white sedan came to life. The tires squealed as the agent slammed on his brakes, and the car slid sideways, blocking the gate. With his Taurus rocketing toward them on a collision course, the act seemed suicidal. They weren't bluffing, though. Casey had killed one of their own in cold blood.

End of the Line

But Farranger wasn't bluffing either. He maintained his speed, bearing down on the patrol car at 70 mph. When the officers held their ground, he swerved onto the shoulder of the gravel road and aimed for the narrow gap between their car and the fence.

It wasn't wide enough.

He clipped the rear of the cruiser and sent it spinning into the fence. The impact crumpled the hood of his Taurus and threw him against the dash as he burst through the blockade.

Gravel gave way to asphalt when he turned onto a four-lane industrial boulevard, where he was immediately surrounded by caravans of the giant tractor-trailers that served the decrepit factories lining the road. The whine of the siren followed him as he wove in and out of the monster rigs, the damaged police cruiser less than a hundred yards behind him.

"Megan, I'm heading for the signal overpass," he said into his packset. "I'll cross over in about three minutes. What's your status?"

"Doing about fifteen up a shallow grade," she replied, her voice strained and weak. "But it's downhill after the signal arch, and I'm already picking up speed."

"Understood." If Farranger didn't catch the train before the downgrade, it would reach runaway speed for sure. And if he failed to get aboard, derailing it would be the only way to stop it. The dispatcher would have to throw a switch beneath the cars or divert it onto a stub track. Either way, Megan was doomed. The sudden deceleration would telescope the train on impact. Even if the hopper didn't explode, her flat would be crushed between the heavier tank cars.

Farranger's pursuers were still right behind him, matching his triple-digit speed as he searched for the cross street, the factory fronts now a blur of red brick. Then he caught a glimpse of a blue rectangular sign a block ahead: LANHAM YARD INTERMODAL FACILITY NEXT RIGHT.

He slowed to 50 mph as he approached the cross street for the overpass and skidded into the turn. Seconds later, he heard the echo of squealing tires as the patrol car maneuvered right behind him. They were closing fast, but the overpass was only half a mile away now. Once Farranger made it across, he'd drive down the access road to the right-of-way, then abandon his car. He'd be running alongside the train before the cops knew what had happened.

As he sped toward the overpass, Farranger scanned the narrow bridge arching over the tracks. It had short guardrails on each side to protect an array of stoplight-like train signals that were mounted at tire level, facing outward for the benefit of the trains passing beneath. He couldn't see their three-light displays, but he could read the candy-striped semaphore arms extending two feet above the bridge that mirrored the signal aspect.

Megan's train was cleared to proceed at maximum speed.

As he started across the overpass, the police now less than fifty feet behind, Farranger spotted her train underneath him to his right. Half the cars had already passed under the bridge. The timing was tight, but he could still make it if he maintained his speed.

He glanced in his rearview mirror, surprised to see that his pursuers had given up the chase and stopped at the foot of the bridge. He immediately discovered the reason. Just ahead, a second police cruiser had barricaded the far end of the overpass.

Farranger slammed on the brakes, skidding broadside to a stop dead center on the bridge. He was trapped, flanked by police officers who were now closing the distance on foot. With their guns raised.

The bridge was vibrating from the weight of the roaring train directly beneath him. Most of the cars had already passed. Only a dozen remained, most of them tanks, and Megan's flat stood out like a sore thumb. Farranger watched helplessly as it approached, then disappeared under the bridge.

The hopper and engine were bringing up the rear. Farranger was only ten car-lengths away, but his view of the locomotive cab was obstructed by a loaded container car. Coupled directly in front of the hopper, the double-stack equipment towered over the rest of the train. As he looked at the oversized car, a plan almost too crazy to consider came to mind.

Farranger stared at the train, visually marking a tank car to time a trial run, but his concentration was broken by a chorus of shouts from the police ordering him out of his vehicle.

End of the Line

Farranger ignored them, focusing on the next tank car behind him as it started under the bridge. He methodically counted the seconds it took for the tank to pass through the blind spot before reemerging in front of him. But as soon as he had etched the count in his mind, he realized it was wrong. The train was accelerating as it crested the grade. The container car he was aiming for would pass more quickly than the tank he'd just timed.

So much for the dry run.

Farranger took another look behind him and saw the leading edge of the intermodal car ducking beneath the bridge. He started his countdown again, but he knew he couldn't rely on it. He'd have to depend on the old switchman's rule: everything takes longer than you think. He prayed that was true. His life now depended entirely on the accuracy of his trainman's internal clock.

The officers were crouched down in firing positions on both sides of his car, yelling at him to surrender immediately. Farranger continued to ignore them, visualizing the position of the hidden container beneath him. He didn't dare wait for it to reappear. By then, it would be too far ahead to serve his purpose. He had to anticipate, make his move while the double-stack equipment was still under the bridge.

His heart was pounding double-time to his silent countdown. When he reached zero, he added an extra switchman's second for luck, revved the engine, and threw the car into drive.

The Taurus skidded in place until the tires caught asphalt, then bolted forward. It sliced through the guardrails, tearing the metal ribbon from its mounting poles, and hit one of the signal arrays. The semaphore arms snapped off like twigs. The impact threw Farranger forward, and he could hear the undercarriage being torn off his car as it scraped over the steel-girder arch.

Then he heard nothing. Just the eerie silence of being airborne.

The Taurus hit its mark. Plowing through the roof of the double-stack container, it crushed the fragile lading before hitting the flatcar beneath it. The tires exploded on impact.

Farranger recovered to find himself in darkness. Boxes of crushed lading covered the car, allowing only pencil-thin rays of sunlight to penetrate the interior. And he could hear the unsettling sound of creaking metal. Overstressed from carrying one midsized car more than the container was designed to hold, the aluminum walls had to be bursting at the seams.

He tried to open the car doors, but they were jammed. Gripping the handle on the driver's-side door, Farranger threw his shoulder against it.

Nothing.

His car was wedged firmly between the container walls.

-34-

Casey gazed out the window as his commuter passed over a steel-girder railroad bridge. He couldn't help but admire the massive structure, a worthy target in its own right. Not only was it an important choke point into Chicago, it was one of the railroad's few remaining swing-span bridges, another dying breed to which he wished he could pay homage. But it was just one of many missed opportunities that weren't quite important enough to make his hit list.

"So much railroad, so little time," he sighed.

He took a last appreciative look at the bridge, then turned his attention to the oversized schedule placard posted inside the compartment. Jasper Siding was the next station, just a mile down the line. It would be an extended stop, a thirty-minute scheduled delay that would ensure the commuter's downtown arrival at the height of rush hour.

Casey intended to rewrite that timetable. He'd take care of a little unfinished business at Jasper, then commandeer the commuter for an early departure. The tank cars would be passing the siding in fifteen minutes. Once they cleared on the main track, he'd give chase in the commuter. He wanted to make sure he had a front-row seat for the main event. He hadn't come this far to watch from the bleachers.

He had found only one flaw in his scenic commuter train. Its reversed locomotive was a huge disappointment. He'd have to run it from the ass end, and he'd have to stick his head out the engineer's window to see around the passenger cars. Not only was it an ergonomic disaster, he'd have a horrible view of the pending detonation. Of course, the explosive flash would blind him almost instantly, but that wasn't the point. It was his show, and he deserved the best seat in the house.

"Jasper Station," the conductor's voice blared over the intercom.

As the train rolled to a gentle stop, the doors opened automatically and all but a handful of passengers stepped off the two commuter cars onto the arrival platform. Casey remained seated, casually scanning the crowd for any sign of his conspicuously absent partner. Casey wasn't worried, though, certain he'd show. There was too much at stake. Casey was the only thing that stood between his inside man at Transcon and a lifetime appointment at a federal penitentiary.

Casey settled back into his seat and rummaged through his explosive-riddled backpack, looking for a diversion. He finally decided on a leftover apple in his lunch bag and almost laughed at the thought of eating it; he'd be dead long before it was ever digested. But after all, he reasoned, you can't create a holocaust on an empty stomach.

He was still munching on his snack when his inside man arrived. Doug McClure stepped into the commuter car, clutching a valise. Transcon's CEO strode by, dismissing him with a fleeting glance. Apparently, he thought Casey's wounds were more the mark of an accident victim than a skilled train-wrecker.

Casey cleared his throat loudly.

McClure turned around, then walked back within arm's reach of Casey and stopped, giving him an icy appraisal.

"We don't all look like Ted Kaczynski, you know," Casey said in a hushed voice. "And it's exactly that kind of stereotyping that gives terrorists a bad name."

McClure calmly sat down beside Casey, adjusting his suit as if he was afraid the upholstery might contaminate it.

"Want part of an apple?" Casey extended the half-eaten fruit toward him.

McClure made a show of looking around at their surroundings in disgust. "What, and get thrown out of paradise?"

Casey frowned. Even death-row inmates had better manners than to refuse the offer of a last meal. For all his so-called breeding, the man was painfully short on common courtesy. Another good reason to kill him.

End of the Line

"Suit yourself," he shrugged, dropping the apple back into the paper bag in his backpack. "I just thought you might want to make this a business lunch."

"I didn't come here to socialize," McClure snapped.

"Yeah, I guess I should've known. You're the classic type A. You really should learn to stop and smell the roses, Doug. Kick back, blow up a few trains, do a little recreational killing. It's very therapeutic. Keeps you centered, if you know what I mean."

McClure shifted impatiently in his seat. "Do you have what I came for, Casey?"

"That's Mr. Jones to you." Casey paused, then pronounced his name slowly. "Keith Christian Jones."

"Is that supposed to mean something to me?"

Casey stared at McClure in disbelief. To think he'd spent the better part of a decade plotting against a man who didn't even remember his name. Well, it was high time to refresh his memory.

"I was a division superintendent for the former Chicago and Memphis—until Transcon fired me. I believe 'downsizing' was the term they used when they gutted C&M."

"Sorry. The name doesn't ring a bell. I fire a lot of people, though. What's another piece of human flotsam more or less?"

McClure's arrogance had Casey dumbfounded. The man wasn't the least bit afraid. He saw Casey as little more than a checkmark in his day planner, a scheduled payoff to a fellow opportunist. The cost of doing business.

Casey considered chucking all his carefully laid plans and strangling the condescending bastard on the spot, but he took a deep breath instead and regained his composure. Lucky for McClure, he didn't have a temper.

"I've been doing a little downsizing myself," he said, his face just inches from McClure. "Why should I spare another piece of human flotsam like you?"

McClure smiled, unfazed. "How about a few million reasons?" He opened his valise to reveal several bundles of freshly minted bills.

Casey gave the money a token glance. It meant nothing to him, just a gimmick to lure McClure to Chicago.

"Damn thoughtful of you, Doug." He took the valise and slid it under his seat. "I'm so embarrassed. I didn't get you a thing."

McClure's face reddened in anger.

"I'm just jerking your chain," Casey laughed, then pulled a small key out of his pocket and handed it to McClure.

McClure examined the key, unsure what to make of it. "Locker at Union Station. You'll find everything I have on you. As a bonus, I've put together a mountain of stuff that implicates Adashek as my partner, including a signed confession that the Feds will have no problem matching my handwriting on. Not that you'll need it; you've given them Adashek tied up nicely."

"The CBO&E," McClure responded. "It took them forever to figure that out, but eventually they cracked the code."

"Can't look too easy," Casey smiled. "It wouldn't look believable. What are the Feds doing now?"

"They found the money trail and will pick up Adashek at the airport. He's leaving for Mexico to talk to our international shippers. Adashek has no idea a reservation was made in his name for Buenos Aires at the same time. He'll have a hard time explaining."

"They'll never believe him," Casey theorized. "Even if they do, they have him on enough securities violations to put him away for life."

Casey leaned into McClure, lowering his voice, all business. "In the locker you'll find records of calls between me and Adashek over the last several months that he has no idea he made. They correspond to key stock trades made in his favor. I'm sure you can figure out an anonymous way to leak this information. That ought to seal the deal."

McClure nodded, satisfied the frame-up was airtight.

"What about the union?" Casey asked.

"I'll be speaking to them in a couple of hours. Things should calm down with them once you exit the scene."

Good luck, Casey thought to himself. In a couple of hours, he and the union would be in the same grave.

"And Farranger?"

"He's back in Dallas minding the store."

Casey knew better.

End of the Line

"I'm curious, Mr. Jones, why did you want me to put Farranger in charge of security? You knew he'd be trouble."

"Wanted a challenge," Casey smiled. He'd got more than he'd bargained for. "Since we're quelling our mutual curiosity, I have a question for you: why would a man who has everything risk it all?"

"There's more to life than money," McClure replied. "I wanted to leave a mark, accomplish the impossible, create what others only dreamed of. We are the greatest nation on earth; we deserve a national rail system."

"So you bribed federal regulators to ramrod approval of all those mergers out of a sense of patriotism?" Casey made no attempt to hide his amusement.

"I don't expect you to understand." McClure shook his head, not the least bit ashamed of what he'd become.

Casey understood only too well. McClure wanted the same thing he did—immortality. McClure had risked his fortune and reputation for a paragraph in the history books. And people called Casey crazy.

He didn't fault McClure for what he did, only the sloppiness in his execution. McClure had thrown too much money around, too quickly, and Casey had caught the scent. The price for his silence had been high, and McClure had been his pawn ever since. Once people started dying, McClure was fully committed.

"Loose ends?" McClure asked nonchalantly as if he was concluding any other business deal.

"A member of the surface transportation board was having a crisis of conscious. He was going to out you."

"And?"

"That problem has been eliminated permanently. All part of the service."

McClure winced. "No one was supposed to die," he objected weakly.

"That was your plan, not mine," Casey replied. He'd sold McClure a bill of goods, assuring him that the terrorist routine could be accomplished without blood or significant damage to the railroad. McClure had believed it because he wanted to believe it. Casey now realized that McClure would have gone along without the subterfuge. The CEO would have done anything to prevent being exposed.

"I expect this is the last time we'll talk, Mr. Jones. After today I expect to put you and the rest of this filthy business behind me."

Filthy business. Casey decided to let the remark slide. It wouldn't be productive to get angry at someone who was going to be dead in twenty minutes. Besides, McClure's insult stemmed from his own desire for immortality. The one thing they had in common.

McClure turned the locker key over in his hand. "There's no locker number," he said, as if he'd caught Casey trying to double-cross him.

"You'll get the number when we get to Union Station." McClure started to object, but Casey quickly cut him off. "I've waited seven years. I think you can wait twenty minutes."

"Twenty minutes, Jones. Not a second more. And then this had better come to an end." McClure stood up and walked to the other side of the cabin. He took a seat directly across from Casey and glowered at him.

Casey grinned. "Don't worry, Dougie, you'll get everything you have coming to you once we get to Union Station."

- 35 -

Farranger's Taurus had come to rest at a steep angle, nose down.
Fighting a sense of vertigo, he climbed into the back, pressed himself against the driver's seat, and kicked the rear windshield.

The safety glass shattered into a thousand fragments but stayed together. Hindered by the darkness, Farranger carefully traced his fingers along the sharp glass until he found the point where it sagged. He memorized the spot, then leveraged himself against the seat and kicked again. The windshield broke apart in marble-sized shards and fell inward, followed by a flood of cardboard and industrial packing material.

Farranger climbed through the opening, digging his way up through a mound of boxes. He suppressed the impulse to panic as the freight shifted. He'd been buried alive for the second time in a week. Damned if he wasn't getting used to it.

He finally reached the surface and got his first look at the remains of the container.

The top of the car was gone, flattened beneath the Taurus. Nothing remained but a jagged perimeter of steel where the sheet metal had been torn from its rivets. The four walls were intact but crumpled downward, and hundreds of pounds of cargo had spilled out of the roofless car.

Though drastically reduced in height, it was still the tallest car in the train, and Farranger had a bird's-eye view of his surroundings. He scanned the right-of-way, then looked south in the direction the train was moving. Bracing himself against the wind, he made a quick inspection of the train he'd been so anxious to board.

It was running on straight track, and Farranger could see all thirty-five cars ahead of him. Megan's flat was a full quarter mile away. To reach her, he'd have to crawl over ten curved tank cars. And even if he accomplished that feat, their only hope for escape would be a 60-mph leap onto the right-of-way.

Somehow he had to stop the train.

Farranger turned away and trampled over the boxes to the rear wall of the container. As he knelt over the edge and looked down through the gap between the container and the hopper, he immediately spotted the uncoupled air hoses. Discovering that Casey had disabled the brake line came as no great surprise, but the chances of stopping the train had just gotten a whole lot slimmer. Now, Farranger would have to make his way to the locomotive behind the hopper.

Peering down into the imposing gap, he considered his options. The drawbar was directly beneath him, twelve feet below his perch. It would make a suitable bridge to the hopper but a narrow target in a twelve-foot drop. One false step and he'd be sliced in half by the rolling wheels. He'd have to do it the old fashioned way, and make a brakeman's leap between the moving cars.

Farranger studied the shorter car and picked an arbitrary target in the center of the sloping roof. Just as he was about to jump, a sudden gust of wind blew him forward. With no hope of regaining his balance, Farranger leaned into the fall and leapt forward. He hit the roof of the hopper on his feet and stumbled, then landed hard on his chest.

He rose slowly, trying to keep his center of gravity low. The normal lateral sway of the car was amplified at the top, making the ninety-foot walk to the engine more like a fun-house ride. He paced himself carefully, taking one step sideways for each step forward.

Farranger stepped over the first of the three fill caps, wondering which one housed the detonator. If he could somehow loosen the eight bolts that held the cap in place, there might be a way to disarm the car from above. But his plan crumbled immediately when he saw the cap in the center.

On top of the hinged access hatch, Casey Jones had written a warning: *Booby trapped for your protection.*

End of the Line

Farranger carefully probed the hermetically sealed cap but found nothing to indicate how Casey had tamper-proofed the hatch. He figured it had to be something simple, like a clothespin setup that would snap two contact points together if the hatch was opened. If he had an acetylene torch and an hour to cut through the hull, it would be easy enough to disarm. Problem was, he didn't have either.

But he did have the dump gates beneath the car. Casey might be clever, but he couldn't beat gravity. He couldn't possibly have rigged a device under the car without letting eighty tons of lading pour through the open gates.

"I've got you," Farranger said. He'd found the hopper's Achilles' heel. He couldn't access the underside of the hopper while the train was moving, but once he'd stopped the train, he could unhinge the dump gates, then slowly roll the train forward and let the ammonium nitrate spill harmlessly between the tracks. With no explosive left inside the car, the detonator would be useless. The plan was brilliant, except for one nagging detail: He still had to stop a 5000-ton train with no brakes.

Farranger ran the remaining forty feet to the end of the car, then descended the ladder to the locomotive platform. He entered the cab to find the train in full throttle, shoving at just over 60 mph. The engine's dynamic and locomotive brakes appeared to be working, but they wouldn't be much help. With forty loaded cars in front of him generating momentum, the brakes would be virtually useless. Given the grade and his current speed, he estimated it would take a good half-hour to get the train under control. The digital clock mounted above the conductor's station read 16:42. According to Megan, Casey had armed the bomb for 17:00. The train would explode in just eighteen minutes.

Farranger froze momentarily. The array of controls, once second nature, seemed almost foreign to him. He hadn't run an engine for almost twelve years and swore he'd never do so again. He'd chosen a hell of a time to get back on the horse.

He flipped the throttle to idle and grabbed the packset off his belt. "Megan, I'm on the train. I'm going to take the slack out, so brace yourself."

Instead of responding verbally, she clicked the transmit button twice, an old switchman's trick, a way of responding when you didn't want to waste time talking. And it was just as well that she didn't say anything. She might've asked how sure he was that he could stop the train, and Farranger wouldn't have had the heart to tell her the truth. With his limited braking, he doubted he'd get their speed under twenty before they crashed into the concrete stops inside Union Station. Presuming, of course, the hopper didn't blow them to kingdom come first. Thinking he had any hope of stopping the train was foolish at best. But he had to try.

Farranger eased into dynamic braking slowly, monitoring the amperage gauge as the electric brakes hummed to life. The engine shuddered as the brakes engaged, then began decelerating rapidly. Too rapidly. The current flow to the traction motors suddenly spiked to full power, throwing Farranger against the control console. The electric load dropped to zero an instant later, whiplashing him back into his chair.

Farranger was shaken and confused by the violent reaction, but he collected his senses enough to see that his locomotive had separated from the rest of the train. The tank cars were free, moving away as if the engine behind them were standing still.

With the tanks already ten car-lengths ahead, Farranger automatically released the dynamic and pushed the lever into the throttle-eight position to give chase. He quickly closed the distance, then slowed when he was a car-length away to make a running coupling. But as he neared to make the joint, he realized he was thoroughly screwed.

The hopper's rear knuckle was gone, leaving only the naked drawbar extending from the rear of the car. It would now be impossible to couple the engine to the runaway cars, much less stop them. The train was a full-fledged runaway.

"Emergency! Emergency! Emergency!" he shouted into the cab's radio. "We have a runaway just south of Lanham Yard on the West Main heading south."

"DS1 copies," replied the dispatcher. "What's the situation?"

Farranger explained as best he could, trying to convey a sense of urgency without sounding frantic. He quickly outlined his plan for dumping the hopper's lading, hoping to stave off the inevitable questions and second-guessing of corporate group-think.

He didn't have time for a debate with the dispatcher. He needed action.

"Farranger, this is DS1. You are ordered to disengage immediately. We'll open a switch and derail the cut."

"Negative," Farranger came back angrily. "The tanks will breech in a high-speed derailment. Check your damn map, see if you can find a good place to derail five thousand tons of explosive gas."

The area surrounding the train was densely populated, and a detonation anywhere along the line would kill thousands of people. Even if the tanks didn't explode on impact, Megan would never survive a 60-mph derailment. Farranger considered telling the COC that she was trapped on the flat but knew he'd be wasting his time. Her life wouldn't mean much to corporate, not when so many others were at stake.

"Run me around the cut," he finally went on. "I can tie on the head end and stop the train."

"Farranger, this is the SYSOP," a familiar voice replied. "No chance on the runaround. I can cross you over to the East Main, but I can't cross you back to the West Main in front of the runaway. They merge into one track about five miles ahead. You'll never make it. You'll hit the train broadside at full throttle."

"I'll make it." Farranger released the transmit button, grateful the SYSOP couldn't see his face. He didn't really believe he could make it either, but he had to try.

He notched the throttle forward, closing in on the runaway. He wanted to be ready to move when the COC gave his plan the go-ahead. And they'd have to approve it. It was the only option they had.

"Prepare to cross over," the SYSOP said after a long silence. "There'll be carmen standing by at Milepost 11 to unhinge the dump gates if you make it. Good luck, Cal. SYSOP out."

"Farranger out."

The SYSOP's next remark was directed to the computer voice-recorder monitoring the road channel. "This is Transcon SYSOP following direct orders from Cal Farranger to operate in violation of sound dispatching practices." He was going on the record to cover his own ass. Not exactly a vote of confidence.

Farranger paced the runaway ten car-lengths behind the hopper. He leaned out the engineer's window to view the switch target for the crossover. The target showed green, the track lined for straight movement. He held his breath, eyes fixed on the rear axle of the hopper as the wheels passed the switch target.

The hopper was clear.

Farranger slammed the throttle to full power, running on a collision course with the runaway ahead. He waited nervously for the first trace of movement from the crossover switch, which was still lined for straight track. What the hell was the dispatcher waiting for?

Just seconds before his lead wheels hit the switch points, the crossover suddenly shifted left. The locomotive hit it at sixty, heeling over slightly as it swung into the passing lane on the East Main. The diesel engine spooled up quickly, and Farranger raced by the runaway cars at 73 mph.

His gut wrenched when Megan's flat came into view. She was on her back, clutching her pinned arm like a wild animal caught in a trap. The planks beneath her were pooled with blood.

Farranger started to reach for his packset, then stopped himself. Megan's face was turned the other way, so she hadn't seen him yet, and she certainly couldn't hear his engine over the noise of her own train. As far as she knew, he was still on the rear of the train. Maybe it was better to keep that belief alive.

But then she turned her head in his direction, and he saw her fumbling for her packset.

"Change of plans," he said before she could speak. "I thought it'd be easier to save the train if I tied on to the head end."

Megan looked ahead to where the East Main dead-ended. "And who's going to save *you*?"

Farranger started to reply, but then the dispatcher's voice came through on the road channel. "Farranger, this is DS1. Prepare to cross over."

The merge was less than half a mile ahead. Farranger was running at maximum speed but still had twenty cars to pass.

He released his grip on the throttle, certain he was now past the point of no return. He'd either beat the runaway to the switch or he wouldn't. If he succeeded, he'd increase his life expectancy by a whopping twenty minutes.

End of the Line

He roared by the lead tank car, just half an engine-length before the crossover. The locomotive swerved right, throwing him from his seat as it ran through the crossover at seventy. He slid across the floor and slammed into the conductor's chair. When he felt the engine settle into straight track he realized he'd won the race.

His engine was now running in front of the tanks.

Farranger scrambled to his feet and went to the engineer's window to take a look behind him. The head tank was less than a hundred feet back, leading a procession of black cars as far as he could see. His proximity to the runaway was unnerving, but the worst was yet to come. He was going to have to get a lot closer.

He eased the throttle to idle in order to cut his speed, bracing himself as the tanks slammed into the knuckle of his locomotive, then coupled together with a violent jolt that vibrated through the entire train.

The slack action at Megan's end of the train would be amplified to a painful degree by the thirty cars between them. Farranger hated to make her situation worse, but there wasn't time for delicate train handling. He'd need every second he had to stop the runaway.

He added full dynamic braking until the gauge redlined at 900 amps. An instant later, the cars slammed into the braking engine in a series of quick jolts as the slack bunched against the locomotive. The vibrations quickly subsided, and Farranger turned his attention to the accelerometer, watching the small black needle on the gauge jumping in concert with the slack action. When the train finally settled, the needle stopped at dead center, indicating neutral acceleration. His speed was now fixed at 65 mph. It wasn't much of an improvement, but Farranger was relieved. At least they were no longer accelerating.

Letting out a breath he didn't realize he'd been holding, Farranger turned from the gauges to the automatic brake handle that controlled the airflow to the train, which was now rendered useless by the open brake line between the cars. His hands were slick with sweat as he reached for the handle that controlled the independent brake on the locomotive, knowing he was about to break the cardinal rule of train handling. Setting the engine brakes without first applying the brakes on the individual cars was a recipe for disaster. The slightest error in judgment, adding too much braking too quickly, would jackknife the engine and derail the train.

Farranger used both hands to inch the lever forward. He watched the air gauge, determined to remain calm and apply a steady application. The brakes were only half set when he realized something was horribly wrong.

The locomotive started to vibrate, bouncing violently on its wheel trucks. Farranger heard a high-pitched squeal, and the sickening stench of scorched metal filled the cabin. He stuck his head out the window and saw a hail of sparks coming from the traction motors. Beneath them, the steel locomotive wheels were glowing white-hot.

The signs were unmistakable. Casey had removed the composite brake shoes, and now the naked steel pistons were cutting into the wheels like giant lathes. Farranger immediately released the engine brake, praying he was in time to stop the damage.

But with every rotation of the wheels, Farranger could feel a subtle bump, a rough spot where friction had begun to grind the metal flat. A few more seconds of braking would destroy the wheels completely, plunging the engine off the tracks at 60 mph. Farranger couldn't risk using the locomotive brake again. He wanted to stop, but not like that.

He stared vacantly at the useless control panel, then looked around the rest of the compartment, hoping to spot some forgotten device, some magical button that would set things right. Finding nothing, he resigned himself to his fate. He was out of brakes and out of hope. Whether or not the train had to be derailed was no longer the question. He had only one decision left to make: choosing the spot where he and Megan would die.

Derailing the train would be the easy part. He'd simply throw the locomotive brake lever and let the pistons rip the wheels apart. Picking the right location to minimize the damage was going to be a lot trickier.

Farranger picked up the locomotive handset. "DS1, this is Farranger. What's it look like ahead? Over."

End of the Line

"Roger, Cal. I've got you cleared all the way to the concrete stops at Union Station. You'll be on the East Main. The track splits back into two main lines just after Jasper Bridge. Anything else?"

The dispatcher's words hit Farranger like a thunderbolt, kindling a tentative hope.

"Yeah. What kind of bridge?"

Casey kept his eyes on McClure sitting across from him, but his attention was focused on the conversation he was hearing through the tiny ear piece connected to his packset. Farranger and the dispatcher were discussing the single option he had overlooked.

He was grudgingly impressed with Farranger's resourcefulness. Improvisation was a sign of genius. Two could play that game, though. He patted the backpack beside him, thankful he'd had the foresight to plan for every possible contingency. "Be prepared," that was his motto. If he hadn't been a terrorist, he'd have made an excellent Boy Scout.

Reaching deep inside the backpack, Casey worked blind. A moment later, he pulled out his lunch bag, which was two pounds heavier now and quite a bit more dangerous.

He glanced at his watch. His timetable had been moved up, but nothing else had changed. He'd already figured out a way to keep McClure on the commuter train while he commandeered the engine. Luckily, he had the perfect bait. Casey dropped the lunch bag next to the stacks of bill in the valise, snapped it shut, then walked across the cabin to McClure.

"I need to tie up some loose ends." Casey threw the valise at McClure's feet. "Watch my bag until I get back."

Without waiting for a response, he walked out the door of the commuter car to the head end of the locomotive and stepped aboard. The crew was gone, taking an extended smoke break. Casey smiled at the irony. Cigarettes had actually saved their lives.

Taking a seat behind the control console, he reacquainted himself with the passenger equipment. He flicked the lever that sealed the automatic doors, then pulled the one-inch knob that activated the locomotive's bell.

He listened to the ring for a few seconds, then depressed the talk button on the intercom and assumed his most dramatic voice.

"Ask not for whom the bell tolls . . ."

-36-

Farranger could see the bridge's superstructure from four miles away. It was half a mile long, crossing the Chicago River at its widest point. The two rigid sections bordering the center span were three hundred feet long and remained stationary, while the quarter-mile middle section rotated for passing ships. A small control booth stood at the halfway point on the bridge, just left of the tracks, giving the bridge operator a panoramic view of his tiny kingdom.

His plan was simple enough. Megan would make a cut on the cars behind her, separating their train from the rear section that held the deadly hopper. Once separated, he'd add speed, putting as much distance as possible between their train and the runaway section that would be close on their heels. When their section of the train was safely across the bridge, the control operator would swing the span open, forcing the hopper and tank cars to crash into the river.

At their current speed, he figured the hopper would split apart on impact, spilling its contents harmlessly into the water. Even if the hopper remained intact and detonated, it wouldn't ignite the tank cars underwater. All in all it was an inspired plan. As far as he could tell it had only one flaw: It wouldn't work.

The bridge was only four minutes away, far too close for the leisurely crossing he'd envisioned. His engine was already near top speed, so there was no chance of getting a mile separation after they made the cut. At this speed, they'd be lucky to get twenty car lengths. Their only choice would be to turn the span just after they cleared, while the runaway section behind them was still on the bridge. This was a major problem.

The bridge operator had told Farranger that it would take a full two minutes to turn the center span. They didn't need a complete rotation, but Farranger was afraid they might not get any at all. No one knew if the bridge would turn under the weight of a train, because no one had ever been foolish enough to try. They'd all find out soon enough, though. The lead wheels of his engine would be on the bridge in three minutes.

Farranger placed a firm hand on the dynamic brake, bracing for what would come next. It was up to Megan now.

"Megan, can you make the cut?" he said over his packset

"I don't think so. I can see the pinlifter, but I can't reach it."

"You've got to. If you don't—" Farranger stopped himself. There wasn't any point in telling her what he planned to do if she failed.

Letting the hopper cross the bridge into downtown Chicago wasn't an option. If Megan couldn't cut away the rear cars, he'd be forced to order the bridge operator to turn the span before they reached it. The entire train would plunge headlong into the river, taking them both to a watery death. There wasn't any other choice. With half a million lives hanging in the balance, they either had to stop the train here or die trying.

Farranger tuned the locomotive's radio to the bridge operator's frequency and picked up its handset. He tensed, enduring a long silence over the airwaves from the packset in his right hand. If Megan didn't answer, he'd have to issue the deadly order to the bridge operator on the locomotive handset in his left. He was about to press her for a response, when her voice broke through the static.

"A little slack, please."

Megan could feel the slack run in as Farranger increased the dynamic brake, bunching the cars behind the engine. Tank by tank, the metallic grinding worked its way through the train. Like a rolling wave, each car in succession bolted forward six inches, fully compressing its drawbar against the car ahead of

End of the Line

it. And the wave was getting closer. By the time it reached her, the full weight of thirty cars would propel her car forward with a violent lurch.

She had no way to brace herself against the coming onslaught, and she watched in fear as the tank ahead of her shot forward. A heartbeat later, slack rippled through her flat with the force of a small earthquake. The forty-ton car snapped taut, throwing Megan forward.

She clawed for a handhold, but found none on the smooth wooden deck. Her body slid along the center axis of the car until her nailed hand yanked her to a stop. She screamed in agony as the shaft ripped a gash in her bloody palm, sending fresh waves of pain shooting through her body.

Once the car steadied, she shimmied closer to the nail that held her prisoner, trying to block the pain by focusing on her singular goal: the pinlifter mounted behind her. Craning her neck over the end of the flat, she saw the straight, six-foot-long metal rod that ran along the trailing edge in both directions from the knuckle linkage, then curved to a ninety-degree angle at both corners, forming crude switchman's handles on either side of the car.

With her free hand, Megan reached for the nearest pinlifter handle at the rightmost corner of the flat, but she grabbed only air. She straightened her arm and rotated her nailed hand clockwise, each excruciating movement shifting her body a few precious inches closer. But it wasn't enough. No matter how she contorted her body, she couldn't reach the switchman's handle.

As she looked at her bloody palm, Megan realized what she'd have to do.

She rolled over on her side and wedged the fingers of her free hand under the knuckles of the impaled one, then yanked hard against the nail. The square shaft tore through her flesh and a new flow of blood pulsated from the wound in rhythm with her hammering heart.

The pain was so intense that Megan nearly passed out, but she kept working the nail back and forth. The head disappeared inside her palm, splintering the fragile bones, but the nail remained firmly embedded.

She was sobbing now, but she struggled to a kneeling position, grabbed her hand by the wrist, and yanked her pinned arm upward. The head of the nail ripped through the back of her hand. She tumbled off-balance from the sudden release, stopping just inches from the edge of the car.

She lay on her side in a daze, one blink away from unconsciousness. But she knew she was free. If she could somehow manage to move, she could still make the cut.

The right-of-way passed by in a dull blur. The world was spinning, the periphery surrounded by a thick black fog that was closing in on all sides. The switchman's handle was out of focus, seemed to be moving as she crawled toward it, cradling her bloody hand.

She collapsed at the edge of the car, groping blindly for the pinlifter. When her fingers finally closed around the metal lever, Megan pulled it up with the last ounce of her strength.

The pinlifter rotated and released the coupled knuckles. The hopper and ten rear cars began drifting away, and her flat slowly pulled ahead of the shorter runaway.

She had done her part.

Now it was Farranger's turn.

She reached for her packset with her good hand, keyed the microphone, then mustered her best switchman's voice.

"Take 'em away."

Farranger forced the throttle to Run Eight. The shortened train responded quickly, running at seventy by the time the lead wheels hit the foot of Jasper Bridge. He anxiously watched the speedometer as the diesel spooled up to full power. He'd have to worry about stopping his runaway later. Right now, he needed all the speed he could get. He had less than a minute to put as much distance as possible between his train and the ten cars following close behind.

He picked up the locomotive handset. "Farranger to Jasper Bridge operator. On my mark."

End of the Line

"Jasper copies."

Farranger picked up the packset on Megan's frequency next. "Megan, timing is everything. I need to know the second your flat clears the turning cutouts."

"Roger," she replied, the pain evident in her voice. "The tanks are right on our tail. Can't you speed up?"

Farranger checked his speed. They were at seventy-three, the maximum speed his diesel could pull. He hoped like hell it would be enough.

"Megan . . . if it looks like we don't have enough distance between our train and the runaway—"

"Then we'll have to turn the bridge while I'm still on it," she finished without missing a beat. "My call, right?"

"Your call." Farranger knew Megan would make the right decision when the time came, even if it meant losing her life. She would never allow the hopper to cross the bridge. If she thought the chase cars were following too closely to rotate the center span after she crossed, she'd order the bridge turned while she was still on it.

The grim scenario played out in Farranger's mind, and he wished he could trade places with her. If the bridge rotated before the train cleared the turning cutouts, the engine and any cars already across would make it. But Megan's flat and the remaining cars would snap away from the head end, then plunge into the river at 70 mph. For once, the locomotive cab would be the safest spot on the train.

Farranger forced the throttle forward, trying to push the thought away. Megan would do her job. It was time for him to do his.

He raced across the half-mile bridge in Run Eight. At 73 mph, the trip took less than half a minute. The engine shot out over dry land, then followed the tracks as they banked around a shallow curve.

Farranger took a last look at the rear of his train. Megan's flat was half a mile back, just starting over the bridge. The runaway tanks and hopper were in close pursuit, less than eight car-lengths behind.

A moment later, the only part of the bridge still visible was the apex of the iron superstructure. The rear of the train was completely hidden by the curve, making him operationally blind. Megan would have to be his eyes now.

Counting down the seconds on the locomotive clock, Farranger tried to estimate the distance traveled by the rear of his train. It was far too crude a measure for the precision maneuver they intended to pull off, but he had to be ready for Megan's signal when it came. Sometime in the next thirty seconds she'd be radioing him to turn the bridge. When she did, he'd have to relay her command to the bridge operator without hesitation. He wouldn't have time to worry about whether or not she was in the clear.

Megan's voice crackled over his packset seconds later. "Get ready."

Her transmission caught Farranger off guard. If he could trust his timing at all, she hadn't even reached the middle of the bridge yet. And then she'd need at least another fifteen seconds to clear before she ordered the bridge turned.

He keyed his packset in a panic. "Megan—"

"Clear," she interrupted.

Farranger grabbed the locomotive handset and keyed the mike, but his finger froze over the transmit button. Megan had freely chosen to die, but in doing so she had also made him the executioner. He knew he had to relay the message, but he couldn't bring himself to do it. He held the handset to his forehead, praying for some kind of last-minute reprieve.

"Clear," she repeated, louder this time.

A few more agonizing seconds ticked off before Farranger found his courage. His voice was choked with emotion when he depressed the transmit button and relayed her order to the bridge.

"Clear."

End of the Line

Megan had issued her order when she was just halfway across the bridge, but the chase cars were too close to risk letting them cross the span behind her. She'd never reach the safety of the rigid section, but there wasn't any turning back now. Any second, the center span would begin turning. She looked at the steep drop to the water below and resigned herself to her fate.

She was a full three car-lengths short of the span's turning cutouts when the swing gears engaged with a jolt, the bridge creaking to life beneath her. As the bridge hydraulics took hold and the center span struggled to turn under the weight of the train, her flat began vibrating wildly. The vibrations soon gave way to a lateral bucking that threw her sideways across the deck. Momentarily forgetting about her injured palm, she threw her arms around the pinlifter, fighting to keep a handhold.

A second later, her flat hit the turning cutouts on the rigid section, where the rotation of the bridge had offset the tracks. The car's one-inch wheel flanges flew off the rails, and the wheels dug into the inlaid wooden planks on the surface of the bridge, spitting up splinters like a buzz saw. The car fishtailed over the hard wood, pulled along by the three thousand tons of train ahead.

Megan couldn't maintain her balance under the rocking, and she started sliding across the deck, anchored only by her tenuous grip on the pinlifter. She prayed that the knuckle connecting her flat to the rest of the train wouldn't let go from the stress. If it did, she'd fly off the tracks at 70 mph.

The steady gyrations of the flat suddenly gave way to a thundering jolt. The car jumped, skidded across the track, then slammed down hard as the wheels caught the rails. The shaking gradually subsided as the flat steadied itself on the rigid section of the bridge.

Megan looked back at the chase cars. The center span had turned a few feet, leaving a small gap between its superstructure and the rigid section of the bridge. She held her breath as the tanks approached the same offset rail that had nearly killed her.

The first car hit the open rail, then skipped across the planks toward the gap. It lodged in the small opening for a second, then shot through the gap from the thousand-ton force of the tank cars behind slamming into it, propelling it off the bridge like a torpedo. One after another, the tanks followed it off the bridge, splashing into the Chicago River below.

Megan cringed as the explosive-laden hopper skipped off the rails, its steel wheels digging into the crossties with such force that the front wheel truck snapped off. The unbalanced car toppled forward and hurtled across the center span at 50 mph. The car ricocheted off both sides of the superstructure. Its hull scraped along the steel girders, tearing gaping holes in its sides. Black sludge oozed out, spewing deadly lading over the bridge as the hopper rolled toward the end of the steel runway.

The shredded car hit the offset track, then vaulted onto the rigid section of the bridge. It sliced into the steel girders, breaking into two pieces that plunged into the river below.

Megan smiled and reached for her packset as the hopper disappeared under the water. "The hopper's in the drink," she said, then depressed her transmit button again as her flat rounded the curve. "See if you can stop this thing, Cal. I'm ready to get off."

Farranger couldn't believe his ears. He looked out the engineer's window behind him and saw the rear of the train rounding the curve. The hopper and rear tanks were gone, leaving Megan's flat dead last. Her survival was nothing short of a miracle, but it was far too early to celebrate.

He still had a train to stop.

Pulling the throttle back to idle, he applied full dynamic brake. The engine lurched slightly as they took hold. Farranger turned his attention to the instrument panel, looking for some sign of deceleration. The dynamic amperage redlined at 900 amps, but the thirty-car train was barely responding, holding firm at 70 mph. The negligible effects of his brake application filled Far-

End of the Line

ranger with despair. The engine's dynamic brakes were simply no match for the three thousand tons of runaway cars behind him.

He started to reach for the automatic brake valve, then remembered that Casey had completely disabled the air-brake system on the cars. The independent air brake on the engine was functional, but it wasn't an option. Even a modest application of air would derail the train by driving shoeless pistons into the wheels. He stared at the useless control console that underscored the unpleasant reality.

He wasn't going to be able to stop the train.

The locomotive clock told the rest of the story. Eight minutes from now the tanks would crash into Union Station and spill a million gallons of flammable gas in the heart of downtown. He and Megan had failed. All their efforts—all Megan's heroics—had bought them only another eight minutes. And now, thanks to his foolish gamble, a good portion of Chicago would die along with them. The disaster would be as much his doing as Casey's. He should have sent the entire train into the river when he had the chance.

The speedometer needle was still glued at seventy, and the tanks were only crash-proofed at fifty-five. Above that threshold, the hulls would breech on impact and unleash their highly combustible cargo. The slightest spark would ignite an inferno.

As his train rounded a shallow curve, he turned toward the window again. Seeing the half-mile of deadly black tanks snaking along behind him, Farranger realized he might still have one slim chance. Assuming he didn't waste what little time he had left.

"Going offline," he advised Megan over the radio, then bolted out the engineer's door with a renewed sense of purpose.

Chicago wasn't going to burn after all. Not on his watch.

He ran down the locomotive walkway toward the tanks. If he was lucky, he might be able to set four or five of the individual handbrakes on the tank cars and get the speed down before it was too late. It was already too late for him and Megan, but he could still try to save Chicago.

Farranger stepped over the knuckle to the first car in his train and grabbed hold of the oversized brake wheel on the tank. He ratcheted the wheel clockwise, a task he'd performed thousands of times as a switchman. He kept his mind on the work at hand, just a railroader doing his job.

There were worse ways to die.

-37-

Casey stood behind the commuter's control console, staring vacantly at the bridge that had been his undoing. Thanks to Farranger's treachery, seven years of planning had gone down the drain, buried in the murky silt of the Chicago River. Had the Unabomber ever had days like this?

The dim flicker of a headlight snapped him out of his melancholy. Farranger's train was closing fast on the East Main, less than three miles away. He must be gloating over his minor victory, having a great laugh at Casey's expense.

But the game wasn't over yet.

Not while Casey still had a million gallons of liquefied natural gas on his dance card.

Casey grinned as the deadly black cylinders rolled into view. The tanks were now the key to his five-kiloton urban-renewal project. Even without the hopper, he could still turn Chicago into an apocalyptic wasteland, though he half wondered if the Southside lowlifes would notice the difference. Luckily, he wasn't interested in the quality of people he destroyed. Just the quantity.

His new plan wasn't without its shortcomings, though. With no hopper to atomize the gas, he'd lose the epic fireball he'd dreamed of. Even though the body count would be roughly the same, he wouldn't be able to use any of the dozen rhymes for "mushroom cloud" that he had come up with to use in his commemorative ballad. Despite these drawbacks, he felt confident that the overall grandeur of his legend would remain intact. After all, it really didn't matter *how* he killed a half million people, as long as the story had a happy ending.

He took a last look at Farranger's approaching train, then hastily emptied the contents of his backpack onto the control console. Working as quickly as possible with the hodgepodge of available parts, he transformed a two-pound brick of plastique into a jury-rigged bomb that would detonate when he toned the singular command frequency. A dozen quick winds of det cord secured the electronic components firmly in place. As a finishing touch, he fashioned the bitter ends of the explosive cord into a bow to give the bomb a more festive look.

After all, 'tis the season.

The device was primitive but sufficiently powerful to demolish the tracks ahead of Farranger's locomotive. Once derailed, the two-hundred-ton engine would dig itself firmly into the ground and provide a solid backstop for the rest of the train. The tanks would crack like eggshells, and their gaseous cargo would roll through Chicago's crowded streets like a deadly fog.

Casey would ignite the lethal mix with one of the fusees so thoughtfully provided by Transcon as part of the commuter's standard safety equipment. The igniting spark would transform the escaping vapors into a napalm-like mist of fire that would incinerate everything in its path. The more he thought about it, the more convinced he was that this new plan was a worthy substitute for the original. He may have lost the mushroom cloud of his dreams, but a river of flaming death wasn't too shabby either.

He visualized the panicked masses trying to outrun their own burning flesh, smiling at the imagery, but then reminded himself that he was being overly romantic. Most would die from asphyxiation. The fire would burn off every molecule of breathable air, replacing it with deadly hydrocarbons. Sure, it might be a less glamorous approach to genocide than incineration, but mass suffocation had a certain Himmler-like efficiency that he could appreciate.

"Say what you will about Fascists," he reflected, "but at least they ran their trains on time."

He threw the engine into reverse with renewed enthusiasm, then throttled up to full power and stuck his head out the engineer's window to look behind him as he shoved the commuter cars south toward the Chicago skyline. The passenger train accel-

End of the Line

erated quickly, forcing open the switch points as it burst through the siding exit. The commuter blasted onto the main track at seventy, just a car-length ahead of Farranger's engine. The two trains roared south together, locomotives nose to nose, less than a hundred feet apart.

Casey looked across the gap to the GE locomotive. He couldn't see Farranger inside, and he chuckled at the image of him frantically setting handbrakes on the runaway train—the last act of the truly desperate. All that remained was to crush the one thin strand of hope Farranger had left, and Casey was only too happy to oblige.

"Hey, Farranger," he called into his packset, eyes on the ninety-foot distance separating the two engines. "If you can hear this message, you're driving too close."

The sound of Casey's voice sent another shudder through Farranger. He released the half-tied handbrake wheel on the lead tank, then leapt down from the car to his engine. Sprinting up the locomotive walkway, he saw the mirror-image of his own locomotive staring back at him, keeping perfect pace with his own runaway. He couldn't see the front platform of the commuter's engine, but he knew Casey was waiting for him. There could only be one reason to run two trains so dangerously close together: Casey wanted to watch him die.

Farranger ran toward the cabin, hating Casey more with each step. As if killing them wasn't enough, Casey wanted to witness the event for his own morbid pleasure. He could have made a clean getaway, put a hundred miles between himself and the train. But he had chosen to follow his sadistic urges at the risk of his own capture. He was a monster, a monster that had to be destroyed. Farranger no longer cared that his own fate was sealed. All that mattered now was finding a way to take Casey with him.

Then it dawned on him. That was exactly what Casey wanted, what he'd wanted all along. He was obsessed with his historical namesake, the heroic engineer who'd clung to the controls of a passenger train and sacrificed his own life to save others. In Casey's sick mind, he believed he was doing the same thing, sacrificing himself to save the railroad from Transcon. But Casey's so-called sacrifice brought with it a sinister promise: *This time everybody gets to die with me.*

Farranger stopped at the rear door of the cab and looked at the train in front of him through the engineer's window. Unable to see Casey, he focused on the commuter, hungry for the premium braking power it contained. Perhaps Casey had unwittingly given him a way out, a way to get his runaway under control. If he could make the coupling between the locomotives, he could use the commuter's brakes to stop the combined train. But the brakes had to be set from inside the commuter locomotive, and the only way to reach the control console was over Casey's dead body, which was fine by Farranger. He had a new ending for Casey's bloody legend: *Nobody else dies if I kill you first.*

Farranger stepped inside the locomotive cab. Crouching down low beside the control console, he grabbed the dynamic brake and partially released it by moving the lever four notches to the right. The engine accelerated slightly, a tiny forward surge that would be invisible from the outside.

But not for long. If Casey saw the engines closing together, he'd add power on the commuter and leave the slower freight train in the dust. To get close enough to jump between the locomotives, Farranger would have to find some way to divert his attention.

Casey was visible now, standing on the platform of the opposing locomotive, leaning nonchalantly against the handrail as though completely unconcerned about the short distance between the engines. He was playing catch with himself, throwing a football-sized object a couple of feet up in the air, then fielding it. It had to be some kind of explosive device, and Farranger had no doubt about how Casey planned to use it. At least Casey appeared to be too preoccupied to notice the closing gap between the engines. But that could change in an instant. If he was going to keep him distracted, Farranger would have to show himself.

He stepped through the nose door to the front locomotive platform. Casey's head turned in a flash, revealing the battle-scarred face he'd received from their previous encounter. The two men stood motionless, momentarily transfixed by the sight of each

End of the Line

other across the ninety-foot divide separating the nose-to-nose engines.

"Welcome, my friend," Casey sang, pressing his lips against the packset microphone like a rock star, "to the show that never ends."

The gap between the engines closed a few feet. Time was every bit as much Farranger's enemy as Casey, his runaway train now only five miles away from the concrete stops at Union Station. Even if he managed to connect to the commuter's locomotive, he'd need every inch of track to stop the combined train. He'd have to leap between two 70-mph trains, couple them together, then set emergency braking. And he'd have to do it all right under Casey's nose.

"Show's over, Casey," he said into the radio. "Guess you should've picked a city without a river."

"You mean the hopper?" Casey shrugged. "A minor setback — just ammonium nitrate under the bridge. Then again, I've always considered myself a glass-half-full kind of terrorist."

"Insanity has sure given you a rosy outlook," Farranger said bitterly, refusing to hide his contempt. It was all he had to keep Casey going.

"I'm sensing some hostility here. Don't tell me you still think *I'm* the bad guy?"

"I think you need help."

"It's Transcon that's going to need help," Casey corrected. "They're about to lose a billion dollars of rail infrastructure that's quite irreplaceable. Transcon will be finished in one bold stroke. It's brilliant, really. Though I'm not surprised you can't see the genius. We visionaries are seldom understood in our own lifetimes."

"You're no visionary," Farranger shot back. "You can't even see past your own wounded pride. So they fired you. Get over it."

"Get over it?" Casey laughed. "'In every day, in every way, I'm getting better.' I learned that mantra from Transcon's post-termination counselors. They were included as part of my insulting severance package to make sure I didn't go postal. All things considered, I'd say Transcon got a poor return on that investment."

The engines were now less than fifty feet apart. Farranger gripped the handrail. As soon as they were close enough, he'd swing underneath, then make the leap from knuckle to knuckle. He had to stall Casey a little longer.

"You've got your pound of flesh," he said. "Why not stop while you're ahead?"

"Sorry, Farranger, this is a through-train. I promised a very special passenger that I wouldn't stop until we reached Union Station. And he paid dearly for the ticket, so I think he deserves on-time service."

"Phil Adashek," Farranger guessed. "Your partner."

"Partner?" Casey spat the word. "God, you're clueless Farranger. Adashek was just following orders, and they weren't even my orders.

Casey looked truly frustrated with him. "Don't worry Cal. I'll explain it all in the next life."

Farranger was thoroughly confused. It sounded like Casey was giving Adashek a pass. What that meant, he had no idea. If he lived though the end of the day, he was sure he'd figure it out.

As a railroader, Farranger could almost understand Casey's fanatical thirst for revenge. Transcon had done more than fire him, they had taken away his way of life. Now, he was a man beyond reason, consumed with hatred and revenge for the railroad he'd once loved. There seemed no way to reach the man inside the monster.

"What about your people on the old C&M?" Farranger asked, recalling Jackson's words about Casey taking care of his own. "They'll die along with everyone else."

"Regrettable," Casey sighed. "But in times of adversity, sacrifices have to be made. I'm afraid they'll just have to take one for the team." He held the bomb in front of him as if checking its weight. "In just a few minutes, Transcon will be extinct. Its death will mark the dawning of a new era, a return to simpler times. The railroad's second Golden Age."

"You'll never live to see it. If these tanks blow, you'll die too."

"I'm already dead," Casey replied evenly. "Keith Jones died seven years ago. It's Casey's turn now."

End of the Line

Just then, Casey noticed the closing gap between their engines for the first time. He smiled at Farranger and waved an admonishing finger. "The old keep-the-madman-talking-until-the-engines-get-close-enough-to-jump-across trick, eh?" he laughed, glancing back at the commuter's cab. "Tantalizing, isn't it? I mean, you're just half a car-length away from a trainload of brake shoes."

Farranger couldn't stall any longer. There was no point in talking to Jones. The man was simply too far gone.

Farranger ducked under the handrail and stepped out on the front drawbar. Even though the locomotives were still 15 feet apart, Farranger knew he'd have to risk the jump soon, no matter how slim the odds. He carefully edged his way over the drawbar until he was perched on the knuckle, then studied the distance and closure rate.

Another ten feet, and he could try the jump.

But then he looked up at Casey and realized he'd never get the chance. The madman was taunting him from the other engine, holding the bomb over the tracks, daring Farranger to make the leap. Time was up. Casey could derail his train any second. And even if Farranger managed the superhuman leap between their engines, he'd never reach Casey before he released the bomb.

There were no more options, no new plan that would save the day. It was over. Casey had beaten him, and they both knew it.

"Why so gloomy?" Casey asked. "I've given you a great honor, a piece of my own immortality. When my epic legend is recorded, your name will be at the very top of the casualty list."

Farranger was too numb to respond. He could only watch helplessly as Casey took the fusee out of his pocket and struck the cap against the deck, igniting a bright red flame.

"Don't think of it as the end of your life, Farranger." Casey flicked a bit of the burning slag between the rails. "Think of it as the beginning of my immortality."

"But what about them?" Farranger nodded in the direction of the city. "They didn't ask to be part of your legend. They want to live."

"Only because they don't know any better." Casey lowered his packset, shouting his parting words across the narrowing gap. "You can take it from me! There's no life without legend!"

Casey returned the packset to his belt and tweaked the channel selector knob to the detonation frequency. Judging by the look on Farranger's face, the significance of this frequency shift hadn't gone unnoticed. They were both well aware of the deadly consequences that would come with his next transmission.

Casey hesitated, waiting for some last-ditch effort by Farranger to thwart the inevitable. But he made no attempt at heroics, no further appeals to reason, not even a pathetic plea for mercy. Farranger knew he was beaten, his mournful expression conveying the depth of his defeat. And he wasn't showing any sign of gratuitous groveling either, so all that remained was for Casey to put them both out of their misery.

He pitched his fusee, watching it fly end over end across the gap. It landed between the rails, then flickered briefly and disappeared under Farranger's train.

Casey removed his packset detonator from his belt, knowing that Farranger's eyes were following its every movement as a dog would follow a piece of meat. Casey's final moment of triumph had come, and he wished he could relish it at leisure. But destiny was calling.

"Casey!" Farranger called out. "I do have one question."

A stall for time? Casey checked the distance between units to ensure that he was well out of reach. "You have ten seconds," he called back.

"What's your favorite number?"

Casey didn't grasp the significance at first, until Farranger held his own packset out at arm's-length.

"Thirty-eight," Casey whispered, as the illuminated frequency number in the LCD face came into focus. He froze for an instant, held hostage by Farranger's thumb, which was cocked over the transmit button, ready to transmit the specific radio channel number that would detonate his bomb. He'd chosen the channel number because it corresponded to the original Casey's Jones' engine numbers and fulfilled his lust for an ironic ending. And it had certainly delivered in the irony department. It would be his own undoing.

Like a gunfighter that was hopelessly outmatched, Casey knew he could never beat Farranger to the draw. But he had one advantage: A complete lack of conscience. He could still unload the

End of the Line

bomb if Farranger's misplaced sense of humanity caused him to hesitate before pulling the trigger. Without warning Casey implemented his plan. He threw the bomb a split second before Farranger managed to send a short burst of static from his packset.

The bomb detonated just below the platform, between the engines in the open air above the tracks. The charge was designed to loosen the rail gauge and far too small to effect the massive trains it detonated between.

The human toll of the ear-splitting blast was another story. The shock wave sent Casey rocketing skyward and Cal tumbling backwards against his engine.

-38-

Farranger was blown off his feet and thrown through the locomotive guardrail behind him. The one-inch steel poles snapped on impact, and the jagged edges sliced a deep gash down the length of his thigh. He slammed into the locomotive nose door, then crashed onto the steel deck of the locomotive platform.

He lay there half-conscious, his eyes filled with lingering flash spots from the explosion. Though his vision was clouded, the vivid image of Casey's death had been etched into his mind. The explosion had blasted the madman off the commuter platform and sent him soaring across the open gap between engines to the tracks below.

If the blast hadn't killed him instantly, the end must have been painful. The wheels of the locomotive would've sliced Casey's body in thirds if he landed on the tracks, and if he'd somehow cleared the rails, he would've hit the ballast at 70 mph and been ground to a pulp. Either way, his train-wrecking days were over.

But Farranger couldn't cheer his death yet. His own situation hadn't improved any. He and Megan were still riding four thousand tons of explosive gas that was hurtling out of control toward downtown Chicago. Their fate would be no less painful than Casey's if he couldn't make it to the commuter engine and set the brakes.

He tried to stand, but his legs buckled and he collapsed on the deck again. Trying to focus his eyes on the commuter engine, he dragged himself toward it, blood running from the wound in his thigh. His train and the passenger equipment were closing and would soon come together. If he could regain enough of his senses, he'd could step across, set the brakes on the passenger equipment, and stop both trains.

End of the Line

Still too dizzy to stand, he pulled his upper body over the edge of the platform beneath the guardrail and tried to grab the drawbar below for leverage to pull himself forward.

Then a hand grabbed his arm.

Casey's hand.

Keith Jones had his chest pressed against the open knuckle of Farranger's locomotive, legs dangling over the tracks. The blast that should've sent him to his death had blown him across the gap to the runaway train instead. He was so close that Farranger could feel his breath.

"This is your stop, Farranger." Casey shifted his grip to Farranger's collar and yanked him off the platform.

Farranger tumbled off the front of the engine toward the tracks below, then slammed into the drawbar. His hands closed around the narrow metal beam, and he held on for dear life.

Casey smiled at the sight of his helpless enemy. One more yank, and he'd be fodder. Once Farranger was greasing the rail, Casey would get a fusee off the freight locomotive and resume his original plan to crash and explode the tanks. The only change now would be that he'd get to ride the tanks to their destruction, the lead dancer in his conga line of death.

But looking into his victim's eyes, Casey saw no fear. The image he saw in Farranger's pupils was not of his own death, but of Casey's, as he saw the reflection of the commuter engine behind him.

The train was practically on top of him. The locomotives were closing to make the joint, and he was still pressed against the open face of the knuckle. He let go of Farranger, but it was already too late. The pincer-like open knuckle was already pushing him forward into its mate.

The engines were going to couple right through him.

The open couplings came together slowly, trapping Casey between them like a vise. The skin around his chest and stomach tightened as the two halves of the knuckle squeezed closer together. His torso caved inward as the trains inched to a joint, steel ripping through his flesh. He could hear the sickening sound of his own ribs shattering. Casey tried to scream, but all that came out of his mouth was a spurt of blood.

He started convulsing as the coupling locked shut with a final metallic bang, then his head slumped downward, eyes fixed on the knuckle now covered in blood and chunks of flesh.

As Farranger struggled to climb over his crushed body to the commuter engine, Casey made a weak attempt to stop his enemy, but his arms wouldn't respond. The strength that had once surged through his muscles was gone. All he could do was watch helplessly as Farranger stumbled over him to the commuter locomotive, the hiss of the commuter brakes shattering his dreams.

His mission hadn't been a complete failure, though. He hadn't brought Transcon down in a legend-making moment of glory, but he *had* dealt them a crippling blow. Probably a fatal one in the long run. Transcon's life-blood would slowly spill onto the tracks, like his, as their shippers continued to abandon them one by one. Even after he was gone, he'd still be draining the life out of them.

It would be a slow death for him, too. He'd seen men coupled before, and they'd lasted for hours, or until they were uncoupled, whichever came first. It would be worth the misery if he fulfilled his dream of destroying Transcon.

But the failure of his other dream—killing McClure, the very soul of the evil beast—was unbearable. McClure was the flesh-and-blood embodiment of Transcon, the man who'd started the war against both Casey and the railroad he loved. He'd needed his help to make his plan work, but now he just wanted him dead. He would go to his death willingly if he could take McClure with him.

If Hell truly existed, he'd be sure to settle the score with McClure there.

The brakes on the commuter set hard. An onslaught of slack action followed, and excruciating pain rippled through Casey with an intensity he thought he was no longer capable of feeling. His body slid sideways, rotating a quarter-turn from the off-center hole in his stomach. The shift left his right arm dangling, brushing against the packset attached to his belt.

He ran his bloody fingers over the radio until he was sure the device was still intact, smiling deliriously at the unexpected discovery. He might be as good as dead, but that didn't mean he couldn't get the last word.

End of the Line

Carefully, he removed the packset from his belt. Union Station was only five minutes away; he could surely hold on that much longer. After coming this far to make his date with destiny, he wasn't about to stand her up now.

He still had one final ace to play.

Darkness engulfed Farranger's train as it pulled into the underground entrance of Union Station. The terminal was eerily quiet, the thousand-foot-long passenger piers jutting out from the rear wall evacuated in anticipation of a runaway.

The added braking power of the commuter cars worked a miracle. He brought the train to a gentle stop at the end of the loading platform, then turned the knob that released the passengers from their prison. As the doors on the commuter cars opened with a whoosh, the silence in the terminal gave way to screams of panic as the passengers ran for safety.

Farranger detrained through the nose door, his only thought to get to Megan as fast as his injured leg would allow. But he stopped short when he stepped down to the boarding platform and caught sight of Casey, who was still conscious, his face ashen and pinched with pain. Blood was dripping from his feet onto the tracks below, his insides spilling down the side of the knuckle.

Farranger had seen men coupled into before. They almost always survived the initial jolt, but then their life-force drained out little by little. The most horrible death imaginable on the railroad. A death Farranger wouldn't wish on anyone. Not even Casey.

He turned away and started to limp toward Megan at the rear of the train.

"Farranger," Casey wheezed.

Farranger turned around angrily, sending a sharp stab of pain through his leg.

Casey motioned with his head, urging Farranger to look behind him.

Farranger saw McClure hustling away down the platform alone. He was carrying a heavy satchel. Cal made the connection instantly, but still had more questions than answers about the CEO's involvement.

Before Farranger could put it together, Casey lifted his packset, punched in a code, and depressed the transmit button.

A thundering blast rocked the walls of the terminal. Farranger watched in horror as McClure was blown apart, a confetti of scorched bills and shredded leather raining down in the spot where he'd just been standing.

"Downsizing," Casey smirked, dropping his packset.

Without an instant of hesitation, Farranger reached between the locomotives and grabbed a firm hold on the pinlifter, never taking his eyes off Casey.

"End of the line," he said. Farranger raised the pinlifter half a turn, until the linkage met resistance against the knuckle.

Casey eyes fell to Farranger's grip on the pinlifter and forced a smile. Using the last of his remaining strength, he dragged a flat palm across his bloody chest, the switchman's hand sign to separate equipment.

Farranger took the dare, giving the handle a firm yank. The knuckle parted twelve inches, releasing Casey from its steely grip. He fell to the tracks below, his body torn apart at his midsection as if some huge hungry predator had taken a bite.

Farranger turned away from the gruesome sight and saw Megan walking toward him, bloody jacket wrapped around her hand.

"Are you all right?" he asked. They were both severely wounded, her hand matching the gouge in his leg.

"I've been better. How about you?"

"Can't complain," Farranger smiled. "Just another day on the railroad."

"What happened to Casey?"

"He tied up at his final terminal." Farranger motioned toward the bloody tracks below.

Megan looked over the edge of the platform and saw Casey lying there. Farranger was surprised to see she didn't turn away. Unfazed by the sight of blood, Megan stared down at the tracks for a moment before turning to Cal.

End of the Line

"Is it really over?" she asked.

"It's over for Casey and McClure."

"McClure?" Megan looked at Cal as if he'd misspoken.

"I think Adashek was just the fall guy," Cal sighed, disappointed. "But what say you and I keep that to ourselves, at least until the Axeman has had his body cavity search."

Megan smiled, until a shot of pain made her hand throb.

"Jesus." Megan winced, cradling her wounded palm. "How about next time, you get nailed to the car and I get to ride the locomotive?"

Farranger tugged on his pant leg, just in case she hadn't noticed it was covered in blood. "The grass is always greener for you union types, isn't it?"

"Aw, did the cushy desk jockey get his hair mussed?" Megan waxed sarcastically. "Don't expect any sympathy from me because you skinned your knee when you were out roughhousing with Casey."

"This little thing?" Cal released his pant leg, pretending it didn't hurt like hell. "This is nothing. What really bothers me is that my insurance rate will triple. Thanks to you, I've totaled three vehicles in a week."

"Since when is it my fault you can't drive, Farranger?"

"You know, I think by now you could call me Cal."

"Could, but won't," Megan confirmed. "So what happens now?"

Farranger wasn't exactly sure. Transcon and the railroad would survive, though he had no idea who would be running things. McClure was out, and Adashek seemed destined for prison, though he wouldn't put it past the Axeman to slip the noose. As for the union—well, Transcon 'wasn't the only one with leadership issues.

"Jackson's going to be finished when his support of Casey comes to light," Farranger said. "I've always thought the international office could use a woman's touch."

Megan shook her head. "I'm through with politics. I think I'll exercise my seniority and go back on the ground somewhere. I hear San Bernardino's nice this time of year. Besides, someone has to keep an eye on you."

Cal was tempted, but didn't take the bait. They both knew that their relationship worked best when they didn't talk.

"So what about you, Farranger?" Megan quizzed. "Going back to the salt mine?"

Though Farranger nodded, he wasn't sure what his future held. He guessed he'd go back to California, try to rebuild what Casey destroyed. It would be a monumental task, but he wouldn't have to do it alone. Megan Langford would be there to second-guess his every move.

As if on cue, Megan tapped his shoulder, interrupting his thoughts.

"Hey cowboy, it looks like our ride is here." Megan motioned toward the terminal entrance, where clots of emergency personnel were rushing toward them at a breakneck pace.

Farranger glanced at the brigade of medics, and then turned back toward Casey for one final look. He realized his fallen enemy had finally achieved in death what he'd wanted all along.

"Congratulations, Casey," Cal murmured to himself. "You're history."

Afterword

The train "incidents" in the book are largely a dramatic retelling of events that have actually occurred at one time or another in railroad history. It is therefore less a question of whether the accidents described in this story could happen than how often they already have.

Some truths are indeed stranger than fiction. Skeptics who doubt the explosive power of a liquefied petroleum gas tank car should start their fact checking with the town fathers at Ardmore, Oklahoma. In 1915, one very small tank car of casing head gas killed dozens, obliterated the entire downtown area, and blew out windows a half mile away. Today's railroads use much larger tank cars and carry cargo with considerably more potential energy.

For you accuracy buffs, I must note that certain "errors" were deliberately introduced into the narrative. Though some authors may well describe in perfect detail the construction of a nuclear weapon, the average person is not likely to come across a cache of weapons grade plutonium. In contrast, almost every garage in America has what is needed to derail a train. I see no reason to make this process easier, or to produce a field manual for the terminally disgruntled. Certain omissions that did not affect the story seemed appropriate. Now, if only I could get locomotive manufacturers to stop mounting step-by-step operational instruction placards on the engineer's control panel.

In fiction, trains run faster, stop quicker, and manage to encounter the exact geography necessary to keep the plot rolling along. In this spirit, the author took certain liberties.

First, and most obviously, there is no coast-to-coast railroad that resembles the fictional Transcon. Likewise, rail management is not rife with union-crushing Nazis who thrive on insider trading, kicking puppies in the gut, and committing generally evil deeds while twisting their handlebar moustaches. No character in the book was modeled after an actual railroad officer. Thankfully, there simply isn't anyone in railroad management who was vicious and dastardly enough to make the cut, not even at the Union Pacific.

Similarly, banking on the odds the general reader wouldn't want a one-hundred-page dissertation on the Railway Labor Act, dramatic license prompted the truncation of a dozen rail craft unions into one global union. Lest the manuscript leave the reader with the wrong impression, railroad labor unions are, in fact, "clean" unions. They are completely devoid of the corruption necessary to build a sub-plot around. As far as the basic premise, there is regrettably less dramatic license in play. Few people appreciate just how vital railroads are to our nation's economy and security. If these avenues of commerce were to shut down for an extended period of time, there is little doubt as to the net result. In technical terms, we would be thoroughly screwed.

Though slightly less than half of total freight moves by rail, this minority stake becomes more important when you consider that certain classes of freight are moved almost exclusively by rail: coal to run electric plants, grain to feed the world, lumber to build our cities, raw materials to run our factories, and just about every toxic substance known to man so that we can all enjoy better living by chemistry.

Rail sabotage is not new. It predates the Civil War, and has continued unabated for a century and a half. Soldiers, spies, outlaws, disgruntled or striking workers, radical groups, and even malicious teenagers have left their mark. The effects vary. In recent history, one lone saboteur nearly shut down the entire German passenger rail system at Christmas time. Another managed to detonate thousands of tons of military munitions at the "Black Tom" rail facility in New Jersey during the First World War. The blast was heard ninety miles away, and caused twenty million dollars in property damage, including one hundred thousand dollars worth of shrapnel damage to the Statue of Liberty.

An Internet search on "railroad" and "sabotage" will return dozens of contemporary stories. Because the number of fatalities is generally fewer than an airline disaster, these incidents, while disturbingly frequent, rarely make the front page. Nevertheless, on any given week, some railroad, somewhere, is a victim of sabotage.

End of the Line

Luckily, those perpetrating these attacks aren't particularly good at it. Most potential rail saboteurs lack technical savvy, imagination, or simply don't have the staying power to be a serious threat. This story merely contemplates what could happen if a sufficiently motivated individual, one who was thoroughly familiar with railroad operations, took it upon himself to create as much mischief as possible.

I am anxious to hear any feedback. I encourage readers to stop by my website at Railtale.com. While you're there, check out the "Rail Tales" section to read railroad anecdotes, most of which are submitted by working railroaders. Leave a railroad story of your own, and perhaps your name will be immortalized in my next novel. My email address is KemParton@railtale.com.

About the Author

After graduating from the U. S. Naval Academy in 1983, Parton served as a shipboard engineer and naval war planner for ten years. In 1993, after achieving certification as locomotive engineer, he spent the next twelve years in railroad management, working a variety of positions in field operations and corporate headquarters. Combining his military and railroad experience, Parton constructed a realistic worst case scenario that highlights the terrorist vulnerability of U.S. railroads, and the devastating consequences of such an attack.

Apparently, the story was too realistic for senior officials at the railroad where Parton worked. He was told to kill publication of this book, or he'd be fired. Parton refused, and is currently unemployed as the book goes to press.